LOSS PROTOCOL

By Paul McAuley:

400 Billion Stars
Secret Harmonies
Eternal Light
Red Dust
Pasquale's Angel
Fairyland
Confluence
The Secret of Life
Whole Wide World
White Devils
Mind's Eye
Players
Cowboy Angels
The Quiet War
Gardens of the Sun
In the Mouth of the Whale
Evening's Empires
Something Coming Through
Into Everywhere
Austral
War of the Maps
Beyond the Burn Line

LOSS PROTOCOL

PAUL McAULEY

First published in Great Britain in 2026 by Gollancz
an imprint of The Orion Publishing Group Ltd
Carmelite House, 50 Victoria Embankment
London EC4Y 0DZ

An Hachette UK Company

The authorised representative in the EEA is Hachette Ireland,
8 Castlecourt Centre, Castleknock Road, Castleknock, Dublin 15,
D15 XTP3, Republic of Ireland (email: info@hbgi.ie)

1 3 5 7 9 10 8 6 4 2

Copyright © Paul McAuley 2026

The moral right of Paul McAuley to be identified as the author of this work has been asserted in accordance with the Copyright, Designs and Patents Act of 1988.

All rights reserved. No part of this publication may be reproduced, stored in a retrieval system, or transmitted in any form or by any means, electronic, mechanical, photocopying, recording, or otherwise, without the prior permission of both the copyright owner and the above publisher of this book.

All the characters in this book are fictitious, and any resemblance to actual persons, living or dead, is purely coincidental.

A CIP catalogue record for this book is
available from the British Library.

ISBN (Hardback) 978 1 399 63556 1
ISBN (Ebook) 978 1 399 63558 5
ISBN (Audio) 978 1 3996 3562 2

Typeset by Born Group
Printed in Great Britain by Clays Ltd, Elcograf S.p.A

www.gollancz.co.uk

And might it not be, continued Austerlitz, that we also have appointments to keep in the past, in what has gone before and is for the most part extinguished, and must go there in search of places and people who have some connection with us on the far side of time, so to speak?
—W.G. Sebald, *Austerlitz*

Ah, so it's true, I didn't just imagine myself, I actually exist.
—Clarice Lispector, *Too Much Of Life*

Suche fantasies ben in myn hede
So I not what is best to do.
—Geoffrey Chaucer, *The Book of the Duchess*

Part One

Cynsea

Early in the morning of the last day of May, an hour shy of dawn, a band of intense rain swept across the Blackwater Estuary. Marc Winters woke as the staccato hammering on the roof of his narrowboat deepened into a jet-engine roar, couldn't find his way back into sleep after the rain had slackened and passed, and brewed a mug of black tea and picked a couple of energy bars from the catering-sized pack and sat out on the little stern deck. Water dropping from the weatherbent Scots pines alongside the mooring pattered haphazardly on the gravel path and the roof of the utility shed. Scant birdsong in the reedbeds and salt willows. Scattered solos where once there would have been a full choir. The river's broad dark sweep flaring to gold as the sun rose.

When it was light enough Winters pulled on his clothes and set off around the perimeter of the island to check for storm damage, following the boardwalks and raised paths that snaked through the marsh and the salt-willow brakes. He visited the bird hide that overlooked a pond circled by reeds, walked to the platform at the far end of the marsh where a pair of composting toilets stood, and climbed through the patchwork woods strung along the shallow rise of the island's backbone.

Cynsea. His little kingdom. A world entire.

The wet planks of the boardwalks were littered with smashed leaves and broken twigs, washouts had bitten into edges of the path to the tidal causeway that linked the island to the mainland, and a freshet snaking downslope had undercut a flight of steps at the seaward end, but there wasn't anything that required immediate attention. Still restless, he stripped the cover from the skimmer and took it out on a loop around the archipelago of mudbanks that curled downstream. Rain had rinsed the air clean. The sky was a cloudless dome of unblemished blue. In shallows fringing the remnants of the island's old breakwater, shoals of tweaked mussels were pumping water through their gills and filtering out microplastic particles, layering them into the world's ugliest pearls. A troop of flamingos, descendants of escapees from a private zoo, browsed at the edge of a mudflat, strutting and dipping like regal stiltwalkers. Swallows traced erratic arcs above the river's flood, their twittering cries carrying faint but clear across the water. And further out, high above the navigation channel, a scattered cloud of airjellies was drifting towards the north shore, their black, fist-sized bells trailing tangles of delicate filaments.

Winters aimed his phone at the cloud and asked his assistant to check its direction and speed, blipped the data to a couple of drones and let the skimmer drift on the outgoing tide as they whirred out from the island, square catchnets strung beneath their landing gear. After they'd made their first cut through the airjellies, he restarted the skimmer's motor and made a wide turn and headed back towards Cynsea, planning to log the sighting and make his daily count of victims of the crab die-off before the island's first visitors arrived.

He was halfway home when he spotted the dark shape on the grassy hump of a mudbank. About the right size for a seal, although seals had vanished from the coasts of England, Scotland and the Principality more than twenty years ago, killed off by a virulent strain of distemper. Still, there was the small possibility that it was a vagrant from the last surviving pods in Norway or Iceland, and even if it was dead it would be a solid tick mark. A mention in the agency's dispatches, might even make the local newsfeeds. As he nosed the skimmer towards the mudbank's blunt crescent half a dozen gulls lofted into the air and tilted away, more than he'd seen in any one place for a while, and the shape shortened and stood up and he realised that it was a person, arms raised above their head and crossing and uncrossing in the classic semaphore for help.

The castaway was a slender androgenous kid dressed in an old, oversized wetsuit, cuffs bunched at wrists and ankles, a long rip in one calf exposing a nasty looking gash. Black hair clipped short, dried in uneven spikes. Brown skin and solemn dark eyes, good cheekbones and a serene, slightly otherworldly air, as if being stranded on a mudbank in the middle of the estuary wasn't especially unusual. No big deal. Their name was S Odice, they told Winters. No, the S wasn't an initial or short for anything. Just S. They/them. On the drift, no fixed address. Reciting these bare facts wearily, as they'd no doubt recited them many times before.

'That's a Bristol accent, isn't it?' Winters said, trying for a connection. 'I grew up not far away, in Gloucestershire.'

The kid's shrug was a minimal twitch of one shoulder. They were standing at the edge of a rippled apron of mud exposed by the receding tide, squinting at Winters and his skimmer riding in shallow water a few metres away.

'Hop on,' Winters said. 'We'll get your leg fixed up.'

'No hospitals.'

'I didn't say I'd take you to one. We'll head to my place, over on the island there. I have a good first aid kit, and I know how to use most of it.'

'Are you some kind of police?'

'I'm a wildlife ranger.'

'Of that island?'

'Cynsea Island, yes. These mudbanks, too.'

'You going to arrest me?'

'For what? You signalled, I came to help. Which is my job, or part of it anyway.'

The kid thought about that for half a minute, then picked up a pair of swim fins, a dive mask and a canvas weight belt and waded out to the skimmer. After they'd clambered aboard Winters handed them his steel water bottle and they sucked on its spout greedily, tilting the bottle to get the last drops, asking him if he had any more.

'There's plenty in my narrowboat.'

'I tried drinking the river water, but it's hella salty.'

'The tides mix it up with seawater. How long were you stuck there?'

'Most of the night.'

'Out in the rain?'

For the first time a trace of animation broke through the kid's laidback demeanour.

'That was interesting. Thought I might drown, or be washed away. Had to dig in and hunch down until the worst was past.'

Winters reversed the skimmer in a churn of silty water and turned its blunt prow towards the island. 'How did you end up there?'

'Was working a car reef,' the kid said, addressing the air off to one side of Winters. 'One of the ones off Mersea? Got caught in a current and swept downstream, washed up here.'

Winters knew about the car reefs, where thousands of scrapped vehicles had been dumped in an attempt to prevent coastal erosion; knew that a crew of local chancers, the Lamb brothers, hired drifters to work as salvage divers, paying them a pittance and selling the electronics and catalytic converters they recovered to the recycling plant over in Gravesend. Blatant exploitation, though legal. But the reefs were more than twelve kilometres away, near the mouth of the estuary, and he thought it more likely that this castaway had been raiding one of the nearby oyster farms. They'd been working alone and got into trouble and ended up here, or had been working with a crew who'd dumped them on the mudbank after some kind of disagreement.

'If you were working on the car reefs, what happened to your salvage?'

'My what?'

'Reef divers usually have net bags they hang from their belt, fill up with the stuff they find. Their salvage. Looks like you lost your air bottle and regulator, too.'

'Didn't have an air bottle.'

'You were free-diving the reefs?'

'I'm a good swimmer.'

'But not good enough to stay out of trouble. Even if you know the tides and currents, you can easily get into serious difficulty out here. You were lucky to have ended up on that mudbank. Lucky I spotted you.'

The kid shrugged.

'If I were you, I'd take it as a sign,' Winters said.

'A sign?'

'That you should find another line of work.'

In the narrowboat's cabin, the kid drank two glasses of water, wriggled out of their wetsuit and, in shorts and a frayed T-shirt, sat with a kind of rigid stoicism while Winters examined the gash in their leg. It was long and ragged but not especially deep, and had mostly stopped bleeding. Winters soaked cotton pads in boiled water and cleaned the gash and patted it dry, painted it with prion solution and closed it up with wound glue and bandaged it. Told the kid to keep it clean, try to keep their weight off it as much as possible and see a doctor if there was any sign of infection, and found them a freshly laundered T-shirt.

'Your feet are about half my size, so you'll have to go barefoot.'

'Okay.'

'I have to ask – how old are you?'

'Old enough.'

'How old's that?'

'Eighteen.'

'You have some ID?' Winters said, because the kid looked a year or two younger than that. A possible school-age runaway from some crisis or horrorshow. There were far too many like that on the drift.

The kid pulled a zipbag from the back pocket of their shorts and took out their ID card and handed it to Winters. Under a long string of numbers and letters, a photo of the kid rotated to the left and rotated back to face forward again. S Odice, born April 28th 2060, non-binary, a Bristol address.

'So you're eighteen, but only just,' Winters said.

The kid shrugged.

'You look younger.'

'I get that a lot.'

'This address, is that where your parents live?'

'Where I was living, once upon a time.'

Winters gave the ID card back to the kid. 'Before you went on the drift.'

The kid shrugged again, dropped the ID card into the zipbag and stuck it in their pocket.

'When did you leave?' Winters said.

'A few years ago.'

'Two years? Three?'

'Something like that.'

'Are you still in contact with your parents?'

'Not really. And it isn't any business of yours.'

'It would have been my business a month ago. Before your eighteenth birthday. But not any longer. Is there anyone who might have reported you missing, might be worried about you?'

The kid shrugged.

'How about someone you could call, ask to come pick you up? If you've lost your phone you can use mine.'

Another shrug.

Winters knew he wasn't getting anywhere and pointed to the head, told the kid that they could wash up there. When they came out, face scrubbed and hair slicked down, the hem of their new T-shirt around their knees, Winters had brewed a pot of tea and was sitting on the L-shaped couch behind the little table, smoking what was left of last night's joint. The kid sat as far away from him as possible, wary as a cat in a strange house, but accepted a mug of tea and an energy bar, asked Winters how long he'd been living there.

'Coming up for two years.'

The kid unwrapped the energy bar and took two big bites. 'Looks like you just moved in, you don't mind me saying. Could do with, I don't know. Some pictures. Flowers. Unpacking those boxes.'

'It suits me,' Winters said, and took a long drag on the joint and blew out a riffle of smoke and offered the stub to the kid.

'I don't do that stuff.'

'Good for you,' Winters said, and licked his finger and thumb and pinched out the stub's coal.

The kid took another bite of their energy bar and said around it, 'You seem pretty cool, for the law.'

'I'm not anything like the law. More a sort of caretaker.'

'Did you set those drones on the jellies?'

'You saw that, huh?'

'Jellies are mostly harmless, aren't they? Why you so down on them?'

'They're proscribed biotech, designed by some hobbyist to absorb pollutants from the air. But they also sweep up insects, so if too many people release too many jellies it could cause all kinds of harm. Crops failing because there aren't enough pollinating insects. Fledglings starving in nests because birds can't catch enough insects on the wing.'

'Everything's connected to everything else,' the kid said.

'Yeah. Kick a rock, start an avalanche. So I had a thought while you were washing up. Someone I know, Teddy Stokes, might need some help. He grows all kinds of produce in his allotment, has a gleaner's licence too. You know anything about gardening, or foraging for wild food?'

The kid shrugged.

'Doesn't matter. Teddy can teach you all you need to know, and he sort of owes me a favour. If you like, I'll give him a call, let him know you're looking for work. He lives over in Tollesbury, but your best bet is to catch him at his stall in the green market. He's there every Saturday.'

The kid ate the last chunk of their energy bar. 'Why are you doing this?'

'I don't know. Maybe it's my turn to help someone out. Reckon you can walk on that leg?'

The kid nodded.

'I'll walk you to the causeway. Take another energy bar for the road. Grab a handful if you want.'

The causeway was a sandy path just wide enough for a single vehicle, raised on a low embankment curbed by boulders and swatches of seaweed and looping away towards the mainland shore like a child's scribble, its far end obscured by a shimmering haze. The freshness after the rain had burned off and the morning was growing ever hotter.

The kid shielded their eyes with their forearm and studied the causeway and said, 'Can't you take me in your boat?'

'I have things to do here. As long as you're quick you won't get washed away again.'

'Really?'

'No, I'm kidding. Tide's just about on the turn, but you have plenty of time to get across. Even with that gimpy leg.'

'My leg's good.'

'Keep that cut clean,' Winters said. 'And don't forget about Teddy Stokes. You can't find his stall in the green market, just ask around. Everyone there knows old Teddy.'

He watched as the kid limped away down the causeway, wetsuit rolled up and tucked under their right arm, swim fins dangling from their left hand, dive mask hung around their neck. A small stubborn figure dissolving into the glare of light on water. Winters sometimes took in injured or exhausted birds, tried as best he could to nurse them back to health, and felt the same way now as when he let one of those birds go. Knowing that it was the right thing to do, but also knowing how hard it was for a broken thing to survive in this world.

'Here he comes, the hero of the mudbanks,' Mic Thomas said, when Winters came into the room, and Embry Clarke turned in his chair and greeted him with a slow handclap and a couple of high-pitched yelps.

'If I had to guess what that was meant to be, a seal would be the last in a very long list,' Winters said.

This was in the back room of Heybridge Basin's harbour office. The monthly meeting of the rangers in charge of reserves in and around the Blackwater Estuary. Half a dozen people in agency jackets and shorts sitting on stacking chairs in a loose semicircle. Evening sunlight burning at the edges of blinds pulled down over a pair of windows. A ceiling fan stirring soupy air.

Embry laid an arm along the back of his chair and smiled at Winters. 'And how is your seal boy?'

'They aren't a boy. Or a girl, either. And they're doing fine, as far as I know.'

'My bad,' Embry said, not at all abashed. 'So were you really hoping you'd found an actual live seal?'

'For maybe half a minute.'

'A grey seal or a harbour seal? Or maybe a Weddell seal, on holiday from Antarctica.'

'Give it a rest, Embry,' Jude Lee said.

'Walruses,' Jon Holderness said.

'Even more unlikely than a seal,' Mic Thomas said.

'They'd visit now and again, back in the day,' Jon said. He was the oldest of the group, white hair pulled back from his weather-beaten face and tied with a black ribbon at the back of his neck. 'Young males, usually, on what you might call a walkabout. Looking for new territory or maybe just seeing something of the world. They'd lounge about on slipways or buoys, climb on boats at anchor. And they're big animals, walruses. Weigh a tonne or more. Nothing you could do if one decided to settle on your shrimper or sailboat. You'd just have to wait until it lost interest and left of its own accord.'

'Well, they're all gone now,' Mic said.

'There's still a few in Canada,' Jon said. 'I don't know if one could make it all this way, but it wouldn't surprise me if it did.'

Embry looked at Winters and said, 'Would you have checked him, excuse me, checked them out if you'd known they were just a drifter from the get-go?'

'What would you have done?'

'I wouldn't have left them there, but I wouldn't have turned them loose until I'd found out what they'd been up to.'

'They claimed they were working on the car reefs.'

'I mean what they'd really been up to.'

'Embry has a point,' Honey Yong said.

'The point being that maybe it's a good thing it wasn't his call,' Jude said.

'It was Marc's rescue, his decision,' Nina Patel, the senior ranger, said. 'And I don't see any harm in treating a drifter with a little kindness. If you're all done with that topic, let's make a start on our actual agenda. We're already running late.'

Winters filled a chipped mug with tea from the big aluminium teapot and took a seat as Nina announced that the first item was a note about the crab die-off.

'Tell me they've finally found what's causing it,' Embry said.

'Unfortunately, that's still undetermined,' Nina said. 'We've been reminded that it is important to collect carcasses from our chosen strips of shore every day, and log species counts as well as overall numbers. Apparently some gaps have begun to appear in the records. I know it's been several months now, and I'm as tired of it as anyone else, but we need to stay on top of it. And also make sure we burn everything we collect.'

The die-off had begun late that spring, when thousands of Chinese mitten crabs had crawled out of estuaries and rivers along the east coast. Aimless armies wandering across mudflats and nearby fields and roads before expiring. At first, there was no particular urgency to investigate. Mitten crabs were a prolific and widespread invasive species that would never make a red list anytime soon, even in these parlous times. But then the corpses of other species, green shore crabs and edible crabs, spider crabs and velvet swimming crabs, began to wash up, there were mass deaths in offshore crab farms and hatcheries, and catches in the few licensed traps still in operation dropped precipitously. Water temperatures along the east coast were no higher than average, there weren't any toxic algal blooms and the crabs weren't suffering from excessive parasite infestations or from shell disease, white leg disease or other common bacterial or viral infections, didn't have unusual loads of dioxins, PCBs, organochlorides or heavy metals. The cause of the die-off appeared to be a synergistic combination of sub-lethal factors. As if the environment itself had become toxic.

'There haven't been so many to collect and count in the past couple of weeks,' Honey Yong said. 'Maybe it's easing off.'

'Or maybe there aren't many crabs left,' Embry said. 'The agency really doesn't have any strategy but watch and wait?'

'I don't like it any better than you do, but those are our instructions,' Nina said, and crisply moved on to the other items on the agenda. Short- and long-range weather reports, precautions for the fire season, and an announcement that the new eelgrass initiative had been green-lit. Which was, Mic Thomas pointed out, no different from the old eelgrass initiative, five years ago. It had failed then, she said, so why was the agency wasting everyone's time by trying again?

'Try again, fail better,' Embry said. 'Our unofficial motto.'

'If you'd read the briefing, you'd know that this is a new strain, with new tweaks,' Nina said. Standing straight-backed at the lectern, fixing her gaze on Embry like a school teacher challenging a disruptive pupil. 'First tested in Spurn Bight last year, now approved for testing in several new locations. Including Blackwater. The team which ran the Spurn Bight project will set up the trial beds, and most of the monitoring will be done remotely. If those trials are successful, the beds will be expanded, creating new habitats for marine life. Increasing species diversity, and also acting as an efficient carbon sink.'

'This is the official word,' Embry said.

'That's what you'll tell anyone who asks about it, yes. No talk about failing better.'

Embry touched his brow with a forefinger. 'Whatever you say.'

'And if anyone asks about disturbances this experiment could cause?' Honey said. 'If fishers and gleaners, the owners of shellfish and kelp farms, are worried about effects on catches and productivity. What do we tell them?'

'The outreach team will be in contact with people who have commercial interests in the estuary,' Nina said. 'But if anybody raises a concern, you can tell them that the project involves only a small number of carefully chosen and rigorously monitored sites. And that it has the potential to increase fish populations and the estuary's overall health.'

'And if it doesn't work out, like last time? Or like the bumblebees?' Embry said. 'What's our script then?'

'It's too early to think about that, but I'm sure the agency has it covered. Planting out the trial beds will begin in four weeks. And we will of course fully cooperate,' Nina said, and asked if there were any matters outwith the agenda.

Mic wanted to know if there had been any movement on her request to repair last winter's storm damage to the causeway to Northey Island, it wasn't getting any better by itself and couldn't be fixed by a few bags of gravel. Nina promised that she'd chase it up, and Jude raised his hand and said that a white-spotted bluethroat had been seen in the reedbeds along the edge of St Lawrence Creek. 'It's only been a couple of days since the first sighting was posted, but it's already attracting birders. We should expect more as word spreads.'

'Remind them that if they want to visit Northey they'll need to book,' Mic said.

'I'm sure they will,' Jude said. 'They're generally a well-behaved bunch.'

'If there's nothing else,' Nina said, and as usual closed out the meeting with the little ceremony, the loss protocol, that memorialised a species recently pronounced extinct in totality.

Most were obscure, because part of the point of the loss protocol was to remember everything that was gone from the world. Not just the charismatic and keystone species, but also the foot soldiers, the marginal and overlooked plants and animals whose disappearance made only the smallest of holes in the world. This time it was the Lesser Lichen Case-bearer moth, *Dahlica inconspicuella*. An image of a drab insect with dusty brown wings kindled in the air beside Nina, and Winters and the other rangers watched in deferential silence as a sequence of short sentences scrolled up, explaining that the Lesser Lichen Case-bearer moth had been locally common in parts of England, but was found nowhere else in the world. The specimen displayed was a winged male. The females had been wingless, emerging from cocoons and mating and laying a clutch of eggs and dying, the eggs hatching into larvae which, protected by cases got up from silk and sand grains and lichen fragments, grazed on lichen and grew and eventually spun cocoons and transformed into short-lived adults.

There were people who had, over years and decades, mapped the moth's locations, catalogued variant styles of larval casings and wing patterns, and monitored its slow decline, but this, the official recognition of its final end, was the only moment when it achieved any kind of significance. An exemplar of all that had been lost. The most beautiful and most wonderful forms that couldn't be saved.

I never knew you, Winters thought, as he often did, but I'm sorry that you're gone.

Later, sharing a joint with Jude after the communal meal, he said, 'I've come to the conclusion that I shouldn't have mentioned seals in my report.'

'It was a nice touch,' Jude said. 'And pay no mind to Embry. He can be an asshole sometimes. Doubles down when someone calls him on his bullshit.'

The two of them were sitting on a bench on the patch of scorched and threadbare grass between the Old Ship pub and the sea lock and floodgates which, at high tide, allowed passage of boats between Heybridge Basin and Colliers Reach and the rest of the estuary. The last of the sunset was fading from the darkening sky. Lights shone on the decks and in the portholes of boats moored two or three deep in the basin and the moon-coloured streetlamps along the basin and the promenade behind the sea wall had switched on.

'What did he mean by that remark about bumblebees?' Winters said.

After almost two years on post, he still hadn't untangled the old disputes and rivalries, the losses and small victories, that informed the back-and-forth between the rangers.

'One of the agency's first attempts at reintroduction hereabouts,' Jude said. 'They bred up two species of bumblebee and released them in the reserves. Both species were once native here, and both died out inside a year. The agency tried it again, same result. Things had changed too much. The bees couldn't hack it anymore.'

Winters passed the joint and said, 'So Embry had a legitimate point, Mic too, if this is the second go-around with eelgrass.'

Jude sucked on the joint and breathed a long riffle of smoke into the hot dark air. He was the youngest of the estuary's five rangers, a calm, amiable, self-sufficient person with elf-locked red hair and a broad sunburnt face who seemed to have unfolded smoothly and completely from child to adult without any of the usual transitional stresses, crises and doubts.

'Maybe this new strain will take hold,' he said. 'I hope it does. But sometimes it's hard to justify trying to bring back what's been lost when we barely have the resources to protect what's survived.'

'That's kind of cynical, you don't mind me saying.'

'It's the nature of our work,' Jude said, and took another puff on the joint and handed it back to Winters. 'What is this weak shit?'

'Goodberry Tea.'

'You're still buying from Teddy Stokes.'

Winters took a long drag on the joint and breathed out smoke and said, 'He's the only one who sells it.'

'He knows what his customers like. Something homegrown, but innocuous. Something that'll give you the same kind of buzz as a nice Chardonnay,' Jude said, and shook his head when Winters offered him the joint again. 'Hit me up in a few days. I should have some new stuff you can try.'

'This would be more of that weird gear peddled by drifters,' Winters said, and took a last quick puff and ground out the nubbin's last spark in the dry dirt between his boots.

'The last batch you tried was pretty good.'

'It was still kicking me in the head the next day, if that's what you mean.'

'I've been told that this new stuff is strong but mellow,' Jude said. '"A ride as smooth as silk" was the sales pitch.'

'I'm not sure if any of it can even be called marijuana.'

'It mostly is. Just tweaked in interesting ways. Speaking of drifters, do you know what happened to your castaway?'

'I made Teddy Stokes an offer. Said that if he threw a little work the kid's way I'd overlook the fact that his gleaning licence had expired a couple of months ago. And so far it seems to be working out. I told the kid to look up Teddy at the green market, but instead, after I turned them loose, they walked all the way to Tollesbury. Found Teddy on his allotment.'

'You've got your castaway working for your drug dealer?'

Winters smiled. It might be weak shit by Jude's standards, but the joint had nicely blurred the edges of the world and set his thoughts adrift, little clouds softly bumping around in his skull.

'Sounds sort of bad when you put it like that,' he said. 'I found them work and a place to stay is all, and they seem to like it.'

He'd pitched up at Teddy's stall in the Green Market, bought his usual bag of Goodberry Tea as a pretext for an unofficial welfare check. Teddy and a couple of his pals were sitting on upturned crates, drinking beer from waxpaper cartons and gossiping, and S was serving customers and seemed happy and well, said that they'd been taking care of their leg and it was almost healed.

'Teddy told me the kid had been double-digging his allotment, and has a fair eye for foraging. Which is high praise, as far as Teddy's concerned. He's paying them minimum wage, as we agreed. Drifter scrip, not credit. S doesn't have a phone.'

'One of those folk who want to drop all the way out of society?'

'Or maybe they have a good reason for not wanting to be found. I didn't ask,' Winters said, and told Jude that he'd also stopped by the produce stall run by the Lamb brothers. There were four of them, operating a variety of dubious businesses, including the car reef thing, out of a smallholding near Mersea. The youngest, Luca, had been manning their stall that Saturday.

'You know him?'

'Scary big fellow,' Jude said. 'But good-natured, as long as you don't get on the wrong side of him.'

'I wanted to check the kid's story about diving one of the reefs, told Luca I'd rescued someone who claimed to have been working for his family, asked if he knew anything about it. And he said that he didn't have anything to do with that side of the business, but might have heard something about one of the divers getting into trouble. In this offhand way, as if it was no big deal, which pissed me off somewhat. S could have drowned, the fucker could care less. I said that as far as I was concerned the reef-diving business should be shut down before someone got themselves killed. Said that I'd found a new line of work for the person I'd rescued, but that might not be the end of it.'

'Oh boy,' Jude said.

'Yeah. As soon as I said it, I thought I was in trouble. But it was okay. I think Luca was amused. Like a kitten had tried to bite him. He told me that Teddy Stokes had returned the diving gear, the kid's share for the scrap they'd brought up had been paid, and that was that. Done and dusted. I think he was relieved that S had been found alive. That there wasn't an inconvenient body he and his brothers would have to answer for.'

'So all's well that ends well.'

'Yeah. And it turns out that S was telling the truth. They really had been diving the car reefs, must have floated all the way to Cynsea. Twelve kilometres, give or take. Pretty amazing.'

Jude said, 'Didn't you once have a girlfriend who was in the life?'

'Briefly. I was nearly on the drift too, at one point. And yeah, maybe that did have something to do with wanting to help the kid,' Winters said. 'But you know how drifters are. Sooner or later they'll decide to move on.'

'No doubt,' Jude said. 'But the way you stuck up for them, going toe to toe with one of the notorious Lamb brothers? I get the impression that you're hoping they'll stick around.'

Although Winters' path to Cynsea Island had been as haphazard and circuitous as any drifter's, he knew precisely where it had begun. The siege of Wakestone Farm, the commune where his sister Izzy lived, his detention by the counterterrorism police and all the rest of the sorry mess. Unlike Izzy, he'd chosen a conventional life. University, employment as a sustainability analyst in the London offices of a construction company, tentative plans to move out of his efficiency pod, the kind that could be hosed down between tenants, and find a place to share with his girlfriend as soon as both of them won the requisite bumps in their salaries. All of that had gone to smash with the siege, which ended in a fire so intense it left no identifiable remains. Izzy, along with her guru and master Kasey Motte, the rest of Motte's followers and the hostages they'd taken, were pronounced dead at the coroner's inquest on the basis of police evidence and Motte's infamous list of so-called saviours. Winters was released without charge, but the construction company invoked the morals clause in his contract and terminated it with immediate effect and no compensation, his relationship with his girlfriend didn't last much longer, and at the age of twenty-five he was suddenly unattached and unemployed, free to reinvent himself but with no idea of what he wanted to be.

Mostly, he wanted to disappear. To escape the media's bottomless appetite for morsels of Izzy's life, the stigma of guilt by association. His uncle, a senior civil servant, arranged an interview with a multinational logistics service provider, and he spent the next three years drudging in minimum wage gigs in mainland Europe. Back-office work in an aid distribution centre in Spain and one of the new ecocities in Albania, organising meals and accommodation for engineers and labourers at the construction site of a desalination plant complex in Greece. Which was where he contracted a new and vicious strain of dengue fever that laid him up in a high-dependency clinic for six weeks.

Serious illness was a different kind of discontinuity. A chance to click pause and reassess. The newsfeeds, citizen journalists and various polders of social media that had once hounded him had moved on to other scandals and moral crusades, and he wanted to believe that he had moved on, too. Had outgrown his shame and remorse and helpless anger, his obsession with the last time he'd met his sister, the stupid fantasies about rewriting the past. No one noticed or cared when he returned to England. He was working as night manager of a factory that farmed black soldier fly larvae, processing them into food-extending protein and turning their frass into fish-food pellets, when a friend tipped him off about job openings for one of the Biodiversity Agency's rewilding initiatives, part of a plan to enrich and expand the National Forest which ran from Cornwall and Devon to Northumberland and the border with Scotland. Winters won a place on the project partly because of his experience in the sustainability business and partly because of his long-standing interest in natural history, rooted in the citizen science projects he'd helped Izzy with, back in the day – plant and insect surveys, bird counts and owl pellet inventories, restoration and renewal parties, and so on. Some might think that ironic, or a rebalancing of karmic forces, but Winters, who in his before-times life had used the metrics of ecological economics to identify and measure the contingent value of ecosystems and the costs of making good losses caused by development and construction, knew that the world was as it was, no more, no less. Transparent, computable and, within the limits of the negative-growth economy, utilizable. Izzy's belief in the world-changing powers of her commune's mushroom dreams, his scary meeting with Kasey Motte, had strengthened rather than undermined this stubborn rationalism.

His first year with the agency, he was part of a crew deployed along the border between Somerset and Devon. Charting numbers and diversity of plant, insect and animal species in tracts of woodland, using chainsaws and industrial strimmers to clear the remains of dense blocks of conifers grown for the timber trade and patches of trees trashed by wildfires and storms, and planting saplings of species adapted to the new climate – horse chestnuts, Turkey oaks and Spanish oaks, wild service trees and grey elms. It was challenging and physically demanding work, but he was fitter than he'd ever been, the crew he worked with was tight-knit and good company, and days and nights spent in the countryside reminded him of the best times in his childhood, when he'd roamed the local common and woods and fields with his sister or his friends.

Sometimes, though, especially while working alone in patches of old woodland, he'd be ambushed by the creepy sense of an uncanny, unseen presence, or the feeling that he'd strayed across some impalpable boundary into woods as old as the world and deep and boundless as an ocean. Faint and fleeting echoes of the hallucinations he'd suffered when Kasey Motte had spiked him with a supercharged strain of shrooms, but deeply unsettling nevertheless.

In the spring of that year he met his first dreamers. A young woman and man on the drift who like others before them stopped by the work camp one evening and were given a share of the workers' supper. A sweet, sincere, other-worldly couple. Vagabond mystics who used shrooms, one of the hallucinogenic species picked in the wild, nothing like Kasey Motte's special strain, to connect with the dreams of the land and memories of its deep past which in a thousand or ten thousand years might return with no need or care for human intervention. They didn't recognise Winters or mention Kasey Motte and his perversion of shroom visions, but he was relieved when they left the next morning.

After the work in Somerset ended, he moved to a project on the English side of the Black Mountains, establishing forests in upland grasslands where biodiversity had been compromised by centuries of sheep grazing. He was a trainee ranger by then, learning about conservation management, prepping for extreme weather events, and basic forestry skills, leading guided walks for visitors and local schoolkids. In the spring

CeCe Craddock joined the crew, and within a couple of days she and Winters were sleeping together. A mutual infatuation between two people who had little in common except for some pretty intense sex and a liking for weed, which Winters had acquired during his voluntary exile in Europe. A classic example of the attraction of opposites, according to CeCe.

She was a drifter ten years older than Winters, a sturdy, spirited woman with pale freckled skin and an uncombed mass of red hair who claimed to be a full-blooded Celt of ancient lineage. She had a trace of a Welsh accent that became near operatic at sexual climax, but wouldn't tell Winters where she had been born and brought up, and warned him at the start of their affair that she was a rambler who refused to be held down by anyone or anything, had no home but the road and places and people she found along the way. She only used her phone, an ancient hard-shell model that predated bionics, when she needed to access credit earned by what she called straight-world jobs, and preferred whenever possible to pay for goods and services with greasy polymer banknotes printed with the likeness of a dead king, the common currency of the drifter community.

On their days off, CeCe and Winters went on long hikes with minimal gear, camping overnight under a groundsheet stretched between a couple of trees for shelter when it was raining, under the open sky when it was not. Sharing a joint by a little campfire, zipping their sleeping bags together, waking at sunrise. Winters, still abed, watching as CeCe squatted naked by the fire she'd rekindled, boiling up wild comfrey tea in a battered aluminium pot.

She wouldn't let Winters consult his phone's agent or satnav on their hikes, had no use for maps. Said that getting lost was the best way to discover something new, and navigated by the sun and instinct and whim, skirting roads, houses and farms as much as possible. It was harder to avoid damage done by decades of wild weather and the overheated climate. Landslips which cut wandering trenches across grassland or carved fresh cirques and slumps into hillsides. Patches of woodland smothered by honeysuckle or dense curtains of Russian vine. Tracts where dead trees stood like congregations of stark white ghosts, or had been uprooted by storms and lay in impenetrable puzzles of broken trunks and shattered branches, all overgrown by bramble and dog rose.

The summer of that year was exceptionally hot and dry. The foliage of heat-stressed trees flamed red and yellow in false autumn and leaves shed to alleviate water stress crackled underfoot and drifted amongst withered clumps of ferns and grasses. One evening, standing on the crest of a ridge burned entirely black, a warm wind blowing siftings of ash past a cairn of stones cracked and broken by the heat of the fire, Winters and CeCe saw the smoke spires of five separate wildfires rising in the shimmering panorama below.

In another life, on another path, Winters might have gone on the drift with CeCe after his contract ended. Might have joined the alternative community of runaways and refuseniks who had chosen or fallen into a low-impact nomadic way of life, owning only what they could carry, taking temporary and seasonal work wherever they could find it. Maybe he would have found happiness on the drift. Fulfilment. A way of healing. Instead, they ran into CeCe's witchy friend, with her weirding ways and her fucking Tarot cards, and that was the end of that.

It was in the last days of summer. They were following a sunken lane that tunnelled through a wood, a holloway first walked by Saxons according to CeCe, and deepened by the tread of feet and hooves and the passage of cart wheels for more than a thousand years since. A hushed place that, in the green shade of trees that clung to steep banks clothed in ivy and ferns and brambles, seemed to stand outside of the ordinary passage of time, haunted by the ghosts of secret histories.

The holloway curved around an outcrop of fractured stone, the slope on one side flattened out, and there, in the shade of a large yew tree, a woman sat crossed-legged, thumbing through something on her phone, looking up as Winters and CeCe approached. They'd met drifters before, lone men or young couples, a raucous crew squatting on a rocky outcrop in unreconstructed moorland. Had always called out greetings and walked on, but this time CeCe surprised Winters by striding towards the woman and giving her a stooping sideways hug, the woman patting CeCe's back while looking straight at Winters. She was in her late fifties or early sixties, her face creased and deeply suntanned, glossy black hair gathered into a loose ponytail splayed across one shoulder. A small blue rucksack stood on the soft duff and an aluminium kettle sat on a camping stove.

CeCe was telling the woman it had been an age, asking why she was so far from her usual beat.

'I got the wandering itch. And maybe I know why, now. Who's your friend?'

CeCe introduced Winters, told him that this was her good friend Ayn. 'Come. Sit. We've some catching up to do.'

The woman, Ayn – whether that was her first, last or only name Winters never knew – studied him with a frank gaze as he settled beside CeCe. She wore a soft leather shirt with red stitching, baggy earth-coloured utility trousers. The soles of her bare feet were black with dirt, toenails painted different colours.

'Where did you find him?' she said.

'We're both working for the agency,' CeCe said. 'Patching in trees here and there, cutting back undergrowth, that kind of shit. Sort of clicked together.'

'He isn't one of us.'

'Partly why I like him.'

'Not from around here, either.'

'But not from that far away, originally,' Winters said, somewhat nettled by being treated like a curiosity. 'I grew up on the other side of the Severn.'

Ayn ignored that, told CeCe that she had some tea and pulled a jar from a hole in the ground. 'Birchbark. Cut the twigs yesterday, let them steep overnight.'

The pale amber tea was cool and faintly astringent. Winters sipped his measure while CeCe and Ayn swapped gossip about common acquaintances, who was on the road and who'd left it, the latest turn in a long-running feud between two sisters, the death of a man they both knew.

'I hadn't heard,' CeCe said. 'Was Freya with him, at the end?'

'He knew it was his time, but didn't tell her when she last visited. Left a note in his bivvy and set off towards one of his favourite spots. Got most of the way there, sat down to rest and didn't get up again. Freya found him the next day.'

'Poor Freya.'

'Was her choice to make that promise. She didn't have to, not after they split up like they did. But now that promise has been fulfilled, and she can move on.'

There was a silence between the two women while they sipped their tea.

'I wouldn't say no to a reading,' CeCe said at last.

'I was thinking it might be necessary,' Ayn said, and reached inside her shirt and fetched out a pack of greasy cards bound with a black ribbon that she undid with slow care and tied around her wrist. She spread the cards in an arc, face-down, and surprised Winters by holding them out to him and told him to choose three.

'I'm not much of a fan of magic tricks,' Winters said, feeling he'd been put on the spot.

'Isn't a trick,' Ayn said. 'Isn't magic, either. Think of a question and pick any three.'

'What kind of question?'

'Up to you. Something you want, perhaps. Or something that's been bothering you.'

'Where I'm going in my life, maybe.'

Perhaps her cards would tell him if he should stick with tree planting or go on the drift for a while, with or without CeCe. Get a feel for that life.

'Everyone who can't think of a real question falls back on that old chestnut,' Ayn said. 'But all right. Hold it in your mind and pick your cards. One for yourself, one for your situation, one for the challenges you face. Pull them out and turn them over. Sideways, not end for end. It's important which way up they are. Whether they're reversed or upright. Set them in front of you as you find them.'

'Go on,' CeCe said. 'Ayn doesn't do this for everybody. She'll tell you something interesting about yourself.'

The cards were hand-drawn, black ink on heavy white stock. Winters chose three at what he hoped was random, setting them down one by one on the carpet of brown needles.

An old man in a black robe trimmed with fur, one hand resting on a telescope aimed through a window filled edge to edge with stars, the other pointing to papers scattered at his feet.

'The Magus, reversed,' Ayn said.

A figure of indeterminate sex with butterfly wings, rising above rippling water into a sky densely cross-hatched with tiny symbols.

'Emergence, also reversed.'

Four swords laid in a compass rose, their points meeting two more swords standing in the centre, lit with a blaze of white in a dark land under a dark sky scribbled with symbols, the moon's crescent cocked high in one corner.

Like the others Winters had chosen, it was upside down. Reversed. When he laid it down Ayn didn't name it but stared at the three cards as if they had suddenly transformed into something loathsome and poisonous and pushed back a little, the heels of her bare feet raising ridges in the duff, her back pressed against the trunk of the yew.

'You shouldn't have brought him here,' she told CeCe.

'It's not as if I expected to find you.'

'But here you are and here he is. And I'd kindly like you to leave and take him with you.'

'What do the cards say?' CeCe said.

'He don't belong here and I shouldn't have done this,' Ayn said. 'Just go. And don't ever bring him back.'

'What did I do?' Winters said.

He was angry and upset. Wondering if the woman had recognised him, knew about his sister. If she believed, because of her stupid card trick, that he was tainted by Kasey Motte's folly.

'It isn't anything you did,' Ayn told him. 'More what you are.'

'If this is about what I think it's about, I didn't have anything to do with it.'

'That's the point. You don't have anything to do with anything. You're here, and you shouldn't be,' Ayn said and turned her head and screwed her eyes shut, as if in child-like denial.

Winters and CeCe had been planning to walk up to the Cat's Back and take in the view, then find a pitch in the woods around Upper Blaen. Instead CeCe turned back towards the work camp and Winters followed her.

'Do you know what those cards were supposed to mean?' he said.

'Not really. If you want, you can look it up.'

'They're just cards. It's crazy to think they mean anything.'

'They're symbols of deep patterns. The shape of the world. The shape of us. And they told Ayn something.'

CeCe was walking quickly, bouncing along the uneven track. Winters, trying to keep up with her, was slightly out of breath. She was seriously spooked. By the cards. By her witchy friend's allegations.

'What did she mean, I don't have anything to do with anything?' he said.

'I don't know.'

'You don't know what she thinks those cards told her.'

'No, I don't.'

'Maybe it isn't anything to do with them. Maybe she thinks she knows something about me. Who I am.'

'And who would that be?'

Winters was briefly tempted to tell CeCe about Izzy, but glossing over his past had become a deeply ingrained habit. And besides, it would most likely make things worse.

He said, 'We're letting that woman's craziness ruin the day.'

'Ayn isn't crazy. Weird, maybe. Weird, and deep. But not crazy.'

'Are you saying you believe her?'

'I don't know what she saw in the cards, but she definitely saw something.'

Later, despite his misgivings, Winters looked up the cards he'd chosen. They weren't part of any Tarot set he could find, but the names of the first two were in common use and he guessed that the third was the six of swords, sometimes called the Navigator, and he plugged their names and the fact that they were all reversed into a site that gave him a free reading. You are between worlds, it told him. The prisoner of a divided situation. You need to make an effort to sharpen your focus so that you can fully understand it and use your special knowledge to take action.

Generalised double-talk. Something which meant everything and nothing, like a fortune cookie message. But he couldn't shake the uneasy feeling that Ayn and her cards had delved into the past he'd tried so hard to put behind him. His entanglement with Kasey Motte's fantasies. His final parting with Izzy. Her madly hurtful dismissal. It didn't help that it ended his relationship with CeCe, who quit work and left the camp the next day. No warning, not even a note. Just gone.

Winters moved on. Maybe the cards were right about one thing. He needed to take action. Realise his potential. He worked on various conservation projects in reserves in the salt marshes of the Thames Estuary and finished his apprenticeship, and soon afterwards saw an advertisement for the post of wildlife ranger for the Cynsea Island reserve, filled in the online forms and attached his CV and sent everything off with a single click. He didn't have much hope of success, but two weeks later he was invited to the agency's head office in Nottingham and quizzed during a walkabout in the model reserve outside the city, followed by a more formal interview with a panel composed of two senior rangers and three administrative officers, and shortly afterwards was offered the job. As someone once told him, you can make all the plans you like, but wherever you end up is where you were headed all along.

Cynsea was the smallest of the three significant islands in the Blackwater Estuary, connected to the mainland by a causeway that was impassable twice a day, at high tide. Its name, like many in that part of England, was a corruption of the original Saxon. Cynesige. Royal Victory. Mersea Island, near the mouth of the estuary, had been used as a holiday resort by Roman occupiers and the remains of Celtic salt workings and fish weirs had been found there; once upon a time Viking marauders had sailed their longships up the estuary and landed at Northey Island, where they'd lost a famous battle with a Saxon army. But all that remained of Cynsea's early history was an oyster-shell midden, a Mesolithic flint adze far from any source of flint, and the hilt of a seax, the long knife commonly carried by Saxon men, found by a metal detectorist in the 1980s. Even the reason for its name, if it had been the site of an unrecorded skirmish in the marshes, perhaps, or part of the settlement of a disputed inheritance, was long forgotten.

In the first quarter of the twentieth century the island had been purchased by a philanthropist who built a half-timbered brick lodge in the local vernacular style and rented the patchwork of small fields to a farmer. On his death, the island had been gifted to a charity and the lodge converted into a sanitorium that was requisitioned by the government during the Second World War and used as a nursing home where injured RAF pilots recovered from their wounds and burns, adjusted to their amputations and facial reconstructions. Abandoned after the war, it was briefly squatted by a hippy commune but otherwise had been left to fall into ruin until, in the economic boom of the 1990s, the freehold of the island was bought by a director of a private bank. He restored the lodge and built a concert hall and cottages to accommodate musicians and guests for exclusive recitals, and the island was used as a holiday home by his family until the middle of the twenty-first century, when the Biodiversity Agency acquired it through a compulsory purchase order.

The lodge had burned down in an arson attack, leaving only the outlines of its foundations and a chimney stack, mostly held up by a thick cladding of ivy, which was the roost of a colony of pipistrelle bats. A beach of imported sand and a significant portion of the fields had been washed away during the Great Storm of '49, and rising sea levels had turned most of the rest into a marsh of mudflats, reedbeds and salt-willow brakes. The roofless shells of the concert hall and the guest cottages, scattered along what had once been the shore, were half-drowned and clad in thick skirts of seaweed. Only the low ridge of the island's spine, its clumps of trees and hawthorn thickets and little clearings, stood above the tideline.

It was a place of shifting and indefinite boundaries. Long perspectives of water dissolving into misty air at a horizon that seemed to be no more than knee-high. Tides and currents rearranging mazy configurations of mudflats and mudbanks. His first summer on the island, Winters had a brief affair with the assistant stage manager of a touring opera company which, on a pair of flat-topped barges anchored side by side off Northey Island and surrounded by an audience aboard every kind of small boat, had given three performances of Britten's *Peter Grimes*. Music and human voices echoing out across the water. The floating stage, illuminated by a choreographed flock of drones, seeming to grow brighter and ever more hyperreal as summer's dusk deepened.

Winters and the other local rangers were tasked with policing the audience's boats. After the technical rehearsal, he fell into a conversation with the ASM, Lyla Stering, they drifted away from the others to share a joint, and ended up in Lyla's narrow bed, in a cubbyhole tucked into a corner of one of the barge's holds.

Each performance of the opera ended with a little piece of theatrical trickery. The lead tenor playing the unjustly accused hero, who committed suicide by scuppering his boat and drowning himself, appeared to climb into a dinghy and sail off down the estuary. But it was really Lyla, a mariner's cap pulled low to hide her face, who took the dinghy around the point of the island while the music of the finale played, so that the tenor could take his bows with the rest of the cast. After the third and last performance, she didn't return to the barges but waited for Winters to catch up with her in his skimmer, and he guided her to Cynsea and his narrowboat's mooring, and followed her into the cabin, his mouth parched with desire and anticipation.

Early the next morning, Lyla insisted on being given a tour and said that the island, its marshes and quaint ruins and narrow ribbon of woods, was the ideal hideout for a gang of children from one of those old adventure books. She could see Winters living there like a castaway, she said. The only inhabitant of his little world, catching fish and robbing bird nests, foraging for berries and mushrooms.

Winters tried to deflect this with a lame joke, saying that Cynsea would be the perfect desert island if it wasn't for the paperwork and the constant stream of visitors, but he felt seen. The job wasn't all it could be. He missed the cheerful rough-and-tumble camaraderie of the forestry camps, was basically a caretaker and tour guide subject to the directives of scientists and bureaucrats, constrained by a thousand regulations and the tireless scrutiny of his supervisor. But at the end of each day, after the last visitors and volunteers had left, he loved to wander along the island's marshy shore or amble through its patchwork woods, listening to wind moving amongst leaves in summer, breathing in the damp and decay of autumn, watching the winter sun rise beyond a lacework of bare branches. And every morning, whether he woke to sunshine and birdsong, to drifts of rain or to haar that shrank his world to a muffled bubble, like the last fragment of a shattered planet adrift in universal blankness, was an affirmation of his luck. His rolling contract was subject to review at the end of every year, and he wasn't certain if he wanted to stick to the job for the rest of his life, but for now he'd found a place of shelter. A safe harbour and useful work. A kind of peace.

When Winters and Jude arrived at the patch where the bluethroat was showing, a hair past seven on a warm sunny morning, there were already several men in high-end outdoor gear and army surplus camo crouched behind their camera tripods, and two local volunteers were standing watch, making sure the visitors picked up their litter and didn't stray from the shore trail or put up drones to triangulate their prize.

The locals were Bob and Will Flowers. Uncle and nephew, birders who kept records of what they called little brown jobs, reed warblers, grasshopper warblers, reed buntings and so on, that went back a couple of decades, and led parties of schoolkids on birdwatching expeditions. Bob, a burly man with a Santa Claus beard, told Winters that bluethroats weren't quite extinct, but the visitor to the estuary was a notable rarity.

'The first seen in England for more than twenty years. Back when young Will was in short pants. They used to pass through on their way to breeding grounds in Europe in spring, or on their way back to wintering grounds in Africa. This one seems to have decided to settle. Shows no sign of Zugunruhe.'

'Zugunruhe?' Winters said.

'It's German. Means migratory restlessness,' Jude said.

'Germans have a word for everything,' Will said.

'Probably have a word for "having a word for everything",' Bob said.

When it appeared, this uncommon visitor didn't seem especially spectacular. Robin-sized, with a blue bib and a dash of white at its throat, pecking about the dusty ground under a patch of gorse downslope from the shore trail. Winters put up his field glasses and tracked it as it fluttered up to a perch on a prickly gorse branch and cocked its tail and carolled a staccato sequence of trills and chirps. Pausing, head tilted, as if listening for the call-backs of rival males or awaiting the cautious approach of a female, before sailing off into the scrub.

'There's a theory that males sing more loudly as numbers of their species drop,' Jude said. 'Trying to cover a larger territory, so they've a better chance of attracting one of the few remaining females.'

'Like in cities, where birds have to sing more loudly to be heard over background noise,' Will said.

'Back in the day, people thought male birds sang to define their territory,' Bob said. 'Competing against other males to prove themselves worthy for female attention. Now, we know they sing when there's a lack of females. Because they're lonely. Used to be, the dawn chorus ended early in summer. Late May. June. When birds had paired off and eggs were hatching and it was all about feeding chicks all the time. Now, you get some males singing into July or August because they still haven't found a mate. If he stays, this one could be singing all summer.'

Out in the scrub, the bluethroat trilled its lone and lovely song again. One of the visitors was holding above his head a big directional microphone attached to a long aluminium pole and sleeved in furry camo. The others had their field glasses up, trying to spot the bird in the briars and dry grass.

'I heard the song of an endling once,' Jude said. 'The last known wood warbler.'

'I know of that one,' Bob said. 'Norfolk, wasn't it?'

'A patch of woods near the River Yare,' Jude said. 'I was new to the agency, temporary assistant to a sound recordist. We set up before dawn for three days straight until we heard it. Singing for a mate it would never find. There hasn't been a confirmed sighting of a wood warbler here or in mainland Europe since then, but the recording's in the agency library if anyone wants to hear it.'

'Stellar little bird,' Bob said. 'Green plumage on top, fresh as a lime, yellow breast, white belly. A mega-tick on a trip I made to Poland some thirty years back. The Białowieża Forest.'

'A migrant like our friend there,' Jude said. 'But none of them learned to stay put.'

'Unable to resist their Zugunruhe,' Will said.

'You ever heard of Weltschmerz?' Bob said to Winters.

'Vaguely.'

'Another German word. Means world weariness, world pain. Coined back in the nineteenth century to describe the grief of poets and painters whose ideals were harshed by reality. A lot of people these days suffer from something similar. What you might call solastalgia.'

'My German isn't all it could be.'

'It's a mix of Latin and Greek. Something someone came up with to describe the feeling you have when you're on your home patch, knowing everything's changing in all kinds of bad ways you can't control, and also knowing that it's only going to get worse. Anticipating a future that's even more fucked up than the present.'

'Yeah, I know that feeling,' Winters said.

'Pretty much every birder does too,' Bob said. 'Every year, our tick lists are shorter than the year before. Question is, does our feathered friend feel the same way? Is it singing to attract a female, or does it know it doesn't stand a chance, but is singing anyway, for itself? And if it's singing for itself, what kind of song is it? Is it hopeful or defiant, or is it grieving for the gone world?'

One night, it was about a week after he'd paid his respects to the bluethroat, Winters was woken by a phone call. It was close to midnight. Absolute darkness pressing at the porthole beside his bed as he groped for the phone. No name or number showing. A voice in his ear saying, after he accepted the call, 'Is she there?'

'Who is this?'

'You know who I mean.'

'No, I don't,' Winters said, although he was wondering if this was, somehow, something to do with the kid, S Odice.

'Are you sheltering her on your lovely little island?'

The voice was crisp and precise and affectless, the male equivalent of his agent's default persona. He'd never bothered to customise or name her, rather liked her somewhat severe manner, its suggestion of an unjudgmental efficiency, but this version seemed calculatedly menacing, like a psychotic computer from some ancient sci-fi film.

'I'm not sheltering anyone,' he said.

'You are claiming to be alone.'

'How did you get this number?'

'Perhaps you don't know yet. But you will.'

'Don't call me again,' Winters said, and cut the link, and asked his agent to give him the caller's number.

'I'm afraid that it has been withheld.'

'You can't trace it?'

'I regret to say that I lack the means to do so.'

He tried to dismiss it. A malicious crank call, nothing more than that. But it reminded him of the media barrage after the siege, the calls and ambushes, notes stuck to the door of his efficiency pod offering to listen to his side of the affair or threatening to tell the real story of his involvement, not to mention the deluge of flat-out trolling, and he found it hard to get back to sleep and woke early the next morning from uneasy dreams of wandering the empty streets of an unknown and depopulated city on an urgent but bootless search for something or someone he couldn't name.

A few days later, out on the river on a routine patrol, checking the mudbanks for fish traps and other signs of poaching, trespassing campers and so on, he spotted a dinghy hauled up on the landward side of a sandbar and steered closer, saw Teddy Stokes standing amongst cord grass and the kid trudging through knee-deep water, leaning into the long handle of a push net.

Teddy touched two fingers to the fraying brim of his straw hat as Winters walked up to him.

'Ranger.'

'Teddy.'

'Another hot day.'

'I see you've got our young friend working.'

'Their third go at shrimping,' Teddy said. 'I believe they're beginning to get the hang of it.'

He was a tall, stooped geezer with a bush of woolly grey hair, barefoot in cut-off blue jeans and an old, unbuttoned cotton shirt. Retired from school teaching after more than forty years, he supplemented his pension by selling produce and weed he grew in his garden and double allotment, and marsh samphire and shrimp and prawns he gleaned along the shore.

'You still haven't got around to renewing your licence,' Winters told him.

'I've been rather busy. Sorting out a place for S to stay, for one thing. They didn't take to sleeping in the house, so we set up a mattress in my shed on the allotment. Cleaned it out, hung curtains, tried to make it homely. And there were clothes to buy, a few necessities. Not to mention smoothing things over with the Lamb brothers.'

'Yeah, I had a word with Luca Lamb, and he mentioned that you returned the kid's gear. How did that go?'

'I know those boys have a reputation, but they've never given me any grief. I taught three of them, back in the day, all but young Luca, and they still call me Mr Stokes. Jake, the elder brother that runs the diving business, told me that S is an odd fish.'

'How so?'

'He didn't exactly explain. Apparently, S had been working on their fruit farm, and one day volunteered for the reef diving gig. Brought up three catalytic converters inside an hour on their first and last outing, big prizes because they contain rare metals. And after handing Jake the third one S went down again and didn't come back up.'

'And drifted twelve kilometres to the mudbank where I found them,' Winters said.

'Hard to believe, but there it is,' Teddy said.

The two of them watching as the kid lifted the push net out of the water and examined their catch, picking out bits of seaweed and throwing them over their shoulder, plucking small creatures and dropping them into their catch bucket, a nylon cylinder clipped to the belt of their waders. The hot wind blew streamers of fine sand along the broad wedge of the beach, combed the mane of cord grass.

'I had a phone call a couple of days ago,' Winters said. 'Late at night, anonymous, sort of threatening. It didn't mention S by name, but I can't help wondering if someone might be looking for them.'

'If they are, I've not been troubled yet,' Teddy said.

'No odd phone calls or messages?'

'Not a one. Do you think the youngblood's in trouble?'

'I hope not. Have they said anything about how they got into the drifter life?'

'Not yet. And I don't intend to pry. Either they'll volunteer it, or they won't.'

'Most likely won't.'

'Most likely. Anyway, what with all that business, and teaching them the ins and outs, sorting out my licence was rather pushed to the back of my mind. But I'll get around to it.'

'Sooner rather than later.'

'Don't worry. I'll get it done.'

Out in the shallows, S had set off on another transect with the push net, and Teddy cupped his hands around his mouth and called to them, told them to come on in. He kicked a hole in wet sand at the water's edge and took the push net from the kid, wedged the triangle of netting strung at its fore edge in the hole and emptied the contents of the catch bucket into it, and he and the kid squatted head to head, sorting through their prizes. A double handful of wiggling brown shrimp, several bug-eyed prawns, and a couple of baby dabs and a small pipe fish Teddy chased into his cupped hand.

While the old man walked into the water to set the fish free, Winters asked S how it was going.

'Okay, I guess.'

'Teddy or anyone else gives you any trouble, you let me know.'

'He's okay.'

'Everything's good, then.'

'Sure. Why not?' the kid said, with a little shrug of one shoulder.

They were both shy with each other. Uncertain of their relationship.

Winters said, 'I hear Teddy gave your gear back to the Lamb brothers.'

Another shoulder shrug.

'Best to stay away from them from now on.'

'I can take care of myself.'

Teddy was coming back, saying that it was time to pack up. 'We have more than enough for supper. And you're welcome to join us. Shrimp, greens from the garden, flatbread warm from the oven. Food of the gods.'

'Another time. I'll see you around, S.'

'I know,' the kid said, and walked off towards the beached dinghy with the long pole of their net resting on one shoulder, a small scrappy figure in the brassy sunlight and booming wind.

It grew ever hotter in the days that followed. Trees restless in scorching winds, the broad sweep of the estuary flecked with white caps, the sunlight unstable. Winters tried to get most of his work done before noon. Meeting parties of schoolkids, giving them his canned introduction to the island. Checking on birders and casual visitors. Patching washouts on the path to the causeway, overseeing a work party dredging rafts of water hyacinth from ponds and channels, meeting with a retired surveyor who'd volunteered to update the island's GPS maps, and a couple of volunteers who were setting up plant identification boards. An awful lot of the work was done by people who gave up their time to do species surveys, lead youth groups, give talks, help with construction work, odd jobs and general maintenance. A good number of them had been volunteering for work on Cynsea and in the other reserves around the estuary for longer than any of the rangers had been in service.

By late afternoon the island lay silent and becalmed under tonnages of suffocating heat. Winters sprawled in the narrowboat's stern deck under a canvas shade or hung off the jetty, submerged in water only a little less warm than body heat. It was even too hot to enjoy a joint – the smoke tasted like burnt chemical waste.

About a week after he met the kid and Teddy Stokes on the river, a thunderstorm drifted in from the west, trailing skirts of rain that mostly evaporated before they hit the ground, and lightning struck a tree on Cynsea and set fire to reedbeds in the Old Hall Marshes reserve. Winters, pitching in with the other rangers and crews from three fire stations, was put in charge of one of the gangs of volunteer workers who, armed with rakes, shovels and long-handled swatters and guided by a drone, located and beat out spot fires kindled by windblown embers. It was a small, localised blaze, nothing like the wildfires which raged through thousands of hectares of farmland and forests old and new every spring and summer, but preventing it from spreading into the grassland and salt marshes beyond

Joyces Head Fleet was hard, hot, stop-and-go work. The firefighters soon exhausted the internal tanks of their engines and coupled long runs of hoses that snaked across dry turf to pumps sucking water from one of the ponds. Sunlight blazing through hazy drifts of smoke spun rainbows around the spray from a dragon drone that flew a hose out above smouldering thickets of bramble and blackthorn. Across the estuary, beyond the floating grids of shellfish and kelp farms, a mountainous range of thunderheads had stalled above the shore, and in their penumbral shadow lightning scrawled bright crooked threads like fleeting fractures in reality. Winters saw several strikes flicker close to the square sepulchres of the decommissioned nuclear power station. Saw a volunteer flinch from a whirl of wings when she trod up a covey of small birds hiding in long grass, saw a dead tree entirely clad in licks of flame, saw a gaggle of the reserve's sheep huddling in a corner of Flying Field like bewildered evacuees.

S Odice was one of the young runners who ferried bottles of water to the firefighters and the volunteers. Twice supplying Waters and his gang, there and gone before Winters could speak to them the first time, the second time handing him the last bottle of water from their net bag and saying that Teddy was filling the bottles from a standpipe in the farmyard, it had been his idea to come out here and help.

'You and him still okay?'

'Sure. Teddy told me to tell you that he'd renewed his licence.'

The kid was breathless and flushed, dressed in baggy shorts and a raggedy, oversized T-shirt printed with the emblem of an extinct car manufacturer. Beaten up nologo sneakers, a faded red kerchief knotted around their neck.

'I hope he's sharing the takings with you,' Winters said.

'A little bit. And I have a place to sleep, and food. So.'

'Teddy's a good guy, but also something of an outlaw. Don't let him exploit you.'

'I won't.' S studied Winters as if seeing him for the first time and said, 'Reckon you're something of an outlaw yourself.'

'Is this about my smoking weed? It's been legal for longer than you've been alive.'

'Not that. Just, I don't know, your attitude.'

'My attitude?'

'The way you bend the rules and such.'

'Sometimes they need a little stretching. You can tell Teddy that I'm glad to hear about the licence. And I should get back to beating out little fires before they become big ones.'

'Can I take a turn?'

'At beating out fires?'

'Why not?'

'I don't have a spare mask.'

The kid lifted the ends of their kerchief. 'I'll wet this, tie it over my mouth and nose.'

'I guess that'll do,' Winters said, and handed them his multi-tool. 'After my crew has dealt with a fire, use this to grub up soil, chop up and smother anything that's still smoking. And if a stray spark restarts the fire, don't try to put it out yourself. Call us over. Okay?'

A quick smile, there and gone. 'Okay.'

The kid tagged behind Winters and his crew for the rest of the afternoon and well into the long evening, hacking at patches of grass burnt to charcoal, digging up squares of smouldering sod and folding them over and stamping them out. Sootstreaked and indefatigably energetic despite the heat. At last, the deputy chief fire officer declared that the incident was over and stood everyone down. Broad swathes of Bale

Field and patches of reeds and grass in the grazing marsh beyond had burned, but the greater part of the reserve had been saved and the fire hadn't spread beyond its seawall.

In the farmyard where the base of operations had been set up, the kid solemnly handed over the multitool and told Winters that they'd see him around and went off to find Teddy. Winters snagged a bottle of water and poured half of it over his sunburnt face and drank the rest and sat with the other rangers and several volunteers, listening to them talk over the high spots of the day while sharing beers and smokes.

Embry Clarke told a story about how the fire service had lost a brand-new bulldozer in a big blaze which had jumped from woods into crop fields and threatened to spread all the way to Heybridge Basin.

'They brought out their new toy, first time in action. Shiny red, like a low slung tractor with this big angle blade. They were using it to scrape a fire line through a soybean field when the wind changed and the fire outflanked it. Driver had to abandon ship, run for his life. Bulldozer was swallowed up by flames . . . ' Embry looked at Winters and said, 'Ever see batteries catch fire? The graphene ones?'

'I don't believe I have.'

'Like something in a war film. Big flash like a lightning strike, then a fireball rolling up and bulldozer parts raining out of the sky,' Embry said, pantomiming the explosion with his hands.

There were other stories. The time when huge rafts of bladderwrack had washed up along the east coast and drifted into the estuary on a king tide and smothered its shores and mudflats in stinking windrows that bred billions of flies. The seaweed couldn't be burned or used as fertiliser because it was contaminated by plastic detritus, arsenic and heavy metals, so it was scooped up by grabs mounted on flat-top pontoons and compressed into bales, and the bales were loaded onto ocean-going barges which sailed north and dumped their cargo in the deep trenches of the Devil's Hole, where the sequestered carbon should remain undisturbed for at least a century. The time when a huge storm got up over the North Sea and swept across the estuary like Hell's own runway train. Thunder like an artillery barrage, lightning everywhere, winds peaking at a hundred and fifty kph. And as the storm was beginning to clear, a waterspout came tottering upriver, its snout sucking leechlike at the cloud base and its column flexing about a footing of foam and spray. It hit land at the head of the estuary and cut along a street at the edge of Maldon, trashing gardens and stripping roofs on one side, flinging broken slates and the sodden contents of bedrooms into the road, but left the houses on the other side untouched. Moved on across fields beyond, and collapsed in a rain of fish and terrapins. There were stories that reached further back, too. How every caravan and mobile home in a holiday park had been washed out to sea during the Great Storm. How the same storm had driven a container ship aground at the east end of Mersea Island, and the ship had stood there for six years, until a Bangladeshi company had broken it up in place. How locals had banded together in a militia to protect farms and market gardens from bandits during Panic Summer. The flocks of swans, wild ducks and other water birds which had overwintered in the estuary or passed through it on migration. Cormorants nesting in trees. A field covered in thousands of Brent Geese. Thousands of starlings lifting off from the mudflats in a great rising wing, darkening the sun as they passed overhead.

Winters liked to listen to those old stories. They evoked a wistful nostalgia for times before he'd been born. A bittersweet, sentimental longing for a past present only in memory and imagination. No doubt there was a word for that feeling. Bob Flowers would know. The world was not as it was and never would be again, but in time, decades or centuries, the losses would abate and some new stable point would be reached. Winters hoped that he was making a small contribution towards making that possible. Hoped that, as the agency claimed, the Old Hall Marshes and Cynsea and all the other reserves were seed bombs from which a better future might grow. It was nice to think so, anyway.

The tree which had been struck by lightning stood at the eastern end of Cynsea, close to the causeway. It was a tall Corsican pine with tufted rafts of needles that began more than halfway up its trunk, and the strike had left a rip of shredded bark spiralling from top to base, exposing a broad pale ribbon of living heartwood. Winters sent photos of the damage to the agency's arboreal management service and decided that it was time he dealt with the steps at the other end of the island, damaged by May's rainstorm. It had been too hot to contemplate the hard labour it would involve but, following on the heels of the thunderstorm, the weather was cooler now.

He made a start early the next morning, cutting back the remains of the steps and marking out the site with a builder's line and pegs. With the help of his agent and a pocket drone he measured the necessary height and horizontal distance, calculated the number of treads and risers needed and pegged lines to mark the backs of treads and roughly shaped them with a spade. He had to break off for a couple of hours to help supervise the visit of a primary school class, an anarchic tribe of seven- and eight-year-old kids in orange safety vests scrambling around the muddy foreshore, searching for the items on their checklists and making drawings of their finds, but by the end of the first day the new course of stairs was dug out and shaped.

He took photos of his progress, told his agent to write a brief piece about the project for the island's diary, and rewarded himself by ordering a drone delivery of cauliflower curry, samosas and pickles, which he ate on the stern deck of the narrowboat while a mosquito coil lofted an unravelling thread of lemon-scented smoke into the darkening air and tree frogs piped and whistled in the salt-willow brakes. An invasive species, the tree frogs. Imported in cargoes of bananas from the Caribbean, back when bananas grew on banana plants rather than being printed from cell cultures, thriving in the warming climate like the red-eared terrapins in the mudflats, the ring-necked parakeets which quarrelled ceaselessly in the trees, and water hyacinth, Himalayan balsam and other super-invasive plants which Winters and his volunteers hacked back three or four times a year.

Before he could resume work on the steps the next morning, he checked in a party of birders and met a graduate student, Shan Cowie, who was making a survey of moth abundance and diversity in the estuary, and helped her lug cases containing disassembled Skinner traps from her cargo bike to sites in the island's pocket meadows and patches of woodland.

According to Shan, moths were seriously underappreciated. Stealth pollinators that serviced a wider variety of plants than bees and butterflies.

'Not that I have anything against bees,' she said. 'But they're charismatic critters with great PR, while moths work away unnoticed. Visiting plants bees ignore, because bees target the richest sources of nectar and pollen sources. If you want a good diversity of plants, you need plenty of moths.'

'How are they doing, moths? I know one species was just declared extinct.'

'The Lesser Lichen Case-bearer? That was sad, but it had been in decline like forever. And wasn't a pollinator.'

'That's what you're interested in. The pollinators.'

'It's why I'm here. Their numbers are much lower than they need to be. Not as low as bees, but still.'

'And you want to fix that.'

'First, I have to find out what needs fixing,' Shan Cowie said. 'This is lovely.'

The path they'd been following through a scrubby patch of hawthorn and brambles had brought them to a long stretch of waist-high honey-coloured grass punctuated by clumps of flowering thistles and the rusty spikes of docks. A tract of day lilies, one of the escapees from the old lodge's gardens, grew along one side of this miniature meadow, clumps of dark green blades punctuated with orange flowers vivid as fireworks. And as Winters and Shan Cowie followed the narrow path that cut through the middle of the meadow several small brown and white moths fluttered up from grass along the margins. Common heath moths, according to Shan. A dayflying species.

'I'm really interested in what comes out at night. But it's a good sign.'

Winters left her to unpack and assemble her traps and collected his tools from the narrowboat and headed over to his half-finished stair project. He dug a shallow slot trench for the footing of the first riser and filled it with porridgy zero-carbon concrete and measured and cut boards to protect the fore-edges of the rest of the risers, sweating through his T-shirt and stripping it off, fixing the half boards in place with wooden stakes hammered into the hard dirt. By late afternoon it had become too hot to work and he took a break for a couple of hours and returned early in the evening, determined to finish the project. Setting the last of the boards in place and shovelling gravel behind each one and tamping it down and levelling it off. Labouring slowly and steadily until, four steps from the bottom, the gravel ran out.

He was close to finishing the damn thing, so took a quick coldwater shower and drove the skimmer up the navigation channel to Heybridge Basin, where he signed out two bags of gravel from the agency store and used the store's sack truck to wheel them to the skimmer. After returning the sack truck and locking up the store, he wandered along the basin in the evening gloaming. The air warm and close. Narrowboats and barges, houseboats and cabin cruisers all packed together. Families sitting out on decks and roofs, chatting, thumbing their phones, grilling food. A man watering tubs of vegetables and cane fruits on the roof of a Dutch barge. A woman sitting on a plank slung from the top rail of a narrowboat's cabin, adding a white rose to a half-finished frieze of painted flowers. Two optimists fishing off the foredeck of a chunky catamaran whose mast towered above the boats anchored around it, and someone somewhere playing a stately, precise piece on a violin. Something by Bach, maybe. Or Monteverdi or Vivaldi. The early to late Baroque music which Julia, Winters' mother, played when she shut herself in the outhouse she used as a studio and was deep in what she called the process. Mum's brain food, according to Izzy. A sign that she shouldn't be disturbed.

Julia Winters had been a painter, although not an especially famous one. She'd turned to art after her husband was killed in a train derailment caused by heavy rain, a landslide and a faulty signal. Quit her work as a teaching assistant, moved with her young daughter and newborn son to a rented cottage in

Gloucestershire, in a village under the brow of a scarp at the eastern end of the Cotswolds. In before times, she'd dabbled in watercolours, mostly still lives of flowers and weeds, hedgerow fruit and fungi. Now, supported by a life insurance payout, she carpentered frames and stretched canvases, and coated them with thick, sculptural layers of black and umber oil paint in which specks and shards of white and yellow shone like birthing stars in galactic dust clouds, gems in subterranean seams, or the final thoughts of a dying brain. In the first flush of her new career, she acquired an agent, shared a gallery show in Cheltenham with two other artists, staged a solo exhibition in a tiny gallery in East London and sold one of her first paintings to a renowned classical composer. That early success was followed by a long tailing off, but she refused her agent's advice to change her style or take commissions. As far as she was concerned sales were incidental. The act of making, rendering in oil paint and canvas the clash between her interior life and the state of the world, was all that mattered. Every painting was part of a long series she called the Emotional Weather Report; when she was felled by her final stroke, she had been working on Emotional Weather Report CXXIV. Winters sometimes wondered if her brain food music had still been playing when her body was discovered by a concerned neighbour, two days after she'd died.

One of the narrowboats had been converted into a café. The owner knew Winters from times when he'd eaten there with the other rangers, and greeted him and led him to a table in a corner, beside an open window. He ate a big bowl of mushroom, lentil and mealworm lasagne and slowly drank a bottle of yeasty alcohol-free beer and paid and walked towards the sea lock and was leaning at the railing, smoking a joint and staring out across the sleeve of open water towards the low dark silhouette of Northey Island, in a slightly melancholic mood because of the music, when his phone pinged and his agent told him that the server which controlled the island's cameras and drones had fallen over.

He didn't think it was a big deal, it wasn't the first time the server had thrown a glitch, but he needed to go home. Reboot everything and go to bed. Puttering back against the incoming tide under a starry sky, steering past the fugitive glimmer of waves breaking over Cynsea's causeway, he felt tired but content. Plugged back into the world. The tree frogs were tuning up, an urchin orchestra equipped with a thousand penny whistles, as he made the sharp turn into the dredged channel that cut through reedbeds to the narrowboat's mooring. The light hung at the end of the jetty contemplated its perfect reflection.

Winters cut the motor and let the skimmer coast to a stop against the mossy tyres hung alongside the jetty and walked to the bow and passed the loop of the painter line over the head of a piling and secured the stern. Put up his pocket drone and followed the splash of light it cast down the springy planks of the jetty to the narrowboat. And saw with a bump of surprise that the double doors to the cabin, which he'd shut before he left, to keep out mosquitoes, were flung open.

The contents of the storage crates had been dumped on the floor, the doors of the galley cabinets hung ajar, and in the bedroom the sheets had been stripped off the bed and the mattress was on its side. Nothing seemed to be missing, but Winters was certain that the person or persons who'd broken in had also used his tablet. He'd shut it down before he'd left, but now it was in sleep mode, lighting up in anticipation as soon as he touched it. Its activity log revealed that around the time he'd been eating dinner on the barge in Heybridge Basin someone had bypassed its biometric security and opened and closed a string of files, and even though the local network was down had somehow managed to log into the island's account on the servers at the agency's regional office.

The network stubbornly refused to reboot, throwing up error messages he couldn't parse, but he was able to access stored footage from island's drones and static cameras. A camera aimed at the causeway had recorded Shan Cowie riding her cargo bicycle towards the mainland, and the birders leaving a little later, but there was no sign of anyone arriving, and neither the rest of the cameras nor any of the drones had captured any trace of human activity before the network crashed and all the feeds cut off.

Winters grabbed his lantern and went topside and counted and recounted the drones clustered like sleepy bees on a pair of charging pads set between the solar panels on the narrowboat's roof. None were missing — their auto-return routines had flown them back to the nest when the network had fallen over. He sent a brief message to his supervisor and remade the bed and shucked his clothes and lay down, and after a couple of minutes got up and lifted the wooden chair away from the shelf he used as a desk and jacked its crest rail under the handles of the cabin doors and went back to bed.

The next morning, he discovered that his toothstick was missing. The local network was still down, still wouldn't reboot, and his supervisor hadn't replied to his message. Probably wouldn't until the agency's offices, over in Colchester, opened in a couple of hours. He brewed a mug of strong tea and carried it outside and saw what he'd missed last night. A message or slogan stencilled in white spraypaint along the side of the narrowboat's cabin.

THE INSTAURATION IS COMING.

According to his agent, the slogan was the trademark of a group of so-called deep dreamers who had begun to make themselves known in the past couple of years. They appeared to have no connection with commonplace dreamers who used shrooms to nope out of the present, like the daffy pair of vagabond mystics Winters had met in Somerset and others he'd encountered in the years since, but were members of an underground clique or collective who used a variety of baroque pseudonyms and claimed to be inspired by the extensive pseudo-scientific speculations about shamanistic rituals, vision quests, shared lucid dreams and reshaping history which Kasey Motte had published before the siege. Their slogan seemed to be a reference to the olden-times philosopher Francis Bacon's unfinished treatise, *The Great Instauration*, which described how humanity could be partially restored to a state of prelapsarian grace and regain its dominion over nature.

'Have they ever mentioned a Great Green Reset?' Winters said.

'I cannot find any reference to that in their literature and postings,' the agent said.

'Doesn't mean they haven't.'

'I'm afraid I don't understand that remark.'

'Absence of evidence isn't evidence of absence, and all that.'

Winters was sitting at the end of the jetty, a mug of tea cooling beside him as he puffed on a joint. Thinking of his sister, and the commune after it had been cuckooed by Kasey Motte. The resets which Motte claimed to have carried out, on his own and with his followers, and had wanted to do again, bigger and better, one last time. The final definitive makeover. This instauration business seemed to be very much like that, the same power fantasies got up in a different garb, and Winters was certain that the break-in wasn't a garden-variety burglary, that it was also connected to that creepy phone call a couple of weeks ago. But what had the intruder been looking for? What had they found?

When she finally returned his call, his supervisor, Aimee Fellows, didn't seem especially troubled by the news. She listened to his explanation of the connections between the deep dreamers and his sister's involvement with Kasey Motte, told him that the agency had been targeted by so-called radical green groups before.

'People who think we are doing conservation wrong, or shouldn't be doing any conservation at all, because Mother Nature will take care of everything. Your break-in might be linked to the new eelgrass initiative. Someone looking for something they can use against it.'

'What about the other reserves? Have there been break-ins elsewhere?'

'You were the only ranger absent from their patch last night.'

'I needed some gravel to finish a repair.'

'I'm not questioning why you weren't there. Merely pointing it out. As far as we can tell, your intruder wanted access to an agency tablet. They saw an opportunity and took it.'

The intruder had accessed only recent images and video footage uploaded to Cynsea's account in the agency's servers, Aimee told Winters, and so far no damage had been discovered. Nothing erased or locked up by ransomware, no spyware or malware inserted anywhere.

'They took out my local network,' Winters said. 'It's still down, and I can't get it back up.'

'One of the technicians will help you with that. Meanwhile, don't use your tablet. Power it down. I expect the police will want to check it for fingerprints and so on. And we'll need to examine it, too.'

'Have you told the police, or should I?'

'It's already done. They told me that someone from the Maldon station will be along today or tomorrow. How many visitors are you expecting today?'

'Some birders. A couple of casuals. And a walking party of natural history enthusiasts. There's also the graduate student with the moth traps. She isn't on the schedule, but I guess she'll want to see what her traps have caught.'

'Message everyone. Apologise for cancelling their visit, tell them it's due to unforeseen circumstances and ask them to rebook.'

'Okay.'

'I'll arrange delivery of a new tablet, and one of our techs will give you a call. So don't go anywhere.'

Winters asked his phone's agent to compose and send the cancellation messages, and took a walk around the perimeter of the island. He wasn't certain what he was looking for, or if he would know what it was if he found it, but he was too stirred up to sit still, was haunted by the idea that someone must have been watching him, might be watching him even now. Holed up somewhere in the reedbeds or inside a patch of salt willows. Tracking him with a drone invisibly high in the cloudless sky. It was the same kind of anxiety which had possessed him when he'd been stalked by mainstream newsfeeds and citizen journalists after the siege and his non-arrest. It had eased during his time abroad, but now it was creeping back, like floodwater seeping under doors and bubbling up between floorboards.

He searched the mudflats for signs that a boat or dinghy had been run ashore, checked the ruins of the old lodge, the roofless bungalows standing in silty water tiger-striped by sunlight and shadow, walked through the patches of woodland. Looking for traces of some kind of hide or cover, somewhere the intruder might have laid up, waiting for him to leave. He didn't find anything, but wasn't reassured. Everything was familiar, everything was the same, but the island no longer seemed like a place of shelter, and as he emerged from the trees at the western end he saw something moving on the path below and his heart gave a little kick before he realised that it was the graduate student, Shan Cowie.

'Didn't you get my message?' he said, when he intercepted her.

'I thought you might make an exception for a fellow agency employee. If I don't check and empty my traps I'll lose valuable data.'

He couldn't be angry with her. 'I guess you have an hour or so before the tide starts to come in. But don't tell anyone.'

'Can I ask what they were, these unforeseen circumstances?'

'Someone broke into my narrowboat yesterday evening. I'm waiting for the police to arrive and do their thing.'

'That's awful. Are you okay?'

'I was over in Heybridge at the time. By the time I came back the intruder was long gone.'

'I hope they didn't take anything valuable.'

'Not really. Just fritzed some equipment,' Winters said. She didn't need to know about the slogan and its implications. 'Did you see anyone while you were putting up your traps?'

'There were some men pottering about the mudflats. One of them was flying this little drone. I went to look because I heard it buzzing around and wondered what it was.'

'That would be the birders,' Winters said. 'They left not long after you did. On your way back across the causeway, did you spot any boats near the island?'

'I think there were some sailboats. But way out in the channel. Is that how your burglar got here? By boat?'

'They didn't walk across. The cameras didn't spot anyone, and the tide was coming in over the causeway. But they could have been hiding somewhere. Watching me, waiting for me to leave.'

'That's creepy.'

'Yeah. If you see any signs of a camp, litter or trampled grass or whatever, let me know.'

'I hope they didn't mess around with my traps.'

'I shouldn't think so. But if you like, I can walk up there with you.'

'I am a little spooked,' Shan confessed. 'This is a lonely sort of place. Isolated. Maybe that's why your burglar chose it.'

Winters thought of the slogan. 'I hope that's all it was.'

A drone delivered a new tablet and an agency technician talked Winters through the remote access setup and assessed the damage to the local network. The result of a botched hack, the technician said, with professional contempt.

'Anyone with the right kind of smarts should have been able to access the root functions of your network remotely. Either your intruder tried to do that and failed, or they didn't know how. So they resorted to a basic denial-of-service attack to crash the network and shut off the cameras and drones. Linked your tablet to their phone so they could log into the Cynsea Island account, and after they finished poking around tried to install spyware in the local network. But they fucked up the network interface in the process, and that's why your reboots didn't work.'

'If they didn't have access to the local network, weren't using it to spy on me, how did they know I wouldn't be at home when they broke in?'

'That I can't tell you. Maybe they had a drone. Or were using Mark One eyeballs. All I know is that it looks like they wanted to leave something that would tap your camera feeds and messages and so on. I'll have to do a complete reinstall. Best set your phone on a charger pad, so it doesn't run out of juice halfway through.'

Winters felt a little better when the network had been restored and the cameras and drones were back in service, but the visit by a detective constable from Maldon's police station was somewhat less reassuring.

'A young woman who looked like she'd just left school,' he told Nina Patel, the next day. 'Asked a few questions, took my old tablet to be checked for fingerprints and DNA, and examined by one of their digital forensics guys. And that was that, apart from taking my prints and a cheek swab for what she called the purposes of elimination.'

'When will you get the results?'

'She told me that forensics are backed up, it might take a week, might take two. And didn't seem to think the slogan meant anything. Told me that it had appeared in several places around Maldon, might be related to drifters moving into the area to do seasonal work in farms and orchards. I asked if it was likely that a drifter would crash the island's surveillance system and get into the agency's files, and she told me I shouldn't underestimate them. The agency doesn't seem much exercised by it either, just wants me to submit a report.'

'A GH20 form or a GH23?'

'GH20,' Winters said.

'Unauthorised trespass, rather than sabotage or a security breach.'

'Yeah. No one's taking it very seriously.'

'Apart from you.'

'Yeah. Apart from me.'

Winters and Nina were sitting in nests of big cushions either side of a low table in her work hut, a small circular timber-framed building with clay lump walls and a conical thatch roof. A curved slit window overlooked one of the reedbeds at the northern edge of the Old Hall Marshes. Foul weather gear hung from a clothes tree by the door; spider plants and air plants hung from shelves packed with old field guides and keepsakes – a clutter of hag stones and water-smoothed shards of driftglass, a car's wing mirror and old bottles crusted with bonewhite barnacle shells and worm castings, a jam jar packed with pale red sand, a piece of driftwood stuck with artificial flowers, framed photographs of Nina's children and grandchildren, an old brasscased barometer and a small ship's bell and a rusted spokeshave, the flight feathers of geese and ducks and gulls sprouting from a wicker pen holder, and a bronze statuette of a crouching soldier in field gear, presented to Nina when she'd retired from the army. She'd served for twenty years, had been a freshly promoted captain in the First Battalion of the Royal Anglican Regiment when the brand-new coalition government declared martial law at the beginning of Panic Summer and she was appointed second-in-command of a unit of ninety soldiers, charged with keeping order and maintaining the security of farms, greenhouse complexes, warehouses, cold stores and associated infrastructure along the eastern coast of the Wash. No easy mission. Armed criminal gangs were roaming the countryside, terrorising farmers, killing and butchering livestock and raiding warehouses and food processing plants. Nina's troops were overstretched and she was under orders to avoid using lethal force, but she'd broken up two of the largest gangs and organised a system of roving patrols that had secured most of the assets in her area. She was brisk and forthright, her manner somewhat blunted by years of service, but her advice was usually fair-minded and sound. Winters wanted her take on the break-in, had decided that a face-to-face meeting would underscore the gravity of the situation.

'I had a notification about additional security measures at the eelgrass trial sites this morning,' she told him. 'The agency may be taking the break-in more seriously than you think.'

'Aimee told me that it might be something to do with the eelgrass thing, but I'm not so sure. Given these so-called deep dreamers' interest in Kasey Motte. And my sister's relationship with him.'

Bringing that up still triggered a queasy little jolt of unease, but he needed to talk about it.

'You think they might be targeting you because of that,' Nina said.

'Do I sound crazy, or are the agency and the police ignoring the obvious?'

'I think you shouldn't take it personally. Or make too much of a piece of graffiti. It could be that you just happened to be the only ranger away from their patch at the wrong time.'

'Aimee said something like that.'

'I know it isn't the answer you wanted, but your supervisor is not often wrong. There have always been people who don't agree with our mission. Don't like what we're doing, or don't think that we're doing enough. Those airjellies you spotted, for instance. There have been two more sightings since then.'

'Yeah, I saw the reports.'

'We might get lucky and catch the culprits in the act, or we might not. A few years ago, someone released thousands of Grayling butterflies. It might have been well-intentioned, an attempt to reintroduce what had once been a common species, but they could have displaced surviving butterfly populations, and they'd been bred from too few individuals and for too many generations. Variation in their gene pool was, to say the least, rather suboptimal. Luckily, they died out pretty quickly, but we never found out who was responsible.'

'Point taken,' Winters said.

'Give the police time do their thing. And try not to be disheartened if no one's brought to book.'

It was sensible advice, but Winters couldn't shake the small but nagging mystery of how the intruder had known he wasn't at home. His stupid feeling that he was still being watched. He tried to distract himself with work. Scrubbing off the slogan, which was easier than he'd thought because the spraypaint turned out to be water-soluble, then hauling one of the bags of gravel he'd requisitioned over to the stair and backfilling the last few steps. When he was done, he sat at the top, sipping from his water bottle and looking out across the salt-willow brakes and the channel that ran through them to the narrowboat. The tide was out. Mudflats along the edges of the willow brakes and the fleet of mudbanks stretching beyond the point of the island glistened in the hot, late afternoon light, and Winters realised that the intruder's hiding place might have been right in front of him all along.

Most of the mudbanks were small hummocks with scanty combovers of cord grass, but a few were larger, crowned with patches of gorse and brambles and salt willows. It would have been easier and quicker to use drones to check them out, but Winters wanted to do it himself. Mark One eyeballs. And besides, it was a little cooler out on the water, and navigating the shallow, mazy channels between the mudbanks, silky chocolate-coloured water purling from the skimmer's bow as he judged speed and distance, was pleasantly satisfying.

At one of the rangers' meet-ups there'd been a canned presentation on the teeming microscopic life of mud's primordial ooze. Predatory flowers and wheel-mouthed filter feeders, iridescent ciliated slippers and shapeshifting plasms, jungle-green and camo-brown photosynthetic units like scattered jewels, or fused into filaments or geometrically precise hollow spheres. More diversity in a dripping handful than in all the plants and animals of the entire estuary. Imagine the adventures you could have if you were able to shrink yourself to the size of those microscopic beasties, Winters had said to Jude, afterwards. He'd sampled one of his friend's specials and was feeling no pain. You could build yourself a little house out of diatom bricks, or take control of one of those spheres, steer it like a submarine or a spaceship. Jude had said that he believed that he'd once read a story like that, observed that what was truly amazing was how Winters could get so baked on a couple of puffs. Yet here he was now, navigating a little world of islands shaped from water and mud, and wasn't he on some kind of quest?

On the first mudbank he targeted there was nothing but the bleached shells of crabs and a scattering of the usual detritus. Shards of ancient plastic and frayed knots of orange polyprop rope. A lobster trap half-buried in silt. The delicate trefoil tracks of birds and a starburst of bloodied feathers left by some ambush, but no trace of human footprints or an anchorage.

There were the remains of a campfire on the second, but they were far too old. Fresh green blades of grass spearing a scatter of charred twigs, ash fused by rain into stony lumps. A pair of common sandpipers raised up from the third and circled, calling anxiously, as Winters walked the grassy crest from one end to the other, finding tattered rags of blue plastic sheeting hung from the branches of a lone salt willow and spotting a dragonfly, the first he'd seen that year, delicately gripping a blade of cord grass. He shook out his phone, managed to catch a good close-up before the insect kicked into the air and zoomed off like a miniature attack helicopter. His agent identified it as a male black-tailed skimmer. *Orthetrum cancellatum*. A species that had once been common in the south-east of England and was now red-listed.

'Write it up for the diary,' Winters said.

'Done. Would you like to publish it?'

'I'm sure it's your usual top-notch work, but I'll check it over first.'

'Of course. Is there anything else?'

'I only have one more mud pile worth visiting. What are the chances that I'll find what I'm looking for?'

He wasn't expecting an answer, but his agent said, 'A fair coin has an equal chance of landing on heads or tails on any single flip, but the probability that it will always land on either heads or tails reduces with each successive flip.'

'Which means I should give this one last go, I guess.'

As he approached the fourth and final mudbank, he spotted a section of bent and crushed blades in the reeds fringing its outer edge, and after he grounded the skimmer found a patch of flattened cord grass at the crest of the shallow slope, where someone might have recently laid up. He knelt beside it and raised his field glasses and saw, beyond the ellipses of several smaller mudbanks, the channel that cut through the fringe of reeds and salt-willows, and a tiny star of light reflected from one of the narrowboat's portholes.

A bank of brambles covered one end of the ridge. He ducked through the briars to a patch of bare dirt at the centre, found a muddle of ridged bootprints and a triangle of small slots, the footing of a camp stool perhaps. A wooden fork, the kind attached to takeaway or readymade meals, trodden into the dirt. The cellophane wrapper of a package of instant noodles caught on a thorny whip.

Someone had been watching him, there was no doubt about it. Camping out on the mudbank for a day or more, waiting for him to leave the island. Weirdly disturbing to think about that. To imagine someone sprawled below the rim of the mudbank's ridge, studying him through field glasses or a camera's zoom lens. Maybe using a drone to track him as he moved about the island.

He called Aimee Fellows and was answered by an out-of-office message, but got through to the detective constable who'd visited the narrowboat after the break-in. Explained what he'd found, said that he had put the fork and the wrapper in separate sample bags and would be happy to deliver them to the police station.

'There are footprints, too. A place where I think a boat was hidden. You might want to see that for yourself.'

'Unfortunately, sir, what you have found is at best circumstantial evidence.'

'Someone was camping here. There's a spot where I think they laid up, with a good view of my narrowboat.'

'My point is that these things could have been left by anyone,' the detective constable said, with the exaggerated patience of someone used to dealing with people afflicted with harmless fantasies. 'A gleaner who stopped over for the night, for instance. Or a poacher.'

'A poacher wouldn't camp this close to me,' Winters said. 'And what if fingerprints and DNA on the fork and the wrapper matches fingerprints and DNA left by the intruder?'

'If they left trace evidence on your tablet, we won't need it from anywhere else. And if we only have DNA from those scraps of litter, there's no way of proving that they were left by your intruder. Which is what I mean by circumstantial evidence.'

'It sounds like you haven't checked out the tablet yet.'

'It's in the system, sir. But as usual there's a backlog, so I must ask you to be patient.'

'Remind me how long I have to be patient,' Winters said. He was beginning to find it hard to control his temper.

'At the moment, we're looking at around three weeks.'

'Three weeks.'

'Yes, sir.'

'And, just to be clear, you don't want to do anything with the evidence I've found.'

'It's not really evidence. If there's a useful result from the tablet, I'll let your employer know.'

When she returned Winters' call the next morning, Aimee Fellows was slightly more sympathetic, but no more helpful. Telling him that she couldn't force the police to speed up the investigation, reminding him that he had plenty of work of his own to be getting on with. He tried his best. Every day at low tide he walked the same stretch of foreshore, picking up every crab carcass he found, burning them in a drum brazier after they'd been identified and inventoried by his agent. He dealt with birders, day visitors, groups of schoolkids. Replaced printed notices damaged by rain and sun and refreshed markers for the island's trails, serviced the composting toilets and the birdwatching hide, helped a couple of volunteers to assemble nesting boxes from flatpack kits and nail them to tree trunks with aluminium nails.

A supervisor from the agency's arboreal management service inspected the Corsican pine which had been struck by lightning, pointed out branches where needles were turning brown, dug several test holes around it, and told Winters that its roots had been damaged when the lightning had penetrated the ground.

'We could repair its bark, but there's nothing we can do about its roots. There's already a significant amount of foliage wilting, and it'll only get worse. I'm afraid that the best thing to do is remove it.'

'It'll leave a big gap in the canopy,' Winters said, feeling an unexpected pang at this death sentence. 'It's one of the tallest trees on the island. There's a hawk that likes to perch way up in it.'

'Being taller than most of the other trees is probably why it was struck,' the supervisor said. 'We'll come back in a couple of weeks and cut it down and dig out its roots. And check the trees around it, too. Then we can think about a replacement. We have some good Spanish oak saplings. Won't grow as fast as a pine, but in twenty or thirty years it'll be on the way to being a good-sized tree. Fine red foliage in autumn too.'

'I know Spanish oaks. Planted a bunch of them in Somerset.'

'The National Forest?'

'Yeah.'

'Spanish oaks aren't native, but neither is this poor fellow,' the supervisor said, patting the trunk of the pine. 'So it goes, these days.'

Shan Cowie came back for the last time, and after she'd counted and identified and released the overnight catch of moths Winters helped her to dismantle and pack up her traps and load them onto her cargo bike. She told him that numbers were significantly lower than the last survey, but she'd found three species which hadn't been recorded previously.

'The agency is planning a breeding-and-release project. My data will contribute to the decisions about which species should be included, and where they are released,' she said. 'It might not be a permanent fix, but we have to try.'

'Definitely,' Winters said, remembering Nina's story about the Grayling butterflies.

A week passed. Still no word from the police. The eelgrass initiative broke ground at a site off the shore of Mersea Island, and Winters and the other rangers visited the team's headquarters in a rented warehouse for the official opening, posing with local politicians for photographs. According to the publicity release, the team would operate a fleet of miniature autonomous submarines that could plant up to ten thousand seedlings a day, eventually covering six hectares of the estuary's bed at the Mersea site and more than twenty hectares at four other sites.

'I hear they'll also be using drones to patrol their planting sites and this warehouse twenty-four seven,' Jude told Winters. 'Looks like your break-in has spooked the agency.'

'Good,' Winters said. 'Because it's still spooking the fuck out of me.'

The next morning the sky was sheeted with low cloud and a thin steady rain set in, striking restless patterns of ringlets across the black water of the channel and pattering on the tarpaulin sheet stretched above the narrowboat's stern deck, where Winters sat cross-legged on a cushion, servicing drones from his small flock. They kept a running inventory of the island's birds and animals and tracked selected individuals, recording the dramas and minutiae of their little lives. Some of this footage, edited by Winters' agent into capsule narratives, was put up on the island's diary, which also featured raw, round-the-clock views from fixed cameras. Nesting birds and their fledgings were especially popular, as was the feed dedicated to the island's lone hawk, the one which liked to perch high up on the doomed Corsican pine, surveying his kingdom with a mad yellow gaze. Even the audio feed of the tree frogs' nocturnal carolling had its fans.

Winters thought that being reincarnated as a drone would be pretty fine. Becoming a cool, disembodied viewpoint free to travel anywhere, observing without judgement, commitment or consequence. Of the world, but not in it. Being reborn as a terrapin, like the dinnerplate-sized grandpa with mossy hindquarters he sometimes saw in the lagoon where the ruins of the old guest bungalows stood, wouldn't be so bad either. They lived a long time, terrapins, thirty years or more, and everywhere they went their houses went with them. Sunlight warming the roofs of their shells on long, lazy days. Rain drumming on them, like the rain on the tarpaulin above his head, while they dozed inside.

The drones patrolled the island day and night, returning to the narrowboat only to refresh their batteries on one of the charging pads or when Winters recalled them for routine maintenance. Testing batteries, cleaning and inspecting chassis, tightening screws, polishing camera lenses, checking that vanes were free-spinning and touching up their bearings with graphene grease and replacing any that were damaged. He was about halfway done when a police launch turned into the channel and glided towards the narrowboat. A shirt-sleeved constable wearing a River Police cap at the helm, three passengers seated behind him. Detective Sergeant Grace Fairbrother, who'd investigated a poaching gang which had hit Cynsea and the Old Hall Marshes last year, and two men Winters didn't recognise, lifejackets buckled over dark suits. With a falling feeling of dismay, he stood up as the launch slowed and reversed, bumping gently against the narrowboat's stern fenders.

'Hey, Winters,' Grace Fairbrother said. 'Been a while.'

'Yeah. Who are your friends?'

The two men in the well of the launch were definitely police or some other flavour of law, studying Winters with shuttered faces impossible to read. One was tall and lean, a grey streak in his severe crewcut; his younger companion sported a neatly barbered beard and a pair of gold-rimmed glasses with round dark lenses. A slim document folder tucked under one arm.

'Colleagues from London,' Grace Fairbrother said. 'They have a few questions for you.'

'Is this about the break-in? The forensics I'm still waiting on?'

'It is and it isn't,' the older man said. 'May we come aboard, Mr Winters?'

'I think you should show me some ID first.'

The two men shared a look, then reached inside their jackets and pulled out black card wallets and flipped them open. Both of them balancing carefully, holding the wallets at arm's length to show Winters their warrant cards. Metropolitan Police, Detective Inspectors.

'Which division?' Winter said, although he was pretty sure he knew.

'Counterterrorism operations,' the older man said. Andrew Sinclair, according to his warrant card.

'If this is about the Wakestone siege, I've nothing useful or new to say about that. It was all hashed out long ago.'

'There's has been a development,' the other detective, Matty Briggs, said.

'We'll tell you everything we know, Mr Winters,' Sinclair said. 'Why don't we get out of this rain?'

The two detectives claimed the couch behind the little dining table and Winters perched on edge of the kitchen chair. He felt underdressed in his shorts and singlet, clamped his hands between his bare knees. He was certain that his visitors weren't about to deliver any kind of good news.

After brief pleasantries about the island and the cosy homeliness of the narrowboat, Sinclair told Winters that their conversation would be recorded and Briggs took out a pocket drone and set it in the air above the table.

Winters looked at it. The blur of its single rotor. Its tiny camera lens, black as a shark's eye.

'Do I have any choice?'

'It's routine procedure,' Sinclair said. 'Please give your name, and state your relationship to Isabel Jane Winters.'

'Marc Winters. Her brother.'

'You live here,' Briggs said. 'On Cynsea Island.'

'I'm the wildlife ranger.'

'And you're the island's only inhabitant, is that correct?'

'There are plenty of visitors. That's partly why I'm here.'

'But you are the only permanent inhabitant.'

'I guess so. You said there'd been some kind of development? What does it have to do with me?'

'We have good reason to believe that your sister is still alive,' Sinclair said.

Winters thought that he'd misheard. 'She died eight years ago. In the siege.'

'Apparently she did not,' Sinclair said, and shook out his phone and flicked his forefinger across its surface and slid it across the table towards Winters, asked him if he recognised the person in the photograph.

Winters leaned forward. A woman sitting at the tiller of a sailboat, squinting into the camera. A blue windbreaker and a canary yellow lifejacket. Her face somewhat rounder than he remembered and her hair dyed candyfloss pink, but it was her. It was Isabel.

He said, 'When was this taken?'

'In July last year,' Sinclair said. 'Loch Awe, Scotland. During a holiday with a friend from her workplace.'

'Her workplace?'

'If you could tell us who you think it is,' Briggs said. The lenses of his spectacles had lost their tint in the cabin's dim light, revealing blue eyes pale as moonlit frost.

'All I can tell you is who she looks like,' Winters said cautiously.

He felt as if he was being slowly anaesthetised. A cool numbness creeping over him as he tried to reconcile two divergent realities. The absolute fact of Izzy's death, and the photograph. Something that easily could have been faked, but why would the police do such a thing?

'We do need a name, for the record,' Sinclair said.

'For the record, it resembles my sister, Isabel. Isabel Winters. But I can't tell if it is real or fake.'

'That isn't all we have,' Briggs said, and unzipped his document folder and lifted out a single sheet of old-fashioned smart paper. It flickered when he touched one corner, displayed a copy of the biographical page of the Scottish passport of someone called Nadine Gulhame, who closely resembled the woman in the photograph. Briggs touched it again to call up a copy of Nadine Gulhame's driving licence. Touched it twice more to show a rental agreement with her signature and a credit statement dated the previous month.

Sinclair told Winters that his sister had been living in Scotland for the past eight years. An Englishwoman with a Scottish passport she'd obtained because she claimed that her mother had emigrated from Glasgow to England just before she'd been born.

'The mother was real, as was the daughter. Who died a few days after birth, in the year your sister was born. It's a common trick to obtain documentation for a false identity.

There are measures in place to prevent it, but there are also people who will, for a fee, bribe or blackmail employees of the General Register office to alter records and issue duplicate birth certificates and other papers. That, and friction between the English and Scottish governments and their respective legal systems, helped your sister to avoid detection.'

'Until now,' Briggs said.

'Yes indeed,' Sinclair said. He had the agreeable, relaxed manner of a kindly headmaster. 'Until now.'

'You're sure this is really her,' Winters said.

'There's no room for doubt.'

'She moved around a good deal, taking a variety of unskilled short-term jobs,' Briggs said. 'A picker on a soft-fruit farm outside Dundee. A delivery driver in Perth. A receptionist in a sailing club in Helensburgh and temporary work in cafés and warehouses and shops elsewhere on the West Coast. Her last job was canteen manager in a displaced persons camp near Aberdour, across from Edinburgh on the Fife side of the Forth. She worked there for the past eighteen months. Rented a static caravan in a nearby farm, made a few friends, even went on holiday with one of them, as you saw. Perhaps she was tired of moving around. Perhaps she wanted to settle down. Live a normal life.'

'She may have thought that she was safe,' Sinclair said. 'That after all this time no one was looking for her. But it seems that someone was.'

'She failed to turn up for work three weeks ago,' Briggs said. 'One of her colleagues, the friend she went on holiday with, filed a missing person's report. The local police followed it up, visited the caravan she rented to make a welfare check, and found it in a state of disarray. It isn't clear if that's how she left it, or if someone broke in after she disappeared, or if there'd been some kind of altercation.'

'Are you're saying that she might have been hurt?' Winters said.

He didn't want to say killed, but the thought was there.

'There's no evidence that she was,' Sinclair said. 'We believe that she escaped from the people who were looking for her, or left before they found her. She purchased a train ticket from Edinburgh to London on the day she went missing. In person, at Waverly Station. And we have video evidence that she boarded the train, and that she didn't get off it at London, but at Newcastle.'

'The local police carried out the usual forensics at her caravan,' Briggs said. 'Which included lifting her fingerprints and sampling her DNA from a toothstick, a routine procedure to distinguish traces left by her from those left by any intruder. When the prints and the DNA profile were fed into the records system, there was a connection with an old cross-border alert, and her real identity popped up.'

'She disappeared three weeks ago,' Winters said. 'But you're only telling me about it now.'

'The Scottish police weren't in any hurry to look for a missing adult person,' Sinclair said. 'And they weren't in any hurry to inform their English colleagues, either. Who in turn were regrettably slow to inform us. Then we had to do some checks of our own, to make sure that the person who called herself Nadine Gulhame really was your sister.'

'Although it seems that someone else got ahead of us,' Briggs said. 'And believed that you might have been helping her.'

'Deep dreamers,' Winters said. 'You're talking about deep dreamers, aren't you?'

'Have you ever met or had any other contact with someone claiming to be a deep dreamer?' Briggs said.

'I didn't even know about their existence before the break-in. Why do they want to find Isabel?'

'They are on our list of suspects, but I can't say any more than that at present,' Sinclair said.

'The anniversary's next month. The anniversary of the siege. Does that have anything to do with it?'

It was also the anniversary of Izzy's death. Except that it wasn't, now.

'It's most likely coincidence, but we can't rule out the possibility of some grand gesture associated with the date,' Sinclair said. 'Which adds a certain urgency to our investigation. I know this news must be a terrible shock, but we do need to know what you know. Every little helps, as they say. Why don't we start with the break-in?'

'I've already told the police everything I know,' Winters said. 'The local police.'

'We should go through it again. There may be something you remembered after you gave your statement.'

Winters took a moment to organise his thoughts, told the two detectives about going to Heybridge Basin for supplies. How he'd headed back after his agent told him that the island's local network had fallen over. How he'd found that someone had broken into the narrowboat and rifled through it, and used his tablet to access its files, as well as files in the agency's servers.

'There was a strange phone call, too. In the middle of the night, about three weeks ago. Someone using a gadget to disguise their voice, asking if I was sheltering someone. "Are you sheltering her." They didn't say who they meant, and I didn't think much of it at the time. But now I'm wondering if the caller might have been looking for my sister. Checking me out.'

'Do you have the number the call was made from?' Briggs said.

'It was withheld. I asked my agent to trace it, but she couldn't.'

'Did you recognise the caller?'

'I couldn't even tell if it was a man or a woman. Or an agent, using a script.'

'Did they say anything else?'

'Not much. I asked them how they got my number. The number of my work phone. And they said that maybe I didn't know anything yet. Something like that.'

'I see. And is there anything else you think we should know?' Briggs said.

'That's it,' Winters said, meeting the man's frosty gaze.

The wrapper and the fork he'd found on the mudbank were cached in separate bags in the freezer compartment of his little fridge, scarcely a metre from where the detectives were sitting. But he wasn't ready to tell them about his suspicion that someone had been watching him. Not yet. He didn't trust them, misliked their superficial smiles and their pretence of concern for Izzy's safety. Counterterrorism police had been in charge of the siege at Wakestone, had arrested and held him on suspicion of aiding and abetting his sister and Kasey Motte, and he was pretty sure they suspected that he was helping Izzy now. And was also pretty sure that they didn't want to find her because they wanted to protect her. No, they wanted to arrest and charge her. Settle an old score.

'Let's get back to the break-in,' Briggs said. 'You discovered it late in the evening, but didn't contact the police until the following day. Why was that?'

'It was on agency property, there's a chain of command. And it was late in the evening, my supervisor wasn't in her office, so I left a message. She called me back the next morning. And also called the police.'

'Do you know what the intruder was looking for? Why they went through those files?'

'Not at first. I thought it was an ordinary burglary. Then, the next morning, I saw the slogan painted on the side of the narrowboat, and found out what it meant. Who it was associated with.'

'And what did you think then?'

'I had all kinds of trouble, after the siege. Not just with the security services and the media. Plenty of crazy people wanted to share their crazy ideas with me. Conspiracy theory types. People who believed that Kasey Motte really could change the world. I thought that slogan was more of the same. And I wasn't wrong, was I? These deep dreamers are crazy too. And they're looking for Isabel, and you won't tell me why.'

Briggs made a show of checking something on his sheet of smart paper. 'After the siege, you left the country. Worked abroad for three years. When you returned, you worked in some kind of factory breeding flies, and then on a number of the Biodiversity Agency's projects. And you've been a ranger here for about two years.'

'Two years this August.'

'And in all that time, while you were working abroad, or planting trees, or doing whatever it is you do here, your sister never once got in contact. Didn't send so much as a text or a card to let you know that she was still alive.'

'No, she didn't,' Winters said, looking straight at the man.

'You said that you live alone on this island,' Briggs said.

'Apart from all the visitors. And the volunteers who help out.'

'Do you decide who can visit?'

'Not really. Visitors have to apply, but no one is ever turned down. It's just a question of making sure there aren't too many at any one time.'

'And what about your volunteers?'

'They generally work here as and when required.'

'They don't stay overnight.'

'Not usually.'

'When they've finished their work and left, you're on your own.'

'I guess.'

'So anyone could pay you a visit out of hours, as it were, and no one else would know.'

'If you mean Isabel, she's never been in contact, never been here.'

'Not even in the past three weeks, after she went on the run?'

'When I was held in custody, after the siege, I told you people what happened on my last visit to Wakestone. The last time I saw Isabel. How badly it went. Do you really think she would have reached out to me after that?'

'You are her brother,' Briggs said. 'Her closest living relative.'

'And she may be desperate,' Sinclair said. 'Afraid for her life. Nowhere else to turn.'

'What about other people from the commune? The ones who left when Kasey Motte took over.'

'We are, of course, checking every possibility,' Sinclair said.

'Do you think anyone else survived the siege? Do you know how Isabel survived it? How she escaped?'

'We are re-examining the evidence,' Sinclair said. 'Hundreds of hours of video, dozens of witness statements, all the forensics.

And we're re-examining the scene, too. What is left of it. All of which will, I'm afraid, take some time.'

'And meanwhile your sister is on the run from people who most likely do not have her best interests in mind,' Briggs said. 'So if she does reach out to you, you should let us know at once.'

'Would she be safer if she was in prison?'

'Have we said anything about prison?'

'Isn't that what this is about? Trying to persuade me to turn in my sister?'

'I realise that it's a lot for you to take in,' Sinclair said. 'We'll let you think it over. Digest the news. I've taken the liberty of sending you my contact details. If you think of anything that might be of help, anything at all, please do let me know. And for the time being, I want you keep all of this to yourself. If the media gets so much as a whiff, it could greatly hamper our work. And might also put Isabel in harm's way.'

'I'm no friend of the media,' Winters said.

'I'm glad to hear it. If there are any significant developments, we'll let you know.'

'Interview concluded,' Briggs said, and plucked the pocket drone from the air.

Part Two

Appointments with the Past

Three days after the visit by the counterterrorism police, Winters went up to London, leaving one of his volunteers, Alice Nakate, the brisk, cheerful woman who ran the local Nature Watch group, in charge of Cynsea. His uncle had also been visited by counterterrorism cops, but hadn't been told much beyond the bare facts that Isabel had been living under an assumed identity for the past eight years, and was now a fugitive, her present whereabouts unknown. He'd called Winters and they'd agreed to meet up, compare notes and strategise, and Winters had also arranged to meet an old acquaintance. Someone who might know if Izzy had reached out to her old comrades for help.

His supervisor had given him time off without asking for any details of the urgent family matter he'd told her that he needed to deal with, but he couldn't help wondering if the pair of detectives who'd interviewed him had also paid her a visit, quizzed her about his habits and recent behaviour, checked visitor records, set powerful agents loose in the island's files . . . His paranoia blues were back, strong as they'd ever been, and his anger was back, too. After he'd been told about Izzy's death in the Wakestone siege, he'd skipped denial, the first of the five classical stages of grief, and gone straight to helpless, unreasoning rage. At Kasey fucking Motte, for deceiving and manipulating Izzy and the others, and the monumental egotism that had driven them to their mass suicide. At Izzy, for allowing herself to be duped. At himself, for giving up on her, and for pushing away anyone who tried to comfort him, which was one of the reasons why his girlfriend had broken up with him.

And now he was angry at Izzy all over again. Everything he thought he knew, everything that had shaped his life in the aftermath of the siege, had been overturned. All this time his sister had been living a secret life, and hadn't ever tried to reach out to him. Had chosen to let him needlessly suffer years of grief and loss. But this time around his anger was muted by the hope that he might see her again, and by anxiety and concern, too. Was Izzy safe, wherever she was? Had the deep dreamers found her? Questions he'd asked the two detectives as they'd got up to leave. Questions they couldn't or wouldn't answer. And he knew from bitter experience that the counterterrorism police didn't need hard evidence to detain anyone. As far as they were concerned, suspicion, association and coincidence were more than sufficient, so it was possible that the break-in by someone who may have been searching for Izzy might be enough grounds to get him banged up all over again.

A taxi took him from Heybridge Basin to the little station at Hatfield Peverel and he caught a local train to Shenfield, where he changed to the Elizabeth Line. Panoramic views of flat countryside and sprawling towns wheeling past under low grey clouds didn't especially register. He'd asked his agent to search for information about Nadine Gulhame, but the only hit was a listing in the staff roster of the Scottish displaced persons' camp mentioned by Sinclair and Briggs. If there was any other information out there, it was either locked inside private polders and walled gardens, or had been redacted by the counterterrorism cops. Even so, Winters reckoned that the detectives had been telling the truth, or some version of it. Couldn't think of any reason why they would have conjured the story from thin air.

In the aftermath of the siege, after his anger had burnt itself out but while he'd still been deep in grief's derangement, he'd wished that there might have been some truth to Motte's craziness. That it might be possible to hack the past, make some small adjustment so that at their last parting he'd been able to find the words that would have persuaded Izzy to quit Wakestone and come with him. And now it seemed that she had somehow managed to escape anyway. He hoped that she'd come to her senses and walked away from the commune before the criminal stupidity which had triggered the siege. The raid and the hostage-taking and all the rest. Hoped that she'd abandoned everyone she knew and loved, cut every tie, and never once looked back. It wasn't impossible. Before she'd fallen for Kasey Motte's fairy tales, she'd always gone her own way.

Winters was five years younger than his sister, born two months before the railway accident in which his father died. Years later, shortly after Isabel moved out, his mother, well into her second bottle of wine of the evening, had let slip that he was the result of a reconciliation after she and his father had come close to divorce. An accident, Julia had said, and hastily qualified it. But a lovely one. A gift.

Julia hadn't been much interested in the routines of domesticity and childcare, had spent most of her time in her workshop with her paintings, or in her bedroom, trying to sleep off the crippling depressions that often followed maniacal bouts of creativity. Izzy had assumed responsibility for cooking and cleaning, making sure that her little brother had clean clothes and got to school on time, and everything else. When he was old enough, she dragooned him into helping her with the housework and her wildlife surveys, and handing out leaflets in the local market with other members of the local cadre of Nature First!, an activist group which combined campaigning for ecosystem restoration and biodiversity protection with a back-to-the-land philosophy. Izzy dug up the lawn and flowerbeds of the cottage and planted vegetables, protested against tree felling and genetically engineered crops, and participated in 'silent witness' actions, she and her comrades mutely standing outside council offices, wearing black armbands and holding signs picturing endangered and recently extinct animals.

In the years after the food shortages, power outages, riots and general civic collapse of Panic Summer, the coalition government had introduced a degrowth economy, ended hydrocarbon dependency and promoted rewilding and a radical plan for food self-sufficiency, but many activists believed that this fell far short of what was needed. The rate of global heating had been slowed, but had not yet been halted or reversed. The Arctic was ice-free for eleven months of the year and ice sheets in Greenland and the Antarctic were still retreating. A billion people had been displaced by coastal flooding, wild fires, droughts and hyperthermal events, famine and war. Pollution by forever chemicals and microplastics was universal and the thinning of the planet's biosphere and the mass extinction of its species was ongoing. And in England, nuclear power was still a backstop for sources of renewable energy and the government's self-sufficiency strategy relied on genetically tweaked crops, while measures to safeguard domestic food security and projects to increase infrastructure resilience had proven to be inadequate, and promises to make major contributions to the pan-European programme to build settlements for climate-change refugees had been undercut by a series of economic crises. And so on, and so on.

General dissatisfaction and unrest climaxed in a protest march in London organised by a coalition of campaigning groups. Izzy and the other members of her Nature First! cadre were caught up in running battles between police and troublemakers, kettled in Golden Square with several hundred other people, and arrested. She was batch processed through Westminster Magistrates' Court, found guilty of breaching conditions imposed on a protest and given a conditional discharge, and returned home three days later, tired and filthy and elated. She believed that the adventure was an affirmation of her badass righteousness, but Julia, who previously had taken little interest in her daughter's activism, told her that she'd been naïve and irresponsible, kicking off the first in a series of quarrels about Izzy's poor record of school attendance, the weekends she devoted to Nature First! meetings and actions, and the housework she no longer had the time or inclination to do.

If he'd been a little older and a little more courageous, a little more passionate, Winters might have sided with his sister, but whenever Izzy clashed with Julia he felt helpless and irrelevant and, obscurely, that he was partly to blame, and avoided the turmoil by going on long and aimless walks or retreating to his attic bedroom. He read enormous amounts of what Julia called escapist literature – multi-volume narratives about strife and skulduggery in pre-industrial kingdoms got up from history, myth, genre tropes and elaborate magical systems, and with three schoolfriends spent hours immersed in an old-school massively multiplayer online sandbox, *Blood+Iron*, set in a medieval otherworld in which the only usable sources of iron were the skystones which fell at irregular intervals in random locations. Lordlings and kings fought for possession of these precious chunks of ore, and some of the skystones also contained demons which could infiltrate and possess the minds of people, or kernels of magic which granted those who found them a variety of powers, or turned them into ravenous monsters.

Winters and his friends were a crew of minor adventurers in this restless world of war and wild magic, resolutely avoiding skirmishes, battles and the baited traps which could drag the unwary into a side quest or the beginning of a major narrative thread. They scavenged equipment, weapons and scraps of armour from the detritus of abandoned battlefields, plodded from village to village and, in exchange for skill points, healing spells and shelter, helped peasants overcome crop failures and droughts, gathered plants and tokens needed to cure plagues, rescued kidnapped children from itinerant traders, exposed and drove out minor enchanters, occultists and other tricksters, and stalked predators which had been carrying off animals and generally causing havoc. Conner pointed out that their adventures were a low-stakes version of an old film, *The Magnificent Seven*, and Sam, with his usual gentle pedantry, explained that *The Magnificent Seven* was a Western remake of a Japanese classic, *The Seven Samurai*. Which Winters tried to watch, but bailed before the end. It was in black and white, subtitled and more than a bit of a downer, though the swordplay and archery were pretty good.

For two years, the world of *Blood+Iron* was as important and real to Winters and his friends as the everyday quotidian. Their avatars developed skills and strength, acquired a small armoury of weapons, several of them uniquely crafted or enchanted, exchanged the chainmail shirts looted at the beginning of their adventures for leather, lace and burnished steel, and rode fierce and tireless horses. Davey joined a mercenary crew fighting for some king or other, and Conner, who'd introduced them to the game, gained a girlfriend IRL and that was the end of his participation in serious team sessions, but Winters and Sam cleaved to their low-key freelance exploration of the obscure corners and crannies of the game's vast imaginarium, were zig-zagging through highland villages towards distant mountains rumoured to be at the edge of the world when a feral AI hacked into one of the game's servers and within ten minutes had taken possession of all the rest, hijacking their computational assets for some mad experiment in exotic physics until the company which owned the game gave up on attempts to evict it and pulled the plug.

By then, Izzy had finished school and moved out of the cottage and was sofa-surfing with friends and fellow travellers or living in temporary squats. She doubled down on her Nature First! activism, supported herself by working as a picker in a local farm, a receptionist and a factory cleaner, stood for election to the local council and lost, was arrested for taking part in an action that involved spraying a field of genetically engineered maize with red dye, and sentenced to a hundred hours' community work. And was arrested again a year later, for sabotaging construction machinery on a greenfield site for new housing. She served eight months in East Sutton Park Prison for that, and after she was released joined a commune in Northumberland, near the border with Scotland. At first she sent Winters texts and brief clips about her new life, and he twice made the long journey north to visit her. She was happy there, had found a belonging place amongst an extended family of like-minded strangers. She'd grown out her hair, a great glossy auburn fall that hung halfway down her back, and had put on weight, most of it muscle. She was in charge of the commune's public-facing educational work, but like everyone else had to put in her share of physical labour, too.

Her new home was built on the bones of an old farm, Wakestone, which had been abandoned after sheep and dairy cattle farming had been curtailed, and purchased by the commune with the aid of a government grant. The dry stone walls which had divided the farmland into a patchwork of fields had been dismantled and the rubble used to construct the foundations of three dormitories and a meeting house, half-buried in the earth and roofed with turf and lit by sunlight piped through optical cabling. Former fields and pasture had been turned into clumps of trees and wildflower meadows and scattered patches of cultivation. Wastewater treated by passage through gravel beds and reedbeds fed into a string of fishponds. Workshops had been set up in the workings of the old quarry which had supplied the stone used to construct the old farmhouse and cottages and outbuildings, and the farmhouse was a visitors' centre, where volunteer workers and guests slept and took their meals. When he visited, Winters was put up in one of its bunk beds, but ate at the long tables in the meeting house with his sister and the other members of the commune, including her partner, a gruff man twice her age. It was a celibate relationship, Izzy told her brother. A union of souls. There were no children in the commune. Its members were strict believers in managed population decline.

It reminded Winters of the villages of *Blood+Iron*, although the commune's dogma didn't prohibit the deployment of technology wherever it was useful. The pillars and beams of the dormitories and the meeting house were shaped from carbon fibre, and rows of wind turbines and racks of solar panels were set up on and between their long, turf-covered mounds. Hydroponic vegetables grew from suspended pipes in climate-controlled polytunnels. One of the workshops used an industrial printer to make tools and spare parts; another used 3D modelling and a hydraulic copy lathe to create the intricately carved wooden bowls, furniture and toys whose sale generated a steady income stream.

The frequency of Izzy' texts and clips had begun to decrease long before Winters' second visit to the commune, and they completely stopped after Kasey Motte joined and took control and began to reshape it for his own purposes. Winters dutifully sent birthday and Christmas cards, but Izzy never replied or reciprocated, and didn't attend their mother's funeral or help with the disposition of her possessions and paintings. By then, Winters was on his own path. Graduating from university and finding employment, meeting his first serious girlfriend. He'd been living and working in London for two years when Izzy broke her long silence with a brief text inviting him to visit the commune and hang out for a few days, she had some news she wanted to share. She didn't reply when he texted back, asking what was up, but his girlfriend told him he should go anyway, it was his sister after all, a chance to rekindle their relationship, and so he went north and met Kasey Motte and discovered the craziness that caused the final unbridgeable rift with Izzy and would later drive the commune to theft and kidnap, the siege and its violent end.

The train was slowing. Creeping through London's rainy outer suburbs, swallowed by a tunnel beyond the glass and steel hives of Stratford. Winters got off at Tottenham Court Road and walked the rest of the way. It was hot and clammy, drizzle not so much falling as condensing from the air. Umbrellas of every colour jostling above the heads of people in hooded capes and slickers, belted raincoats and ponchos. Hundreds of strangers swarming along this one street in a city of more than twelve million people, a world of ten billion. The human herd he'd once been part of, in its typical urban habitat.

Bicycles and cargo trikes and the occasional bubblecar moved through the crowds, trams glided down the centre of the street with an electric tingle of bells, and a steady stream of cargo drones passed overhead, silhouetted against giant screens displaying government-sponsored clips of forests and mountains, waves smashing against rocks, horses galloping across a beach, birds in flight against a sunset, and impossibly beautiful people smiling and gesturing behind streaming captions about recycling and upcycling, water conservation, three ways to keep homes cool without air-conditioning, blackout schedules, how to sign up for volunteer work and neighbourhood improvement schemes . . .

The trams were shabbier than Winters remembered, several shops were boarded up and beggars sat in shuttered doorways with their appeals hand-lettered on squares of cardboard, and a police drone hung at rooftop level above the intersection at Cambridge Circus, blue lights steadily flashing. He was sweating under his agency-issue poncho by the time he reached Trafalgar Square, but it was a little cooler in the green shade of trees planted around the fountains and the base of Nelson's column and a faint breeze was blowing from the river. He was a little early and sat for a few minutes on a bench, fired up a joint and burned through it in half a dozen long drags, and then it was time to go.

Whitehall was likewise tree-shaded, and far less busy than Tottenham Court Road's main drag. Winters turned down a side street, found the Gothic red-brick of his uncle's club. The hive noise of the city dropping away as he entered a cool, dimly lit lobby. A woman in antique uniform took his name and hung his poncho in an alcove and directed him to the bar, and there was Daniel Seddon, Uncle Danny, at a table at the far end of the long wood-panelled room, rising to greet him.

Winters had never been especially close to his uncle. Daniel had sent expensive gifts on birthdays and at Christmas ('conscience tokens' according to Julia), but otherwise was mostly an invisible presence. His distance from his sister and her family, and his seniority in the civil service and work in the Ministry of Carbon Budgeting, meant that he'd barely been touched by the debacle of the Wakestone siege, and he'd used his contacts to help his nephew escape his trial-by-media by helping him to get work abroad with a logistics service provider. The last time they'd met had been shortly before Winters had left for his first posting, a hasty lunch in a cheap pasta joint in Victoria Street, Winters feeling like an apprentice spook being briefed for his first mission, Daniel making his apologies and leaving early because there was some kind of crisis at his ministry. And here they were eight years later, once again brought together by Izzy. Daniel emitting a waft of complex citrussy fragrance as he reached across the table and deftly poured a glass of ice water for Winters, telling him that he had taken the liberty of ordering lunch, explaining that the club was a storied sanctuary where no one could eavesdrop on them. A tradition more than a century old forbade Members of Parliament from crossing its doorstep, so that senior civil servants could freely discuss matters of administration, policy and conduct out of earshot of their masters, and because its members were prime targets for foreign agencies the club employed a private firm to sweep the place regularly for spyware and bugs.

'Even if any of the relevant agencies know that we arranged this meeting,' Daniel said, 'anything we share here will stay between us.'

A tall, trim man in a pale yellow linen suit, immaculately groomed and barbered, he made Winters, whose good blue shirt was damp with sweat under his agency work jacket, feel like a cloddish yokel. They exchanged pleasantries, Daniel asking about Winters' work on Cynsea, Winters asking about his uncle's husband and their two children, before Daniel turned the conversation to the reason for their meeting.

'The detectives who visited me said that Isabel was last seen getting off a train at Newcastle,' he said. 'Do you have any idea about where she might have gone after that?'

'Not really. But I know some of the people who left the commune after Kasey Motte took over. And there are her old friends in Nature First!, too. I could ask around, see if she's reached out to any of them. Perhaps find some way of letting her know that I want to help.' Winters paused, then said, 'You haven't heard anything from her.'

'If I had, it would have been my duty to inform the police. And to tell her that she should do the right thing, and turn herself in. The first step towards minimising or even overturning any charges brought against her. And you know what her answer to that would have been.'

'Yeah.'

'I was her only uncle. And by no means her favourite.'

It was a line Daniel had used at the memorial service. The one without a coffin, or a body. Only a charcoal sketch of Izzy that her mother had made years before, wreathed in wild flowers. Everybody there wanted to remember her as what she'd once been, not what she had become.

'She quite wilfully refused to understand the difference between a civil servant and a politician,' Daniel said. 'The concept of neutrality. Wanted me to subvert this, make a stand against that. Said that if I couldn't do anything else I could at least find something I didn't like, and resign in protest.'

'She didn't – doesn't, I guess – like any form of compromise,' Winters said.

Both of them were having trouble with their tenses.

'I very much doubt that she has changed in that respect,' Daniel said. 'I don't suppose she has reached out to you for help, either. Just to be clear.'

'No, she hasn't. But someone definitely thinks that she might have, and I don't mean the police. Which is kind of why I'm here.'

Winters told his uncle about the weird phone call in the middle of the night, a few days after Izzy had gone on the run, told him about the break-in. The island's network falling over, the hacking of his tablet, the message spray-painted on the side of the narrowboat.

'"The Instauration Is Coming." It's the slogan of this mad little crew who call themselves deep dreamers. From what I can tell, they seem to be trying to reboot Kasey Motte's crazy plans.'

'The business with mushrooms and changing history.'

'Yeah. The Great Green Reset. The police wouldn't tell me if they were investigating them, but I reckon they have to be the prime suspects.'

There was a pause while the waiter set down plates of vegetarian moussaka, a glass of white wine for Daniel and a glass of mineral water for Winters.

'I asked for fake cheese,' Daniel said, as he unfolded his napkin. 'Couldn't remember whether or not you were vegan.'

Winters, who wasn't even vegetarian, except in the way most people were most of the time, thanked his uncle for his thoughtfulness. Daniel looked at him over a forkful of aubergine and lentils and said, 'Do you think that Mr Motte might still be alive? That he has something to do with these deep dreamers?'

'I think we'd know if he survived the siege. The kind of person he was, he'd want everyone to know. But the deep dreamers are definitely fans of his. And Isabel was close to him, once upon a time. Was part of his inner circle. Perhaps they found out that she was still alive, wanted her to help them. Tell them everything she knew about Motte's stupid ideas. The shrooms and the reset and all the rest of it. But she didn't want to cooperate, and got away.'

'Because she is no longer a believer, given what happened.'

'Or because she's still loyal to Motte, and doesn't much care for the deep dreamers' plans. Reckons that they're some kind of, what's the word? Renegades. Heretics,' Winters said, thinking that maybe that sneaky pre-meeting toke hadn't been a good idea, it had made him sort of fuzzy around the edges.

'Mmm,' Daniel said, and took a sip of his wine.

'I know it sounds crazy. But these are crazy people.'

'I don't know enough about Mr Motte's arcane theology to make a judgement. But I have been wondering if Isabel might have been working for the police, or MI5. I looked into it after the siege, in fact, but didn't get very far.'

Winters, misliking this idea, said, 'If she was some kind of police informant, why didn't she ask them for help?'

'Perhaps she doesn't trust them. Feels that they have failed her in some way. Or perhaps, if she was working for MI5 or some other flavour of spook, she did get some help, and her helpers neglected to inform the counterterrorism police.

It might explain how she escaped from the siege, and why she helped you get away, after you fell into Motte's clutches.'

When he'd been detained by the counterterrorism police after the siege at Wakestone, Winters had told his interrogators about that last visit, explaining how Motte had tried to convince him that the Great Green Reset could change everything and make the world a better place, how the man had dosed him with shrooms so that he could see what was behind the veil, how Izzy had set him free. But he hadn't told them about Izzy's coldness when they'd parted. Her terrible last words. He'd never told his uncle about them either, and he didn't want to get into it with him now, even though the idea that Izzy had been secretly working against Kasey Motte might explain her cruel dismissal. She'd needed to save her brother, but she'd also had to drive him away, make sure that he didn't compromise her . . .

He said, 'I was hoping that you could help me find out more about the deep dreamers. Exactly who they are and what they want. Whether they caught up with Izzy. All the stuff the police wouldn't tell me.'

Daniel had efficiently cleared his plate. He set his fork down and patted his lips with his napkin and said, 'You must understand that there are boundaries I cannot cross. If a senior civil servant was found to be interfering with the work of the police it would cause quite the scandal. But I have an acquaintance who may be of some help. Someone who also has a personal connection with Mr Motte and the Wakestone siege.'

'What kind of connection?'

'Her son was one of Motte's followers. Like Isabel, he was pronounced dead after the siege.'

'Does she know about Izzy? Have you told her?'

'The counterterrorism police gave her the news before they told you and me. I think it would be mutually beneficial if you shared what you know with her. She will be very interested to hear about your break-in and that disturbing phone call, and may have some of the answers to your questions. She isn't able to come here, but we can go to her.'

'And who is she, exactly?'

'Talia Armstrong. Lady Armstrong, to give her proper title – her late husband was a KBE. She was a barrister once upon a time. Retired now, but still quite formidable.'

'And who was her son?'

'William. William Armstrong.'

Winters didn't remember meeting anyone by that name at Wakestone, but people in the commune hadn't always gone by their birth names, and the last time he'd visited there'd been a lot of new faces.

He said, 'So, given the news about Izzy, I guess this acquaintance of yours thinks her son might have survived the siege as well.'

'It has lent her some small hope. You came to me for help, Marc. This is the best I can do.'

Winters was sympathetic to his uncle's position, the problems Isabel's reappearance could cause him, but he felt as if he'd been somehow pushed into a corner. Manipulated. Out-manoeuvred. It was like the aftermath of the siege. He'd been grateful that Daniel had helped him get out of the country and escape the incessant media attention, but he'd also suspected that his uncle was getting rid of an embarrassment that might compromise his career. Still, what harm could meeting this friend do? She might be able to make good on Daniel's promises, and there was also the matter of the two specimen bags tucked in the breast pocket of his jacket.

'I was kind of hoping for some practical assistance,' he told Daniel.

'What sort of assistance?'

'The forensic kind. Fingerprints, DNA analysis, so on.'

'Is this to do with your break-in?'

'Before we get into that, maybe I should meet your acquaintance. See what she has to offer.'

'I promise that you won't regret it,' Daniel said. 'I'll make a couple of calls, let my secretary know where I'll be and so forth, and we can be on our way.'

'You want me to go meet her right away?'

'Of course. No time like the present.'

'How long will it take?' Winters said, thinking of the other meeting he had arranged.

'Not very. She lives quite near here. Let me make those calls.'

A water taxi took them upriver to the fortifications of the Chiswick Mall dyke and they walked along the road in the dyke's shadow to a three-storey detached house, overgrown with bougainvillea, that stood behind a tall brick wall. The steel flood gate swung open after Daniel tapped a code into a keypad, revealing a cobbled courtyard and a woman in blue tunic and trousers waiting for them at the front door.

'Good afternoon, Ida,' Daniel said to her. 'How is she today?'

'As good as can be, Mr Seddon. She's waiting for you in the drawing room.'

Daniel led Winters upstairs, past the rail of a stairlift fitted beneath massive oil paintings in gilt frames, mostly of military men in antique uniforms, to a room with a pair of tall windows that overlooked the top of the dyke and the muscular flow of the river beyond.

The woman they'd come to meet, Lady Talia Armstrong, sat in a wheelchair jigsawed from curved, slotted carbonblack struts, like a throne fashioned from the skeleton of some extinct giant bird. Riding on four pairs of small, fat-tyred wheels, it carried her noiselessly over the threadbare carpet to her visitors. She was frail and gaunt and crook-shouldered, dressed in a pale green polo neck sweater and an ankle-length plaid skirt. Winters could feel the small bones under her cool skin when she shook his hand.

Daniel had briefed him about her during the water taxi ride. A former barrister and widow of Sir Antony Armstrong, a senior member of the Diplomatic Service, she had spent a great deal of time and credit trying to find out what had happened to her only child, despite being stricken by a species of progressive ataxia. Her illness had robbed her of speech, but her right hand skated over a tablet strapped to the armrest of her wheelchair, tapping shorthand icons that were translated into a warmly-inflected machine-generated voice. She introduced Winters to Bailey, the private investigator who worked for her, a compact, burly person who stood in a shadowy corner of the room, and explained that her son had graduated with First in Philosophy, Politics and Economics at Oxford University, had been an assistant employed by a Member of Parliament when he'd had some kind of breakdown and disappeared. Walked out of the flat he shared with his boyfriend one evening and didn't come back. He'd been arrested for begging in Peterborough nine months later, but was released without charge the next morning, and by the time Lady Armstrong and her husband had learned about the arrest and tried to follow it up, he'd disappeared again.

'That was the last I knew about his whereabouts until the siege at Wakestone Farm, when the counterterrorism police told me that he was one of the people who had broken into the spaceport in Northumberland. I went there at once, but I was not allowed through the police cordon and had no way of contacting William, and the next day it was all over.'

'I'm sorry,' Winters said.

'You visited the commune on several occasions. The last time was after Mr Motte took charge. Perhaps you met William then.'

Spotlights kindled in the ceiling, illuminating a row of photographs in silver frames set on top of a darkwood sideboard. Candid shots and formal portraits charting the progress of Lady Armstrong's son from boy to adult. Black ribbons fastened over the top righthand corner of each frame. A vase of canna lilies set in the middle of the row. Winters studied the last photograph in the series. A young man in academic gown and mortarboard cap, holding a scroll slantwise. High cheekbones and a long narrow nose and a confident gaze.

'I'm sorry,' Winters said again. 'I don't remember him.'

'Bailey interviewed several former members of the commune,' Lady Armstrong's synthetic voice said. 'One, who left just two months before the siege, said William was part of Motte's inner circle. Apparently, he went by the name of Billy X.'

'I know the name from Motte's list of saviours, but I don't remember meeting him. There were quite a few new people in the commune when I last visited it, but I wasn't introduced to any of them. And I wasn't there for very long.'

'But you did meet Mr Motte.'

'Yes, I did.'

'What was he like?'

'Calm, confident, very sure of himself. Gave the impression that he really believed in what he was telling you.'

'Yes. As others have described him. A preacher, but not the kind given to ranting and raving. Did he want you to join his congregation?'

'That was the plan, apparently. But it didn't come up when we talked. He wanted to convince me that the things he claimed to have done were true and real.'

'And the state of his sanity? What was it? In your opinion.'

'Oh, he was definitely crazy. Not just because of what happened, at the end, but because he truly thought that he'd changed history.'

'By the ceremonial consumption of psychoactive mushrooms.'

'That was part of it.'

'Did you witness or participate in one of those ceremonies? William may have been present.'

'I never had any first-hand experience of an actual ceremony. I only know what Motte told me about them.'

Winters was thinking of how he'd been spiked, the Green Man and the Wild Hunt and the rest, but didn't want to get into that.

'And your sister,' Lady Armstrong said. 'I understand that she was also part of the inner circle.'

'That's what I was told. But she didn't want me to join Motte's thing. His congregation. His plan. In fact, she helped me escape.'

'You were being held prisoner?'

'Not exactly.'

'But you needed help to leave.'

'It was sort of a complicated situation. Can I ask you a question?'

'Of course.'

'How did you and my uncle meet?'

'It was shortly after the siege,' Lady Armstrong's synthetic voice said, as the thumb and forefinger of her right hand brushed across the tablet on the arm of her wheelchair. 'William was amongst those missing. I was told that he died in the explosion, like the rest of the holdouts. The so-called saviours. But because no trace of his body was ever found I had some small hope that he might have survived. That with the help of sympathisers he was hiding from the police. Badly injured, perhaps, but alive. Daniel was one of the people Bailey contacted on my behalf. A little later we met and became friends, united by loss.'

'As I'm sure you remember, I was trying to find out what happened to Isabel,' Daniel told Winters. 'Talia, very kindly, gave me a little help.'

'I remember you didn't find anything,' Winters said. 'I don't remember being told that you had help.'

Lady Armstrong was working her tablet. 'Bailey would have interviewed you, Mr Winters, had you not moved abroad. And perhaps we would have met and joined forces then. As it was, I didn't find anything that contradicted the official version of events. And then my husband passed. I did not entirely give up on my investigations, but they were scaled down. And that is how things stood until I learned that your sister is still alive. I would very much like to meet her and find out what she knows about William. She may be able to help me to find him, if he is still alive. Or might know exactly what happened to him, if he is not.'

'There it is. That's why we're here,' Daniel told Winters.

'Let me ask a few impertinent but necessary questions,' Lady Armstrong said. 'Did you know that your sister survived the siege? Did you ever meet her, or have any contact with her, after she went on the run? And do you know where she is now?'

'The last time I saw her was on my last visit to Wakestone,' Winters said. 'When I met Kasey Motte. I didn't know she was still alive until the counterterrorism police paid me a visit, and I have no idea where she is now. But I think I know why she went on the run.'

He told Lady Armstrong what he'd already given up to his uncle. The phone call and the break-in, the spraypainted slogan and its association with the deep dreamers.

'I am familiar with the slogan, and the deep dreamers,' Lady Armstrong said. 'Latter-day followers of Kasey Motte. One of several such groups.'

'It looks like my sister broke cover after they found out she was alive. I don't know why they're looking for her, maybe they think she knows something they need to know, but it's clear that she doesn't want anything to do with them. That as far as she's concerned they're some kind of bad juju. You want to find her because of your son. I get that. But if I can, I want to help to keep her out of the hands of these deep dreamer people.'

Daniel said, 'I have suggested that the best way of helping Isabel would be to persuade her to turn herself in to the police.'

Winters ignored that, said to Lady Armstrong, 'If we can track down these deep dreamers, we might be able to find out what kind of trouble she's in, and put a stop to it. Find out where she is, where they're keeping her, if they've caught up with her. The other reason I came here, I have something that might help with that.'

He explained that he'd suspected that that the intruder must have been watching him, waiting for him to leave the island. How he'd searched the mudbanks near his narrowboat and found signs of a camp or watch post.

'I also found these,' he said, and plucked the pair of specimen bags from his jacket, one containing the cellophane wrapper, the other the wooden fork, and held them out towards Lady Armstrong.

'I could pay for private testing, but even if it found DNA or fingerprints, I don't have any access to the databases and files the police use to make a match. But if you do, if you can help me, we might be able to identify the person who broke into my narrowboat. And they might lead us to the rest of the crew.'

'Let's have a look,' the private investigator, Bailey, said from the shadowy corner of the room. It was as if a statue had spoken. A statue with a gravelly South London accent.

Winters handed over the specimen bags, watched nervously as Bailey held them up to the light falling through the windows. As if this was a test he might well fail.

'Fork's obviously been in wet dirt, which won't help,' Bailey said. She was in her fifties, with a shrewd, pugnacious face and a close-cropped frizz of iron-grey curls, dressed in a dark blue suit and an open-necked yellow shirt. 'But my man's pretty good. Even if the DNA's degraded, he might be able to stitch it back together. Might be able to pull a fingerprint from the wrapper, too. Was there any shit?'

'Shit?'

'If someone were watching you for more than a day, they would have had to take a dump at some point.'

'I didn't look for anything like that.'

'Might have to, if this doesn't yield anything. Do the police know about it?'

'I told the local police, but they said it was circumstantial evidence at best. They took my tablet to be swabbed and fingerprinted. As far as they're concerned, that's all they needed to do.'

'If you told the local plods what you'd found, they might have passed the info to counterterrorism. The detectives who interviewed you, did they mention it? What did you tell them?'

'It didn't come up.'

'Then maybe you got lucky. Maybe the locals didn't include it in their file. Could be their own forensics yielded a hit. If so, the counterterrorism boys and girls will be ahead of us. But even if they are, I think it's worth giving this a go.'

'How long will it take your man to do the work?' Lady Armstrong said.

'Couple of days, if I get him on it right away. And if he pulls out something useful, I know someone else who can run it through the national database. If this intruder has a criminal record, was ever detained for whatever reason, or was in the services, we'll find them. And if they aren't in the database, we can look for familial matches with the DNA of any close relatives who are.'

Lady Armstrong touched her tablet. The synthetic voice said, 'Despite the unfortunate circumstances, it was a pleasure to meet you, Mr Winters. I found our conversation very useful and hope that you did too. And I think you will agree that we share a common interest in your sister's well-being.'

'I guess,' Winters said, wondering if she had prepared different versions of that bland little speech. One expressing sorrow that it hadn't worked out, another threatening him, telling him to give up Izzy or else . . .

Lady Armstrong was working her tablet, conjuring something new. 'Thank you especially for your candour, and the trust it implies. I look forward to talking to you again, once Bailey has the forensic results. Whatever they may be.'

The investigator walked Winters and his uncle down the stairs. 'I looked up that island of yours,' she said. 'You have a lot of static cameras, don't you? Not to mention all those drones tracking birds and whatnot. I put in countermeasures here, I'm pretty sure no one was listening in to your conversation with her ladyship. But when you get back home, you might want to think hard about who you meet and what you say to them. Counterterrorism can easily plant spyware in your drones, and they have plenty of other resources. Drones that can loiter a kilometre up, with cameras that can track a fly and laser interferometry capabilities that can pick up the buzz of its wings. Or they could dust the place with pin cameras and mikes, record everything in 3D and surround sound.'

'I did wonder if the police might be watching Marc,' Daniel said. 'Which is why I suggested we meet at the Civil Service Club.'

'I'll be careful,' Winters said.

'One last thing,' Bailey said. 'I'll shoot the forensic results to you as soon as I can. And if you decide you don't want to take it any further as regards cooperation, that'll be fine by me. But if you do your own thing, make sure that you don't get in my way.'

Back on the pavement, the flood gate rattling shut behind them, Winters said to his uncle, 'Lady Armstrong, she's something more than an acquaintance, isn't she? You know the gate code, her nurse knows you . . .'

'We've stayed in touch over the years. And I helped Talia whenever I could, in case her investigations turned up some new information about Isabel.'

'And never told me about any of this.'

'I didn't want to give you false hope, Marc. But things are different now, and I truly believe that this is your best chance of finding Isabel. And if it works out, will it matter who helped you?'

'It will if it puts Izzy at risk. Who exactly is this Bailey character? She comes on like she's some kind of police.'

'That's because she is. Or was. A detective inspector who retired from the Metropolitan Police and took up work as a private investigator for Talia's chambers, before illness forced Talia to retire.'

'I let her take those scraps I found because I don't know what else to do with them. But I'm not sure if I want to go all in with her and your friend. I get the feeling it won't exactly be an equal relationship.'

'Bailey can be somewhat unfiltered, I know, but she is also very good at what she does. And Talia has the resources you need, and she is going to search for Isabel with or without your help. Handing over that material was an excellent first step towards establishing mutual trust. And knowing Talia as I do, I really don't think you'll regret it.'

But it wasn't just about whether he could trust Talia Armstrong, Winters thought, as the sleek pod of a black cab carried him east. His uncle wanted to help, but also wanted to put as much clear blue water between himself and his troublesome nephew as quickly as possible. And if his friend decided that giving up Izzy to the police would the best way of finding out what really happened to her son, whose side would Daniel take then? He was glad now that he hadn't told him about the meeting he'd arranged with Charlie Lowe, a former member of Izzy's commune. It might give him a different angle of attack, some advantage over Talia Armstrong and her bulldog.

Charlie Lowe worked in a taxi garage in Hackney, one of the small businesses that occupied the arches beneath a railway line. Despite the diversion with Talia Armstrong, Winters arrived early and found a café close by and drank a mug of builder's tea and smoked a joint, idly watching passers-by, thinking about the commune and last time he'd seen Izzy, Kasey Motte's attempt to draw him into his mad conspiracy.

After he'd received the invitation that had broken her long silence, his travel arrangements had been confirmed in a brief exchange of texts, but his attempts to call her, talk to her directly about the trip, were unsuccessful. That wasn't unusual — members of the commune didn't have their own phones, and communication with outsiders was often erratic — and he wasn't especially worried when Izzy didn't reply after he texted to let her know that his train was running late, or when he discovered that she wasn't waiting for him at Berwick-upon-Tweed station. Which was also par for the course. It was only when he arrived at Wakestone after a taxi ride that put a considerable dent in his credit and was told that his sister was meditating and couldn't be disturbed that he began to wonder if his trip had been a mistake.

He was in the meeting house, picking at a bowl of cracked wheat and stewed greens, when Izzy's partner, Rob Copely, found him and said that Kasey Motte wanted to talk to him.

'Right now?'

'He'll find you when he wants to find you is how it works,' Rob said, giving Winters a starry smile that showed the gap between his front teeth. A skinny guy, barefoot in dirty coveralls, hair done up in short tight braids that stuck out in every direction, as if he'd recently jammed his finger in an electrical socket. Some grey in those braids now, and in his straggly beard.

'What about Izzy? When can I see her?'

'Maybe when she's finished getting her head straight.'

'Is that what everyone else is doing?' Winters said. 'Getting their heads straight too?'

There were only a scant dozen or so people eating supper in the meeting house. The last time he'd visited there'd been five times that number.

'Mostly,' Rob said. 'We're sort of in the middle of getting ready for something big.'

'What kind of something?'

'Something world-changing. Beyond that I can't say, so don't ask.'

'Maybe you can at least tell me this – was it really Izzy who invited me here?'

'Why would you think she didn't?'

'I came all this way, and you're telling me I can't see her. That Kasey Motte wants to talk to me instead.'

'Well, she's kind of caught up in this thing. We all are.'

'But she's okay. She know that I'm here.'

'Kasey'll straighten you out about everything. And man, will you be amazed.'

'I'm getting the idea that things have changed an awful lot since I was last here.'

Rob smiled his starry smile. 'Have they ever.'

'All because of your dear leader.'

'Man planted the seeds of change, but everyone here helped them grow. Speaking of which, I'd love to stay and chat, but I've got stuff to do. Later.'

Winters had a bad feeling, but was curious about the man who'd cast some kind of spell over the commune, and this mysterious world-changing thing of his. And he was worried about Izzy, wanted to see her, find out if she was all right. As on previous visits, he bunked in the old farmhouse, but this time there were no other guests and it looked like there hadn't been any for a good while. Floors unswept, cobwebs in the corners of ceilings, a blown lightbulb in the hallway, the bedding damp and musty. He woke early the next morning. A cool and overcast day towards the end of March. Fine rain blowing in gusty billows under a blank sky, half-erasing the wooded slope that rose beyond the commune's fields. In the cheerless daylight the place looked even more desolate. Weeds in the gravel paths, on the turf roofs of the half-buried meeting house and dormitories. Half the polytunnels empty and the blades of several of the wind turbines unmoving.

Two men loitering by a trash fire in an oil drum watched Winters as he walked towards the meeting house, one saying something he didn't catch, the other spitting into the flames. No one came over to greet him or deliver a message from Kasey Motte while he worked his way through a bowl of oatmeal porridge, and when he was finished he asked the woman at the service hatch, someone he vaguely remembered from his previous visits, Sarah something, where he could find Rob Copely.

'He'll be over at the mushroom farm,' the woman said.

'The mushroom farm?'

'What used to be the Barn Owl dormitory before we converted it. Rob's in charge of it.'

'Growing mushrooms.'

'All kinds,' the woman said. 'Sacred and mundane.'

Winters hoped to prise more information out of Rob, but the door at the foot of the steps down to the half-buried former dormitory was locked. On previous visits to the commune there'd been no locks, everything was shared and trust was the default assumption, but here was a keypad lock that looked new, and a camera angled above it. Winters banged the side of his fist on the door and sat on the steps and waited and when no one came he banged on the door again and at last it cracked open with a gust of warm musty air and a young man, hardly more than a kid, long hair and bad skin, peered through the narrow gap and asked Winters what he wanted.

'Is Rob there?'

'That depends.'

'Either he is or he isn't.'

'Why do you want to know?'

The kid had the same slow, dazed manner as everyone else in the commune. The same sly smile. As if they were all stoned on something especially potent. Sharing a secret cosmic revelation.

'You know who I am?' Winters said.

'You're the one thinks he's Izzy's brother.'

'Tell Rob I'm going to wait out here.'

'Probably best not to wait too long,' the kid said, and shut the door.

With nowhere else to go, Winters sat on the steps for a while. No one came out or went in, and at last he gave up and saluted the camera and wandered along a narrow path winding between clumps of vegetable plots and clumps of trees. The rain had more or less stopped. His breath smoked in the damp air. Bare woods rising along one side of the repurposed fields. Bridal-white clouds of blackthorn blossom here and there. Scatterings of fresh green where trees were coming into leaf.

A woman Winters thought he recognised was using a hoe to root out weeds between rows of cabbages and he asked her if she knew where his sister was.

The woman leaned on her hoe and studied him and said that Isabel was meditating and couldn't be disturbed.

'How about your leader? I've been told that he wants to see me. Know where I can find him?'

'Best if you wait for him to find you.'

'Do you know why he wants to talk to me? Why I was invited here?'

'I'm sure there's a good reason. Be patient, friend. Kasey'll see you when he sees you.'

It was like talking to a hopped-up child.

Winters said, 'Do you like it here? How things have changed?'

The woman raised a hand and waved it in a vague circle, as if conjuring the entirety of the damp, chilly morning. 'Who wouldn't like a world as fine as this one?'

Lunch was an omelette loaded with wild garlic and chunks of bland, slippery mushroom. Winters had just finished eating when there was a small stir amongst the people dotted around the other tables, everyone turning to watch the person walking down the centre aisle. A small, slender man who didn't seem to grow any taller as he drew near, somewhere in his early thirties. Long blond hair parted down the middle, large black-framed glasses, square lenses tinted purple, a denim jacket that hung unbuttoned over a black T-shirt, black utility trousers.

Winters stood as he approached, knowing who he must be. The man smiling, saying, 'I'm so glad you came.'

'I'm here to see my sister.'

'And you will.'

'I get the feeling that she didn't send the invitation.'

Kasey Motte clasped his hands prayerfully and tapped his lips with his forefingers before he replied. As if considering how to frame the answer to a tricky question.

'To be honest? She didn't want you to come. Thought it was a bad idea. I've been trying to persuade her otherwise, but I'm sure you know how stubborn she can be.'

'If she doesn't want to see me, what am I doing here? What do you want from me?'

'What do I want? I want to show you something. Let's walk and talk.'

Kasey Motte set an eager pace, leading Winters along a path winding through a scrub of brambles and gorse towards the wooded slope that loomed above the commune. Asking him if Isabel had ever mentioned that he, Kasey, was one of the so-called dreamwakers.

'I don't believe so.'

Winters was trying to ignore the two sturdy men who'd fallen in behind them. He wanted to believe that as long as he played nice nothing bad would happen.

'Do you know how dreamwakers came to be?'

'Was it something to do with one of the Covids?'

'The doctors called it encephalitis somnium. Dreaming sickness. Similar to the sleeping sickness epidemic in the first quarter of the last century. Sleeping sickness caused a variety of neurological symptoms, including overwhelming and frequently fatal fatigue. Many survivors were left disabled, and a good number were stuck in a sleep-like state – becoming speechless living statues. Dreaming sickness also caused a sleep-like state, but with permanent REM activity. Continuous dreaming. And while sleeping sickness could be temporarily relieved by injections of L-dopamine, there was no cure for dreaming sickness. Most sufferers died, and most of those still alive are locked in permanent comas. But a few, the dream-wakers, were blessed by spontaneous remission. And as far as

I know I am the only dreamwaker who remembers anything of their long dreaming.

'It was of a world at a slant to this one,' Motte said, his voice softening in recollection. 'Or I should say, the one before this. A beautiful quiet green world, absent all human presence. I spent years wandering in it and never found any other inhabitants, or any trace of the hand of man. No ruined cities or overgrown highways, not a house or a hut, not even a single footprint. I was utterly alone in a world of forest and grassland under a sky untroubled by drones or planes. A world with pristine beaches at the edge of a sea which cast up only seaweed and driftwood. I was skyclad and barefoot, living on blackberries and hazelnuts, windfall apples and bird's eggs and mushrooms. And then, without warning, on a winter's day after the first snow had fallen, I awoke, and that lovely green world was gone. I mourned the loss of it for a long time, and my ordinary dreams never took me back there. But at last, after much trial and error, I discovered that it could be reached by another path.'

Several months later, after the siege, after he'd been taken into custody and released, Winters discovered that this part of Kasey Motte's story was true. He really had been struck down by encephalitis somnium, really had woken from months of sleep-like dreaming. Most of the other survivors suffered from lasting physical and mental disabilities, and none of them had reported any vivid, detailed, seamless dreams like Kasey Motte's, or claimed that they had learned to control their dreams and use them to change reality. Winters thought that the man's rambling monologue was a long way from any kind of sense, but he could understand why the story of a pristine dreamworld had captured the commune. It spoke directly to their utopian ideas about self-sacrifice and regreening, and Motte's account was delivered with the quiet conviction of a true believer in a righteous and necessary cause. Saving the world in the only way it could be truly saved.

As he led Winters through the woods, following a muddy path that scrambled between leafless oak and birch trees, clumps of dark green yews and outcrops of mossy stone, Kasey Motte talked about consensual hallucinations and synchronised mental states, the illusion of reality and how superposition of quantum states, when measured, yielded a random but statistically significant instance of the swarm of possibilities they contained. How entangled pairs of quantum particles and larger quantum systems – atoms, molecules, objects – were intimately linked to each other, even when they were separated by great distances. How, if there was no size limit to this entanglement, the universe itself could be a quantum totality. Change one part, no matter how small, and everything else instantly adjusted to the new state.

'All of us change the world all of the time. Collapse possibilities moment by moment simply by being. That's what the observer effect is. More or less. Your basic double slit-screen experiment. Collapsing the wave function of a quantum state by measuring it. Forcing it to choose one possible state over all the others. And if two particles are entangled, then collapsing the wave function of one half of the entangled pair also collapses the wave function of the other. Instantaneously. No matter how much they are separated. A metre, a light-year, it doesn't matter. It's nonlocal. Can happen everywhere all at once. Even if the entangled particles are in two different quantum fields. Do you see?'

'I'm trying,' Winters said, although he had no idea what the man was talking about.

They had left the upper edge of the woods behind and were walking up a slope of unreconstructed heathland, tramping across a tough carpet of bilberry and heather towards a crest of bare rock that stood against a locked-down sky of low grey cloud. The two burly sidekicks followed a little way behind. Winters was breathless and dizzy. Had to concentrate on each step. His feet were numb and seemed a long way off and bright cross-hatchings were beginning to crowd into his sight. Shifting sideways and floating back when he tried to blink them away.

'The point is this,' Motte was saying. 'You don't need consciousness to collapse a wave function. It's a simple matter of statistics. Probabilities. But if you want a specific outcome, then that's where the combination of consciousness and the observer effect comes into its own. Amplified consciousness. Directed consciousness. Collective consciousness entrained and focused by discipline and certain aids.'

He stopped and took off his glasses and wiped them on the sleeve of his denim jacket and put them on again. Gestured at the wooded slope below and the patchwork of the commune spread beyond, like a conjuror invoking his prestige.

'With the right kind of entrainment, we can reach into the past and change history. Go to sleep in this world and wake in another.'

Winters squinted at him through swarming luminous static. The man's expression was pure and open, as if a revelation had been injected by divine force into his brain.

'You're wondering how I know this,' he said. 'Here's how it happened. This is the secret I've shared with your sister and everyone else in the commune. The secret I'm going to share with you. When I woke from my dream of that wild and lovely green world, the world in which I woke was not the world in which I had fallen asleep. It was a little while before I understood that. Before I discovered that while everything was still fucked up, it was not quite as badly fucked up as it once had been. And when I finally realised what had happened, what I'd done, I tried to change it again. And eventually I succeeded. In a small way at first, and then on a global scale, with the help of some special shrooms, and my followers. And only we know what we did, because we were at the dead centre of the change. Only we remember how the world once was. How bad everything had been and how we made it less so. But not yet perfect. And that's why we'll do it again.'

The ground was rising under Winters' feet like an endless wave. He swayed forward, clutching at Kasey Motte for support, and the two sidekicks moved in and with surprising gentleness seated him on a stone slab.

'It's beginning to come on, isn't it?' Motte said.

'What have you done to me?'

'We put a small dose of my special shrooms in your omelette.'

'You fucking dosed me?'

'To help you see. And I've taken the same dose, so we can take that journey together.' Motte squatted in front of Winters, his gaze serious behind the square purple lenses of his glasses. 'You're special, too. Did you know that? Did Isabel ever tell you?'

'Tell me what?'

'It's why I invited you here.'

'Because I'm Izzy's brother?'

'You don't know, do you? We'll talk about it tomorrow, when you'll be able to process it properly. When you aren't as elevated as you are now. I spent a long time searching for a way of invoking and controlling the kind of changes I'd made to the waking world during my long dream of that green world. I tried all kinds of psychedelics, but at last found a shaman in Ulaanbaatar who grew strains of psychoactive shrooms handed down from father to son over many generations. You've partaken of one of them. A strain that opens the doors of perception in the waking world. Tell me what you see. What you're seeing that you couldn't see before.'

'This is mad crazy.'

'Telling the truth in a world of lies can make a person sound crazy to the unenlightened. Do you see lights? Patterns?'

'What if I do?'

'That's the aura. The sign that the shrooms are beginning to alter your perceptions. Look around. What else do you see?'

'Sky and rock and a crazy person.'

Motte pushed to his feet. 'Let's take a walk in the woods. It often helps.'

He set off down the slope and his sidekicks helped Winters to his feet and gave him a gentle shove and he started down the slope too. Stumbling on feet grown horribly distant. Like trying to walk on stilts. Following the man back into the woods, trees thickening around him, their naked arms raking the cloud ceiling. The damp air packed with a rich odour of earth and slow vegetable decay. The snow of crosshatchings was bright and sharp now, like light bleeding in from a different, more vivid reality.

Kasey Motte was standing with one foot propped on the mossy curve of a fallen tree trunk half sunken in dirt and leaf mould, pointing towards a cluster of ash trees.

'Do you see?'

'See what? What am I supposed to be seeing?'

'The shadows in the shadows . . .'

It was hard to see through the luminous snow, but for a moment, Winters thought he saw something moving through the murky footings of the ash trees. Figures like drifts of smoke, there and gone.

'If you saw what I saw, that was the Wild Hunt,' Motte said. 'Just a glimpse before it moved on. There are other avatars. The Burning Bear. The White Stag. The Green Man, with his hair and beard of leaves. Let's see what we can see.'

Motte stepped onto the fallen tree trunk and stepped down on the other side, and his sidekicks urged Winters to follow. He hadn't gone very far when he thought he glimpsed something behind a mass of Russian vine that sheeted a leafless tree. A face, bearded, leonine and deep green, framed by tangles of hair like dark green ivy, large eyes so black they seemed to be all pupil, their bottomless gaze turning towards him. He froze, skin clammy, heart pounding, luminous flecks pulsing urgently as they drifted aslant, and with a sudden rush of terrible clarity the face pushed through the mass of vine leaves and swooped towards him and he cried out and stumbled backwards and fell full length on his back and after a timeless interval came around in a small storeroom, lying in a nest of blankets on a concrete floor.

Industrial shelving packed with cardboard boxes and catering-sized cans loomed above him. An LED ribbon stuck to the ceiling cast a sharp white glare. The luminous static was gone but he was sluggish and weak, a headache pincered his skull and there was a foul taste in his mouth. He got to his knees by stages, used the shelving to pull himself upright. The heavy door had a lever handle that didn't yield when he tried it.

His phone had been taken, and his keys and his card wallet. Nothing left in his pockets but loose threads and lint.

Three waxed cardboard boxes of water and a roll of toilet paper stood beside a covered pail. He opened one of the boxes and rinsed his mouth and spat into the pail and sat on the blankets, sipping water as he tried to put together his last memories. Kasey Motte's crazy monologue about dreams changing the world. Following him through the woods. The glimpse of shadows moving in shadow. The leonine face rushing out of its nest of vines.

He told himself that none of it was real, it had been nothing but shroom dreams and suggestion, but he didn't like to look at the shadows behind the shelves of boxes and cans. And he was locked in here because Motte had plans for him. Wanted to dose him with shrooms again, play more mind games. Force him to take part in some weird ceremony . . .

He startled awake when the door swung open. Squinted at the person framed there.

'Izzy.'

His sister stepped inside and held out a hand and they gripped each other's wrists and she hauled him to his feet. He fell against her, tried to hug her, but she pulled away. She was dressed in jeans and two flannel shirts, a yellow check shirt open over a red shirt buttoned to the neck. Her hair was cut shorter than he ever remembered, shaved at the sides and back. Her face pale and grim.

'Can you walk?'

'I think so.'

'Then come on.'

He followed her through a shadowy kitchen, past prep tables and a double sink and an industrial dishwasher. A pair of six burner ovens. Fridges humming to themselves in their sleep.

'He dosed me,' he said.

'I know what he did.'

'Talked crazy talk about sharing dreams. Changing the world.'

'No doubt.'

At the far end of the kitchen, Izzy cracked a door open, peered around its edge, told Winters to follow her and keep quiet.

'Where are we going?'

'I'm getting you out of here.'

'Are you coming with me?'

'Didn't I tell you to keep quiet?'

It was dark and still outside. The moon, half-full, tilted behind thin strips of cloud in a kind of temple of pale light. Winters followed Izzy up a short flight of concrete steps and across a stretch of muddy grass to a quad bike parked between two polytunnels, and Izzy swung into the saddle and told him to climb on behind her. He found the pegs for his feet and wrapped his arms around her waist and she switched on the motor and they were off, jolting over grass in a rush of air and the thin whine of the quad bike's electric motors. Passing between rows of solar panels and the parallel humps of the meeting house and a dormitory, the steps to their sunken entrances lit by yellow lamps. Passing the shuttered and lightless farmhouse and following the track beyond it, Izzy switching on the bike's headlight as they plunged between stands of dark pines.

Winters leaned against her back, feeling her solid reality and warmth. Breathing in her familiar smell.

'It's so good to see you again,' he said, with an unreasoning surge of affection.

'Depends what you mean.'

'What I mean?'

'By again.'

The bright wedge of the quad bike's headlight lit tree trunks streaming by on either side of the track, and a gate appeared at the far end and rushed towards them. Izzy braked hard and swerved to a halt beside it. The five-bar gate he'd passed through the day before, weather-grained lichen-spattered wood lit with harsh particularity.

Izzy said that this was as far as she could take him, and swung off the quad bike and opened a pannier and handed him his windcheater and a plastic bag holding his phone and keys and card wallet. Pulled out his overnight bag and dropped it at his feet and walked through the glare of the bike's headlights and unlatched the gate and dragged it open. There was a muddy pull-off and a tarmacadam country road beyond. The carbon silhouette of a high hedge on the far side.

'Wait here. I called a taxi,' she said, and took a step back when he moved towards her, held up a hand.

'Don't.'

'I came here to see you, Izzy. It's been a while.'

'I didn't invite you. That was Kasey. He shouldn't have done it, but his curiosity got the better of him. And you were a fool to accept.'

'I know that now. Kasey told me you thought it was a bad idea. That you didn't want to see me. Is that true?'

'What else did he tell you? Did he say why he thinks that you can help us?'

'He said that he was going to explain everything tomorrow. But you know, don't you? You can tell me.'

'He's planning to dose you again. Have one of his special one-on-one struggle sessions. The first step in making you one of the gang. That's why I'm helping you to get out. The only reason.'

'You don't have to stay here. You can come with me.'

'That's the last thing I want to do.'

Izzy's face, bleached in the glare of the quad bike's headlight, was as shuttered as a mask.

'Have you ever taken those shrooms he fed me?'

'They're part of the process.'

'Everyone here takes them and dreams of a better world, and somehow makes those dreams real.'

'In a nutshell.'

'He made you believe in it somehow. Or maybe it's something to do with the shrooms. Like an addiction. But I think that you know, deep down, that it isn't true. It can't be.'

'But it is. We dreamed of a better world and made it so. And here we are and here it is. And soon enough we're going to change it again. And we don't need you to help us do it.'

Winters tried another tack. 'This is like the arguments we used to have when we were kids. You always claimed you were right, and most times you were. But when you weren't, there wasn't any way of telling you otherwise.'

'We have so much less in common than you think.'

'I helped you hand out leaflets, was your assistant in those surveys you signed up for. You hardly ever needed to use your phone to identify something. Flowers, insects, birds – you had it all down. I loved those times. I learned so much.'

'I didn't ask for you to be born. And I don't need anything from you or want to have anything to do with you.'

The matter-of-fact coldness of her voice, her look, cut through him. He said helplessly, 'I know what I know. And I think you know it too.'

'The taxi will be here in a few minutes. It'll get you to the station in time for the last train to London. Go home. Enjoy your little life while you can,' Izzy said, and swung onto the quad bike and twisted its throttle and turned it in a tight arc and sped off and left Winters standing there, watching as the unsteady beam of its headlight was swallowed by the darkness under the trees.

In the aftermath of that last visit, on the train back to London, Winters had discovered that the Wild Hunt and the Green Man were common figures in English folklore. One a gang of ghost riders led by an old god or a long-dead king, the other a symbol of rebirth whose likeness was often used as an architectural decoration in churches. The first image of a Green Man he pulled up, a famous example in Lincoln Cathedral, was uncannily like the face he'd seen in the wood, and he wondered if he'd seen it somewhere before and forgotten about it until, triggered by Kasey Motte's shrooms, the memory had resurfaced as an hallucination. That's all it had been, he told himself at the time, a weird trip, and eight years later it was still hard to understand why Izzy, sensible, practical Izzy, had fallen for Motte's bullshit fantasies. That she could ever have believed that mushroom dreams could create a fresh green paradise. After the siege, in the long slough of his grieving, Winters had returned to that last conversation with her over and again, looking for a way he could have moved it in a different direction and persuaded her to leave with him, feeling shame and guilt for having failed. And now, now that he knew Izzy had survived Motte's last mad grand egotistical act, he couldn't help hoping that somehow he'd planted a seed of doubt in her mind after all, that if he found her she would confess that she'd been wrong. Wrong about Motte and his fantasies of dreaming new worlds into being. Wrong to have dismissed her brother so coldly, and to have spurned him ever since.

At six o'clock, he walked back to the railway arches. The taxi garage was shuttered and Charlie Lowe was standing outside, a skinny, nervous fellow in his forties, hair cropped to grey stubble. He squinted at Winters as he walked up, saying, 'You're late.'

'You must have closed early, because I'm dead on time. I found a café around the corner. We could have our little chat there.'

'Let's go the pub. I'll need a stiffener for this. More than one, probably.'

There was an old brick-built pub on the main road. On the way there, Charlie told Winters that the police had paid him a visit the day before. Two detectives from counterterrorism operations, Sinclair and Briggs.

'They visited me, too,' Winters said.

''Course they did. They're hot to find Isabel, aren't they?'

'What did you tell them?'

'The truth,' Charlie said. 'That I didn't have a clue she was still alive. Hadn't laid eyes on her since I left the commune, a good two years before that fucking foolish mess at the end of it. And I don't suppose you've seen anything of her either, or you wouldn't be here.'

In the pub, Winters bought a pint of beer for Charlie and a tomato juice for himself and they bagged a corner table. Charlie drank half his beer in three gulps and blotted his mouth with the back of his hand. He was older than most members of the commune, a drifter who like many such had turned up at Wakestone one day because he'd heard that its commune offered free meals, and had stayed on, doing odd jobs and eventually taking charge of maintaining the wind turbines and solar panels and storage batteries. He'd quit and gone back on the drift soon after Kasey Motte had arrived, not wanting to have anything to do with his nonsense, but even so was haunted by survivor's guilt. Like Winters, he'd left England for a couple of years, had been driving trucks for an NGO when they'd run into each other at the aid distribution centre in Spain where Winters had been working. They'd stayed in touch, Charlie relaying news and rumours from other former members of the commune, but this was the first time they'd met face to face in more than four years.

'You really had no idea Isabel was still alive,' Charlie said.

'I really didn't.'

'All this time, she never got in touch.'

'Things had changed between us. Did the police tell you about her alias, where she'd been living when she disappeared?'

'In Scotland? Yeah.'

'Does anyone from the commune live there?'

'You mean anyone who might have been helping her? I don't think so. But it's not like I've been keeping tabs on everyone.' Charlie sipped his beer and said, 'When they paid you a visit, did the cops say anything about how she escaped from the siege?'

'No, they didn't.'

'It's possible she isn't the only one. There could be other survivors. Maybe even you-know-who.'

Charlie still couldn't or wouldn't say the name of the man who had driven him from the commune.

'If Motte's still alive, he's kept unusually quiet for the past eight years.' Winters took a sip of his tomato juice and said, 'There's something else.'

'I might have known.'

'Just before the police visited me, someone broke into my narrowboat. They'd been watching it for a little while beforehand, I guess because they hoped my sister might turn up. They got into my work files, spraypainted a message on the side of the boat. "The Instauration Is Coming."'

Charlie shrugged.

'It's like a calling card for people who call themselves deep dreamers,' Winters said. 'Ever heard of them?'

'They follow you-know-who, don't they? His teachings, anyway. All that stuff he put up before what happened, happened. Nutters, mostly, from what I've heard. Don't really know anything about the shrooms, or about the resets either. Just think that they do.'

'Have you ever met any of them?'

'A couple of them bothered me one time. Wanting to know what it was like, living in the commune. What you-know-who was really like. I told them I was never a believer. That I'd seen through all that nonsense. Knew it for what it was from the beginning and upped and left. You think they might be after Isabel?'

'I think it's very likely. I'm sort of caught up in this, Charlie. And I want to help Isabel if I can. I think one of the ways I might be able to do that is by finding who is looking for her. Which is why I was hoping you might know some of these deep dreamers. Or know someone who does. Someone who can help me to get in touch with them.'

Charlie drank half his remaining beer. 'The two who bothered me, that was getting on for a year ago. Haven't seen them or any of their friends since. But as it happens, there is someone who might know something. Remember Dash Baker? Looked after the electrics and such in the commune.'

'I think so.'

She'd been clattering about in the workshop when Izzy had shown him around the commune, the first time he'd visited, and he'd also seen her at meals in the meeting hall, eating with the same small group of women or taking her turn behind the counter, serving food. A slender young woman dressed in dungarees and sleeveless T-shirts who'd taken absolutely no notice of him. Winters had been young enough back then for that to matter.

'She left right after the so-called first reset,' Charlie said. 'Doesn't have much to do with the rest of us. But she gave me a call a couple of days ago. Just after you called me, as a matter of fact. Said she'd heard about Isabel, and might know something about the people looking for her. Said that I should mention it if you came asking around.'

'Did she tell you what she knows?'

'Nothing specific. But I know she still uses shrooms now and then. Some kind of self-medication thing. So maybe there's a connection.'

'It sounds like I should talk to her. Do you have her number?'

'I can do better than that. I'll give her a call right now, let her know what's going down. And while I'm doing that, you can fetch me another pint.'

When Winters got back to the table Charlie told him that Dash was trying to set something up, she'd call back in a few minutes, but it was close to half an hour, Charlie had nearly finished his third pint and Winters was about to give up on the idea, when the call came. Charlie listened to the person on the other end, saying *I know* and *I won't tell a soul*, and *he's right here*, before handing his phone to Winters.

'I hear you've been having trouble with the deep dreamer crew,' a woman, presumably Dash Baker, said. 'I know someone who might be able to help.'

Winters rode a packed and overheated Overground train from London Fields to Edmonton and found his way to the address Dash Baker had given him, a flat above a second-hand clothing and furniture shop on the corner of an intersection, across from a red-brick Greek Orthodox church that loomed above the streets of terraced houses like a ship stranded on a coral reef. The door to the flat opened as Winters approached and Dash's contact, Hari Pacek, ushered him inside. A gruff, sturdy man in his fifties, barefoot in shorts and an uncinched purple sateen dressing gown like the garb of some minor religious order, he led Winters up a narrow flight of stairs, explaining that he had installed a CCTV system that watched every approach because it was best to see trouble coming before trouble saw you, and in the cramped kitchen lifted books from a chair behind a battered pine table and asked Winters to please sit and disappeared into the depths of the flat.

The table was covered with uneven stacks of books and old journals, most of them about the physiology of sleep, sleep disorders, or dream interpretation. Winters spotted a water-stained paperback copy of Francis Bacon's *The Great Instauration*, the root of the deep dreamers' slogan, various editions of Freud's *The Interpretations of Dreams* and Jung's *Dreams*, and an ancient volume, *Dreambook and Fortune Teller*, handsewn with twine, its cracked browned cover depicting a crone in bonnet and shawl instructing a wide-eyed young couple in Victorian dress. A pack of cards, larger than ordinary playing cards and wrapped in an elaborately embroidered silk handkerchief, triggered a shiver of memory. There was an amethyst agate geode on top of one irregular heap of loose papers, a glass pyramid filled with what looked like black sand weighed down another, and more books, boxfiles and loose papers were piled high on the kitchen counter, the draining board of the sink and the cooktop of the oven. The air was warm and close. A faint odour of spoiled milk. The dusty sash window overlooked a small garden mostly occupied by an ancient caravan. A balding man sat on a concrete block by the caravan's open door, thoughtfully vaping, sparking in Winters a craving for a joint or a soothing bubblepipe. Even a gummy would do. It had been a long day, and he was far from being done with it.

He could hear music elsewhere, and the low grumble of a voice, wondered if there was another person in the flat or if Hari Pacek was talking to someone on the phone. When at last the man returned he sat across from Winters, settling the wings of the dressing gown around himself. A bell of black hair fell to his shoulders and thick black curls matted his bare chest. A band of arcane script was tattooed around his neck and there were stylised eyes on the backs of his hands that reminded Winters of people in an Ancient Egyptian frieze he'd once seen in Bristol Museum, on a school trip at least fifteen years ago.

'So,' Pacek said. 'My friend Dash tells me that you are looking for your sister.'

'And she told me that you're writing a book about end-time cults, including the deep dreamers. I guess she was right. You have a lot of books about dreams here.'

'It's a deep and mysterious subject. We spend a month of every year dreaming. An essential activity. People who are deprived of sleep, especially the type of sleep associated with dreaming, begin to exhibit signs of psychoses and eventually die. And dreams are not peculiar to human beings. All mammals dream. Birds. Even some insects. Bees, for instance. Bumblebees especially.'

'Those that are still around.'

'Yes. The thinning of the biosphere's diversity is also a thinning of the diversity of dreams and dreamers. But although dreams are a vital and necessary part of consciousness, there is no agreement about their exact function. Someone once said that our dreams are where we can truly be ourselves, and everything else, our entire waking life, is simply a support system. The deep dreamers would certainly agree with that. Kasey Motte also. I believe that you are here because your sister was one of his disciples. And I understand that you met him.'

'Just the once.'

'And sampled his infamous shrooms.'

'Not by choice.'

'Were you fully awake, or did he put you in a trance?'

'That doesn't have anything to do with why I'm here.'

'If you answer my questions, I will do my best to answer yours. That's the deal.'

'Okay.'

'So. Awake or in a trance?'

'As far as I know I wasn't put in any kind of trance. I was fed an omelette spiked with shrooms.'

'What did you see?'

'Patterns of light, to begin with.'

'Visual precepts. Basic entopic forms.'

'Yeah. Lots of tiny ones. Like a kind of geometric snow.'

'Grids? Dots? Zig-zags like lightning?'

'Sort of like hashtags, mostly.'

'Very good. What else?'

'When he knew that the shrooms were working in me, Kasey Motte took me on a walk through some woods. I saw what might have been something moving in shadows. And a face inside some vines. You know those Green Man carvings in churches?'

'Of course.'

'Like that.'

'He is far older than those carvings. Did Kasey Motte tell you what was in the shadows?'

'He said it was the Wild Hunt, but it could have been anything.'

'I see. And afterwards, that night or any of the nights following, did you dream of these things? Or dream of a green world?'

'As in Motte's dream?'

'Yes. A world he wished to dream into being.'

'I don't remember any dreams. Just the things I saw, or thought I saw, after I'd been spiked. Hallucinations.'

'The things the shrooms help you to see are neither hallucinations nor dreams. They are the fourth state.'

'I don't know what that means.'

'Waking, dreaming, deep and dreamless sleep – those are the three states of consciousness familiar to most people. But there is a fourth, the ground state on which the other three are based. Sometimes called turiya, or svapna. Kasey Motte's shrooms help you to access this ground state, and to manipulate it if you are sufficiently trained. You, I think, are not.'

'I left before he got to that part.'

'What a shame you did not stay longer. You might have learned something useful.'

'I don't think so.'

'You are not a believer.'

'I'm whatever's the opposite of that. But my sister,' Winters said, wanting to change the direction of the exchange. 'Isabel. She was a believer. Back then, at least.'

'And unlike other disciples of Kasey Motte, it appears that she survived the siege. And has avoided arrest in the years since. Do you know how she survived?'

'No, I don't.'

'And do you have any idea about where she may be now?'

'If I did, I wouldn't be here.'

Hari Pacek's questions, the stuffy kitchen and its battlements of opaque and useless knowledge, the man loitering below the kitchen window and the idea that there might be someone else in the flat, were giving Winters the fear, making him feel that he'd walked into some kind of trap. Like one of those dreams where he urgently needed to get away from someone or find something, but was paralysed by a stifling inertia.

He said, 'It looks like the deep dreamers had something to do with my sister's disappearance. So I'm looking for any information about them, their beliefs and activities and plans. How I might be able to find them.'

'There are three parties to consider,' Pacek said. 'First there are the ordinary dreamers. Lotus eaters who use ordinary magic mushrooms and lose themselves in trivial solipsistic reveries about the great dreaming of Mother Earth and other nonsense. They have some skill in variants of the dream yoga method and clear light practices, but essentially they are no more than moths who batter against a garden lantern and believe that they have discovered the sun or the moon. And then there are the self-styled rivals of the deep dreamers. People who use Kasey Motte's strain of shrooms to practise lucid dreaming and refine their pseudo-scholarly theories of mindfulness and the nature of dreams and dreaming. Like the commonplace dreamers, they wish to change only themselves, and refuse to believe that Motte's teachings are anything other than fantasies. The delusions of a superego subjugated by the primitive desires of the subconscious, according to their archaic Freudian jargon. And lastly there are the deep dreamers themselves, who are refining Motte's methodology. His use of shrooms. Do you know what they are planning?'

The man was treating him as a recalcitrant pupil, but Winters played along because he believed that he was beginning to get somewhere.

'I heard they were trying to copy Motte's idea about some kind of reset. Dreaming a different history into being. Trying to complete what Motte failed to do. Which is why, I guess, they have an interest in my sister. She's the only known survivor of the siege. The last of Motte's inner circle.'

'Someone who may know secrets thought to have been lost in the fire,' Pacek said. 'What do you know of his Great Green Reset?'

'Only what was in those writings of his. He wanted to save the world by dreaming up a version of history in which the human race had never existed.'

Winters hadn't read any of the stuff Motte had published before the siege, but he'd read articles by people who had.

'Exactly so,' Pacek said. 'He claimed that his reset was the world's last best hope. That the only way to make good the damage caused by the murderous greed of our species was to dream us out of existence. No one, not even Kasey Motte and his little tribe of dreamers, would pass across into the new green world they would create. Hence the cleansing fire. Although there are some who think that, despite his claims, he planned to cross over anyway. Given his nature, he could not conceive of a world in which he did not exist. And that meant his followers would have to cross also, for what is a messiah without disciples?'

'So are the deep dreamers planning some kind of rerun of that, with this instauration of theirs?'

'They want to use Kasey Motte's methods, but to a different end. One that's not quite so radical. I am a scholar, not a detective or some species of cheap psychic. I can't help you find your sister, but I do have some information about the deep dreamers that may be of some use.'

'What do you want in return?'

'The opportunity to meet your sister, should you find her. It would greatly help my research.'

'If I find her I guess I can ask if she'll agree to that. That's the best I can do.'

Hari Pacek scratched at the thatch on his chest while he considered that, saying at last, 'I know the names of some of those who claim to lead the deep dreamers. The names they have given themselves.'

'Okay.'

Pacek closed his eyes and recited sonorously, 'Oniros. The Eighth Gate. The Six. The Marquis d'Hervey. Voidrider.'

Jesus, like characters in some comic book. Winters said, 'What about their actual names?'

'They are no longer the persons they once were. The first thing they do, after they have mastered Kasey Motte's procedures, is to change themselves. Write themselves out of common history.'

'You mean like erasing their personal information from databases?'

'Deeper than that. Making small but significant changes in our common consciousness. Rewriting the Weltstoff.'

'Is that German?'

'Its literal meaning is world stuff. The fundamental essence of the universe, according to Pierre de Chardin.'

'I see,' Winters said, although he didn't. The conversation had taken a turn into unintelligible weirdness. 'Well, thanks for giving me your time.'

'Before you go, I would like to give you a reading.'

'A reading?'

'Using these,' Hari Pacek said, and unfolded the silk handkerchief to reveal a pack of Tarot cards.

The legs of Winters' chair squealed on the vinyl floorcovering as he pushed back from the table.

'No way.'

'It will not take long,' Pacek said, and began to shuffle the cards. It was the standard Rider-Waite deck, with coloured faces and backs crosshatched in blue and black. Worn from much handling.

Winters thought he heard something elsewhere in the flat. A faint creak, like someone putting their weight on an old floorboard. He said, 'I had a reading a few years back. It didn't end well.'

'Deep dreamers use the cards to explain their dreams and visions, and I also find them useful. Here,' Pacek said, and fanned the cards and held them out to Winters. 'You have only to pick one. It will tell you something about your search.'

'And then I'll go.'

'Of course.'

With prickling caution, Winters picked one from the middle.

'Put it on the table.'

Winters laid it on top of a short stack of books. Pacek folded the fan of cards and set them down and turned over the one Winters had chosen.

Six swords standing with their points embedded in the well of a flatbottomed skiff or punt bearing two hooded figures, an adult and a child, and a boatman leaning into his pole as he propelled his craft towards a sparsely wooded shore. A different iteration of the last of the three cards that Winters had chosen when Ayn, CeCe's friend, had done a reading. The six of swords, reversed.

'This is some kind of trick,' he said.

'The card is the card you freely chose. I will not say at random, for it is your significator. But there was no trick involved. Only what passed between you and the cards. Do you want to know what it means?'

'I think it means you know Ayn. The weird woman who camps out in woods, brews tea from twigs and does sort of weaponised Tarot readings.'

Hari Pacek ignored that. He touched the card with his forefinger. 'Upright, this would suggest that you were closing on your goal. That although you might be in need of guidance, you were moving forward easily, like a boat crossing calm water towards a welcoming shore. But the card is reversed, and the water is choppy, not calm. You feel trapped. Trouble is coming. Relationships are in peril. Travel will be disrupted. In short, everything in your life is upset and unstable. And yet, there is still hope. The possibility of a slow healing at the end of your journey.'

'I made a mistake, coming here,' Winters said, and stood up and stepped around the table. He half-expected Pacek to try to stop him, or for an accomplice to be waiting in the short hallway, but the hallway was empty and so were the stairs. He clattered down them and turned the latch of the door's lock, but although the door rattled it would not open. He heard footsteps behind him, saw that there was a chain and ratchetted it back, turned the latch again, wrenched the door open.

'Pay attention to your dreams!' Hari Pacek called out as Winters stumbled out into the perfectly ordinary street. 'They will tell you everything you need to know!'

Every seat was taken and passengers were straphanging with weary resignation and squatting in gangways and crowding up against doors as the train rolled east though suburbs and edgelands. Braced beside a bicycle rack at one end of a carriage, Winters reviewed the day's frustrations and reversals. Despite everything, he didn't seem to have made any headway in finding Izzy or discovering who the deep dreamers were, what they wanted from her. Or from him. His uncle had palmed him off on Lady Talia Armstrong and her bulldog, and he couldn't trust anything Hari Pacek had told him, the man seemed to be a charlatan trying to run some kind of con, and the thing with the Tarot card couldn't have been anything other than a trick. The kind of close-up sleight of hand used by street magicians. Forcing the card or palming it, simple as. Except, how had Pacek known which card to force?

After the encounter with CeCe's witchy friend in the woods, after she'd up and left, Winters had tried to rationalise it, find an explanation that didn't have anything to do with mystic woo and his last parting with Izzy, and reckoned that it had been down to nothing more than simple malice. Ayn had taken a disliking to him, thought her friend shouldn't be wasting her time with this lame straight guy, and had decided to interfere. To fake a reading she knew would upset CeCe, like putting a hex on him. Or maybe the whole meeting had been a setup, CeCe wondering about a more permanent relationship and using her friend and her cards to vet him, and not getting an answer she liked.

It was possible that Hari Pacek had some kind of connection with Ayn — she had definitely seemed like the kind of person who'd be into shrooms and dream magic. Or maybe the story about the Tarot cards selected by the brother of the infamous Isabel Winters, their so-called significance, had circulated in the drifter and dreamer communities, and Pacek had heard about it and incorporated it in his con game, tried to trick Winters into believing that he possessed esoteric skills which, for the right price, could be used to find the deep dreamers and Izzy.

What he didn't want to think about, what it couldn't possibly be, was that the reappearance of that fucking card was down to something deeper than a mundane trick. Something weirder.

No. All in all, he reckoned that he'd had done the right thing by bugging out before whatever kind of scam or trap the man had been devising snapped shut. He shook open his phone, checked the comic-book tags Hari Pacek had claimed to be the true names of prime deep dreamers, and was surprised when he got a couple of relevant hits. Oniros was the name of a French Dream Society, and the Marquis d'Hervey was some long-dead French guy who'd studied Chinese culture and customs back in the nineteenth century, and was also, apparently, the father of the modern study of dreams, especially of lucid dreaming. Which was sort of interesting, but wasn't much help in figuring out whether they were true names or fictions, part of Pacek's game.

The train crawled into a station and Winters shrank back as someone hoisted a bike from the rack and people crowded out of the doors. As the train started off again, his thoughts turned, for about the millionth time, to that last conversation with his sister. He'd read a little about cults, afterwards. The nature of them. The nature of people who led them and the nature of the people who joined them, or just sort of fell in. The lovebombed and the lost. Those searching for some kind of structure and control. Those who thought that they had discovered a superhuman saviour, or believed that they were wolves possessed of secret knowledge in a world of sheep, and those who had no idea that they were part of a cult. The normalisation of extremes. The sunk costs of misguided conviction. He hadn't read much. Just enough to realise how naïve he'd been, back then, thinking that he could persuade Izzy to walk away from Kasey Motte and the commune.

Thinking that he could help her now was probably no less naïve, but she was his sister, flesh and blood and bone, and besides all that she'd helped him to escape from Motte. The way she'd cut him loose had been brutally hard-hearted, but in the aftermath he'd wondered if she knew what was coming and didn't want him to have any part in it. And maybe his uncle was right, maybe she hadn't been a true believer after all, had been leaking information about Motte and his plans to the police or some species of spook. It was one of the things he wanted to ask her, if he ever found her. One of the things he needed to know. Like, why she hadn't ever reached out to him while she'd been on the run? Was it because she didn't want to put him in danger, or because she didn't trust him? Or was it just part of her rejection of her former life? The life before Kasey Motte.

Do you really owe her anything?

Yeah, you know you do.

Should I try to help her, despite those hard last words?

Yeah, you know you're going to try.

Which brought him back to Talia Armstrong, the uneasy alliance he'd been sort of forced into by his uncle. His growing regret about trusting her and her investigator with those scraps of evidence. There wasn't any point in trying to tap Charlie Lowe for another lead, he'd been burnt once and didn't want to get burned again, but Hari Pacek's condescending lecturette on the hierarchy of the dream biz suggested another way of connecting with the deep dreamers, chancy and frail though it was. Winters hunched closer to the racked bicycles, trying to gain a little privacy, and called Jude, asked if they could meet up.

'I need to ask a favour. Make use of your contacts in the drifter community.'

'Is this about your break-in, or your trip to London?'

'How did you hear about that?'

'Your supervisor told Nina you'd been given the day off. And Nina mentioned it to me, asked if I knew what was going on. So, what's going on?'

'I sort of don't want to talk about it over the phone. Can I swing by first thing tomorrow morning?'

'As long as you promise to tell me everything.'

'I'll tell you as much as I can.'

The train's speed was much reduced, now, and it was shuddering to a halt outside every station and standing there for a minute or two before crawling at a walking pace to the platform. After Brentford, Winters snagged a corner seat, thinking that he'd soon be home, but then the train stopped again, this time in the middle of the countryside. The driver explained over the PA system that there was a problem with the power lines, she hoped it would be fixed shortly, and for a long while nothing else happened.

The other passengers made calls, engaged in low-level grumbling – it seemed that delays like this were commonplace. Winters' thoughts drifted back to that Tarot card. Hari Pacek telling him that it meant that his travel would be disrupted.

No, it was just a coincidence. Had to be. Trains broke down all the time. Ancient rolling stock, infrastructure weakened by heat and extreme weather events, decades of zero-growth, make-do-and-mend economics.

Thirty minutes passed. An hour. A field of wheat glowing in magic-hour light on one side of the carriage, oilseed rape on the other. Birdsong. The train's backup batteries gave out and the lights and air-conditioning cut off. People fanned themselves with hands and hats and books. A few foresighted folk broke out little battery-operated fans. Several small children chased each other to the end of the train and turned around and chased each other back to where they'd come from. At last, the driver announced that the onward journey was terminating here, passengers would alight and walk to the nearest road, where buses would pick them up. There was a brief flurry as people gathered their belongings and the driver walked along the carriages, cranking open the centre doors, and everyone clambered down steps set in place by community volunteers, mostly teenaged schoolkids with armbands, who handed out cardboard cups of water and escorted the passengers along the edge of the railway line to a rural lane that led to a dual carriageway where a small convoy of buses, most of them at least as old as the train, was parked up. Winters, carrying the suitcase of a woman who was traveling to Chelmsford because her ninety-one-year-old mother had suffered a bad fall ('That's the last time she'll be allowed to use a step-ladder'), was one of the last to board. As soon as he sat down the bus made a U-turn in a gap in the trees which divided the carriageways, and joined the east-bound traffic.

There was a wait of more than an hour in Chelmsford for the next bus to Maldon. Winters bought a satay tofu wrap from a street stall and ate it and lit up a joint, was watching passers-by and people waiting under the slant roof of the transport interchange, playing a not entirely unserious game of spot-the-spook, thinking that he'd have to be careful, try to stay under the radar, make sure he didn't lead the police or Talia Armstrong's investigator to Izzy, when his work phone buzzed in his pocket. Someone he didn't know who claimed to be with the Live Force news agency, asking if he could spare a moment to comment on the BBC story about his sister, Isabel.

He dropped the call and the phone buzzed again and he switched it off. Took a long drag on his joint and slowly breathed out smoke and brought up the BBC feed and found, in the breaking news section, a brief stub put up thirty minutes before. 'Police have discovered that Isabel Winters, previously believed to have died at the explosive end of the Wakestone Farm siege eight years ago, has been found to have been living under a false identity in Scotland. Her current whereabouts are unknown, but police are urgently searching for her, more to come . . .'

A quick search found variations of the news in half a dozen other feeds. Winters didn't think that it was likely that the counterterrorism police had gone wide with their investigation, and his uncle had his own reasons for wanting to keep it quiet. Which left either a leak by someone in the local police, or Talia Armstrong. Who wanted to find Izzy by any means necessary, and almost certainly had contacts in the BBC and elsewhere. Winters took a last drag on the joint, thinking that at least he no longer had to worry about disobeying DI Sinclair's request to keep the news about Izzy secret. He could only hope that the inevitable media feeding frenzy would pass as quickly as possible, and try to get on with his own thing.

It was late evening, dusk's last bloom fading, when he reached Maldon. He snagged a community bike and cycled across the bridge over the River Chelmer, through the streets of Heybridge and along the footpath beside the long straight channel of the Chelmer and Blackwater Navigation to Heybridge Basin. He was walking towards the berth where he'd tied up the skimmer in what seemed like another age, when someone called his name. A young guy loping towards him with a broad, eager smile, saying, 'Mr Winters. Marc. Can we talk?'

He was barely in his twenties, radiant with false goodwill and dressed in immaculate white trousers and a pink shirt with comically voluminous sleeves. With a plunging feeling Winters knew what he was and what he wanted, heard a whisper in the dark air and looked up. A drone was taking station a couple of metres above his head, its LEDs clicking on, pinning him in a column of blueish light like a UFO abductee.

'Is it true your sister has been on the run for the past eight years, Mr Winters? Do you know where she is now?'

'I have nothing to tell you,' Winters said, and turned away, started to walk along the quay. The drone followed, matching his speed perfectly, keeping him at the centre of its spotlight, and the young citizen journalist quickened his pace, asking him breathlessly if it was true that Isabel was a key figure in the deep dreamers' movement, and was he helping her hide from the authorities?

'I want to give you the chance to present your side of the story, Marc. It'll take hardly any time.'

Like most of his kind, this eager young man was driven by an old and dangerous hunger. The need for views and any kind of feedback. A bottomless longing to be seen. The same hunger for attention which had polluted the old internet, amplifying grievances, weaponising gossip and rumour, prizing fake news and bad takes over fact. Even so, Winters realised that he might be useful, and stopped and turned and said that he wanted to make a brief appeal.

'Before I do, you have to promise that you'll include all of it in your piece.'

'Of course.'

'All of it. Whole. Uncut.'

'And will you answer my questions?'

'Just the appeal. No questions. Yes or no.'

'Whatever you like.'

'I'll take that as a yes. Follow me.'

Winters walked down the long jetty to his skimmer, untied its mooring lines and climbed into it, looked up at the young man.

'Are you ready?'

'It's not a great angle. Can I bring the drone lower?'

'Leave it where it is,' Winters said, and looked into the drone's bright light and said his piece, and when he was done started the skimmer's motor, ignoring the questions the journalist called out, and powered away in a wash of muddy water. He wanted to count it as a victory, but knew that it wasn't even close. The news about Izzy was out in the world, he couldn't trust the journalist to keep his promise, and knew that this was only the beginning.

Winters' little speech went live overnight, and by the next morning his personal phone, the cheap nologo model he'd bought when he'd returned after working abroad and hadn't had much use for after he'd started work with the agency, had soaked up a full charge and accumulated more than twenty messages, most of them from various newsfeeds and agencies, but a few spiteful rants from anonymous hatemice too. Nothing yet from Izzy, but it was early days.

There were more messages on his work phone, and he was checking and deleting them one by one when his supervisor, Aimee Fellows, called. It seemed that several news outlets, including the BBC, had contacted the agency's media centre and requested an interview.

'Is it true?' Aimee said. 'Are the police are looking for your sister?'

'That's what a couple of detectives told me,' Winters said.

'And it's why you had to go to London.'

'As I said at the time, there was a family emergency.'

'And you didn't think that you should have told the agency about the true nature of that emergency.'

'The police gave me the impression that I should keep quiet about it.'

'But you haven't kept quiet about it, have you? Our media people found out about the appeal you made last night. They aren't happy about it.'

'I was sort of ambushed. And it felt like the right thing to do. Given the circumstances.'

Winters thought that it had come out pretty well. He'd kept his gaze on the drone and spoken as slowly and cogently as he was able, telling Izzy that he believed that she was in some kind of trouble, that if she wanted to reach out to him he would do all he could to help her, and giving the number of his personal phone and a way of confirming her identity. It was preceded by footage of the journalist's ambush and brief pursuit, and followed by a long straight-to-camera commentary, but Winters had watched only a minute or so of that before turning it off.

'I understand that the situation isn't your fault, but you should have cleared it with me first,' Aimee said. 'It could cause a serious problem. An unwelcome distraction from the agency's work.'

'So what happens now?'

'Our media people are going put up an additional statement on your behalf. A brief announcement that you have no further comments to make until the police have completed their investigation. And you will have to attend a disciplinary hearing. Meanwhile,' Aimee said implacably, 'you'll sit tight on Cynsea. Continue with your work, and don't talk about this with anyone.'

'If I stay here, it'll make it easier for journalists to find me.'

'You can organise your volunteers, get up a rota for safeguarding the causeway, make sure that only genuine visitors are allowed onto the island.'

'And if some journalist gets the idea to hire a boat?'

'You'll refuse to answer any of their questions, refer them to our statement, and ask them politely to leave.'

'I have a better idea,' Winters said.

Part Three

A Man Out of Time

Walking down the jetty towards Winters, Jude Lee said cheerfully, 'Here he is, the infamous outlaw.'

Winters was tying up his hire boat. 'Is that what people are calling me?'

'The general impression is that you've been irredeemably tarred with your sister's notoriety.'

'We don't have to do this if you think you might get spattered with some of that tar.'

'Oh, I'm too desperate to hear your side of things to worry about that.' Jude set down the thermos and cups he was carrying and took up the slack in the boat's stern line and whipped it around a post. 'Smart ride. Where did you get it?'

It was a five-metre aluminium-hulled jet boat, red livery and yellow speed stripes, a knife-edged bow and raked windshield.

'Doyle's,' Winters said.

'I hope you they gave you a good deal.'

'Just the usual ranger's discount. I thought I might need something that can outrun any journalists who thinks to give chase.'

'Looks like a fun ride.'

'Yeah. There's also that.'

'Flat bottom?'

'With a delta pad and a fifty-centimetre draft. If I can't outrun them, I can lose them in the marshes.'

'Is that where you're hiding out?'

'No, the Old Ship. The room they keep reserved for agency folk.'

'First place anyone would look, when they discover that you're no longer on Cynsea.'

'They haven't found me yet.'

'I have coffee,' Jude said, picking up the thermos and cups. 'Real coffee from real beans, grown by some hydroponic outfit in Cornwall. One of my birder friends slipped me a couple of hundred grams. Let's go sit in the shade, and you can tell me everything.'

They settled under a canvas umbrella off to the side of the old boat shed which served as Jude's office and home, with a view of the mudflats of the foreshore and the estuary's sun-starred main channel. It was a little before ten in the morning. Already hot. Brassy sunlight threw their shadows against the weathered clapboard of the shed's wall. Winters in the short-sleeved blue cotton shirt and stone-coloured cargo shorts he'd worn for his meeting with Uncle Danny, Jude in workwear shorts and his green agency T-shirt and green canvas agency jacket, unruly curls of red hair poking out beneath the brim of his bucket hat.

'You'll take it black,' Jude said, as he poured coffee from a steel thermos into the two small, thick-walled cups. 'Milk of any species would be sacrilege.'

The brew's oily bitterness reminded Winters why he wasn't a coffee drinker. The last time he'd tried it, at a meeting with a local politician in Albania, it had been served with a spoonful of gritty brown sugar, but he guessed that as far as

Jude was concerned sweetening the taste would even worse than adding a drop of milk.

'So is it true?' Jude said. 'You've been suspended over this business?'

'Not exactly. There'll be a disciplinary hearing, I'll have to justify what I did. I suggested that it would be a good idea if I made myself scarce in the meantime, asked for two weeks of the leave I'm owed. The agency agreed, and Aimee came through, arranged a replacement to babysit Cynsea inside a day. I think she's happy to be shot of me for a while. I guess I can't blame her.'

'Who's the replacement?"

'Theo Bennet. I think you know him.'

'He covered for me a couple of times. Cynsea'll be in good hands.'

'I hope so.'

'Must have been a shock, when you got the news about your sister. I mean, I can't imagine thinking someone close to me was dead and then finding out they aren't.'

'I've had a little while to come to terms with it, but yeah.'

One rainy August, thunderstorms bashing about the Cotswold scarp just about every day, Winters, then twelve years old, had discovered a set of C.S. Lewis's Narnia novels in one of the storage boxes his mother hadn't unpacked since they'd moved from London. Seven foxed, fragile paperbacks, his grandmother's signature and the dates she'd read them neatly lettered in blue ink on their forepages, February through April in the antediluvian year of 1997. He'd devoured them inside a week. In the last book, the children who'd become the magical realm's heroes and rulers were jolted back into it by a fatal railway accident, which was how kind of how he felt now. As if he'd been pitched headlong into a different history created by one of Kasey Motte's resets, with conflicting memories and events clashing in his head.

Jude drained his cup of coffee and carefully refilled it and offered the thermos to his guest.

'That's okay. I'm still working on my first.'

'Don't let it go cold.'

'I won't.'

'The agency sent a note around, telling us not to speak to any journalists. Damage limitation, even though that horse is long gone.'

'Yeah.'

'Pretty bold, giving up your phone number,' Jude said. 'How's that working out?'

'Around a hundred calls and texts so far. Mostly citizen journalists and reporters from mainstream newsfeeds.'

With the help of his agent Winters had set up a simple filter in his old phone that would log everything, send crazy or malicious messages to a junk file, and alert him if the call he was hoping for came through.

'But no luck yet, I guess, or you wouldn't be here,' Jude said.

'Not yet. But the clip's out there, and other newsfeeds are copying it. Hopefully, my sister will see it soon. Get in contact. She's in bad trouble, Jude. And not just because the police want to find her. Do you know anything about Kasey Motte, the guy who took over the Wakestone commune? His ideas about using dreams to change the world?'

'I saw a thing on one of the newsfeeds that mentioned it.'

'He claimed that only he could save the world. Dismissed the collective efforts of governments and billions of ordinary people.'

'Not an especially modest fellow.'

'I met him once. The scariest thing was, he truly seemed to believe his own bullshit about dreaming a better world into existence.'

'But he blew himself up instead.'

'Yeah, he did. But now there's some kind of group or cult, people who call themselves deep dreamers, who are into the same shit. You know about my narrowboat, the slogan spray-painted on its side. That was one of theirs. It seems likely that they found where my sister was hiding out, want to get hold of her. And I've been sort of dragged into it.'

'Is this where you ask for that mysterious favour? The one you couldn't tell me about over the phone.'

Winters told Jude about discovering that the intruder who'd broken into his narrowboat had been spying on him from a nearby mudbank, how he'd found a fork and wrapper they might have discarded, the local police's disinterest. His trip to London, and the meetings with Lady Talia Armstrong and the charlatan Hari Pacek, the latter more comical than menacing in hindsight.

'Maybe the forensics on those scraps of litter will identify my intruder. Meanwhile, there's something else I want to chase up. They needed a boat to reach the mudbank where they set up camp – I found the spot where it had been dragged ashore. If they aren't from around here, they might have borrowed it or hitched a ride from someone who is. Another deep dreamer, or someone sympathetic to the cause. So I was wondering if you have any contacts with the local dreamer community, if there is such a thing.'

'I'm not exactly part of that scene.'

Winters knocked back the rest of his coffee, which tasted no better cold than hot. 'I was thinking of your drifter pal. The one who supplies you with those weird strains of weed.'

'He isn't exactly a drifter, and he doesn't have anything to do with dreamers. Sells selected small-batch strains of weed grown by drifters and amateur gardeners. What he calls experiments in hedgerow chemistry.'

'But he might know someone who grows shrooms, or the people who use them.'

'If you don't mind me saying so, it seems awfully tenuous.'

'The one useful thing I learned from the guy I told you about, Hari Pacek, is that there's a group of dreamers who are sort of rivals of the deep dreamers. They use the same special shrooms, but only to control their dreams, tap into deep levels of consciousness or whatever. And think that the beliefs of the deep dreamers are nothing but crazy fantasies. So I was wondering if there were any of those dreamers living hereabouts, if they might know anything about the person who broke into my narrowboat. Who they are, if they had any local help and so on. And maybe also tell me what they know about the deep dreamers.'

'Have you discussed any of this with the police?'

'If you're worried that this might get you into trouble, I understand. There's someone else who might be able to help, although I reckon your friend is the best bet.'

'I tried shrooms once,' Jude said. 'The ordinary kind. Your basic, untweaked magic mushrooms. It was back when I was in university, in Brighton. A friend and I cycled out past Seaford and we sat on top of the cliffs there and ate the shrooms with some dirty rice and shrimp. We'd been told it was best to eat something when we took them, it made it less likely that you'd throw up. It was a very calming high at first. Blissful, even. Sitting there on the grass, feeling every blade pricking my skin, grokking the waves and the sunlight and the sky. But then it started to become too much, all this light and flow everywhere. Full-on sensory overload, a serious panic attack. My friend tried her best to calm me down, but I was racing around in little circles, full-on bugout mode, screaming and crying, thinking my heart and my head were going to fucking explode. I only started to calm down after I made myself throw up. Never tried shrooming again. Haven't been able to eat shrimp since then, either.'

'I guess I'm missing the point to this story.'

'You sort of remind me how I must have looked, when our shroom trip took a wrong turn. Raggedy and wild-eyed. Overloaded. I get why you want to help your sister. Why you feel like you have to do something. But you've had a tough couple of days, you turn up on yonder scarlet beast and tell me crazy stories about deep dreamers and so forth, and I'm worried about what you might be getting yourself into.'

'Whatever it is, I'm in already the middle of it, what with the break-in and the police, and now this trouble with the media. The deep dreamers know about me, and there are other people, like Talia Armstrong and Hari Pacek, who want something from me. And there's family stuff, too. Unresolved stuff that I might have a chance to put right. But if you can't help me, if you're worried about blowback or whatever, I totally understand.'

Jude gave Winters a long careful look as he screwed on the top of his thermos.

'I didn't say I wouldn't help,' he said. 'And I can't promise anything, but I guess it won't do any harm if I tell my friend you'd like to have a word. It isn't likely that he knows anything useful. But if he does come through, promise me now that you'll take a deep breath and think long and hard before you decide what to do next.'

★

But Winters couldn't stay still, there was someone else he needed to see, and he took the jet boat across the estuary and headed downriver, hooking left into Tollesbury Fleet and left again into the winding channel of Woodrolfe Creek, throttling back the jet boat's motors and burbling past the old lightship to the mud berths of Tollesbury Saltings and the flood defence wall.

Teddy Stokes was working in the garden of his bungalow, methodically hoeing rows of sweet potato, callaloo and spinach in the vegetable patch beside the polytunnel where he cultivated his Goodberry Tea plants. The strain of weed he'd inherited from his mother, who'd in turn inherited from her father, Teddy's grandfather, who had, according to family lore, smuggled the seeds from Jamaica by hiding them in a packet of loose-leaf black tea.

'What can I do you for, Mr Winters?' Teddy said. 'Is it business, or have you run out of the good stuff?'

'Private business, kind of. I'm on leave right now.'

'I have lemonade. Made from lemons I picked this morning, from the tree in my allotment. Let me fetch it.'

They sat sitting on a bench, in the shade of gnarled apple trees by the back wall of the garden. Winters drained the first glass straight off, ice cubes clacking against his teeth. As Teddy refilled it from the sweating pitcher Winters asked after S Odice, and Teddy said they were around somewhere or other.

'How are you two getting on?'

'They come and go as they please, like a fledgling getting ready to fly. One day they'll leave and not come back. But not yet. Meanwhile, they've been making themselves useful on the allotment and out in the marsh. Which I certainly appreciate, what with not being as spry as I once was.'

Teddy had taken out his pouch of weed and papers and was expertly rolling a fat joint. Twisting the ends, lighting it with a kitchen match struck on his thumbnail and drawing in smoke and breathing it out in a cloud that enveloped his head. He passed it to Winters, who took a small sip to be friendly and handed it back.

'So what kind of private business brings you to my door?' Teddy said, and took another deep draw, the burning end of the joint crackling and sparking.

'Have you heard about the news about my sister?'

'Might be I've heard a little something. Must be a strange time for you.'

'Pretty much,' Winters said, and explained why he believed that his sister's return from the dead was connected with the deep dreamers, asked Teddy if he knew anyone who might know anything about them.

Teddy's third draw just about finished the joint. He held in the smoke until it began to leak from his nostrils and blew it out and shook his head. 'I would help if I could. But that kind of thing I know nothing about.'

'Do you know anyone who might? Someone who uses or sells shrooms, for instance.'

'I do,' another voice said, above their heads.

It was the kid, S Odice, hanging upside down amongst leaves and small hard green apples in one of the trees shading the bench.

'They do that,' Teddy said. 'Appearing out of the thin air from who knows where.'

'I was in the marsh,' the kid said, and swung down from branch to branch and landed beside Teddy. They were dressed in an oversized T-shirt and black Lycra shorts, holding up a plastic bag packed with dark green spikes of samphire. 'Here. It'll go good with the fish you bought.'

'I'll pretend you didn't say that, since I know you don't have a licence,' Winters said.

The kid shrugged. 'If you want to find someone who sells shrooms, I know someone who might be able to help.'

'A dreamer?'

'More of a dealer. Sort of a friend of a friend.'

'What's their name? Where can I find them?'

'I can take you there.'

'That's not how it's going to work.'

'He's after more than shrooms, youngblood,' Teddy said. 'Wants to find someone who knows something about some bad people.'

'Deep dreamers. I heard that part. If you're going to ask her about them, I really should come with,' the kid told Winters.

'Maybe you didn't hear the part where I told Teddy this is personal business. Just give me the name of this dealer, tell me where I can find her. I'll do the rest.'

'You sound like the law, even if you're not on duty. And I'm sort of a friend of one of her customers. She knows me, and I can vouch for you.'

'Isn't going to happen,' Winters said.

'It's lunch time,' Teddy said. 'Why don't I fry up this nice dab I caught – legally – with this samphire. We'll break bread like civilised people and discuss how to make this work.'

After he reached the main channel Winters opened up the jet boat's throttle, standing at the wheel with hot wind and spray smacking his face as he drove it up the estuary towards Heybridge Basin. S Odice sat on the bench seat behind him, legs tucked beneath them and hands nested in their lap, as self-contained and unreadable as a stone Buddha as they watched the shore go by. They'd refused to tell Winters the name of the dealer or where she lived until he'd promised to let them come along, and even now he knew only that they were heading to a hobbiton west of Maldon. The fast ride blew away his exasperation. The kid's stubbornness was kind of admirable, really. Implied a certain strength of will. And they sort of had a point. 'If you cause trouble and it gets back to me,' they'd said, 'it'll damage my reputation. And reputation is all that people like me have.'

After docking at Heybridge, Winters and S pulled two community bikes from the parking bay and cycled to Maldon and caught one of the little local buses. Their destination was near the end of the bus's route, an irregular grid of the kind of smart igloos used in the first settlements for heat refugees along the Mediterranean coast. Built thirty years ago as temporary housing for people displaced by coastal erosion and flooding, still in use because of the perennial housing shortage, it looked like a shabby holiday camp stranded amongst cropfields.

S led Winters at a confident pace down the main drag, past domes painted in their original palette of primary colours or splattered with jagged throwups or patterns of lines and dots borrowed from Australian aboriginal art, augmented with jerry-rigged lean-tos and sheds, porches strung with hammocks and furnished with tables and chairs, fridges and chest freezers and washing machines. It was late in the afternoon, beastly hot. People were sitting outside, chatting or interrogating their phones, sinking a beer or two. Snatches of conversation and music and TV blending into a general buzz, like a sleepy beehive. A man squatting on a low stool was lifting dumbbells with mechanical repetition, shaved head and bare torso gleaming with sweat. Two women were working on the motor of a cargo bike. Old men seated around a table snapped dominoes down in a cascade of decisive clicks, taking no notice of a gang of shrieking children running past.

Winters followed S through the shadows of a cluster of wind turbines, their vanes stilled in the hot moveless air, to an igloo with a peeling, sunfaded green paintjob. The little vegetable patch off to one side had mostly gone to weeds. A motorbike leaned on its stand by the front door, its battery casing decorated with flames and a screaming skull.

'Hang back and let me do the talking,' S told Winters, and rapped on the door.

It was wrenched open by a sturdy young man in shorts who glared at the kid and said, 'What?'

'Is Megan around?'

'What if she is?'

'Tell her Dovy's friend is here.'

'Who's he?' the man said, aiming his chin at Winters.

'Someone who wants to ask her something. He'll pay,' the kid said.

'He looks like a cop.'

'He's my friend.'

'Tell Megan I'm Isabel Winters' brother,' Winters said.

'Wait there,' the man said, and banged the door shut.

'That wasn't hanging back,' S told Winters.

'If this dealer knows who my sister is, she'll want to know why I'm here.'

'And if she doesn't?'

'Then we're probably wasting our time.'

An old woman sitting in front of the igloo on the other side of the path was watching Winters and the kid as if they were a rare kind of entertainment. Shaking her head when the kid smiled at her. At last, the door opened again and a young woman in a pale blue thigh-skimming robe stepped out.

'I'm Dovy's friend,' S told her. 'I was here that one time for her stuff, when she was sick?'

'She any better? Haven't seen her around.'

'She got fixed up and rambled on. Not sure where, but she was talking about going home for a while.'

'London, wasn't it?'

'Some place in Kent.'

'Oh yeah. Kent,' the woman, Megan, said. 'I think I remember you, but him I don't know.'

She was barely in her twenties, slender and smooth-skinned, the fringe of her straw-blond hair cut just above her eyes, studying Winters with a hazy squint. He wondered if she was high on her own supply.

'He's looking for a little help,' the kid said.

'What kind of help?' Megan said.

Winters said, 'I'm trying to find my sister. Isabel Winters.'

'Don't know her.'

'She was involved in the Wakestone siege, eight years ago. Was believed to have died in it, but it turns out she didn't. The story's all over the newsfeeds.'

Megan shrugged.

'Deep dreamers are looking for her. I'd like to meet them. Discuss our mutual interest. I've been told that you deal in the kind of shrooms dreamers and deep dreamers use. That you might be able to put me in touch with someone who might know something.'

'Was this your idea?' Megan said to the kid.

'I sort of owe him a favour.'

'If you can help me, I'll pay you for your trouble,' Winters said.

'And you're . . . Who did you say who were? Some kind of relative?'

'I'm Marc Winters. Isabel Winters' brother.'

'Got any ID?'

Winters handed her his agency card and she bent over it, moving it close to her face and then further away, as if she was having trouble focusing. Her robe parted a little, giving Winters a shadowy glimpse of her breasts. She smelt of musk roses and sex.

'Says here you work for the Biodiversity Agency,' she said.

'I'm the ranger over at Cynsea Island.'

'That anything like police?'

'Nothing like. I want to find out what kind of trouble my sister's in, help her if I can.'

'Wait here,' Megan said, and ducked back inside the igloo.

'How do you think it's going?' Winters said to the kid, and the kid shrugged.

The old woman in her front-row seat across the way said loudly, 'She shouldn't be selling that stuff. Not where other people live. People and their children. It isn't right.'

'I wouldn't know anything about that,' Winters said.

'Drugs are what it's about, young man. And all kinds of visitors, day and night. I was living in Norfolk before I was sent here. A little seaside village near Great Yarmouth. Very friendly. Lovely community. We retired there, my husband and me. Had a beautiful bungalow. Walked our dog on the beach every day. And then the sea took away the beach, and started on the dunes behind it. Coming closer and closer to the village. And one night there was a storm and the sea broke through the dunes and flooded most of the village. Our garden was washed away, our bungalow was ruined. And that was that. Our beautiful forever home all gone to smash. Condemned and demolished. We'd already lost our boy in the war, the one in Greenland, and now we were homeless. Brett, my husband, had two heart attacks over it and he didn't survive the second. And I was moved here, and here I am. And I have the dropsy too, and glaucoma in both eyes. They gave me the injections, the special T-cells that stop it getting worse, but that didn't fix the damage already done. I can't see too good, but I can see well enough to know what goes on there.'

'You mind your business, Mrs Tyler, and I'll mind mine,' Megan said, stepping from her igloo.

'Drugs,' the old woman said. 'And who knows what else.'

'We've been over this in community remediation. What I sell isn't illegal.'

'It isn't just the drugs,' the old woman said, appealing to Winters and the kid. 'It's all the coming and going and toing and froing.'

'Just friends I like to help,' Megan said.

'Is that what you call it?'

'That's what it is,' Megan said and stepped closer to Winters and lowered her voice. 'I should feel sorry for her, what with her son getting himself killed and all. But she's a sour old thing who doesn't have a good word for anyone. A right pain in the proverbial.'

'What's she saying about me now?' the old woman said.

'I'm telling my visitor about your son's ultimate sacrifice, Mrs Tyler,' Megan said.

'He didn't die so you could sell drugs to all and sundry, Megan Rix. And if he was here, God rest his soul, he'd tell you the exact same thing,' the old woman said, and unhooked a walking stick from the arm of her chair and planted it between her feet and levered herself upright and turned her back on Megan and Winters and S and hobbled towards the door of her igloo.

'I try to be a good neighbour, but that's what I have to put up with,' Megan said, and handed Winters his agency card. 'So I checked you out. You seem to be who you say you are. Found a couple of pieces about your sister, too. She was kind of famous, wasn't she?'

'Now you know who I am, can you help me?'

'I might know someone who can. Before we get to that, I believe you said something about payment.'

'I have cash,' Winters said, and pulled out the roll of greasy plastic notes Teddy had exchanged for credit.

'Perfect. You got five hundred there?' Megan said.

'We were thinking three. As long as the information's good,' S said.

'It's good. And I'll take five for it.'

'That's fine,' Winters said, and counted out eight fifty pound notes and five twenties and handed them to Megan.

'So, I just now had a word with someone who'd like to talk to you,' she told him.

'Are they a deep dreamer?'

'They grow shrooms. Pretty good stuff, by all accounts.'

'I'll need a name and an address. And a phone number.'

'That isn't how it's going to work. They'll get in contact with you, tell you where to meet.'

Winters gave her the number of his crappy old nologo phone, and Megan promised that she'd pass it on right away.

'Good luck and all that,' she said. 'And hey, kid? Don't bring any more of your friends here. I don't think Mrs Tyler could stand the excitement.'

As they walked through the hobbiton towards the bus stop, S said that they thought it had gone pretty well, but Winters wasn't so sure.

'I don't like having to wait for the shroom grower to contact me. I don't even know if they exist outside that woman's imagination.'

'She doesn't have any reason to lie.'

'I can think of five hundred reasons.'

'It would take a lot more than that for her to risk her reputation.'

'She's a drug dealer, kid. And I'm pretty sure not just of the legal kind.'

'That's why she needs her reputation more than most.'

'Yeah, but I'm not part of her social network. As far as she's concerned I'm just a regular citizen. A gullible mark.'

'When home is wherever you lay your head, you have to believe in the kindness of strangers.'

'Sounds like a quote from something.'

'It's how we live.'

'You like life on the drift, don't you?'

'I like the people. This could still work out, as long as we let it take us wherever it takes us.'

'Thanks for the help and everything, kid, but there's no "us".'

'I think I should be there, when you meet this person.'

'And I think I'll have to think about that.'

They were waiting for the bus back to Maldon when Winters' phone rang. It was Jude, explaining that he'd had no luck with his dealer friend.

'He just doesn't move in those circles. Makes a point of steering clear, in fact.'

'Well, thanks for trying.'

'There's something else,' Jude said. 'Someone stopped by, asking after you.'

'A journalist?'

'She told me she was a private investigator. Said that she was working with you.'

'Bailey.'

'So she was telling the truth. I wondered.'

'What did she want?'

'She told me to tell you she has some news. She also asked me all kinds of questions, wanting to know why you'd gone on leave, was it anything to do with your sister, and so on. I said she'd have to talk to you.'

'Does she know where I'm staying?'

'Theo Bennet told her. She was over at Cynsea before she came here.'

'Then I guess I'll be seeing her soon. But thanks for the heads-up.'

'Trouble?' the kid said, as Winters put away his phone.

'I don't know what it is yet.'

The bus took a while to arrive. Winters bought himself and the kid a takeaway supper of rice and peas at a café in Maldon before they cycled back to Heybridge Basin. As they wheeled their community bikes towards the parking bay, one of the people sitting at the tables outside the Old Ship pub called to them. It was Bailey in her dark blue suit, looking like a crow amongst the rainbow flock of tourists.

'I heard you were looking for me,' Winters told her. 'Hope I didn't keep you waiting.'

'Part of the job,' Bailey said. 'Where's your friend gone?'

Winters turned around. No sign of S but their bike lying on its side.

'They're kind of shy with strangers,' he said. 'If this is about the results of the forensic tests, you needn't have gone to all this trouble. A phone call or text would have been fine.'

'The only number I have for you is your work phone, currently in the possession of Mr Bennet,' Bailey said. 'Why don't we find a seat inside? We need to catch up.'

Bailey was at the bar and Winters was sitting at a small table in a shadowy corner of the busy pub when a text popped up on his phone. A time and a place, and a question, *y/n*? Sent from a withheld number, but it had to be Megan Rix's shroom grower, wanting to meet where there weren't likely to be any other people around. Winters was still thinking it over when Bailey set down their drinks, a cup of green tea for him, cloudy cider in a dimpled pint glass for her. She sat on the other side of the table and said, 'Your young friend?'

'Work,' Winters said, and tapped *y* and rolled up his phone and put it away.

'I thought you were on leave.'

'I am. But you know how it is.'

Hard to tell if that satisfied Bailey, her face was as closed as a fist, but she didn't pursue it.

'Saw that clip you made,' she told Winters. 'The appeal to your sister. Can't decide if it was dumb or smart, but it was definitely bold. And the thing about asking for the name of your neighbour's dog was a nice touch.'

'Yeah, I thought so too.'

Izzy hadn't believed in owning pets. Thought that it was a kind of enslavement. But their neighbour had been more or less permanently unwell, one of those long-term post-viral things, and whenever she was bedridden Winters and Izzy would take turns walking her dog. Skye, a cute, inquisitive Border Terrier. Winters wasn't sure that his sister would remember the dog's name, but he was certain that no one else would be able to discover it.

'So did it work?' Bailey said.

She was trying to sound nonchalant, but there was an eager glint in her gaze.

'Not yet. But it's out there, if Izzy is looking for a way to get in touch.'

'It's probably pissed off the terror police,' Bailey said. 'Which is a plus as far as I'm concerned, but could cause problems down the line.'

'If they've seen it, they haven't said anything about it to me.'

'Best to assume that they know about it,' Bailey said. 'And that they've tapped your phone.'

'There are ways of working around that,' Winters said, with a plunging feeling. Making the little speech had been a spur-of-the-moment thing. He hadn't given any thought to the counterterrorism police's reaction, and wondered now what else he'd overlooked.

'As previously discussed, they've probably set up some kind of watch on your island,' Bailey said. 'I paid a visit myself, it's how I found out you were on leave. Luckily, the fellow in charge pointed me in this direction. Nice place, that island. A nice little hideout.'

'I like it,' Winters said cautiously.

He was trying to seem unflustered, but the text and Bailey's warning about the counterterrorism police had thrown him off-balance.

'I couldn't decide if it was a genuine patch of wilderness or some sort of abandoned garden,' Bailey said.

'A bit of both, I suppose.'

'So not one of your actual wild places.'

'The point is to try to save as much biodiversity as possible. Everything and anything, because all of it is important. It all knits together.'

'"Save the tigers." That's what I remember when I was a kid. Tigers and elephants and so on. Back when there were still elephants and tigers outside of zoos. Save the pandas, too. And gorillas, penguins . . . But it didn't help most of them in the end, did it? And now it's all about saving us. Saving the humans.'

'I don't think you came here to discuss my work,' Winters said, trying to move things along and get to the point of this, whatever it was.

'You could say this is the getting-to-know-you stage of our relationship.'

'Yeah? What kind of relationship do you think we have?'

'We don't need to be friends, but we could be good allies. Lady A gave her word that you'd get the results of the forensic tests on those scraps of litter you handed over. I'm here to make good on that promise. Spirit of cooperation and so on.'

'What did you find?'

Now Winters was trying to sound nonchalant.

'The wrapper was a washout,' Bailey said. 'No DNA or fingerprints. But there was enough DNA on the fork to work up a partial sequence. Enough for my contact to get a hit on the national database.'

'You're saying that you've identified who was watching me. Who broke into my narrowboat, accessed agency files.'

'I am,' Bailey said, and shook out her phone and held it towards Winters.

It displayed an image of a woman in her mid to late thirties, pale skin and sharp cheekbones, cropped dirty blond hair half hidden by a scarf. A wary, edgy look, as if she misliked having her picture taken, had been surprised or tricked by the photographer. Winters hadn't seen her for fourteen or fifteen years, but recognised her right away.

'You're kidding me,' he said.

'So you know who she is.'

'Yeah. Dash Baker. Are you sure about the forensics?'

'The DNA lifted from the fork matches the requisite core STRs in her police record. Good enough for court, if it ever comes to that. She was a member of the Wakestone commune, wasn't she? One of your sister's comrades, back in the day.'

'She had longer hair,' Winters said, stupidly.

He was wondering if Bailey knew about Dash Baker's connection with the charlatan, Hari Pacek. And was trying to relate that to the idea that she was his intruder. Had been watching him from the mudbank and had broken into his narrowboat, searched his tablet and the agency's files, looking for anything that would give her an idea of Izzy's whereabouts. Had left the deep dreamer slogan. If she was a deep dreamer, what was Hari Pacek?

'Was she a friend of your sister's?' Bailey said. 'Were they close?'

'If they were, my sister never mentioned it.'

'After Kasey Motte moved into the commune, Ms Baker stayed on for a year or so, but left before everything blew up,' Bailey said. 'Was detained, like you, when it did, and released without charge. Again, like you. Her DNA profile's on record because she was arrested when police raided a group of activists who were making banners and effigies and the like for a protest march, and found a number of tweaked phones which could have been used to interfere with police comms. She has a degree in electrical engineering and may or may not have had something to do with those phones, the police couldn't make that stick. But it might have some relevance to your break-in.'

Winters remembered Charlie Lowe telling him that Dash Baker had looked after the commune's electrical systems. He said, 'So she could have taken down the island's net, and got inside the agency's servers.'

'One of the many things we need to discuss with her. Her last known address was some kind of sustainable community in Gloucestershire. The Forest of Dean. Not too far from where you and your sister grew up, I believe. Sometimes, when people are in trouble, they head for a familiar place. It's a reach, I admit, but maybe your sister had that itch.'

'Can I ask you something?'

'Of course. Within reason.'

'If you find Isabel, with or without my help, would you arrest her?'

'I don't have power of arrest. Lost it when I turned in my warrant card. All I want is a nice quiet friendly talk with your sister about Lady A's son. What went on, in those last days. Whether or not William managed to escape too. And if he did, where he might be found. What happens after that will be up to you.'

'You don't have any plans to turn her in to the police.'

'I might suggest to her that surrendering to the police would be the sensible thing to do. Especially as she appears to be on the run from some dodgy characters. But I won't put her in a headlock and march her to the nearest station.'

'Will you swear to that?'

'If I tell you I won't do something, you can rest assured.'

'I need to think about all of this.'

'Sleep on it. But we're not the only people looking for your sister, time is of the essence and all that, so I'll be travelling west tomorrow. With or without you.'

Winters was too wired to sleep after his conversation with Bailey. He walked back and forth along the waterfront in the hot summer evening, trying to make sense of everything. If Dash Baker had broken into the narrowboat, she must have been working for the deep dreamers, either as a fully paid up member or a hired hand. Which meant that aiming him at Hari Pacek had something to do with them too. The man's wandering conversation and questions, the trick with the Tarot card, it had all been a set-up, a way of unsettling him, extracting information from him. What he knew about Izzy, his intentions.

He briefly wondered if Charlie Lowe was part of it too, but no, if he was he wouldn't have needed to involve Dash Baker. He called Charlie anyway, asked him if he knew where Dash was hanging out these days.

'Last I heard, some commune or such in the West Country,' Charlie said, sounding sleepy.

'In the Forest of Dean.'

'That rings a bell.'

The man sounding cautious. Furtive, even.

'Mind giving me her number? I need to follow up on that meeting she arranged.'

'I meant to give you a call, ask how that went. Was it useful?'

'It was interesting. How about that number?'

Charlie gave it up, but Winters got an out-of-service message when he called it. He didn't think it likely that Dash had returned to the Forest of Dean, reckoned that she was still nearby, keeping watch on Cynsea in case Izzy finally pitched up. And it wasn't likely that Izzy was hiding out in their old neighbourhood, either. After she'd joined the Wakestone commune she'd never once come back home. She hadn't even returned when their mother died.

Julia had suffered several small strokes in her last years, but insisted on her independence. She'd taught herself to paint left-handed after her right side was affected, clattering about the cottage in a walking frame, venturing out only for hospital appointments, and died from a massive cerebral haemorrhage one day early in summer, was found sprawled on a divan in her studio by the housekeeper she'd hired to clean and cook twice a week. When Winters had phoned Izzy to give her the news she'd been cool and distant, refusing to come to the funeral, telling him that the small amount of credit she'd inherited and her share from the sale of any of the paintings Julia had left stacked in her studio should be donated to Nature First! Said that he could do what he liked with the rest of their mother's stuff.

'I'll tell her agent about the paintings,' Winters said. 'But what about mum's ashes?'

'Did she leave instructions?'

'I haven't found any.'

'Then do what you think best,' Izzy said, and that was that, until Winters received her invitation to visit the commune. The invitation that hadn't been from her after all.

No, wherever Izzy was hiding, it wasn't anywhere near their childhood home. Bailey's plan to head west was almost certainly a dead end, but that was her problem, not his. He had his own lead to follow, still believed that the best way to help Izzy was to discover everything he could about the deep dreamers and turn them in to the police before they caught up with her.

He slept fitfully, got up at first light and used the bathroom and checked his old nologo phone. Some twenty-odd new messages, still nothing from Izzy or anyone who might be of any help. After copying a few numbers from the contacts list he'd ported over from his work phone he buried the old phone at the bottom of his kitbag – it was his best chance of finding Izzy, he didn't want it to fall into the wrong hands if the rendezvous backfired – and snuck down the back stairs of the pub. He had almost half a day to kill, and cycled into Maldon, found a café that was open and dawdled over breakfast, sat in a park for a while and had a smoke. Wondering if by now Bailey had realised that he wasn't going to meet up and ride along with her. Feeling a smudge of guilt, thinking of Talia Armstrong and her son, but fuck it, that deal was done. He'd handed over the litter he'd found and Bailey had organised the forensics and shared the results, and neither side had made any promises about what would happen after that. Bailey had her thing, and he had his.

Shops were beginning to open. Winters bought a drone in a place called Hobby Heaven and a no-contract phone in a supermarket. Used it to call Teddy Stokes, and after Teddy passed his phone to S told them about the text message and the rendezvous, then called Jude and asked him for another favour. Jude offered to come along and Winters told him he had that covered, agreed that he was crazy, and did his best to reassure his friend that, given the dubious nature of the source, the meeting he'd agreed to most likely wouldn't come to anything.

He cycled back to Heybridge Basin, taking the long way around so that he could approach the waterfront without passing the Old Ship, just in case Bailey was still waiting for him. Glanced back several times as he walked down the jetty towards his rented jet boat, expecting to see the investigator marching towards him. That fear easing, replaced by a childish sense of elation, as he steered the jet boat out into the navigation channel between the mainland and Northey Island, cutting past the half-drowned ruins of the old leisure park, passing Cynsea Island, puttering down the length of the estuary to West Mersea. He tied up the jet boat in the harbour, amongst fishing boats and about a hundred small sailing boats, and in a park in the shadow of the seawall downloaded an app on his new phone and put the drone through its paces. It wasn't much more than a toy, delicate and gossamer light, and its cameras weren't half as good as the pocket drone he'd handed over when Theo Bennet had taken charge of Cynsea, but he reckoned that it would serve. By now it was closing on noon. He found shade under an ailing cypress tree and smoked a joint, then ambled along the seawall and ate lunch at the fish shack, returned to the harbour and took the jet boat across the mouth of the Tollesbury Fleet and up Woodrolfe Creek to the Salting, where S was waiting for him.

'So where are we going?' the kid said, as they headed back down the creek.

'A derelict place the other side of the river. Did you bring the cash?'

The kid dug into the pocket of their baggy lemon-yellow trousers and handed Winters a roll of plastic notes fastened with a fraying elastic band. 'It cleaned Teddy out. He had to borrow some from a friend to make up the difference.'

Winters stuffed the roll of notes into the inside pocket of his jacket, on top of the slim roll left over from yesterday's excursion. 'Let's hope it's enough. I doubt that this acquaintance of Megan Rix will accept credit.'

'Do you know who they are?'

'The shroom grower or their proxy, I guess.'

'The text didn't say?'

'Just gave a time and a place. Nothing about who or why, but we'll find out soon enough.'

The kid thought about that, said, 'Teddy told me to tell you that he'll hunt you down if you get me in trouble.'

'You'll be fine, as long as you do as I asked.'

'Stay out of the way and keep watch.'

'Yeah. Find a good hiding place and use my drone to record the meeting. And if it goes sideways, keep your head down and call my friend Jude Lee.'

'The ranger of the St Lawrence Creek Reserve. I haven't forgotten.'

'He'll probably call in the police, but you don't have to get involved with them. Just drop the drone someplace, tell Jude where you left it, and get out of there.'

No need to explain that the police would take a wildlife ranger more seriously than a drifter kid.

S said, 'Does the woman from last night have anything to do with this?'

'Sort of,' Winters said, and told them who Bailey was, who she was working for and why, and what he'd learned from her.

'I thought she looked like police,' S said.

'You impressed her, the way you slipped away.'

'So she did this DNA thing on that stuff you found, but you aren't working with her now.'

'I shared the evidence with her so I could get it analysed, but that's as far as it goes. Which is why I need your help. I don't expect any trouble. I don't even know if this person will turn up, or if they'll have anything useful to tell me if they do. But if things do go wrong, for whatever reason, stick to the plan.'

'You're taking this very seriously.'

'I'm meeting someone I don't know, on the recommendation of a drug dealer. You bet I'm taking it seriously.'

Winters cut close to the shore, pointed out Jude's boat shed as they passed it and eased back the throttle, skating along the edge of mudflats to an old concrete slipway near a shoreside property development which had been abandoned after it had been comprehensively trashed in the Great Storm. The rendezvous was at the end of a street at the development's riverside edge, roofless wrecks of bungalows strung along one side and the remains of an old embankment on the other. The roadway was buckled and cracked and overgrown by grass and weeds and volunteer saplings, and the front gardens of the bungalows were littered with broken furniture, bricks and shattered tiles. The rusted shell of a car was skewed sideways in a driveway, floated there by the storm surge and overlooked by reclamation crews. The untidy platform of an old stork nest was snugged against a chimney.

Winters gave his new phone to the kid, said that he'd put Jude's number on speed dial, showed them how to use the app which controlled his new drone.

'All you have to do is make sure its camera is pointed in the right direction, and press this button to start recording when the person I'm supposed to meet turns up.'

'Okay.'

'Give me the phone back for a second.'

Winters sent the drone straight up and locked it in hover mode fifty metres overhead, returned the phone to the kid and told them to get lost. 'We're good and early, so you have plenty of time to find the best spot to hide. Don't come out until I call you. And don't worry. I'm pretty certain this'll turn out to be a big fat nothing.'

'I'm not worried,' S said and knuckled their forehead in mock salute and scooted off between two bungalows.

The end of the road dipped into a shallow lagoon that had once been a recreation ground. A half-drowned slide and swing set stood in the middle of the muddy water. A heron hunched patient as a sentry at the edge of reeds on the far side. Winters wandered along the strandline of sun-dried seaweed and scattered crab shells at the water's edge, wandered back. Studied the row of bungalows, couldn't see any sign of the kid.

Thirty minutes passed. The ruins baked in the growing heat. Off in the main channel, a two-masted ketch with sails the colour of dry blood passed by on its way to sea, and a few sailboats were tacking back and forth.

Winters pulled down the bill of his agency ballcap to shade his face, sipped from his water bottle. The forlorn, haunted loneliness peculiar to abandoned places was beginning to spook him; his anticipation was fraying into anxiety. The shroom grower, if that was who had texted him, was now officially late. Not quite late enough to make him believe that Megan Rix had cheated him, taken his money and given him a false lead, but late enough to make him wonder about the foolishness of this enterprise, the inadequacy of his preparations and precautions. He told himself that he'd stay until the drone's charge ran out and it dropped down on autopilot. If no one had turned up by then he'd try to fix up a new meeting, and if that didn't fly he could call Charlie Lowe again, try to track down other survivors of the commune. Something he should have started on earlier.

He watched the sailboats out in the estuary, wondering, when one swerved shorewards, if it was crewed by the person he was supposed to meet. But it was already turning back, its sail slackening and filling as it caught the wind, and something, some kind of primal instinct or glimpse of movement that scarcely registered in his consciousness, pricked up his hackles. He turned, saw the heron on the far side of the lagoon unfurl its wings and launch itself into the air, ungainly as a pterodactyl, and the reeds parted like a curtain as someone moved through them and set out across the lagoon.

They were shrouded in an earth-coloured suncloak, their face hidden by its hood. At first Winters thought that they were following a path sunk just beneath the surface of the water, but then saw they were skate-skiing towards him on the broad pads, ridged with inflated pods, of a pair of Jesus boots. They paused several metres from the shore. Swaying a little as they kept their balance, asking Winters if he'd brought anyone with him.

A woman's voice. He wanted her to be Izzy, even though he knew how improbable that was.

He said, 'I came as agreed. And you, are you alone?'

'As you see,' the woman said and came towards him, stepping ashore with exaggerated care and kicking off her Jesus boots. Her feet were bare, her toenails painted black. A scarf or mask wrapped around her mouth and nose inside her cloak's hood. Only her eyes were visible.

Winters said, 'I was told that you know something about the deep dreamers. I'm also wondering if you know someone by the name of Dash Baker.'

'Oh, I know her, all right,' the woman said, and poked what looked like a toy crossbow through the folds of her suncloak, a pistol grip and a T-bar that with a crisp snap fired a length of smart plastic cord, striking Winters' legs below the knees, coiling tightly around them and delivering a high-voltage shock that shot up his spine. Black light exploded in his skull and then he was on the ground, unable to move, skin prickling all over. A shadow fell over him and the woman said, 'This would have been so much easier if fucking Hari Pacek hadn't let you walk out on him.'

Winters knew then who she was and tried to say her name, but his tongue was as numb as the rest of him. He was lying on his back, vaguely aware that his ballcap had fallen off, had a slant view of the street and the ruined bungalows simmering under the hot white sky. A small truck turned a corner and drove towards them, banging over broken tarmac, smashing a path through crackling weeds and stiff tufts of grass. He searched the sky for the drone but couldn't see it, hoped it was recording everything, hoped that the kid would have the good sense to stay hidden, that they were already speed-dialling Jude.

'You wanted to meet the deep dreamers,' Dash Baker said. 'Welcome to the first part of your journey.'

Winters' wrists and ankles were bound with zip ties and Dash patted him down, finding the two rolls of notes, asking him where he'd hidden his phone.

'Didn't bring it,' Winters said. The numbness was wearing off, but his tongue was heavy and clumsy. 'Police.'

'Police? What do you mean, police?'

'Might have hacked it.'

Dash appeared to accept the lie, told her accomplices, a pair of amiable young bravos, that they needed to get going before trouble found them. They hoisted Winters into the back of their little truck and drove at speed along winding country roads to one of the drainage channels that emptied into the coastal floodplain west of the Blackwater estuary. Past some kind of camp or way station for drifters, tents pitched on the embankment beside a cluster of decrepit boats, to an equally decrepit cargo barge.

A desolate and lonely country. In one direction a vast level expanse of mud and mazy creeks, dotted with clumps of cord grass and sickly saltwillows, stretched towards the shimmering line where sea met hot sky. In the other, beyond the drifter camp, a row of wind turbines and the white cube of one of the pumping stations built to reduce saltwater intrusion into the coastal aquifer defined the border between the floodplain and arable fields not yet claimed by rising sea levels.

Dash wandered off towards the bow of the barge, talking to someone on her phone, and her accomplices dumped Winters on a sleeping bag under a tattered sheet of rust-brown canvas stretched above the rotten planking of the stern deck, cut his zip ties and lit up a fat joint to celebrate the success of their operation. They called each other by their nicknames, Brick and Purdey, but that was about as far as any attempt at anonymity went. Winters quickly learned that they were cousins who'd gone on the drift to escape the shithole town where they'd grown up, didn't know much of anything about Izzy, deep dreamers, or Kasey Motte. According to Purdey, they'd thrown in with Dash for the thrills and spills, and a share of the cash money she'd been promised. He had no idea who she was working for, she'd said it was best if they didn't know.

'You aren't even slightly curious?' Winters said.

He was trying to massage some feeling back into his legs. His kidnappers didn't seem to be much of a threat. They hadn't found the kid or spotted the drone, and their tactics, seemingly borrowed from the low end of popular crime fiction, might have left an obvious trail.

'It beats picking tomatoes and fucking salad leaves,' Purdey said, and drew hard on the joint and passed it to his cousin.

Winters made the time-honoured finger twiddling gesture and Brick grinned and handed the joint to him. It was as strong and weird as any of Jude's specials, and the two cousins nudged each other when Winters coughed out the smoke almost at once.

'Here's how you do it,' Purdey said, after he'd reclaimed the joint, and drew on it until its tip flamed and sparked and held in the smoke for a good half minute before blowing two dragon plumes from his nostrils and passing the joint back to Brick.

'I get why your cousin's called Brick, seeing as he's built like the proverbial outhouse,' Winters said. 'But why Purdey?'

'After the people who make the best kind of shotguns,' Purdey said.

'He's a fighter,' Brick said. 'When one of his crosses connects, you go down. Like you've been hit with both barrels.'

'One two, the end of you,' Purdey said, miming a quick left-jab-right-cross combo.

'How did you boys hook up with Dash?'

Brick breathed out a cloud of smoke and passed the joint to Purdey. 'We got some work in this place where she lived.'

'In the Forest of Dean?'

'You know about that?'

'Heard something about it.'

'She was looking for a couple of likely lads could help her out. Purdey and me fit that description.'

'Plus,' Purdey said, 'Brick was fucking her.'

'Just the one time,' Brick said amiably.

The two of them had been loosened up by their loco weed. Winters asked them if they'd ever used shrooms and Purdey grinned and said, 'You name it, we've tried it.'

'How about the kind of shrooms used by dreamers?'

'We prefer the kind found growing in nature,' Brick said, taking the nubbin of the joint from his cousin.

'How about Dash? Is she a dreamer? Maybe a deep dreamer?'

'Why don't you go ask her?' Purdey said, pointing towards the bow with his chin. 'Now she's done with her phone call.'

Dash Baker surprised Winters by lighting up her own joint, small and tightly rolled. She'd shucked the suncloak, was dressed in a fraying denim jacket and a long, layered muslin skirt, seemed strung out and jittery. She told him that she wasn't any kind of dreamer, deep or otherwise, she'd had enough of that shit long ago, which was why she'd quit the Wakestone commune after the fucking weirdness which had gone down over the first reset, so-called.

'But it was you who broke into my narrowboat, spraypainted one of their slogans on its side. Or was that supposed to be some kind of misdirection?'

'You think that was me?'

'I know it was,' Winters said, and told Dash about the DNA extracted from trash she'd left behind on the mudbank, omitting Bailey's role in the forensic analysis.

Dash was more amused than upset, shrugged when he said that he hadn't told the police about it.

'Tell them what you like. I'll say I was, I don't know, bird-watching. Unless you have something that puts me on your boat, it'll be your word against mine.'

'I'm not planning to tell the police anything. I want to find my sister before they do, and help her if I can. That's why I agreed to the meeting.'

'And how's that working out for you?'

'I think you were hired by deep dreamers to do their dirty work, and you were talking to one of them just now. Was it that fraud you aimed me at? Hari Pacek, with his trick pack of cards?'

'You'll find out soon enough.'

'Or was it the person who sells you shrooms?'

'What makes you think that?'

'I was told that the person I was put in contact with, the person who set up our meeting, grows them. You already have the cash I was carrying. I'll double down on that if you turn me loose and tell me who you're working for and where I can find them. So I can meet them on my terms, not theirs.'

Dash took a little sip from her joint. 'I can't tell if you're some kind of simpleton or have the biggest balls.'

'It's a genuine offer. You have all my cash, so anything extra will have to be credit, but I'm good for it.'

Julia's gallery still sold one of her paintings now and then. Not for anything like as much as they used to fetch, her work was out of fashion, but it was always a pleasant surprise. Winters gave half of what was left after taxes and the gallery's commission to Nature First!, honouring Izzy's request, and stashed the rest in government bonds he mostly hadn't touched since he'd started work at Cynsea. He reckoned that he could easily afford to bribe Dash to take his side, but she wasn't having any of it.

'You don't have to worry about finding the deep dreamers,' she said. 'They've already found you.'

'So you are working for them.'

'I didn't say that.'

'Before you hand me over or whatever, you should seriously consider my offer.'

'I don't need to think about it. The answer's still no.'

'If it's about the amount, or how it's paid, I'm prepared to negotiate.'

'That isn't it.'

Winters thought about trying to scare her into taking his deal by telling her that someone had been watching him, that by now the police would know about what had gone down. But if she took him seriously it might get him into deeper trouble, and if she panicked and dumped him he'd lose his best chance of finding out why the deep dreamers wanted to find Izzy, why they wanted to get hold of him. So he tried another angle, saying, 'If Hari Pacek is a deep dreamer, why didn't he snatch me when we met? What's changed?'

'I wish I fucking knew, the trouble it caused me. All I can tell you is they've changed their mind about you, and here we are.'

'How about Charlie Lowe?'

'You think Charlie's one of them? Are you serious?'

'He put me in touch with you. And you put me in touch with Hari Pacek.'

'Charlie's a sweetheart. Everybody's friend, always eager to help. I figured you might reach out to him, so I asked him to put me in touch with you if you did, told him I could probably help you. Told a few other old-timers from the commune the same thing. And that's all there is to it, as far as Charlie's concerned, so leave him out of this,' Dash said, and took a last drag on her joint and snubbed it out on the rim of the hold with a quick stabbing gesture. She hadn't offered Winters a single puff.

'You didn't have to involve Charlie. You could have called me yourself.'

'I would have, if the thing with Charlie hadn't worked out. But I wanted to be sure that you were looking for Isabel, and Charlie came through, as I knew he would. Like I said, he's eager to help.'

'And why did you point me towards Hari Pacek?'

'Maybe because he asked me to.'

'You mean because he paid you. Because he's either a deep dreamer, or moves in the same circles.'

'Lot of supposition there, Sherlock.'

'Is that why you painted that slogan on my narrowboat? To put me on the hunt for them?'

'It sped things along, didn't it?'

'And the phone call, asking about Isabel?'

'Wasn't me.'

'So it was one of the deep dreamers.'

'Your guess is as good as mine.'

'I'm getting the feeling that you like to play games. Manipulate people.'

'Maybe I'm easily bored.'

'Or maybe you're the kind of person who thinks she's smarter than everyone else.'

'I'm pretty sure I'm smarter than you.'

'Aren't you worried that this instauration thing might work? Given your history, why you left the commune. Why you're still using shrooms.'

Dash lit up another joint. 'Charlie told you about that, didn't he? The fucking blabbermouth.'

'He said that you were self-medicating. I guess because of what happened to you with Motte's so-called reset. The shrooms and his one-on-one talks and all the rest.'

'What would you know about any of that?'

'Motte slipped me a dose of his so-called special shrooms, the last time I visited the commune. Took me for a walk in the woods, gave me a lecture about world-changing dreams.'

'He did?' Dash said, looking at Winters with a frank spark of interest. 'What did you see, in the woods?'

'The shadows of what might have been the Wild Hunt. And the Green Man, at the end. A face with crazy hair and a long beard, looking out at me through a tangle of leaves.'

'You didn't see anything else?'

'I don't think so.'

'There are others. The Harrowhound and the Woodwose. The White Stag and the fucking Burning Bear . . .' Dash took a long, crackling draw on her joint. Held the smoke in and said, her voice pinched, 'There's this neurologist who wrote a paper on the special shrooms. She got hold of some after the siege. Studied the effects of their psychoactive molecules on these little brain organoids. Blobs of neurons and such grown from human stem cells in test tubes. You're looking at me like I'm crazy.'

'Tiny brains in test tubes does sound sort of crazy.'

Dash blew smoke sideways and said, 'People have been using them in experiments for years and years. It seems that the psychoactive chemistry of those shrooms embeds itself in what the neurologist called the base layers of neural ecology. Generates novel small RNAs similar to the kind that regulate long-term memories. It's all very detailed and technical, but the short explanation is that Kasey's special shrooms rewire your head. Trigger all kinds of strange activity that your brain interprets as things like the Wild Hunt or the Green Man.'

'I kind of figured Motte might have planted the idea of seeing them in my head. That I saw what he wanted me to see.'

'It's more complicated than that. If you saw the same things I did, that all the other poor fuckers who took his magic shrooms saw, they must have some kind of basic reality. Archetypes. Fundamental patterns hardwired into our brains and conjured up when the shrooms alter our brain chemistry.'

After the siege, when he'd been trying to make sense of Izzy's death, Winters had trawled through conspiracy sites and discovered that Kasey Motte's special shrooms had more than one origin story. There was the one about the shaman in Ulaanbaatar, which Motte had told him in their walk and talk in the woods. Another about an unnaturally long-lived magician who cultivated them in his cliffside palazzo near Palermo. One in which Motte had been guided by a gaucho, the last of an obscure tribe, to a secret spot in the tropical grasslands of central Paraguay, and yet another in which he'd stolen them from a very technical guy who lived in a decommissioned missile silo in Nebraska. And so on. An article by a level-headed journalist suggested that it was most likely that Motte had got up these fabulations to obscure the mundane facts – that he'd purchased the shrooms while he'd been part of a network of enthusiasts, including biohackers who cultivated rare, ofttimes illegally tweaked varieties, and used elements pillaged from a mad range of sources, from lucid dreaming techniques to astral projection experiments by the CIA in the 1960s, to cobble up his rituals and communal dreaming sessions. Winters reckoned that Dash's junk science was the same kind of bullshit, an attempt to justify her jones for the shrooms, and felt an unexpected pinch of pity. She was still fucked up, still lost in the maze. Telling him now that he'd been lucky.

'You only had a taste. We took those fucking shrooms just about every day. Like church communion. Sometimes I need to go back. Try to find the green world – did Kasey tell you about that? The world he dreamed about in his long dreaming?'

'The world without any people in it.'

'The world within the world, waiting to be born. Sometimes I can catch glimpses of it. Calms me down when weed can't. And that's why I still use shrooms every now and then. The only reason.'

Dash put the joint to her lips, took it away, looked at its burning tip, then ground out the coal and stuck the remains in the breast pocket of her denim jacket.

'He hypnotised every one of us. Like a snake with so many mice. It wasn't just shrooms. He used acid too. Would dose you and deliberately give you a bad trip by ridiculing you in front of everyone else. Tear you down until you were defenceless,' she said, something ugly and naked showing in her face for a moment. 'Then tell you that he loved you and could put something true and real into your life.'

'Did he believe in any of it?'

'I think he did. But you have to remember that he was crazy. It broke my heart, you know? What he did to the commune. The thing we built together. He took it and he twisted it into something else.'

Winters tried to get her to talk about Izzy, her role in Kasey Motte's inner circle, why and how she'd escaped before the bitter end, but Dash wasn't interested in discussing any of that, saying abruptly she was going on a food run, calling to Brick and Purdey and telling them to make the prisoner secure.

Purdey fastened a band of soft white plastic around Winters' ankle and Brick demonstrated how it worked by gripping Winters' elbow and walking him down the gangplank and along the embankment. Quite soon the skin under the cuff began to prickle, and after a few more steps the prickling developed into a scalding circlet of throbbing unbearable heat that had Winters yelling for mercy, though when he grabbed the cuff it was no warmer than his skin.

Dash showed him the transponder that the cuff was linked to, told him it had a range of thirty metres or so, and beyond that he'd be in a world of pain, and handed the transponder to Purdey and drove off along the embankment. She returned an hour later with a big bag of bean burgers and fries, a pack of bananas, and a watermelon Brick chopped into neat segments with his hook-bladed knife. The two men chomping their way through a couple of burgers and munching watermelon while Winters tried and mostly failed to get more information out of Dash.

He asked her about the place where she'd been living, in the Forest of Dean, but she batted that away, saying that it wasn't anything special, just happened to need someone who could take care of their storage batteries and keep their wind turbines spinning.

'But that isn't all you've doing, since you left Wakestone,' Winters said.

He was hoping to prompt further confessions, but Dash shrugged it off, saying, 'A girl's got to make a living.'

'By working for people who think Kasey Motte had some good ideas, and want to finish what he couldn't.'

'It's strictly business,' Dash said.

Brick and Purdey were watching this to-and-fro like spectators at a tennis match. Winters knew that Dash was toying with him, but he tried one last sally, said that he was wondering, since she'd stayed in contact with Charlie Lowe and other survivors who left the commune before the bitter end, if she knew whether any of them were part of the deep dreamer thing.

'Are you wondering if your sister is still a loyal follower?' Dash said.

'I'm trying to understand what I've been caught up in. How big this thing is.'

'To tell you the truth, I don't know. And I'm not interested in finding out.'

Winters had been imagining some kind of sinister underground conspiracy with tentacles everywhere, like in those old movies, but if the deep dreamers needed to hire outsiders like Dash and her two sidekicks maybe it was more of a homespun affair. Kasey Motte hadn't commanded any kind of army, after all. Just a couple of dozen people he'd mindfucked into believing that they were a special crew armed with world-changing knowledge, like every crazy sect there ever was. And maybe that was what this deep dreamer thing was, too. Maybe there wasn't a masterplan, or networked cells of fanatics working with common purpose towards a shared goal. Just a bunch of people stumbling about the way people usually did, spending most of their time arguing about their homebaked ideology and conjuring elaborate schemes that usually came to nothing, now and then acting on opportunities that presented themselves.

He was woken next morning by the whine of electric motors, sat up in his sleeping bag as, with Dash at the wheel, the truck sped off along the embankment in a caul of dust that was still spreading and settling out after it had disappeared from view. The sun was low and red at level horizon, glowering like an inflammation amongst filigrees of cloud which had drifted in from the North Sea during the night, and the moveless air was already hot and a lone reed warbler was chirping somewhere in the bullrushes on the other side of the channel.

The two sidekicks were still asleep, though Brick roused a little when Winters shucked his sleeping bag and stood up. The big man squinting at him before heaving over and going back to sleep. Winters peed over the side of the barge, sending concentric ripples widening across the black water of the drainage channel. No drones in the sky, no blue lights flashing in the distance. No sign of rescue. If S had called Jude and told him what had happened, if Jude had alerted the police, they'd either failed to track Dash's getaway route or for some reason hadn't taken the abduction seriously. Whatever he'd gotten himself into, however it was going to play out, he'd have to deal with it on his own. An unsettling, lonesome conclusion.

Breakfast was the last of the bananas and warm bottled water. Neither of the sidekicks knew where Dash had gone or why, when she'd be back or who she might bring. 'I guess we just hang,' Brick said, unconcernedly.

People were leaving the drifter camp, heading towards the world on foot or riding bicycles and scooters. A little later, Winters saw what he thought at first was a thread of black smoke rising from one of the drifter boats, spreading out into a patch of discrete flecks that floated off across the floodplain in the direction of the estuary.

Brick and Purdey kicked a football about on top of the embankment and Winters sat nearby, his ankle stinging whenever Purdey and the transponder strayed too far. When he asked if he could join in, Brick and Purdey put him in goal and took turns at defence and offence, a hard-charging, full-contact game that for an hour or so made Winters forget his forebodings.

The clouds burned away and the morning grew ever hotter. The air unmoving. The stop-and-start sizzle of crickets hidden in the grass. Winters dozed in the scant shade of the tattered canvas sheet while Brick and Purdey shit-talked about acquaintances, was woken by laughter and howls of pain. Brick and Purdey had strapped on spare ankle cuffs and were trying to find out who could bear to walk the furthest from the transponder.

Winters refused their invitation to join in the competition, chugged down a bottle of water, and saw, a long way off, a small shape piece itself from the shimmering shards of heat haze, swiftly resolving into the little truck. It braked hard in a squall of dust and gravel and Dash climbed out. Brick and Purdey were trotting towards her, but she ignored them, pointing to Winters and saying, 'Time to go.'

Winters sat in the cab, beside Dash, as the truck jostled along the top of the embankment, with Purdey and Brick squatting in its loadbed amongst the gear from their hide-out. Dash was in a grim mood, strangling the steering wheel and driving too fast, refusing to tell Winters where they were going and who they'd meet there, passing the drifter camp, cutting around a cluster of wind turbines and skidding onto a narrow tarmac road.

'The offer still stands,' Winters said.

'Forget about your stupid offer.'

'And there's still room for negotiation.'

'What did I say?'

'Is there some kind of problem? Anything I can help with?'

'I wanted to deliver you myself, but there's been a change of plan,' Dash said, barely slowing the truck as it shot through a crossroads.

'So what's happening instead?'

'You're still going to the same place. To meet the same people. But someone else will be dealing with the handover.'

'Someone else?'

'The guy who hired me. The middleman.'

Winters braced as the truck banged over a serious pothole. 'You mean the shroom grower.'

'Okay, yes. The shroom grower.'

'Who is he? What do I need to know about him?'

'Just be careful,' Dash said.

She wouldn't elaborate, but it was clear that she'd tried to make some kind of deal, it hadn't played out, and Winters was going to be turned over to someone Dash didn't trust. Like her driving, it did nothing to ease his nerves.

They headed south and west, threading a network of back roads to Burnham-on-Crouch. Dash parked the truck on the high street and opened a pocket knife and cut the tie around Winters' wrists, reminding him that he was still wearing the ankle cuff.

'I have the transponder right here in my pocket, so don't try to run off.'

'I won't.'

'Don't cause any trouble, either.'

'It would help if I knew where we're going.'

'We're taking the ferry,' Dash said, and unlocked the truck's doors.

Purdey drove off in the truck and Dash took Winters' arm and walked him towards the riverside quay, Brick wheeling a community bike behind them. The river ferry was a flat-bottomed, steel-hulled cockleshell with benches along either side and a big outboard motor at the stern. The three of them boarded with a group of tourists and as everyone was taking their seats the last passenger arrived, a slight figure with the hood of their oversized skyblue cagoule pulled over their head. It was S, taking a seat at the end of one of the benches, very carefully not looking at Winters. Neither Dash nor Brick seemed to take any notice of them and Winters turned sideways as the ferry cast off, pretending to be interested in the view, but as it powered up the broad calm river towards its landing station on Wallasea Island, the tourists taking pictures of each other and pointing out sights, he snuck a couple of quick peeks at the kid, who sat with their head lowered, fists balled in the pockets of their cagoule, never once looking at anyone else. Winters couldn't figure out how they'd tracked him down, and although it was reassuring that he'd been found, he was worried that S might be planning to do something stupid and decided to play down the trouble he was in, turning to Dash, asking her for the loan of a joint.

'This isn't the time,' she said.

'I just need a quick puff to ease my nerves.'

'If the man's got the jitters, it can't hurt,' Brick said. 'You don't have anything, I got makings.'

'Your shit'll put him into orbit,' Dash said, and speared two fingers into the breast pocket of her denim jacket and pulled out a skinny joint and handed it to Winters. Brick flicked his lighter and Winters sneaked another glance at S as he bent to apply its unsteady flame to the twisted end of the joint. He drew in a hot riffle of smoke and held it, blew it out and drew in another. One of the tourists, a young woman, was giving him a look of stark disapproval and he turned and blew smoke into the ferry's slipstream and turned back and smiled at the woman until she looked away. The kid gave no sign that they'd seen this little pantomime. Winters took one more puff and snubbed out what was left of the joint on the heel of his boot and handed it to Dash.

'That's all you get,' she said.

'It was all I needed,' Winters said.

S was the first off when the ferry docked at the other side of the river, walking away without a backward glance, somehow disappearing almost at once amongst steel-walled sheds and boats on trailers or blocks and general industrial clutter. No sign of them as Dash led Winters and Brick through the boatyard to a bubblecar parked outside the gate, steepening Winter's anxiety about their plans.

Dash clicked a key fob and told Winters, as the front half of the bubblecar lifted up like a clamshell, that it would take them the rest of the way.

'The person who arranged this likes to play stupid games,' Dash said, with no trace of irony or self-awareness. 'Likes to show he's in control. There's only room in this thing for you and me, and I don't exactly know where we're going, but don't worry, I have a workaround.'

'That's why the bike,' Winters said.

'I'll be right behind you,' Brick said.

Dash and Winters climbed into the bubblecar, sitting shoulder to shoulder, knee to knee on the bench seat, and Dash pulled down the clamshell and pressed the starter button. The bubblecar made a laborious three-point turn in self-driving mode and turned left at the end of the service road, onto a narrow country road. Brick managed to keep up for a short while but began to fall behind as the bubblecar picked up speed, following the road through a salt marsh dissected by wandering creeks. Winters, nervy and slightly stoned, an unsettling combination, watched the marsh give way to fields, a scatter of houses on stilts, a block of wind turbines. After a couple of kilometres the bubblecar slowed and turned onto a lane that ran off through a stand of windbent trees, and Dash killed the motor and grabbed the tiller, taking control of the bubblecar as it drifted to a halt.

'Are we walking from here?' Winters said.

'We're waiting for Brick,' Dash said, and restarted the bubblecar when her sidekick, breathing like a steam engine, T-shirt dark with sweat, caught up with them a few minutes later.

The bubblecar backed up, as if reorientating itself, and set off down the dead centre of the lane, flashes of sunlight flickering in the branches and leaves knitted overhead, and slowed and stopped at a steel bar gate set in tall security fencing. Beyond it, a concrete yard and a bungalow clad in white weatherboard baked in an avalanche of heat and light. An airboat on a trailer and a pickup truck with French numberplates were parked alongside three greenhouses packed with tall plants.

Brick pulled up beside the bubblecar and Winters and Dash climbed out. A dog chained outside the nearest greenhouse, some kind of hypermuscular pitbull cross, roused and began to bark, and a woman came out of the bungalow and walked halfway across the yard and told the dog to shut the fuck up. It stopped barking but strained at the end of its taut chain, quiveringly watchful, as she bent over her phone. The gate lock clunked and as the gates swung inwards Brick dropped a hand on Winters' shoulder, holding him in place. Dash was staring at the woman with imperious distaste.

'Where is he?' she said. 'And who the fuck are you?'

'I'm right here,' a man said, and stepped out of the slice of shadow in the bungalow's doorway.

He was dressed in a sleeveless T-shirt and jorts, hair shaved to a greasy stubble the way some men of a certain age tried to disguise male-pattern baldness. When Winters realised who he was, the shock was an order of magnitude greater than the shock of seeing the kid boarding the ferry.

'You're supposed to be dead,' he said stupidly.

'I get that a lot,' Rob Copely said. 'What's with the big fellow? Do I detect a lack of trust?'

'You have company too,' Dash said.

'I don't think I ever told you about Cleo, did I? She's my wife, and this place is hers as much as mine.'

'And I'm not looking for any trouble,' Dash said. 'As long as you stick to what was agreed.'

'That's a bit rich, coming from you. But don't worry, you'll get your due. Come in, all of you. I'm sure young Marc has all kinds of questions he wants to ask me.'

Brick was banished to the kitchen and Winters and Dash followed Rob Copely into the living room, where Cleo delivered a sweating jug of lemonade and three tall glasses packed with ice cubes before making herself scarce.

'The lemons are from a tree she grew from a pip,' Copely said, as he carefully filled each of the glasses. 'Has a green thumb, our Cleo. And not just for the weed you no doubt clocked in her greenhouses.'

'I heard that you're also in the shroom business,' Winters said. Although he was dry-mouthed and overheated, prickling with nervous anticipation, he ignored the glass Copely pushed towards him across the glass coffee table. The room was small and airless and packed with oversized furniture and mermaid-themed memorabilia. The wallpaper featured repeating patterns of anime mermaids with drifts of blue hair and overlarge oval eyes peeping coyly behind clumps of seaweed and barnacled rocks, plastic and porcelain mermaid figurines crowded the shelves of a pine dresser, a mobile hung with mermaid and angel fish cut-outs turned slowly back and forth against the French windows, and mermaids decorated the shade of a big standard lamp and the cushions of Copely's overstuffed armchair and the sectional sofa where Winters and Dash perched. A claustrophobic overload of kitsch.

'Got it in one,' Rob Copely said, and raised his glass of lemonade in salute and drank half of it down and belched.

Izzy's partner, back in the day. The two of them living together in a celibate marriage. Copely had acquired a confident gaze and an air of indulgent authority since then, and had put on weight, too. His face was broader and coarser than Winters recalled, and a wedge of pale belly bulged between the hem of his T-shirt and the belt of his blue denim jorts.

'The shroom business is why I'm still walking up and down in this world,' he said. 'Kasey gave me the task of saving his special stock. The beta strain and various specials, including the special special. Backup in case his plans went awry. Which was prescient, considering. I didn't want to leave, I wanted to be part of the birth of the new green world, was ready and able to make the ultimate sacrifice for it. But I had my orders, so leave is what I did. Took off as the final preparations for the Great Green Reset got under way, and you know how that went. I managed to stay under the radar, have been taking care of the shrooms ever since.'

'Here, or in France?' Winters said.

'So you noticed my numberplates. Yes, like your sister, I chose to make a new home in another country, but I visit my wife on the regular. Checking on our dealers and their customers, fixing problems. We supply dreamers from Southend to the Wash with good old beta. The strain that lets you see, but doesn't let you do. The one all sorts of chancers grow, because Kasey gave away chunks of mycelium to anyone who asked. I'm not complaining. Man was a visionary. Spreading the word and spreading shrooms that gave people a glimpse of the world to come. Forming the base, as he called it. A kind of background psychic field. The grounding for everything he wanted to do. But the real deal, the stuff that enables you to make a difference, the specials and the special special, I'm the only one that grows them. They were entrusted to me and I have kept that trust to this very day.'

'Don't listen to his bullshit,' Dash said. She was perched on the edge of the sofa, and although she was clutching her glass of lemonade in both hands she hadn't taken a sip. Maybe, like Winters, she was wary of being spiked. 'He sells shrooms to anyone who has enough money.'

'Including you.' Copely paused for a beat, and when Dash didn't respond he told Winters, 'I'm keeping Kasey's legacy alive, and she's no more than a gun for hire. And not an especially trustworthy one either, as it turns out.'

'I've done things to survive that I'm not proud of,' Dash said. 'Having to work with you isn't the worst of them, but it's up there.'

Winters said to Rob Copely, 'Megan Rix is one of your dealers. She told you about me, and you told the deep dreamers.'

'Bingo.'

'They were already paying Dash to keep watch on me. And after you told them about me they paid her to kidnap me and bring me here.'

'Matter of fact it was me who employed her. Out of charity, and the mistaken belief that we were still friendly. Still shared a common cause. And then she turned around and tried to do a deal behind my back. Don't try to deny it, darling,' Copely told Dash. 'The person you met did the right thing and told their higher ups, who insisted on sticking to the original deal. No doubt they didn't want to upset the man who controls supply of the special strain they need. Something you should have thought about when you decided to chance it.'

'I brought him here, didn't I?'

'Along with the bully boy in the kitchen, despite my request to bring young Marc on your lonesome. But that's all right. I forgive you.'

'As if you're any better,' Dash said, with a flash of disgust. 'Pretending to be sympathetic to the deep dreamers, and all the while gouging them for the shrooms they need.'

'Making a living on the dark side is costly. And even though you know full well where my money comes from I didn't hear any complaint when I gave you your advance.'

'You give me the rest, I'll leave you to get on with delivering our friend here, and you won't hear from me again,' Dash said.

'Until you need more of the special special,' Copely said.

'I'm here because I want to find out about Isabel and the deep dreamers,' Winters told the man, irritated by the pair's bickering. 'How she escaped from the siege. What the deep dreamers want from her and why she doesn't want to give it to them. And I'm wondering, given your relationship with her, back in the commune, whether you can help me.'

'You're wasting your time,' Dash said.

'She's right, for once,' Copely said. 'I gave my word that I wouldn't discuss certain matters. But I'll give you this much for free. Kasey entrusted me with preserving the shrooms, but he didn't divulge the secret of how to use them to what you might call their full extent. Not just dabbling on the shore, making little sandcastles and splashing in rock pools, but swimming far out into the ocean. Mastering its storms and its depths. Its monsters. Or as Kasey once told me, learning how to guide and synchronise the psychic energy of dreamers of world-changing dreams. I had the skill and the magic touch needed to grow and propagate the shrooms, but I was never made part of the inner circle, and they were the only ones privy to that knowledge. So I don't know how to change the world, but I do know that it can be changed, having been one of the dreamers of the first reset. Having been right there at the hinge-point. The still centre of the turning, as Kasey called it. You only know the world as it is now, but I remember it as it once was. And so does Dash, because she was there too. We have our differences, but we have that in common. And I know she'll agree when I say that you should be glad you know only this world, this history. The other, well. Here and now, things are bad, but not as bad as they could be. As they once were. The world's two degrees Celsius warmer than it was in preindustrial times, but the rise has topped out and if things keep going right it'll start to fall in the next century or so. Before our first reset, though, the global temperature was a tad over four degrees above where it should have been, and still rising. Which doesn't mean things were twice as bad. No, they were much worse than that. Much, much worse. Billions dead, and more dying every day. Hurricanes at the poles. Hyperhurricanes everywhere else. Coasts gone. Not just beaches and a bit of beachfront property, but just about all the coasts everywhere that had been at sea level, and a lot of the land behind them too. And on top of all that, there were wars everywhere. Over food, over water, over ground that wasn't flooded or burned. That's what I remember. What Dash remembers, too, and everyone else involved in the turning point of the reset. Because we didn't make the change here. We made it in the world that was and no longer is. Because we set history on a new and better path, and we would have done more if we'd been allowed. Well, I say we. I mean the commune. The friends I had to leave behind when I was sent out into the world. The people Dash left behind when she ran away. You probably don't believe a word of that, and I don't blame you. Unless you were there it's hard to credit. But it's true. Every word of it. And I hope, I really do, that the deep dreamers can take up the torch. And that, not any commercial consideration, is why we're here.'

After the siege, when Winters had been trying to understand what his sister had believed in, whether any part of it could possibly be true, he'd read interviews with members of the commune who had left before or after the first reset. He'd also read the report of a forensic psychologist, who had concluded that under the control and guidance of Kasey Motte his followers suffered from a hallucinatory suite of false memories, a shared, highly detailed consensual fiction reinforced by continuous intake of psychoactive substances and forced participation in talking circles and self-criticism. The psychologist's clinical analysis of the commune's beliefs, with references to similar events, similar behaviours, similar shared narratives, placed it in a pathological spectrum shared by other cults. But experiencing the force of Rob Copely's deep and very real belief in the truths the commune had constructed and inhabited, like another presence bodying forth in the hot, close little room, was something else. Powerful. Astonishing. Frightening.

Winters said, 'What do the deep dreamers want with me? Dash said that they changed their plans, but wouldn't tell me how or why.'

'That's because she doesn't know,' Copley said, looking at Dash as if daring her to contradict him.

'And you do.'

'You'll find out soon enough,' Copely said, with a sly smile.

'Is it something to do with the time Kasey Motte shroomed me? The walk and talk in the woods?'

'If that was the reason, we'd all of us be candidates. It was the last time we met, I believe,' Copley said to Winters. 'You had a glimpse of what would have been revealed to you if you'd stayed on, but Isabel got it into her head that you shouldn't be there, and sprang you.'

'Did she get in trouble because of that? I always wondered.'

'Kasey was unhappy about it. Words were had, et cetera. But he let Isabel stay on, although he would have been well within in his rights to kick her out. In the end he said that it wasn't meant to be and we should all move on. As we did.'

'Speaking of moving on,' Dash said. 'If you pay me what I'm owed, I'll be on my way.'

'I haven't forgotten,' Copely said, and raised his hands and clapped twice.

His wife, Cleo, appeared in the doorway a moment later. As if she'd been lurking there, waiting to be summoned.

'How is he?' Copley said.

'Spark out,' Cloe said.

'What's going on?' Dash said, and pushed to her feet as Cleo stepped towards her.

'Your friend's asleep is all,' Copely said. 'Let's get this done.'

Cleo grabbed Dash, crooked an arm around her neck and raised a syringe that reflected a brief star of window-light. Dash, seeing it, kicked backwards. The two of them crashed into the dresser and dozens of miniature mermaids tottered and fell, showering down around their heads and shoulders. Winters jumped up, ready to take Dash's side, and Copely heaved out of his armchair, muttering forfuckssake, and shoved him back into the sofa. He felt a bee-sting in his shoulder, the man had jabbed him with a syringe, and he tried and failed to stand up. Copely and his wife were struggling with Dash, a clumsy waltz that blundered towards the French windows and sent the mobile swinging wildly. Mermaids were swarming everywhere, darkening the air as Copely lowered Dash to the floor, and then, like passing from one part of a dream to the next, Winters was strapped in the passenger seat of a pickup truck with his wrists fastened behind his back and Rob Copely beside him at the wheel, the man watching the side mirror as he backed up. When the nose of the pickup cleared the gate Copely braked and leaned out of the window to talk to Cleo, cutting off her complaints, telling her that Dash and her large accomplice probably wouldn't remember anything, and even if they did they couldn't do anything about it.

'They kidnapped our friend here, so they're hardly going to go crying to the police, are they? And if they find their way back here, try to cause you grief, just give me a call. I'll send someone who'll sort it.'

Cleo started to say something about not agreeing to any of this, and Copely interrupted her again. 'You signed up for it long ago. You just didn't realise it until now.'

The trees on either side seemed to be multiplying, a forest unfolding into vast green distances, and Winters had a sense of birds passing overhead, a river of birds beating fast and low above the endless trees, and when he came around again the pickup truck was moving along a country road and hot air was howling through the open windows. Flat fields on either side and a green wing floating at the horizon like the ghost of a lost continent.

'How are you feeling?' Copely said brightly.

When Winters tried to speak drool spilled from his mouth. He wiped his chin on his shoulder and tried again. 'What did you do to me?'

'A little shot of fentanyl and muscle relaxant to quiet you down, plus a soupçon of my special shroom extract. Same mix I gave Dash and her pal, but not quite as strong. They're sleeping it off in back. I wouldn't bother,' Copely added, when Winters shifted from side to side, testing his bonds. 'Even if you could get loose, I have Dash's transponder. Get any distance from me and your ankle cuff'll start hurting. What they call a gomer in the trade. Works by selective stimulation of the nerves. Dash always was a technical girl.'

Winters wondered vaguely how much trouble he was in now, but didn't feel afraid. He was still floating on the hot shot. 'Where are we going?'

'You know where.'

'Deep dreamers.'

'Bingo.'

'You're part of it, aren't you? The deep dreamers. The Instauration.'

'I never stopped believing. Unlike some other people we know.'

'You really believe that you changed the world. Changed history.'

'We did the heavy lifting together. One mind, one dream. Changed the world and made it a better place.' Copely paused, then said, 'There were smaller changes, too. What you might call individual touches. I brought back tigers.'

'Tigers?'

'Yeah, tigers,' Copely said, with a smile that dared Winters to challenge this improbability.

'What kind of tigers?'

'What do you mean, what kind?'

'I mean the different subspecies. Siberian? Sumatran? Bengal?'

'All of them I guess.'

Rob Copely's smile didn't change, but there was the slightest wobble in his gaze.

'I know you didn't bring back Siberian and Sumatran tigers,' Winters said. 'They're definitely extinct.'

'What about Bengal tigers?'

'There are still a few. Not in the wild. In zoos.'

'Well, that still counts. No need to thank me, by the way.'

'What did Isabel change? What was her individual touch?'

'She didn't tell you?'

'She didn't tell me anything about the reset. So if your friends think I have some kind of special secret knowledge, if that's why they want me, they're going to be disappointed.'

'This isn't about what you know.'

Copely was in high good humour. Smiling at Winters, fingers tapping on the steering wheel.

'Then what is it about?' Winters said. 'Come on. It won't do any harm to tell me now.'

'I'll tell you this much. It's about who you are. What you are.'

'Because I'm Isabel's brother?' Winters said, and remembered asking Kasey Motte the same question, after the man had tricked Winters into coming to the commune, had given him a shroom omelette. Motte had promised to tell him everything once the effects of the shrooms had worn off, but Isabel had set him free instead.

'That's part of it,' Copely said.

'Is it a genetic thing I share with Isabel? Something to do with the way we dream?'

'Nothing to do with genes. Try again.'

'You could just tell me.'

'I'll say one thing. Then no more questions.'

'Okay.'

'You're a man out of time.'

'What do you mean, out of time?'

'My friends know more about this than I do. I'm sure they'll want to explain everything.'

They drove in silence for a few minutes. Eventually, Copely said he'd noticed that Winters kept looking out the window. Asked him what he saw out there.

Winters had been watching the silhouette of the ghost continent at the horizon, half-expecting it to drift closer, or spread across the actual landscape like a tidal wave.

'I don't know what it is,' he said.

'But you see something. Something that shouldn't be there.'

'You should know, since you're the one who dosed me.'

'Don't be like that. I answered your question, didn't I?'

'Not exactly.'

'It was more than I should have said. So, what does it look like?'

'A sort of floating green world. But it isn't really there, so why does what it looks like matter?'

'It matters because it's a sign of things to come,' Copely said, and beat a tattoo on the steering wheel and laughed. 'Signs and wonders heralding great changes, as dreams begin to come true.'

They stuck to B roads, heading roughly north. Only a little traffic, mostly trucks and farm vehicles, a few bubblecars. Winters tried to ignore the shroom hallucination, if that was what it was, concentrated on the road ahead. He didn't know where he was going, but as long as he knew how he got there he could find his way back. Hedgerows, fields. Small villages rearing up out of nowhere and spinning past and disappearing. They were passing through woodland when Copely braked and turned the pickup onto an unmade track, wallowing through ruts and potholes for a short distance before stopping.

'Time to deal with our friends before they come around and start kicking off,' he said. 'I'll need a hand. Me and Cleo had a devil of a time getting the big guy into the back. Don't want to bang him up too badly getting him out.'

'I'm not sure if I'm up to that.'

'Do your best. And remember that cuff is still around your ankle, so no theatrics,' Copely said, and told Winters to lean forward and severed the zip tie around his wrists with a box cutter.

Winters climbed out of the pickup carefully, his legs uncertain, his hands tingling as blood rushed back into them. Beech trees on either side of the track. A carpet of last year's leaves, a scatter of broken branches. Patches of ferns and brambles. The air was as hot and moveless as Cleo's living room and Winters had the creepy feeling that there was something out there, skulking in the deep shade under the trees or crouching inside the glossy green tangle of a big holly bush close to the track, preparing to spring at him like a feral jack-in-the-box.

Rob Copely lowered the gate at the back of the pickup's loadbed and whipped away a ragged square of blue tarpaulin, revealing Dash and Brick lying on their sides facing each other, ankles and wrists bound with zip ties, socks stuffed into their mouths. Copely pulled himself up into the loadbed, and paused, standing between his victims and looking over the top of the pickup's cab as a bubblecar bumped down the track and stopped a few metres away.

For a moment, Winters had the wild idea that Cleo had been following them, but this bubblecar was buttercup yellow and it was Bailey and S who climbed out of it. Bailey walking at an unhurried pace towards the pickup. Aiming a pistol, no, it was a taser, at Copely, who started to raise his hands in the moment before she triggered it.

'What were you thinking?' Bailey said to Winters. 'If you knew where Dash Baker was, why didn't you tell me?'

'The meeting was arranged by text. No names. She was about the last person I expected to turn up. And why I agreed to it, I wanted to get on the inside with the deep dreamers. Or at least, with someone who knew them. And I sort of did.'

'Only if your definition of "getting on the inside" is the same as "being snatched by".'

Bailey wasn't exactly angry, but she'd made it clear that she was exasperated by the inconvenience Winters had caused her, the lack of trust it implied.

'Rob Copley was taking me to people involved in this instauration business,' Winters said, in a last-ditch attempt to justify himself.

'Did he tell you who they are? Where he was taking you?'

'Not exactly.'

'So he didn't.'

'If you hadn't stepped in like you did, I would have found out.'

'It seemed very likely that he was up to no good when he turned off into these trees, so of course I stepped in. And I plan to find out everything he knows, but this isn't the place for that. Are you done with your horse whispering, S?'

'I think so,' the kid said. They were kneeling on the ground beside Dash, holding one of her hands in both of theirs. She'd had a panic attack after Winters and Bailey had hauled her out of the pickup, thrashing about and shouting, 'They're in the trees! They're in the trees!' until S had sung a long, soft, wordless song that had calmed her down.

Winters asked Bailey if they should call the police, turn Dash and Brick over to them, and Bailey said fuck no.

'I have no intention of spending the rest of the day justifying my involvement in your foolishness. We'll do what your friend Mr Copely was planning to do. Leave them here, let them find their own way back to wherever it was they came from,' she said, and cut Dash's zip ties with a penknife and told the woman that she was on her own, no thanks needed for the rescue.

Dash sat up, rubbing her wrists. Her eyes were raw from weeping and there were leaves caught in her hair. She said, 'What about Brick?'

The man was still spark out, snoring and muttering and every now and then shuddering all over, like a broken engine trying and failing to start.

'He's your problem, not mine,' Bailey said.

Dash looked at Winters. 'We need to get him to a hospital. I think Copely's witch of a wife overdosed him.'

'Good luck with that,' Bailey said, and told Winters and S to get in the pickup, it was time to go.

'If Brick needs treatment, he should get it as soon as possible. Rather than cause, you know, complications,' Winters said. He had some sympathy for the big guy, caught up in something he didn't fully understand, damaged in the line of duty.

'You could let me use that bubblecar,' Dash said. 'But I'll need help getting him into it.'

'I don't think so,' Bailey said.

'Then at least give me back my phone, so I can call my other friend. He has our truck, was supposed to come collect us.'

Bailey pulled out the phones she'd taken from Copely after she'd tased him. One of them looked like the phone Winters had bought a couple of days ago. She showed them to Dash, asking her which was hers, and Dash pointed, said, 'The silver one.'

Bailey held it out to Dash and told her to unlock it, asked if her friend was in its contacts list.

'He calls himself Purdey,' Winters said.

'Like the shotguns?' Bailey said, poking at the phone.

'Yeah.'

'And you let yourself get kidnapped by these people,' Bailey said.

She called Purdey, telling him no, this wasn't Dash but if he shut up for a moment she'd tell him where to find her, gave directions and said that he'd better hurry because his pal was having a bad trip, and stuffed the phone into the pocket of her suit jacket and told Winters and the kid that it was time to go.

'I think you have my phone, too,' Winters said. 'It's the cheap black one.'

'You don't need it right now.'

'Yeah, I do. My jet boat's moored not far from my friend Jude Lee's place of work. He'll probably have seen it by now, will be wondering where I am. I should give him a call and let him know everything's okay before he gets it into his head to call the police.'

Bailey studied Winters for a moment, then sorted through her little collection and tossed his phone to him. 'Be quick. And switch it off and hand it back when you're done. I don't want anyone using it to track us.'

Jude answered on the second ring.

'It's me,' Winters said.

'Marc? Where are you?'

'I guess you saw where I left the jet boat,' Winters said, giving Bailey a look she ignored.

'It's hard to miss,' Jude said. 'You're okay?'

'I'm fine. On the move, following a lead. Can I ask – have you been in touch with the police?'

'No, but I was beginning to think that I should.'

'I would have called earlier, but I was sort of caught up in something. Listen, I might not be back for a while. Could you call Doyle's, ask them to take the jet boat back? And tell them I'm good for whatever I owe, rental and the fee for retrieval and whatever, but they should send the bill to this number. I left my other phone back at the Ship, and I'm not sure when I'll be back.'

'No problem.'

'Thanks. I swear I'll find some way of returning the favour when this business is over. There's one other thing,' Winters said, and told Jude about the drifter camp and the swarm he'd seen rising from one of the boats.

'You're sure it was airjellies you saw?'

'Positive. Released from one of the narrowboats there. The blue one. I don't know if the jellies were grown there or bought in, I didn't have time to check it out.'

'I guess I can take a look,' Jude said. 'Good luck with whatever it is you're up to.'

Bailey held out her hand, and after a moment Winters handed the phone to her. He needed her help, there was no sense in making a thing about it. She switched the bubblecar to self-driving mode and dispatched it to the hire company, and they set off in the pickup. Copely was in the footwell of the crew cabin's rear bench seat, hogtied with the cords he'd used to secure Dash and Brick, gagged with one of his socks and wrapped in the blue tarpaulin sheet. They were heading towards a place where, according to Bailey, they could rest up and question the man.

How she'd found Winters: in the course of her background checks and enquiries she'd discovered that he'd recently rented a boat, and put up a couple of drones to search for it after he'd done a bunk. It wasn't long before one of the drones spotted the boat in West Mersea harbour, and it had followed Winters as he picked up S and headed downriver to what was obviously some kind of rendezvous. By the time Bailey got there, driving around the head of the estuary in her rented bubblecar, Dash Baker and her sidekicks had snatched him and made off. S had tried and failed to track them with Winters' cheap drone, but before it ran out of charge it had captured a clear image of their truck's licence plate and given a rough idea of where they were heading, and when Bailey had turned up the kid decided it would be better to cooperate with her and give chase right away rather than involve Jude and the police. Bailey had called in a favour to gain access to the area's traffic cameras, her agent quickly located footage of the truck driving along the road at the edge of the floodplain, and she and S had checked out farms and drifter camps and by the end of the day had found the barge where Winters was being held. They'd staked it out because Bailey had wanted to see if Winters' abductors would lead to what she called bigger fish, and the next day tailed Dash's truck to Burnham-on-Crouch. S followed Winters and his captors to the ferry, stole a bicycle on the other side of the river and chased after Brick to the bungalow; meanwhile, Bailey drove the long way around, Rob Copely's pickup passing her in the other direction just before she met up with S. And the rest, she said, was history.

Winters told her about the conversation in the bungalow, explained that Dash Baker had been working for Copely, and he in turn was working for deep dreamers who were planning a rerun of Kasey's Motte's final reset, changing the world through dreams and so on.

'I'm familiar with the fantasy,' Bailey said.

'It isn't a fantasy,' S said. They were scrunched sideways on the rear seat, hugging their knees to their chest so they wouldn't have to rest their feet anywhere near Rob Copely.

'I think they wanted to find my sister because she'd been part of Kasey Motte's inner circle, knew all about the resets,' Winters said. 'But then something changed, and his friends decided that they could use me instead.'

'Is anyone else from the commune involved in this? Did you think to ask Copely about Lady A's son?'

'I had other things on my mind at the time. And Dash and Copely weren't exactly, what's the word, forthcoming. But now the tables have been turned, maybe you can get answers to the questions you think I should have asked.'

'We're going to have a very crunchy conversation, Mr Copely and me,' Bailey said. 'I have years of experience in dealing with people like him. And I have plenty of leverage, too, what with him still being wanted for involvement in the Wakestone siege, not to mention his cross-channel drug business and your kidnap. He has any sense, he'll talk in exchange for being allowed to go on his way. Tell me everything and tell it straight.'

'That all sounds fine, as long as I can ask some questions about my sister.'

'Don't worry,' Bailey said. 'Lady A still wants to talk to her, and I haven't forgotten about our quid pro quo.'

'As I said before, that'll be up to Izzy. If we can find her.'

Winters was grateful for the rescue, but also resented the way Bailey had used him as bait to catch Rob Copely, and knew that she didn't see him as any kind of equal partner. For one thing he was still wearing the fucking ankle cuff, and the transponder was in Bailey's pocket. For another, he didn't know how that quid pro quo might change if Copely could answer all of Talia Armstrong's questions about her son.

They turned north off the A12, stopped at a charging station on the outskirts of a village for a fast top up. Bailey told Winters to sit tight and make sure their hostage didn't cause any trouble, and she and S headed off to the station's shop, which still bore traces of the signage of the petrochemical company which had once owned it. Rob Copely lay quiet and still in the footwell, wrapped in his tarpaulin shroud like the chrysalis of a giant bug. Winters resisted the temptation to take a peek, make sure the man was still breathing, and paced around the pickup, trying to walk off his anxiety. His ankle cuff faintly tingled and he wished he'd thought to ask Bailey to buy a pack of joints.

It was early evening, still light. The air packed with heat, quiet countryside spread all around. Cropfields, rows of greenhouses, the gleam of a solar farm. Like a factory floor after the workers had gone home. Winters had forgotten how regulated most of it was. Every square metre put to use, growing food or biomass, generating electricity. The shot of shroom extract seemed to have worn off, the ghostly green land floating at the horizon was gone, but he still felt a weird floating detachment. As if the world had thinned, or his engagement with it had weakened. As if he'd been halfway to somewhere else and hadn't come all the way back.

Bailey and the kid returned with sandwiches and cardboard cups of tea. S asked Winters if he wanted brown sauce or red, they'd brought sachets of both, and Bailey said that he also had a choice of beansprout salad or seitan bacon.

'I'm old enough to remember when bacon was actually bacon, but the seitan stuff isn't bad. Or maybe my standards have slipped over the years.'

Winters took the salad. After they'd eaten and used the charging station's bathroom, they climbed back into the pickup and Bailey cut away from the main road, taking a crooked course along crumbling B roads and country lanes. By the time they reached their destination the sky was darkening and Venus's steady star burned low in the bloody afterglow of sunset. A lane pinched between trimmed hedges led to a small industrial estate islanded amongst fields of corn and oilseed rape. Steel-framed sheds, different sizes, stood along one side of a concrete slab roadway. Machinery hire, 3D fabbing, a gin distillery, a place that converted shipping containers into workshops and offices, and at the far end a small airfield, its landing strip a long lane of mown grass between dense plantings of corn, lights burning in the small office in the lee of the first of three blister hangars.

Bailey told Winters and S to wait in the pickup and crossed over to the office and shook hands with the man waiting in the lighted doorway. They walked to the nearest hangar, pulled one of its big sliding doors open and went inside. Winters' ankle cuff started to tingle again; Bailey was still carrying the transponder. He opened the pickup's door, prepared to jump out if she strayed too far, told the kid that he was grateful for their help, but they needn't have come this far or put themselves at risk, the way they had on the ferry.

'I don't mind. It's interesting.'

'As Bailey might say, that's an interesting definition of "interesting".'

'I couldn't ask before. But now she isn't here, do you think I did the right thing, involving her?'

'Don't worry about it. She was already involved. And if you'd called Jude, and he'd called in the police, we might not have found out that Rob Copely was part of this thing.'

'She said she was your friend. But you don't trust her, do you?'

'We both want to find my sister, but for different reasons. And things could get tricky from here on in. So you don't have to stick around, and I won't blame you if you take off.'

'I want to see what happens next,' the kid said.

After a couple of minutes, Bailey and the man came out of the hangar. While the man walked back to the office, Bailey climbed into the pickup's cab, said that everything was in hand, told Winters to shut the damn door.

'This would be a good time to tell me what you're planning.'

'It's been a long day. We'll get some rest, let our friend think about his situation, and talk to him tomorrow. Find out what he knows about Lady Armstrong's son and your sister, who he was supposed to deliver you to. Take it from there,' Bailey said, and started the pickup and drove it into the hangar.

Most of the space was taken up by two single prop aircraft. Cot beds had been set up beyond a clutch of oil drums and a workbench cluttered with antique tools. The blue booth of a portable toilet unit, folding chairs, a table with a kettle, microwave and a cool box packed with microwavable meals and cartons of beer and soft drinks, and a pair of antique floor lampstands with fringed shades that cast dim circles of light in the shadows beneath the roof.

Bailey pulled the big door shut and Winters helped her drag Rob Copely out of the cab and hoist him onto the pickup's loadbed. She pulled off his tarpaulin wrapping and fitted him with an ankle cuff improvised from zip ties and padlocked it to one of the loadbed's tether rings, cut the cords from his wrists and ankles, squatted in front of him and unravelled the sock from his mouth and told him that he would be spending the night there.

'As long as you don't give me any trouble you won't get any trouble from me. Are we clear on that?'

The man started to tell her that she was the one who was in a lot of trouble, and she slapped his face, hard enough to raise an echo.

'I'm in charge. Understand?'

Copely rubbed his cheek and said sullenly, 'There was no need for that.'

'You won't cause any trouble. Say it.'

'No trouble.'

'Good boy,' Bailey said.

She fetched a couple of blankets and a plastic lidded bucket and a roll of toilet paper, bottles of water from a coolbox and left-over sandwiches from the cab, tossing everything carelessly into the loadbed and telling Copely if she heard one word from him she'd gag and bind him again, and then she rummaged amongst the tools on the workbench and found a fearsome pair of boltcutters and told Winters to take a seat and stretch out his leg.

'I trust you won't run off on some bootless enterprise again,' she told him, her flat stare devoid of any trace of humour.

'I've learned my lesson.'

'I hope you have,' Bailey said, and worked one of the boltcutters' jaws under the strap of his ankle cuff and severed it with a fearsome snap that travelled up Winters' spine to the back of his skull.

'Let's check out Mr Copely's stuff,' she said. 'You never know, we might find something resembling a clue.'

Winters and the kid watched as she briskly ransacked the man's possessions. A day bag containing toiletries and a change of clothing. A French national identity card, a French driving licence and a French passport, all in the name of Simón Bolívar. A leather wallet that when unzipped revealed ampoules and glass syringes held in loops, and a pack of sterile hypodermic needles. Bailey had already taken the man's phone, and when Winters asked her about it she told him that she would check it later.

She zapped a portion of chickpea curry in the microwave and forked it up between sips from a carton of beer while Winters picked at the remains of the charging station salad he hadn't been able finish earlier. It had been a long and freaky day, he was completely whacked and badly jonesing for a joint – there weren't any in the hospitality package, a major oversight as far as he was concerned.

The kid was walking around the two aircraft, ducking under the wing of one, standing on tiptoe to look into the cabin of the other, running a hand along the shapely blade of the propellor at its nose.

Bailey called out to them, asked if they liked planes.

'I think so.'

'The one whose prop you're fondling, that's a Piper Cherokee Charger almost a hundred years old, found in a barn and rebuilt with an electric engine. The other, it's based on Charles Lindbergh's *Spirit of St Louis*. The first plane to cross the Atlantic Ocean, a hundred and fifty years ago. Give or take.'

The kid turned to look at it. The polished aluminium fuselage dimly reflecting the glow of the floor lamps. The slit windscreen peering under its high wing.

'Can it still fly, after a hundred and fifty years?'

'It isn't the original,' Bailey said. 'It's a kind of replica. A tweaked retro-modern design built at the turn of this century. Pretty old for a plane, even though it's half the age of the original. But to answer your question, yes, it's completely airworthy. Wouldn't be here if it wasn't. This place isn't a museum, and these planes may be rich people's toys, but they're functional. Practical, even. Take off from here, you can be in France or Scotland inside a couple of hours.'

'Does your boss have one?' Winters said.

'She's just a good friend of the person who owns this place, is nowhere near wealthy enough to afford one of these babies. But I've worked for the kind of people who can. The kind of people who, despite all the shit's that gone down, still have the same kind of lifestyle, more or less, that their grandparents and great-grandparents enjoyed. The price for maintaining that is way more than it once was, but beyond a certain level of wealth the price of anything ceases to matter. You hold out your hand, the thing you want drops into it, you don't have to worry about what it costs.'

'What kind of work was it?' Winters said.

'I don't tell war stories. Client confidentiality and so on. Also, most of what I do is boring. Routine grind. This is the most fun I've had in a long while.'

'So this is your idea of fun.'

'Putting down the bad guy and freeing his hostage, what's not to like?' Bailey said. She had taken off her suit jacket and was sprawled in her folding chair, her legs stretched out and crossed at the ankles.

'Does Talia Armstrong know you're here?' Winters said. 'What you've been doing?'

'I gave her a quick call back at the charging station. Brought her up to speed.'

'And she's okay with everything.'

'Let's say she was encouraged by my progress. We didn't get into the details.'

'Aren't you worried about breaking the law? You being ex-police and so on.'

'I operate in grey areas with specific aims and set boundaries.'

'Tasering someone, gagging them and tying them up, for you that's just a grey area.'

'I would say that it depends on who's being tasered.'

'How far would you go, to solve a case?'

'"Solving" isn't a word I'd use.'

'What would you call it, then?'

Bailey took a measured sip of beer, thinking about that. This was for her a serious topic.

'Closing, maybe,' she said. 'Though if you ask me the idea of closure is oversold. Oversold and overrated. Because really, when does something end? Back when I was a working cop, I'd do my best to find out what happened and why, gather enough evidence so that when I brought in the doer I could make the charges stick. Hand them over to the system, and let it take its course. Which shouldn't be confused with actual justice, given that in many cases it doesn't deliver what is wanted or expected. The doer goes to prison or is put on workfare, maybe has to pay a token sum meant to be reparation, but that doesn't mean it's over for the victim, the client. There's some relief in knowing that someone has answered for their crime. But if the victim has lost someone, if their life has been changed in some terrible and irreversible way, they still have to come to terms with that. The damage. The hurt. Life goes on and all that shit. Grief fades. People become accustomed to it. Habituated. But it never goes away.'

'You sound as if you're speaking from personal experience.'

'If I am, it's no business of yours.'

'Okay.'

'What I'm saying, if we do find your sister, that probably won't be the end of it.'

'It'll be the end of something. Possibly, I guess, the beginning of something else, but I can't think about what that might be until I know what's happened to her.'

From the shadows under the Piper Cherokee, the kid said, 'Do you think the bad guys have found her?'

'I know they want to,' Winters said. 'But she's smart, she managed to stay out of trouble for eight years. And she got away when they came for her.'

'If our man Copely knows where they are, I'll make sure we find them and ask them some questions,' Bailey said, and took another sip of beer. 'Do you believe in any of that stuff? Changing the world, the power of dreams, all that?'

'My sister did, back in the day. I don't know if she does any more.'

'But at one time she and her pals really thought they had dreamed a whole new history of the world into being.'

'Yeah. Replacing one a lot worse than this,' Winters said, thinking of Rob Copely's passionate declamation.

'Which still sounds like pure fantasy,' Bailey said.

'That things could be worse?'

'No, that's not hard to believe. It's already worse for a lot of people. I mean that some crazy cabal getting high on weird little mushrooms could share a collective dream, let alone make it real.'

A memory of Hari Pacek's hot, airless kitchen surfaced in Winters' mind. The old book, *Dreambook and Fortune Teller*, amongst the other books and magazines and papers on the cluttered table. Its crude cover illustration of the crone instructing the young couple. Explaining what their dreams had revealed.

He said, 'As I understand it, there's a taxonomy of dreams. Studies of the various common types. The things in the world that they represent, and what dreaming about them means. So maybe it's possible that people who were taking part in a ceremony, all of them high on the same drug, could have shared the same dream at the same time.'

'Even if they did, it was still only a dream. It couldn't change the world,' Bailey said, and looked past Winters. 'What about you, S? What kind of dreams do you have?'

Winters turned, saw that the kid had come up behind him, soundless as a cat.

'I don't dream,' they said.

'Everyone dreams. Maybe you're one of the people, like this friend of mine, who doesn't remember them.'

'No, I just don't have any.'

'How can you be certain, if you don't remember them?'

'You told me about these planes. But can you fly one?' the kid said.

'That isn't the same thing.'

'I think it is. And besides, I have some experience of other people's dreams, and where they can take someone if they aren't careful. That woman we found tied up in the pickup? She was in a bad place. Stuck between two worlds. I sang her back into this one.'

'That's a nice little notion,' Bailey said. 'But in the real world where everybody else lives, dreams don't mean anything. They're just your brain trying to make sense of hallucinations as it sorts through the garbage of the day. They can't change the world, or move people from one dimension to another, or whatever it is that Kasey Motte and his crazy cabal believed in.'

'You don't have to believe in it,' Rob Copely said. 'But that doesn't mean it isn't true.'

He was standing on the pickup's loadbed, looking at them over the roof of the cab.

'Another crazy person heard from,' Bailey said. 'Have you forgotten what I said about talking?'

'I know what you want to find, but I can't help you unless I know why you want to find it,' Copely said, and flinched when the beer carton Bailey threw at him struck the pickup's windscreen and bounced away.

'We'll talk about all of that and more tomorrow,' Bailey said. 'Hold your tongue until then, or I'll find that fucking sock and stuff it back in your mouth.'

Winters slept deep and long, woke to grey morning light filtering through the dusty skylights in the curved roof high above. The hangar's sliding doors had been cracked open and Bailey and the kid were gone.

'On that bench behind you,' Rob Copely said, from the pickup's loadbed, 'I believe you'll find a pair of boltcutters.'

'I'm not going to help you escape.'

Copely smiled. He was leaning on the roof of the pickup's cab, a blanket wrapped around his shoulders. Tousled and unshaven but alert.

'I know what that retired cop wants, and it doesn't have anything to do with you. What you want to know. We both need to get out of this, get back on the right track. I'll tell you what I know about Isabel, and take you to people who can help you find out more.'

'You're going to tell me everything soon enough,' Winters said, and went outside, Copely calling after him, telling him that he would be a better friend than that ugly bitch, saying that he was offering cash money too. Gold coins, untraceable, easily converted to any kind of credit.

Bailey was standing outside the office in the warm damp air, drinking coffee from a mug blazoned with the name of an aviation tools supplier. It had rained in the night. The runway's long strip of mown grass was wet and on either side of it dark green fields of corn stretched away under low clouds. Winters glimpsed a flash of a spectral glow at the horizon, looked away. It wasn't real and it would pass, it would pass, it would pass.

'What was our friend shouting about?' Bailey said.

'He was offering to tell me about my sister if I helped him escape.'

'I thought it might be something like that.'

'I do need to know.'

'And you will.'

'When do we make a start?'

Winters had the same pit-of-the-stomach mix of anticipation and dread he'd felt at the beginning of every school term.

'There's fresh coffee inside,' Bailey said. 'Also bread rolls and croissants. Little pots of jam and honey, if that's your thing.'

'I'm more of a mug of builder's tea guy.'

There didn't seem any point in asking about a calming joint.

'I'm sure Ivor can stretch to that.'

'Ivor?'

'You saw him last night. The man who runs this place. We both got a call early this morning, while you were spark out. Lady A's flying in.'

'Actually flying?'

'By helicopter. A favour from another of her friends.'

'You don't seem especially pleased about it.'

'She wants to take charge of questioning Copely. I advised against it, but she dealt with all kinds of criminals in her former life, thinks that this won't be any different.'

'I guess I don't have any choice about it.'

'No more than I do. There's something else. How you and our young friend S first met. They told me that you rescued them, after they got themselves stranded on a mudbank.'

'Yeah, I spotted them when I was out on the river.'

'And this was six or seven weeks ago.'

'More or less. What is this, you don't believe the kid? I know it's kind of a mad story, but it's what happened.'

Bailey ignored that, saying, 'Are you often out on the river?'

'It's part of my work. Routine patrols of my patch.'

'Routine patrols. So S could have put themselves out there day after day, knowing that sooner or later you'd show up. It's like a film. The two of you meet cute, form a bond. And when the time is right, S gives you up to the people they're working for.'

'Wait. You think they're working for someone? For the deep dreamers?'

'It occurred to me last night, when they chipped in about dreams.'

'Except that it was my idea to have S keep watch when I met Dash. And they helped you to rescue me from Rob Copely. Why would they do any of that if they were involved with the deep dreamers?'

Winters didn't want to believe Bailey's notion, it was flat-out crazy, but he was thinking of the kid's implausible story about drifting all the way downstream from the car reef. How they'd led him to the woman, Megan Rix, who'd given him up to Rob Copely. Their insistence on sticking around after Bailey took Copely down . . .

'There could be rival factions, each with their own batshit ideas about changing the world,' Bailey said. 'Maybe Copely belongs to one, S to another.'

'Or maybe you just don't trust anyone.'

'That's generally good practice in my line of work. Maybe there's nothing to it, but still, it's something to bear in mind, going forward. And obviously, don't tell S.'

'Yeah, it's definitely something they don't need to hear. Is there a bathroom in this place?'

'There are two. One for employees, and something fancier for clients.'

'Does either of them have a shower?'

It had begun to rain, thin irregular spits condensing out of the warm clammy air, when the helicopter arrived. A hard fluttering sound swelling somewhere in the low cloud before the machine materialised beyond the far end of the runway and drifted towards the hangars and settled in a squall of downdraft that flattened a perfect circle in the wet grass. Winters, showered and shaved, watched from the shelter of the office doorway with S as one of the airfield's mechanics dragged a thick yellow recharging cable to the helicopter and plugged it in, and Bailey and the carer, Ida, lifted Lady Talia Armstrong out of the helicopter's bubble cabin and settled her into her skeletal wheelchair.

'She must be a Power,' S said.

'She's definitely scary,' Winters said. 'Be careful about what you say to her.'

'Don't give any secrets away.'

'Exactly. Remember that she's only on our side so long as she thinks we're useful.'

'Like Bailey.'

'Yeah. A more polite and refined version of Bailey,' Winters said. He hadn't told the kid about the investigator's allegation, felt bad for wondering if there might be some truth to it.

Talia Armstrong was rolling towards them in her wheelchair. Bailey and Ida followed behind, Ida lofting a large green umbrella to shelter her charge.

'I believe that you helped to lead Bailey to our guest,' Talia Armstrong's machine voice said to S, after Winters had introduced them.

The kid shrugged.

'They're being modest,' Winters said. 'Bailey couldn't have found me without their help.'

Talia Armstrong was wearing a thin black leather jacket and matching black gloves. A tartan blanket tucked around her legs. The thumb and forefinger of her right hand tapping and skating on the tablet strapped to the arm of the wheelchair, conjuring words and phrases. The synthetic voice saying, 'Bailey told me that you were being held prisoner.'

'It was a bit more complicated than that,' Winters said.

'Did you learn anything about your sister, or my son, from your captors?'

'Rob Copely hinted that he knows a few things about Isabel, said that I would find out more from the people he was taking me to. I don't know if he was telling the truth, or if he has any new information about the siege. He told me that he left Wakestone before the raid on the spaceport and all the rest. Was ordered to by Kasey Motte, because Motte wanted him to take care of the special strains of mushroom he and his followers used.'

'Does he strike you as a truthful person?'

'I think he wants to seem more important than he is.'

'My impression also,' Bailey said. She had turned up the collar of her suit jacket, was sort of hunched in the gusty rain. 'He wants to be thought of as a proper villain. Old school. But he came over from France on his own, has no backup apart from his wife, who looks after his grow-ups here. I think he's a small-time grower and distributor with some kind of connection with the deep dreamers, he heard about Mr Winters and his search for his sister, and decided to make a play.'

'The person who kidnapped me was on his payroll,' Winters said. 'But she'd also been working for the deep dreamers, keeping watch on where I lived and worked in case my sister turned up. And then the deep dreamers decided that they needed me too, and here we are.'

Talia Armstrong's hand moved on the tablet. 'In short, Mr Copely is potentially useful, but possibly untrustworthy.'

'He's still a believer,' Winters said. 'He took part in Motte's first reset, and it did something to his head – it did something to everyone involved, including my sister. He really thinks it changed the world, and the deep dreamers' instauration thing will change it again.'

'Nevertheless, he is also a kind of business person. He wanted to make a deal involving you and these deep dreamers, so I may be able to make a deal with him.'

'I hope you're not still thinking of paying him,' Bailey said. 'If he's given so much as a sniff of credit, he'll most likely tell you anything he thinks you want to hear.'

'We are going to try your way first,' Talia Armstrong said. 'Offer to free him without informing the police of his various transgressions, in exchange for a candid conversation. I expect that he will want more than that, but it is a good starting point. How does that strike you, Mr Winters?'

'As long as that candid conversation covers what he knows about my sister.'

'Of course. Are we ready to begin?'

'Give me a couple of minutes to make him presentable,' Bailey said.

Rob Copely was courteous to begin with. Bailey had moved him off the loadbed of the pickup and sat him in one of the folding chairs, and although he was zip-tied at wrists and ankles he jacked to his feet as Talia Armstrong rolled towards him, and sketched a bow and apologised for his situation.

'This is not how I would have chosen to meet anyone. And certainly not someone as distinguished as you.'

'So you know who I am,' Talia Armstrong – her synthetic voice – said.

Winters and Bailey were standing behind her wheelchair. S had been parked in the passenger lounge, with Ida. Bailey's idea. There was no need to burden the kid with more than they already knew, she'd said. All the overhead lights in the hangar had been turned on, brighter than the rain-dimmed daylight.

'One of the grieving parents whose children were lost in the fire,' Copely said. If he was surprised by Talia Armstrong's wheelchair and voice generator he didn't show it. 'The leader, I believe, of the group campaigning for a new enquiry into police actions during the siege. I wish you all the best with that, seeing as I also have reason to dispute the official version.'

'Please sit down, Mr Copely,' Talia Armstrong said. 'We have much to discuss, and I don't want to get a crick in my neck.'

Copely studied her for a moment, his smile fixed in place, then sat. 'I admit I'm surprised to discover that someone like you is involved in something like this. I truly am. I mean, a former barrister, her late husband a knight of the realm, commissioning yonder bulldog to kidnap me, hold me against my will? Police wouldn't look kindly on that if they found out.'

'And who will tell them? Not you, Mr Copely, as it would put you in considerably more jeopardy than me. Forcible administration of unlicensed drugs, conspiracy to supply. Abduction of Mr Winters, which forced my employee to act as she saw fit in order to rescue him. And if the counterterrorism police and the National Crime Agency find out that you are still alive, they will want to question you about your involvement with Kasey Motte and the siege of Wakestone Farm.'

'Ancient history, seeing as I had nothing to do with it.'

'I'm certain that the authorities believe otherwise.'

'As for Marc, I rescued him from his actual kidnappers. Was in the process of taking him where he wanted to go when your bulldog tased me and took me prisoner.'

'That's one point of view,' Winters said.

'Not to mention I'm a French citizen,' Copely told Talia Armstrong. 'So there's a diplomatic angle you need to consider.'

'I see from your passport that you presently go by the name of Simón Bolívar.'

'Because it's my actual name. Had it officially changed.'

'I wonder what the leader of the liberation of former colonies in South America would think of you taking his name in vain.'

'If you want to ask him, you'll have to dig him up first.'

'I could make a deal with the counterterrorism police. They would not especially care about how I acquired you. And do you really think that the French authorities would come to your aid, given your real identity and the terms of the bilateral extradition treaty?'

Rob Copely didn't answer. Rain rattled on the high roof. Somewhere inside the hangar, water was steadily, monotonously, dripping into water.

'This is what I propose,' Talia Armstrong said. 'You will help me by giving full and truthful answers to my questions. And I, in turn, will help you return home.'

'You're saying you'd get me back to France. Wouldn't turn me over to the authorities. To be clear.'

'You are in something of a pickle, Mr Copely. But I can help you to get out of it.'

'And the police? Not just the counterterrorism mob, but also the ordinary variety.'

'Would not need to know about any of this.'

Copely pretended to think about that. 'What kind of answers are you looking for?'

'You knew my son. William Armstrong.'

'Billy X was the handle he went by in the commune. If I tell you what I remember about him, you'll let me go?'

'Also everything you know about the deep dreamers, and what they want from Mr Winters and his sister.'

'Everything you wouldn't tell me,' Winters said.

'All you have to do, Mr Copely, is answer my questions as honestly as you can,' Talia Armstrong said. 'And then you can be on your way.'

Copely leaned forward, splaying his bound hands. 'Shake on it.'

Talia Armstrong scooted her wheelchair closer and they shook hands and she scooted back.

'So where do we begin?' Copely said.

Talia Armstrong tapped her tablet with her forefinger. 'My son's name – his assumed name – was on Kasey Motte's list of so-called saviours. Your name was on that list, too. As was the name of Mr Winters' sister. Both of you survived the end of the commune. Is it possible that my son also survived?'

'Why I'm here, talking to you, I wasn't there at the very end. Nor was Isabel for that matter. But I do know that when I left Billy was at the very centre of it all. Was part of Kasey's inner circle, one of the crew that raided the spaceport. Could he have survived? It's possible. But given how close he was to Kasey, the depth of his loyalty, it isn't likely.'

'In your opinion.'

'My informed opinion. Sorry to be the bearer and all that, but there it is.'

After a pause, Talia Armstrong's thumb and forefinger tapped at her tablet and her synthetic voice said, 'What else you can you tell me about my son?'

'What else would you like to know?'

'Everything you can remember about him.'

'He turned up at the commune a year or so before Kasey took over. He'd been on the drift, heard about the place from someone who'd heard about it from someone else, thought he'd check it out. He was already calling himself Billy X because he wanted to be rid of the family name. He never said why, he didn't like to talk about his old life, but I suppose he had a falling out with you and your husband. Pardon me, your late husband. He'd been to university, had Billy. Oxford, Cambridge. One of those places. Was on the first rung of the career that was supposed to take up the rest of his life. Something in politics, wasn't it?'

'PPE. At Oxford.'

'He said that he'd burned out, trying to keep up with what he was expected to be. He couldn't face it. Didn't want it. Revolted against it and dropped out, went on the drift, and acquired a bad habit that numbed the war in his head. As in good old heroin. He was smoking, not injecting, but still, addiction's addiction. He was in a fair old state, let me tell you, when he arrived on our doorstep.'

'So far you haven't told me anything I haven't already heard from other former members of the commune.'

'Who would those former members be?' Copely said. 'If you don't mind me asking.'

Winters was wondering about that too. Wondering if Charlie Lowe was one of them, and what that might mean.

'I think it best if they remain anonymous,' Talia Armstrong said. 'Please, continue.'

'You couldn't help Billy, but we could. He turned up at the commune in a right old state, as I said. He'd tried to get the monkey off his back before, tried going cold turkey, but it didn't take. We helped him get clean, properly clean, and gave him a chance to prove himself. As he did. He ended up working for me. Growing Kasey's shrooms. You might have met him,' Copely said to Winters, 'when you came a-calling for the last time.'

Winters flashed on the young man who had opened the door to the half-buried mushroom farm, on that last visit to Wakestone. Long hair and a surly manner, that was all he could recall.

'If I did, I didn't know who he was,' he said.

'We were his found family,' Rob Copely said. 'A relationship stronger than blood because we were forged in the same fires. Had similar problems to overcome. Understood each other in ways other folk never could.'

'You cured him of his heroin addiction,' Talia Armstrong said. 'And then you got him hooked on something else. These shrooms of yours.'

'We all took them. It was part of our thing.'

'Kasey Motte's cult,' Winters said.

'Other people called it that. We never did. We were a family.'

'And Motte exploited that. Your found family. Got inside it, took it over.'

Winters would have said more, but Bailey touched his shoulder and quietly reminded him who was running the show.

Talia Armstrong worked her tablet. 'You are claiming that William was an integral part of this thing of yours.'

'Very much so,' Copely said. 'At the core of it, you might say. The inner circle. Which I never was, even though my work was essential. Even though I had the skills and the knowledge that Billy lacked.'

'You must have resented that.'

'It was what it was. For the common good.'

'Was that why you left? Because someone younger and less skilled had been given the recognition you felt that you deserved?'

'It wasn't anything like that.'

'What was it like, then? Remember that you promised to be candid.'

'There'd been a lot going on. Not only preparations for the Great Green Reset, but a fair few knockbacks, too. A good number of people had left. Then there was the thing with you,' Copely said, looking at Winters. 'Kasey inviting you to the commune, wanting to recruit you. Your sister interfering, turning you loose against Kasey's express wishes. He really did want to bring you into the fold, you know.'

'Then I had a lucky escape.'

'Wasn't so lucky for your sister. Did you know that she and Kasey were lovers?'

'I didn't,' Winters said, thinking it was probably a lie.

Copely smiled. 'I suppose there were all kinds of things she didn't tell you. I said, didn't I, that Kasey let her stay on after that business with you. And so he did, but he put an end to their relationship. And kicked her out of the inner circle, too.'

'Is that when she left the commune? How she avoided the siege?'

'No, she stayed on. She was still a true believer. At that point, at least. Just didn't want you to be involved.'

'How did you feel about her relationship with Kasey? You were handfasted to her, after all.'

It was a cheap shot, but so was Copely's dig about Izzy's secretiveness.

'That was in name only,' Copely said offhandedly. 'We weren't even living together. And Kasey was Kasey.'

'He could do what he wanted.'

'Why not? He was the man,' Copely said, and turned back to Talia Armstrong. 'And on top of all that, there'd been some heated discussions in the inner circle about the Great Green Reset. There was a faction who wanted to make a number of smaller resets. Reduce what Kasey called the human overburden in stages, so that we could be certain of what we were doing. While Kasey and the rest of us wanted to go for broke. One and done. Although it wasn't clear until later exactly what that entailed.'

'You mean the suicide pact,' Talia Armstrong said.

'Yes. The translation. But Kasey didn't reveal that until later. Anyway, there was a fair bit of back and forth, bad blood building, until Kasey had had enough. The man didn't usually get angry,' Copely said. 'But he blew up after one too many meetings of the inner circle, and that night the woman who'd been championing the gradual approach disappeared. Sarah Semple, maybe you remember her,' Copley said, looking at Winters.

'Yeah, I do.'

She'd served him the omelette laced with Kasey Motte's special shrooms, before the walk and talk.

'Kasey said she'd been kicked out,' Copely said. 'Exiled. But most of us believed that she'd been killed, and buried somewhere in the woods.'

'Did anyone challenge him about that?' Talia Armstrong said.

'No one dared. He was the man. And he had his bodyguards, who'd probably done the deed, to back him up. I'm not defending him. It was a bad decision. But we were getting closer and closer to the Great Green Reset, and the strain of holding everything together, the weight of it, was beginning to show. The man was short-tempered, gave orders that contradicted each other, long speeches about the forces arrayed against him . . . And he was doing shrooms more or less constantly, and drinking too. Alcohol, that is. Not a good mix. By then, the clock was ticking down, there were communal dream sessions and other exercises to get us all in synch. And at last Kasey explained how we'd save the world and what was expected of us. Our ultimate task and ultimate sacrifice, as he called it. The final reset, and the translation. How we'd reach far back in history and make the change, and pass over into the soul of the new green world. He told us anyone who wasn't on board with that could leave, join the mundane billions who'd be erased when the Great Green Reset was dreamed into being. At the time, bearing in mind what probably happened to Sarah, it didn't seem like it was much of a choice. Kasey made us swear an oath, absolute loyalty to the cause, and we all did.'

Talia Armstrong tap-tap-tapped on her tablet. 'Did William swear this oath? Did he stay?'

'Everyone did. Everyone was on board, including Billy. He was in charge of rehearsals for the raid,' Copely told Talia Armstrong. 'Did a pretty good job, too. You should be proud.'

She ignored that. 'You still haven't told me why you left, despite the oath that you swore. How you survived, while William, according to you, did not.'

'I'm just coming to that. And I didn't break my oath. Everything I did was for the good of the cause. One night, just before the raid, Kasey sent for me. He told me that he had chosen me for a special mission, said that he wanted someone to safeguard samples of his shrooms. He was ninety-nine per cent certain that everything would go as planned, but there was a possibility that Sarah Semple had been a police spy. That the authorities had some idea of what we were planning, and might try to intervene. So he wanted me to leave right away, take samples of his shrooms and keep them safe.

'And he wanted Isabel to go with me,' Copely said, turning to look at Winters. 'Because, you see, she knew how to use them, how to organise mass dream sessions and all the rest. And also, after what happened with you, because he was worried that she wasn't completely devoted to the great project. She'd been saying things that made her loyalty suspect. Made him think that she might be thinking of quitting. Running away. Maybe even going to the police. He didn't want to disappear her. That they'd been lovers was probably part of it. He had a generous heart. He told me that he was sending her away with me not only because of what she knew, but also because he didn't want any upset so close to the end of things. And said that he trusted me to do the right thing if it came to it. If she proved to be troublesome in any way. Put his legacy at risk.'

'In other words, he wanted you to kill her,' Winters said.

'Only if it was necessary. I wasn't too pleased about that, or any of the rest of it, either. But Kasey had put his trust in me, so what else could I do? He told me that if the reset went as he hoped it would, he'd make sure that I would still join the world soul. But if the worst came to the worst, as of course it did, I was to use the shrooms and Isabel's knowhow to start everything over. And we wouldn't have to worry about the police looking for us, because our names would be on his rollcall of saviours. So I gathered up what was needed, and Isabel and I set off.'

'She agreed to this,' Winters said.

'She did. Gladly.'

Talia Armstrong punched her tablet with her forefinger. 'What about William?'

'I wish I could tell you what you want to hear. I really do. But like I said, I left the commune before the siege and everything that led up to it.'

'How long before?'

'Two days.'

'So you have no way of knowing if other members of the commune left after you did.'

'In all the years since I've never heard a whisper that Billy or anyone else quit in those last days. And if they did, if they're still knocking about, they never once thought to give me a call. But if you like, I can ask around,' Copely said, leaning towards Talia Armstrong. 'I have contacts your bulldog doesn't. If Billy is still alive, if he's hiding somewhere, I'm your best chance of finding him. Maybe you can tell me what that's worth to you.'

'Two former members of the commune have already made the same offer, but neither found anything useful.'

'They wouldn't have known Billy like I did. What with working alongside him, almost to the end. Wouldn't know how to begin to find out whether he's still alive.'

'Even though, in your informed opinion, it isn't likely that he is,' Bailey said. 'This man can't be trusted, ma'am.'

'I know. But I think he's given an honest account, all the same.'

Talia Armstrong and Rob Copely talked a little more, going over details of his story. Copely wouldn't or couldn't tell her much more about her son's relationship with Kasey Motte, saying that it was the business of the inner circle he'd never been a part of, but was more forthcoming when Winters asked him about what had happened after he and Isabel had left the commune, saying that they'd crossed the border into Scotland, using a route Isabel knew to avoid surveillance, and camped in a forest, waiting for the world to end.

'We were wondering what it would be like to be translated into the world soul,' he said. 'And frankly, I was wondering if Kasey had fixed it for her the way he promised he'd fix it for me, or if he wanted her to fall into oblivion along with all the unbelievers. What happened instead, Isabel woke me on the second night, showed me her phone. Some newsfeed about a siege at Wakestone. I still believed that there was a chance Kasey could pull it off, but no. The place went up, as planned, but the world was still the world. Nothing had changed except everybody I knew and loved was dead.'

Copely paused. He seemed to be genuinely affected by the memory. Eyes shining with unshed tears.

'Isabel was very cold about it,' he said. 'Said that Kasey had betrayed our trust in him. Had failed us. Asked me if I believed that what he'd planned was ever possible. I mean, after all we'd been through together? The first reset, all the work we'd put in . . . It was very cold. I didn't even want to argue with her. I went to sleep, and when I woke the next morning she was gone. Hadn't taken the shrooms, or any of the cash money Kasey had given me. Just upped and left. I didn't see any point in looking for her. I hid out for a few days, until I was certain the police weren't after me, and then I headed south, and did what I had to do to survive.'

'Selling the shrooms you'd been entrusted with,' Winters said.

'And looking for likely people who could help me do what Kasey had trusted me to do. As eventually I did. And now I'd like to know how you're going to get me home,' Copely said to Talia Armstrong.

She poked at her tablet. 'I have a few more questions.'

'I've told you everything I know, and more.'

'These are about the deep dreamers, which you also agreed to talk about. Answer as best you can, and then we can discuss your travel arrangements.'

'There better not be too many.'

'Where were you taking Mr Winters?'

'To a drop-off, of course.'

'A drop-off?'

'The place where I'm supposed to hand him over.'

'To the deep dreamers,' Winters said.

'That was my understanding.'

Bailey said, 'How did you contact them? Do you know their names?'

'They've never given up their real names, and I've never met them,' Copely said. 'We exchanged messages in a deepnet chat group. End-to-end encryption, erase on reading, secret agent stuff. But for the right inducement I could tell you where I was supposed to meet them.'

'There's no need,' Bailey said. 'The coordinates are in the navigation app of the phone I took off you.'

'So you got around to looking at it,' Winters said.

'I wouldn't mind having it back, now you're done with me,' Copely said.

'It doesn't have many contacts on it,' Bailey said.

'Well, I wouldn't bring my actual phone on a business trip such as this, would I?'

'There's a number for Dash Baker – the person who originally kidnapped Mr Winters,' Bailey said. 'One for your wife. And one other. Tagged with the initials M.D.H. Who might that be?'

'I might be able to recall that. For the right inducement.'

'Marquis d'Hervey,' Winters said.

Bailey and Talia Armstrong looked at him.

'It came up when I was trying to find the deep dreamers,' Winters said. 'An alias borrowed from a long-dead French guy who wrote a book about dreams.'

'The Marquis is one of the original deep dreamers,' Copely said, trying to get back in the game. 'They're well known, if you move in the right circles.'

'Do you know their real name?' Bailey said.

'I wish did. I really do. But, talking of moving in the right circles, we really should get down to discussing terms for employing me to find out more about Billy. William. If his last days really were his last days, and where he might be if they weren't.'

Talia Armstrong spent a little time on her pad. 'I think not,' its synthetic voice said. 'I will reward you for the information about William that you have disclosed, slight though it is, by arranging for your return to France. A short flight, courtesy of the custodian of this airfield, to a private airfield near Calais. And that will be the end of our relationship.'

'And what about my pickup? Not to mention some kind of compensation for this illegal detention, and losing my deal with the Marquis and his pals.'

'He could take me to this Marquis person, as planned,' Winters said. 'He'd get to keep his pickup and collect his fee, and we'd get a chance to find out about the deep dreamers. What they're planning. Whether they've found Isabel.'

'I could do that,' Copely said.

'It's a crazy idea,' Bailey said.

'Do you have a better one?' Winters said.

'Matter of fact, I do.'

After Talia Armstrong and her carer had departed in the helicopter, Bailey told Winters that it had gone about the way she'd expected.

'The man was playing her,' she said sourly. 'Having fun. Lady A knew it, she was trying her best to get past his bullshit, but she's out of practice and this isn't a courtroom.'

'The story about being entrusted with Motte's legacy could be true. It would explain why Isabel survived the siege.'

'It's a good story, but without some kind of corroboration that's all it is. And Lady A made a deal with the shitweasel. Shook on it, for fuck's sake. Which means I don't have any leverage with him now, and he knows it. If I question him, try to substantiate anything he told us, he'll laugh in my face.'

'So what next? What's this idea of yours?'

'A little something I set up before Lady A's intervention.'

'Am I part of it?'

Winters had been fretting about it ever since Bailey, with uncharacteristic coyness, had refused to discuss it in front of Copely. He was worried that she'd made a pre-emptive move that would either minimise his involvement or exclude him altogether.

'You're still here, aren't you?' Bailey said, and told him that one of her friends, a very technical guy, had helped her to unlock Rob Copely's phone. They'd found two texts, the ordinary, unencrypted kind, sent by Copely's contact, and Bailey had replied to them. Apologising for the delay in delivery, making up a story about complications involved with evading the police, asking if it was okay to meet in the same place. A new text had arrived almost at once, giving a new location at the edge of Thetford. Bailey's friend had traced the contact's phone to a nearby Travelodge, and loaded an app into Bailey's phone so that she could keep track of it.

'The meeting place isn't a bad choice,' Bailey said. 'Out of the way, exit routes to different main roads. But we won't need to use it if Copely's contact is holed up in that hotel for the night. I don't expect to learn much. Given the lack of security precautions, this is probably some kind of foot soldier, not one of the high command. But you never know.'

She assured Winters that she'd do all of the heavy lifting.

'Best case, I can ambush them in their hotel room, persuade them to have a nice little one-on-one chat. Find out where they're supposed to be taking you and for what purpose, see where that leads us. That's what half of my work is – talking to people. The rest, it's mostly going through records and archives. Very little of it amounts to what could even remotely be called excitement.'

Even so, Winters was worried about what he'd got himself into, resented her assumption that she was in charge, the way she'd been making plans and taking actions without bothering to consult him.

'This is still about removing the deep dreamers as a threat,' he said. 'Making sure they won't be able to get hold of my sister. And then, hopefully, finding her. Helping her in any way we can.'

'It's also about finding which parts of Copely's story are true. Finding out exactly what transpired at Wakestone in those last days, so that I can tell Lady A what happened to her son. Which is why she gave this the go-ahead.'

'Does she still believe he might be alive?'

'Hope is often hard to kill. We'll bring S along, too. What comes next might prove whether or not they're part of the deep dreamers' game.'

'I know that they aren't.'

'Whatever they are, they aren't your usual drifter.'

'This is what, your police sixth sense?'

'I know you know it too. Before we hit the road, I need to ask Ivor for a little favour with regard to Mr Copely.'

She told the airfield's manager that she'd set up a meeting with one of Rob Copely's associates, said that it would be a big help if he held on to the man for a couple of days before flying him back to France.

'I want him to be kept incommunicado until everything's done and dusted. And of course I'll pay you for the extra trouble.'

'It won't be a problem,' the manager said. 'I have a client coming in this evening from Switzerland, but nothing else until the weekend. Will flying your friend out on Thursday evening fit with your plans?'

'We'll be done by then. One way or another.'

'Good. Meanwhile, I'll keep that hangar locked. Your friend can kick off all he likes, no one will hear him.'

'Will there be any difficulties with the other people working here?'

'You can trust them to be discreet. And I'll fly him to France myself. I'm a partner in the limited company which owns the Cessna your friend is currently sharing quarters with,' the manager said, with a slight smile. 'A perk of the job.'

'You might want to take someone with you,' Bailey said. 'Someone who can take care of him if he tries anything.'

'He'll be restrained until we land. And if there is any unpleasantness, all I have to do is tilt the plane sixty degrees. The door swings open, I hit the snap on his harness . . .' The manager fluttered a hand downwards. 'Problem solved.'

Winters couldn't tell if he was joking or not. Maybe working for the rich made you cynical about every variety of human foolishness.

'Now there's someone I wouldn't mind doing business with again,' Bailey said, when they were outside again. 'You go get S, and I'll fetch the pickup and tell Copely what I've arranged for him.'

'I'd like a word too,' Winters said. 'There's something I want to ask him.'

'Then we'll say goodbye to the shitweasel together.'

'I'd rather talk to him alone. It'll give me a better chance of getting an answer.'

'What's the question?'

'It's kind of private. Something about me and my sister. Copely might be able to shed some light.'

'He's also an asshole who'll most likely flat-out lie, just for the fun of it.'

'I know. But I want to try.'

S showed Winters how to coax a measure of thick black coffee from one of the spouts of a machine that squatted like an antique brass dragon in the lounge's kitchenette, how to add a froth of steamed milk. Winters carried the heavy porcelain cup to the hangar, shielding it from the rain with one hand. Rob Copely dipped his nose towards the offering, inhaled appreciatively, eyes half-closed, and said, 'Got any sugar?'

Winters found several packets amongst the remains of last night's supper and emptied them into the cup. Copely cradled it in his hands and took a small sip, then a larger one, and said, 'So what's this in aid of?'

The overhead lights had been turned off and he was lounging in the camping chair in semidarkness and the hulking presence of the two aircraft, wrists and ankles still bound. Rain's white noise seething on the roof.

'You owe me an answer to a question,' Winters said. 'Something I asked you about yesterday. Before Bailey intervened.'

'Intervened. That's a nice way of putting it.'

'I asked you why the deep dreamers thought I might be useful to them, and you said that I was a man out of time. I'd like to know what that means. If it had anything to do with the way Isabel behaved towards me, the last time we met.'

'You mean when she set you free.'

'She set me free, and refused to come with me. Said she didn't want to have anything to do with me ever again. Words to that effect. She wouldn't explain why, but I think it was something to do with the first reset. So-called. Either something had changed, or she thought it had.'

Rob Copely took another sip of coffee. 'She didn't tell you what that change might have been.'

'No, she didn't. Which is why I'm asking you.'

'And Kasey, he didn't tell you either. Didn't explain his interest in you.'

'No, he didn't.'

'What will I get out of it if I enlighten you?'

'I didn't come here to make a deal. I'd just like to know.'

'I'm not sure that you would.'

'So you do know.'

'Yeah, I know.'

'So what changed? Why did she do what she did?'

'It's simple. You're here now. As real as anyone else. But once upon a time you weren't.'

'You mean before the reset.'

'In the before time, as Kasey called it. The time that everyone involved in the reset remembers, but no one else does. Especially you, because you weren't around in that before time.'

'Isabel thought . . . what did she think? That I had died, before the reset? And afterwards, somehow, I hadn't?'

'If that's all there was to it, I have no doubt she would have welcomed you back with tearful joy. But this was something deeper than death,' Copely said, giving Winters a sly look, daring him to guess.

Winters realised what he must mean. 'She thinks that I didn't exist, in that before time of yours.'

'Bingo. According to Isabel, you were a creation of the reset. In the before time, you had zero history. You were nothing. Less than nothing. Nada. An egg that was never fertilised. Or if it was, one that never took. As for Isabel, she was an only child. But after the reset, when she woke for the first time in the world she helped to dream into being, she suddenly had all these memories of growing up with her brother. And she still had memories of the before time, too. The time when you weren't. So you see the conflict.'

Winters laughed. It was so completely ridiculous and Rob Copely was so fucking serious.

The man saying now, 'Sorry to be the bearer, et cetera. It must be a hard pill to swallow. But all of us who were at the heart of the change remember the world as it was as well as the world as it is now. And Isabel remembered being an only child in that world.'

'Which is not how I remember it,' Winters said.

'Well, you wouldn't. For one thing, you're a creation of the reset, so how could you have any memories of a time when you didn't exist? For another, the only people who remember how it was in the before time are the people who were at the heart of the reset. I was there. I helped to dream this world into being, and I know that there was another world, another history, before the world as it is now. The original world. The original history, that only we remember. The commune as it was before we changed everything. The struggle for survival. The terrible things we had to do in a world on fire. Both are real. Both are true. But which one feels realer, truer? The world we lived in most of our lives, or the world we dreamed up?'

'You're saying that Isabel knew that I was her brother, but she couldn't or wouldn't believe that I was real.'

'We all went a little crazy after the reset. Each in our own way. Some couldn't handle it at all, and left. Like Dash. The rest of us learned how to cope, in our different ways. Kasey told us we should forget the past and embrace the new world we'd made, and that's what Isabel was trying to do when you turned up. No longer just an inconvenient memory, but living breathing proof that the shape of her life had been completely altered. Can you imagine the rude shock of that? Why she couldn't embrace it?'

'So,' Copely said, with a cheerful smile, 'does that answer your question?'

'Did he give up anything useful?' Bailey said, when Winters found her.

'I'm not sure.'

'He tried to play you, didn't he? Got under your skin.'

'That's one way of putting it.'

'Well fuck him. He's history, far as we're concerned. We have better things to do. Give me a few moments with him, and then we'll be on our way.'

As they drove north and east along country roads in gusty rain, Bailey gave S the bare bones of her plan, told them that she was relying on them for backup. 'Nothing dangerous or difficult. Keeping watch on entrances and exits, and so on.'

'No problem,' the kid said.

'Two words I very much like to hear,' Bailey said, looking sideways at Winters, as if daring him to object or tell S about her suspicions, the real reason why she wanted them to ride along.

While Bailey and the kid fell into a conversation about videos, the classic animes that she liked and the meditative, impressionistic mood pieces circulating in the drifter community, Winters brooded about Copely's claim that there had been a world before this one. A world in which Izzy had been an only child. A world in which he hadn't been born. Had never existed. Was it something Copely had made up to hurt him, or was it something Izzy and Kasey Motte had really believed, the reason why Motte had sent that bogus invitation? The man's claims about the power of dreams, his resets, were nothing but wild, self-aggrandising fantasies. Had to be. There was only one world. One life. This, and no other. But if Izzy had believed that her brother was an unwelcome imposter shaped out of her shroom dreams, it would explain her rejection, why she'd wanted to get him away from the commune and out of her life, why she'd never tried to get in touch with him after the siege. *I didn't ask for you to be born . . .*

Winters hoped that there was a more prosaic reason for her silence. But if that was what she still believed, if she hadn't seen through Motte's lies and mindfuckery after all this time, he'd have to find some way of convincing her that the memories they shared were real. That he was real, as real as she was. That they could find some way of regaining the closeness they'd once had, the history they shared. Those long hot sunny days on the common and in the fields and woods around and about, birdwatching, ticking off plant and insect species, hunting for fossils in the little quarries. Both of them in T-shirts and shorts and sandals, faces and arms slathered in sunblock. The stupid sunglasses with star-shaped frames that Izzy wore one whole summer. Her hair tied back with rainbow strings. She could identify birds by sight or song, knew the formal and common names of most grasses and flowers, and most of the ones which had been lost, too. Winters remembered the spot on the far edge of the common where she liked to sit, with its view across the floodplain of the Severn, and the hills and woods of the Forest of Dean on the far side of the river. Remembered her running over scorched turf, arms out like an airplane, or delicately wading through the barbed-wire margins of a bramble patch as she picked blackberries, or sitting in her favourite armchair during one of the power cuts, headlamp strapped to her forehead as she read a secondhand book she'd bought in the covered market.

The last summer they'd been together, just after Izzy's nineteenth birthday, they'd spent a weekend at a reconstruction rave. Riding there on an old coach with soft suspension and hard seats and no air-conditioning. Hot wind blowing through open window inserts, people singing old songs, 'Cripple Creek Ferry', 'Tub-Thumping', 'Shake It Off', and more, all the way to a spit of land in a loop of the Severn, one of the retreat zones where attempts to prevent flooding had been abandoned and the land had been given over to rewilding.

Their coach parked up alongside a couple of others in a rough meadow and everyone pitched their tents right away because they'd been warned that they'd be too tired to do it at the end of the day. On the far side of the field people were moving to and fro under canvas sheeting, and music thumped from a sound system on the back of a truck. Beyond, broad stretches of reeds, swales of coarse grass, and slants of mud ran along the river's edge, marshy land which was flooded whenever the

Severn was swollen by runoff after heavy rains, or by the largest of its famous bores, when high tides after every full and every new moon were funnelled into waves which raced upriver.

The rave had been organised to plant alder and willow saplings to stabilise the margins of the retreat zone and create patches of woodland that would soak up rainfall, slow erosion, and provide habitats for birds and small mammals. Most of the participants were in their late teens and twenties, but there were a couple of dozen kids around Winters' age or younger, and some older people from local Nature First! groups, too. Winters, like the rest of the kids, was tasked with handing out spades and stakes and dripping sacks of bare-rooted saplings to newcomers, and then carrying saplings to teams labouring along the edge of the retreat zone. Flags marking out sections flew from flexible poles in the hot wind. The DJ, barechested in a kilt, a cowboy hat clamped on his head, played raw beats that set the pace of the work, and red and green clouds burped from smoke generators and blew in ragged ribbons across the meadow and the marsh. After the lunch break, Winters was dispatched to the field kitchen to help prepare the evening meal, which was where he met Matty Holdness, almost exactly his age, with an electric smile and a frizz of golden curls held down by a scarf. Matty wasn't the first girl he'd kissed, but she was the one he remembered most fondly, remembered how they'd fooled around in long grass at the edge of the meadow as late evening reddened and faded and lights on and around the sound truck brightened and people swayed and twirled to cool-down music.

Everyone was back on the line early the next morning, Winters and Matty pairing up and working all day to keep the teams of tree planters supplied, and after supper Izzy found them and said that she'd arranged a special side-trip. One of the wildlife rangers overseeing local rewilding projects, a lanky, amiable guy in his twenties named Winston Collins, drove her and Winters and Matty several kilometres west in the long summer evening light, his fat-tyred runabout following an old tarmacadam road and a newly-laid track of recycled telegraph poles and steel mesh that ran through watermeadows of lush grass and tapestries of wildflowers and climbed a long shallow rise and passed through a belt of old woodland.

They parked in the turnout at the far edge of the woods and Winston told his guests to keep as quiet as possible and led them along a path through banks of bracken to the rushy edge of a pool. When he pointed out a mound covered in a thatch of broken reeds and twigs and branch stubs on the far side of the water Winters realised with a thrill of delight why they'd come here and Matty must have realised too, because her hot grip on his hand suddenly tightened. The mound was a beaver dam, one of more than a dozen in the local area, Winston said, diverting and slowing the course of one of the tributaries of the Severn and creating a meandering landscape of marshes, ponds and patches of woodland.

They sat in silence for a while, Winters and Matty leaning together, swatting at blackflies, stealing quick kisses, until Izzy suddenly startled and pointed. A beaver was moving steadily through the water towards the lodge, dividing a patch of duckweed and leaving a long vee-shaped wake that was still spreading across the pond when it reached the dam and clambered out of the water. Pausing for a moment, raising up on its hind legs to look around before diving into a gap between crossed branches and vanishing. They waited a while longer, as the sun began to set and the air darkened, but nothing else moved in or around the pond and at last Winston said it was time to go.

In the back of the runabout, Winters told Matty about the family of talking beavers in his grandmother's books, and they solemnly agreed that the real thing was equally magical, and much more important than anything in books. An agent of change, a glimpse of a better world. The next day was the last of the reconstruction rave, and at the end of it Matty told Winters that she liked him a lot, she really did, but she had a boyfriend in Bristol. So that was that. And a little later that summer Izzy left home, taking a path which eventually led to the commune in Wakestone and Kasey Motte and fantasies about dreaming better worlds into being. In years to come, Winters sometimes wondered if he remembered that brief sighting of the beaver because of Matty, or Matty because of the beaver. But both had been equally real, as real as anything or anyone else he could call up from memory, and he decided now that when he caught up with Isabel, if he ever did, memories of that evening in a summer long past would be one of the first things he would try to share with her.

The pickup was on a main road, four lanes cutting through conifer plantations in the rain and gloom of the day's long dying. Bailey drove at exactly the speed limit, passing trucks and road trains outlined in constellations of little lights, surfing drenching wings of spray. As they neared Thetford, Bailey turned off the road at a roundabout and trundled into a charging station. Winters and S followed her to the adjacent supermarket and in the café tucked in one corner of its airy glass and steel shed she bought them tea and wraps and checked the tracking app, said that the contact's phone was still off, but it didn't signify.

'No reason why they've moved, seeing as the hotel's close to where we arranged to meet. Which we'll check out, just in case, before I confront them and have a friendly little chat.'

'What do you want me to do?' the kid said. They'd eaten their sprout and yeast curd wrap in half a dozen big bites, were slurping iced tea from a cardboard cup.

'The hotel will have a service entrance. You'll hang out back there, keep watch. Let me know if anyone enters or leaves in a hurry. And you,' Bailey told Winters, 'can watch the main door.'

'I have another idea,' Winters said.

'If you want to swap around, watch the service entrance instead of the front, that'll work too.'

'Or you and S can watch the doors,' Winters said. 'While I go inside and find this contact.'

'I don't think so,' Bailey said.

'Why not? I'm the reason for this meeting. The package, as this contact of Copely's put it. If I turn up on my own, I can ask them to tell me everything they know in exchange for my cooperation. All you have to do is wait a short while, then step in.'

'And what am I supposed to do if they have pals? March you out of the hotel mob-handed, threaten to harm you if I try to intervene?'

'You can hang back and follow them. If they're some kind of foot soldier, they'll take me to the people they're working for.'

Bailey laughed, a low rasp like a motor trying and failing to start. 'If you think I can crash into some kind of deep dreamer lair and single-handedly overpower everyone in it, you've been watching the wrong sort of film. And the risk that Copely's contact might snatch you is exactly why I want you to keep out of the way.'

'While you do all the talking.'

'I don't know all the ins and outs of your job, but I doubt that negotiating with bad actors ever comes up.'

'I've had to deal with poachers more than once.'

'Not exactly in the same league as kidnapping and mad ideas about the power of dreams, is it?'

'You set this up without consulting me. And now you want to talk to Copely's contact without me. Even though we're supposed to be in this together.'

Winters had raised his voice in frustration. An elderly couple at a nearby table were looking at him and S smiled and stuck out their tongue and they looked somewhere else.

'And here we all are, getting ready to make our play,' Bailey said. 'And you need to do your part, and let me do mine.'

'If I let you do all the talking, I could at least come with you instead of standing outside in the rain,' Winters said, hating himself at that moment because he knew it sounded weak, knew he'd lost the argument.

'I get why you want to be in the room. I do. But as discussed, it's too risky,' Bailey said. 'And besides, it's more or less stopped raining.'

'You think you have an answer for everything.'

'Standing watch is an important part of jobs like this.' She reached into her pocket, took out Winters' phone and handed it to him. 'You or S spot any sign of trouble, text me. Text, not call.'

'S doesn't own a phone,' Winters said. 'That's why I lent them this one.'

'I'll add it to my to-do list. Meanwhile, stay cool. If Rob Copely is a typical specimen, it'll be a piece of cake. We'll be dealing with amateurs.'

Bailey's jaunty confidence didn't make Winters feel any better. His bladder was full, and after he'd emptied it in the supermarket's bathroom he did that thing that people in films do, studying himself in the mirror, assessing his readiness, affirming his reality. Well, there he was, looking back at himself with a haunted expression, and it didn't help any. He used the credit stored in the phone to buy a packet of five joints and a book of matches, found S waiting outside the exit, under the raked canopy.

'Where's Bailey?' Winters said.

'She went to the bathroom too. And said she'd get me a phone,' the kid said, watching as Winters lit up and took a long drag, shaking their head when he offered the joint to them.

'I forgot, you don't partake,' Winters said. 'Sorry about losing my temper in there.'

'It's okay.'

Winters took another drag on the joint, the smoke hot and sweet in his mouth. It was a commercial blend that was even weaker than Goodberry Tea, but he could feel it beginning to blur the edges.

'She's working for Talia Armstrong, so she has different priorities. And her attitude, the way she acts as if she's in charge, doesn't exactly help either. Which is why we're supposedly working together, but actually pulling in different directions.'

'You're finding it hard to trust her.'

'She's made it pretty clear that she doesn't trust me. And it's likely that she doesn't entirely trust you, either,' Winters said.

'Well, she used to be police. They're not big on trust.'

'Why did you come along? I mean, this isn't your hunt. You don't have any skin in the game.'

'I still owe you.'

'Because I hauled you off that mudbank? That was my job. No need to take it personally.'

'And you found me a berth with Teddy.'

'Which you repaid by steering me towards that Megan woman.'

'That didn't work out so well, so I don't know if it counts. And anyway, it's all very interesting.'

'You're a mystery, kid.'

'I don't mean to be. Here she comes.'

Bailey handed a phone to S, told them she had plugged in her number. 'It's the only one you need. There aren't many minutes on it, so use it only when you have to.'

They drove a short distance along the main road, to the next junction and the industrial estate where Bailey had agreed to meet Rob Copely's contact in the morning. She pointed out the spot, a parking lot sheltered by a hawthorn hedge, and spent a little time driving back and forth along stub roads between industrial sheds and warehouses and trade suppliers. Everything gleaming in the glow of streetlamps like a hyper-real set in a film or a game.

'Plenty of hiding places,' S remarked.

'For us as well as them,' Bailey said. 'If the hotel is a washout, we'll come here early. Set up a couple of hours in advance, check that no one is waiting for us, make sure that if things go wrong we have a way out.'

'I'll find anyone who tries to hide from us,' S said, serious and serene.

Bailey drove back to the ring road and took the second exit for the town, following a circular route to avoid the pedestrianised centre and coming at the hotel from an odd angle, slowing as they went past. It was above a row of shops, two storeys of metal-framed windows and stained concrete panels facing a bridge across the river which ran through the town. The bridge was guarded by a camera filter signposted against traffic other than bicycles and emergency vehicles, and Bailey made a left turn onto a narrow road that ran parallel to the river and stopped and told Winters and S that this was where they got out.

'Get to your positions, stay out of sight and stay alert. You're my eyes and ears while I'm inside. Anyone you don't like the look of comes in or out, you know what to do.'

'Text, don't call,' S said.

'There it is.'

Winters watched as Bailey drove off and took the next left, circling back to the hotel, and when he turned to the kid they weren't there. He took up station at the corner, with a view of the road and the bridge, and the lighted entrance of the hotel at the end of the row of shops. Apart from a pair of strollers on the walkway on the other side of the river no one was about. After a couple of minutes the pickup returned and angle parked outside the hotel, and Bailey climbed out and walked purposefully into the entrance.

Winters studied the scattering of lighted windows above the shops, wondering if the contact was behind one of them. Who they were. If there was more than one person waiting. What they'd say when Bailey knocked on their door. Or kicked it in. She hadn't explained what he and the kid were supposed to do if she got into trouble. More of her bullshit control freakery, her overconfidence in her ability. It occurred to him that she might give him up to the deep dreamers if she thought it would help her find out what happened to Talia Armstrong's son. Not a good thought to have while standing alone in the warm damp dark of this strange town.

Five minutes passed. Ten. He was wondering if something had happened to Bailey, should he text her, when two figures hurried out of the hotel entrance and scrambled into a bubblecar and shot off towards the bridge, triggering a flash from a traffic cam as it passed through the filter. Winters shook out his phone, was thumbing a text when a scooter cut past him, its rider's face hidden by the visor of their crash helmet, and set off another flash as it zipped across the bridge. Moments later, Bailey came out of the hotel and trotted towards the pickup, and Winters ran across the road and swung in beside her as she kindled the headlights. S was already in the cab, leaning forward on the bench seat behind Bailey, explaining that the scooter's rider had run out of the service door at the back of the hotel.

'Two people came out of the front,' Winters said. 'Left in a bubblecar.'

'Which way did they go?' Bailey said.

'Over the bridge. Like the scooter.'

The traffic cam's flash flared in the windscreen as Bailey eased the pickup through the filter. There was a market square beyond the bridge and the scooter was sitting on the far side, caught squarely in the pickup's headlights and suddenly on the move, swerving off down a narrow street. Bailey slowed, looking left and right, and turned in the opposite direction, another traffic cam flashing as she cut around a planter. Saying, as the pickup scraped between bollards, that the fuckers wanted her to try to run down the scooter, it was an obvious diversion, and this was the only other way out of the square.

'What if the bubblecar went the same way as the scooter?' Winters said.

'Trust me, it didn't.'

When they reached a junction with a main road Bailey paused before driving straight across, into a long, narrow residential street. The pickup's motors whined as she accelerated, and Winters spotted the bubblecar at the far end of the street, its tail lights briefly flaring as it turned right. Bailey took the corner at speed, Winters' seat belt digging into his shoulder and chest as she braked hard, stopping the pickup a bare couple of metres from the entrance to a pedestrian underpass that tunnelled beneath a road embankment.

Bailey slammed out of the pickup and trotted towards the underpass. Winters and S followed her into a dimly lit arched tunnel clad in corrugated steel, thickets of graffiti glowing and blinking on either side, a block of lettering catching Winters' eye as he tried to keep up with the kid. Following them out of the far side into the damp night air, Bailey standing foursquare in the middle of a cycle path pinched between the embankment and back-garden fences, aiming her taser at the dwindling tail lights of the bubblecar.

'I underestimated them,' Bailey told Winters and S as she drove them back to the hotel. She was in a sour mood that hadn't been improved when Winters pointed out the spraypainted slogan, THE INSTAURATION IS COMING!, as they walked back through the underpass. 'They were prepared for trouble. Had an escape plan. I should have scouted the hotel first, instead of banging straight in.'

It was the kind of cheap place that didn't have a desk clerk or any other human staff on the premises out of hours, she said. Where guests booked by phone, and a couple of housekeepers on basic wages came in every morning to set out tea and croissants, make up vacated rooms.

'I started to knock on doors, telling anyone who answered that I was security, following up on a reported robbery. There were only a couple of guests on the first floor and none of them seemed likely, so I went up to second, and there was a fellow using one of the vending machines at the far end of the corridor. I looked at him, he looked at me, and he booked. Banged straight through the emergency exit. I tried to give chase, but he had a good head start and I'm not built for speed. He must have alerted his pals, and here we are.'

'Do you think they'll come back?' Winters said.

'To the hotel? No chance. But I hope that the deep dreamers will pitch up at the rendezvous tomorrow. That they're still expecting Rob Copely to hand you over. So why we're going back to the hotel, we need a place to stay for the night. And also, I want to find the shitweasels' room, see if they left anything behind,' Bailey said, and told Winters and the kid to wait in the pickup while she did a quick recce.

After she'd left, Winters powered down the side window and lit one of his supermarket joints. He didn't care if Bailey kicked off about it. He needed something to ease his jitters, and anyway, the pickup wasn't hers.

'This thing about bubblecars is interesting,' S said.

Winters blew smoke into the dark air beyond the open window. 'What thing is that?'

'I've never given bubblecars much thought before, but now I've been in two chases involving them.'

'There was a scooter, too. The bubblecar thing is just a coincidence.'

'Maybe. But coincidences often reveal deeper patterns.'

'What pattern do you see here? Anything that might help finding the deep dreamers?'

Winters, remembering Bailey's suspicions about S, was wondering if he could draw them into revealing something, but the kid shrugged and said that if Bailey was right, if the deep dreamers turned up at the meeting place, he'd be able to find out who they were and what they wanted.

'I hope so,' Winters said. 'But I have a feeling that everything's gone to hell.'

He was thinking of Rob Copely's mad story about his unbirth, or whatever you wanted to call it, wondering if the deep dreamers really believed that it gave him some kind of special power. If they did, if they were as crazy as Kasey Motte, it might be for the best if Bailey's failed ambush scared them off. If he gave up this wild quest before he got himself into some real trouble.

'It's been fun, though, hasn't it?' the kid said. 'The three of us working together.'

'Better not say that to Bailey. This has put a bad dent in her professional pride.'

When she returned, Bailey said that she'd found the shit-weasels' room, door wide open, but all they'd left behind were a couple of wet towels on the bathroom floor.

'It's possible I walked us into some kind of setup. Baited by a phone that in hindsight was too easy to track. They might have been spooked by the delay in delivering you, or I didn't come on like Rob Copely, or failed to use an agreed safe word. So they decided to lure me in, see who I was.'

'So they weren't amateurs after all,' Winters said.

'Oh, I think they very much were. Professionals wouldn't have cut and run. They would have tried to take me down, find where I'd stashed you. Only smart thing I did was insisting on keeping you out of harm's way.'

'Yeah, I know now that I shouldn't have asked to go in there on my own,' Winters said.

'We both got things wrong,' Bailey said. 'The difference is, I'm being paid to get things right. I booked a room. You want to finish that joint you stubbed out when you saw me coming, you'll have do it before we go in. I don't want to pay a cleaning fine.'

Winters took the double bed, S curled up on the floor, and Bailey staked out the lobby all night, like a cat at a mousehole after the mouse had escaped. Nine in the morning, they drove to the car park in the industrial estate. Bailey sat in the pickup, waiting for the shitweasels or their bosses to turn up, and Winters and S lurked in the bushes. The time agreed for the rendezvous came and went, no one showed and no one answered when Bailey texted the contact's phone, and at last she drove Winters and S to the nearest railway station and turned them loose. Shaking hands with Winters, saying that she was sorry that things hadn't worked out, she'd be in touch if Lady Armstrong decided to continue the investigation, and drawing him into an unwelcome clinch and whispering that she couldn't tell if S was some kind of holy idiot or an especially sly stool pigeon, but maybe Winters should keep an eye on them.

It took Winters and S several hours to get back to the Blackwater Estuary. Two changes of train and a bicycle ride from Maldon to Heybridge Basin, where they parted. If Rob Copely had been telling the truth, which was a big ask, Winters had learned something useful about how Izzy had escaped the siege, but he'd also been told something he didn't care to believe, and knew it was going to nag at him. Otherwise, the adventures of the past three days had pretty much been a comprehensive disaster. Chaotic, randomly terrifying and, at the end, with the farcical car chase and the pointless stakeout in the liminal space of the industrial estate's car park, humiliatingly absurd. Even S was subdued, although they perked up a little on the first train ride, leaning their head against the window and watching scenery unspool, remarking that it had been years since they'd travelled like this.

'How do you usually get about?'

'Walking, mostly. Sometimes strangers will give you a lift, or you can jump a road train, but mostly walking.'

'You started off in Bristol,' Winters said. He still knew very little about the kid. Why they'd left home, the places they'd been and the things they'd done, the people they'd met along the way.

'That was another life.'

'And you've been walking ever since. That's a lot of road.'

'Not all of it was on roads.'

'You must have seen all kinds of places.'

'I've never been to Thetford before,' the kid said, as if it had been a notable addition to their itinerary.

'Nothing against the place, but I'm not planning to go back,' Winters said.

'What are you planning to do?'

'I don't know. I've kind of run out of leads.'

'Will you be seeing Bailey again?'

'I think we're done. And I'm pretty sure she feels the same way.'

When they reached Heybridge, the kid cycled off to Teddy Stokes' place and Winters took a shower in his room in the Old Ship and more out of habit than hope checked the phone he'd left behind, the one whose number he'd given out when he'd made his public appeal. And there it was, highlighted amongst messages from journalists and a scatter of trollish threats and insults that had escaped the filter. The thing he most wanted, waiting for him all the time he'd been chasing it elsewhere. A message from his sister.

Part Four

Wakestone

'She put the name of our neighbour's dog in the header,' Winters told Jude. 'To make sure it would grab my attention.'

'So does she want to see you? Does she need your help?'

'I don't think so. And kind of.'

Izzy had sent the message two days ago, around the time Bailey had been driving Winters and S to the airfield in Rob Copely's pickup, with Copely trussed up on the floor of the cab. He'd hesitated before opening it, feeling that he was at some kind of hinge-point, and when he did a low resolution video began to play and he was gripped by a whole-body shiver because there she was. Izzy, leaning close to the camera, her face filling the window, the bill of a green cap pulled low over her eyes, nothing but deep shadow in the marginal space behind her. Her lips were moving but there was no sound until Winters, with a flutter of panic, turned the phone's volume all the way up.

'. . . don't try to find me, either,' she was saying. 'But if you want to help, you could try to do something about the Marquis. They want to get hold of me and they're planning something big and stupidly dangerous. Find out who they are, or tell the police to get on to it. And if the police are watching your phone, which they probably are thanks to your stupid stunt, they should know that I didn't have anything to do with taking hostages and I was never at the siege, I left Wakestone before that shit show. Okay, bye. And don't worry about me. I have friends. I'm safe,' Izzy said and the video's window folded in on itself.

Winters told Jude that the message was still on his phone, but the link to the video was futzed and he couldn't find a way of replaying it. It wasn't in the phone's download folder, wasn't in the bin or the spam folder, wasn't anywhere, and when he'd tried to send a reply it had bounced right back.

'The important thing, Isabel's safe and well. The deep dreamers haven't caught up with her. And maybe she doesn't want to meet up, but she does want me to find out who this Marquis character is. Which is what I've already been trying to do,' Winters said, and told Jude how he'd discovered that the Marquis d'Hervey was a pseudonym of one of the leaders of the deep dreamers. 'And what Isabel said, about leaving Wakestone before the siege? Someone who was part of the cult told me she was supposed to help them look after Kasey Motte's legacy, but ran off when it became clear that Motte's crazy plans had come to nothing.'

They were sitting in the shade of Jude's boathouse. Late afternoon, hot and humid. Swallows swooping above flooded mudflats. A million points of sunlight dancing across water bright as hammered steel, Cynsea Island and the far shore of the estuary shimmering mirages in the rippling haze. Winters had returned home, but he still had people to find, unfinished business to settle. It was an odd, lonesome feeling to be unmoored, virtually a drifter, in a place he knew so well.

'If you came here to ask for my advice, I think you already know what it is,' Jude said.

'Yeah, I do. And you're probably right, but it's complicated.'

'I don't see the problem. All you have to do is tell the police what you've just told me, let them take it from there.'

'I'm worried that they'd be more interested in using Isabel's message to try to trace her, rather than look into the deep dreamers. And there are other people caught up in this. I could get them in trouble.'

If it came to it, he was certain that Talia Armstrong and Bailey could look after themselves, but he didn't want to endanger S. And he was going to have a hard time explaining how he knew what he knew. Rob Copely wasn't anyone's idea of a reliable source, and if he gave the man up to the police they'd almost certainly find out that he'd been kidnapped, held against his will.

Jude took a sip of iced tea and said, 'Do these other people know about the message?'

'You're the first person I've told.'

'So it isn't anything to do with them. And if it leads the police to wherever your sister's hiding, would that be so bad? If she really didn't have anything to do with the siege, maybe it's time she gave herself up.'

'There are a couple of loose ends I want to check out. If they don't lead anywhere, then yeah, talking to the police should be my next move.'

'That would be my first move, but okay.'

'I really do appreciate the advice. And your help with sorting out the boat rental.'

'Consider it fair exchange for the tip about the airjellies.'

Winters had forgotten about that, asked how it had worked out.

'I passed it up the line, said you'd seen something suspicious and asked me to deal with it because you were on leave. I got to ride along with the enforcement crew and the local police, and when we raided that barge we discovered that the people squatting there had just acquired a fresh batch. They've been charged for possession of illegal bioforms, but so far have refused to say where they got their little pets. Hopefully, their solicitor can persuade them to give up the breeder in exchange for a reduced sentence. But however it works out, it was a good catch,' Jude said. 'Earned you some good will. Please don't squander it on something hopelessly quixotic.'

'I'll be careful. It won't help Isabel if I get into trouble.'

'You better not. If you get yourself fired for crossing a line, I'll have to find another smoking buddy. And it won't be easy to replace you.'

S was waiting for Winters when he left the Old Ship the next morning, perched on the rail of the sea lock, reading a paperback book. As Winters crossed towards them, one of the ravens that hung around the pub, snaffling scraps left by visitors, flapped away.

'I didn't realise you were a reader,' Winters said.

'Teddy has a box of his mother's books. This one's about olden times in Jamaica. There's a preacher who can fly, and a woman who can see bad things before they happen, and all of it's told by another woman who's dead. It's interesting.'

'What are you doing here?'

'Was wondering what you were planning. If you needed help,' S said, with their usual cheerful insouciance. They were wearing the same baggy yellow pants, but had swapped their T-shirt for an overlarge blue Ipswich Town home shirt, its hem belling in the warm breeze.

'The past few days were so much fun, you've come back for more,' Winters said, wondering what the kid had told

Teddy about their adventures. He liked the old man, but if you wanted the entire estuary to know about something, all you had to do was mention it to Teddy, and wait.

'They were definitely interesting,' S said.

'Any new ideas about those unseen patterns of yours?'

'I'll tell you if I think of something. How else can I help?'

'I'm planning to see your dealer friend again. You want to, you can come along.'

Winters was wondering if the kid's interest was motivated by simple curiosity or whether, as Bailey believed, they had some kind of secret affiliation with one of the players in this tangle of intrigues and crazy conspiracies. If so, if he kept them close, he might learn something useful. And besides, things might go more easily with someone else at his back.

'She wasn't really a friend,' S said.

'But you know her, might be able to help me strike another deal. If she can't tell us anything about this Marquis, maybe she knows someone who can. And maybe she knows where we can find Dash, too.'

Winters was wondering if Dash Baker might have returned to the Forest of Dean after all. If he went looking for her there, he could make a detour to his childhood home and all of the old familiar places. Check in with Izzy's old Nature First! comrades, just in case.

'Let's go get a couple of bikes,' he told the kid. 'We have some distance to cover.'

They cycled to Maldon, and when their bus arrived hooked their bikes to its rack. But when they reached the hobbiton, they discovered that Megan Rix wasn't there. According to her neighbour, Mrs Tyler, she and her no-good boyfriend had moved out yesterday.

'A man came in a van, they loaded a few things on it and took off. I don't know where. I do know Megan didn't look too pleased about it,' Mrs Tyler said, with grim satisfaction. She was sitting in her lawn chair, a frail but triumphant sentinel, face shaded by the brim of a bucket hat. Telling the kid, 'We weren't introduced the last time you visited. I'm Blossom. Blossom Tyler.'

'S,' the kid said.

'Essie? One of my aunts was called Essie. Short for Esmeralda.'

'Just S.'

'Like the letter,' Winters said, and asked Mrs Tyler if she knew who the man with the truck was.

'Are you the police?'

'I guess you could say I'm an investigator,' Winters said, thinking of Bailey.

'Like one of those private detectives?'

'Yeah. Like that. I'd be really grateful if you could tell me what you know about this man.'

'He was a large person. Swarthy, with long black hair. And there may have been tattoos on his neck.'

'Blue tattoos? Like lettering?'

'I didn't see them very clearly. It was late in the evening and growing dark.'

'What about the backs of his hands? Did he have tattoos there?'

'I don't remember seeing his hands.'

'Tattoos of eyes.'

'I don't recall,' Mrs Tyler said. 'But I took a picture of the van. I try to keep a record of all her visitors. Just in case there's trouble.'

She fussed with her phone, a hard-shell model that reminded Winters of CeCe's old phone, eventually managed to locate the photograph. It was crooked and somewhat out of focus, but the van's number plate was readable and Winters made a note of it.

'You make a good witness, Mrs Tyler.'

The registration number wasn't much use, he didn't have the kind of contacts who could help him to track it down, but it might give him some useful leverage with Bailey if he was ever desperate enough to ask her for help.

'Is Megan in trouble with the law?' Mrs Tyler said. 'I mean more than the usual trouble.'

'I think she might be in trouble with someone else. Nothing for you to worry about,' Winters said, and gave her the numbers for both his phones, asked her to give him a call if Megan came back.

'Sounds as if you know who helped Megan,' S said, as they rode their bikes through the hobbiton, towards the road.

'Fellow name of Hari Pacek. Dash Baker pointed me at him before the kidnapping business, when I was trying to find out about the deep dreamers and this instauration thing of theirs. Told me he could help. Though as it turned out he was more interested in what I knew than in telling me anything useful. Megan Rix knew Rob Copley, and he was employing Dash. They're all connected with each other, though exactly how and why I still don't know.'

Winters was remembering the claustrophobic kitchen and Hari Pacek's creepy vibe, how he'd got the fear and bolted. He'd been lucky that time, but then he'd visited Megan Rix, and she'd given him up to Copely. And because Copely was in France at the time he'd asked Dash to organise a crew and carry out the snatch, the two of them survivors of the commune with a common interest in shrooms. It was possible that Pacek was this Marquis character, or was close to them. And although Copley had denied being a deep dreamer, he'd said that he was sympathetic to their cause, believed that Kasey Motte's resets were the real deal . . .

As usual, Winters knew just enough to glimpse what might be the edge of one of S's deep patterns, but had no idea what it meant. He hoped that he'd learn more from Copely's wife, the next loose end on his short list. He and S caught a bus back to Maldon and cycled through back roads towards Burnham-on-Crouch, high hedges and small fields giving way to an expanse of crop fields that stretched towards the blighted floodplain in a dazzle of late morning sunlight. A row of wind turbines in the distance, standing knee-deep in heat shimmer. A glimpse of what might be the blockhouse of a pumping station, maybe the same one Winters had seen from Dash's decrepit barge.

It was hot work, despite the assist from the bikes' electric motors. They stopped at regular intervals to drink from the bottles of water Winters had bought at the bus station, and when they reached the town they visited a café for iced tea, snacks and a little confidence-building session. Rehearsing what he needed to ask Copley's wife, Cleo. Knowing that she'd be hostile, hoping that threatening to go to the police about her role in his kidnapping, the illegal shroom grow-ups Copely had boasted about, would be enough to break her down. Telling himself it needed to be done, especially in the light of Megan Rix's flit.

The kid made a kale salad disappear in five minutes flat, but Winters was too nervous to eat more than a few bites of his wrap. They finished their iced teas and refilled their water bottles and took the ferry across the river and cycled to Cleo

Copely's bungalow. Winters' heartrate bumping up as they turned off the tarmac road onto the lane, passing through shafts of light prying between the windbent trees that overhung it, leaves glowing like a host of tiny green lanterns that he didn't like to look at. There seemed to be faces flickering in there, a host of watchful eyes.

When he and S reached the security fence and swung off their bikes the dog skittered around a corner of the bungalow and ran straight at them. It wasn't chained this time. Winters stepped back as it slammed into the gates and reared up on its hind legs, claws scraping at steel bars, spittle frothing between yellow fangs. Winters told it to take it easy and it stared at him with eyes black and lifeless as a shark's and slammed against the gate again. S stepped towards it, hands lifted, making sounds with their tongue. An irregular pattern of clicks and tocks that reminded Winters of the chatter of crows. The dog growled at them, but more in peevish complaint than fury. Dropping to all fours as the kid knelt in front of it and reached out, holding its gaze, letting it snuffle their fingertips.

Behind it, across the concrete apron, the front door of the bungalow cracked open and the woman, Cleo, stepped out and asked them what the fuck they wanted. Winters told her that he was sorry for the intrusion, he wanted to make sure that her husband had got home safely.

'He told me some ex-copper tased him and took him prisoner,' Cleo said. She was standing in a narrow slice of shadow, but Winters could see that her face was bruised and both her eyes were blacked.

'Yeah, she did. And after he told us everything he knew about the deep dreamers he was given a free ride back to France, instead of being turned over to the police for kidnapping me. I seem to remember that you had something to do with that,' Winters said. 'But if you help me out now we can call it even.'

'Call the police for all I care. It'll be your word against mine,' Cleo said.

'Not exactly. My friend here saw Dash Baker and her sidekicks ambush me. Followed her when she brought me here.'

'That's true,' the kid said. They were still squatting in front of the dog. It was squatting on its muscular hindquarters, panting hoarsely.

'Oh it is, is it? I don't even know who you are,' Cleo said.

'I can't help noticing your bruises,' Winters said. 'Are you in some kind of trouble?'

'That's none of your business,' Cleo said, with freezing dignity, and called to her dog. 'Vic! Leave it off. Come here! Come now!'

'Go on, Vic,' the kid said softly, and the dog turned and trotted towards its mistress.

'Did Dash and her friends came back?' Winters said. 'Looking for their fee, and a little payback for those hot shots. Or was it deep dreamers? A man named Hari Pacek, maybe. I know he has something to do with the deep dreamers, and he was seen not that far from here yesterday.'

Cleo pushed out her lips but didn't reply.

'Were you punished because Rob failed to deliver me to them? Did they warn you to keep quiet about their plans? If you can tell me anything useful about them, who they are and where I can find them, I won't trouble you again. Especially if it helps me find my sister. Isabel Winters – do you know who she is?'

'Oh I know her, all right. And I know that's she's beyond help. Yours or anyone else's.'

'What do you mean? Have the deep dreamers found her?'

'Rob was a fool,' Cleo said. 'Thinking that he could make a deal with crazy people. And you'd be a fool to keep at this. You got away this time, but you might not be so lucky again.'

'If the deep dreamers have my sister, I need to find them. Any help you can give me, I'd really appreciate it.'

'You really don't know, do you?' Cleo said.

'What don't I know?'

He was pleading, he knew. Not a good way to play this, but he was pretty sure that threats wouldn't work. Was pretty sure that she had been warned to keep quiet by someone who frightened her a lot more than he did.

'Your sister,' Cleo said flatly. 'She's dead.'

'What do you mean, dead?'

'Sorry to break it to you,' Cleo said, not sounding sorry at all.

'Are you sure? How did it happen? When?'

Anger was rising in him, hot and fast. He wanted to break through the fence and shake the truth out of the woman.

'You should give this up. Go home,' Cleo said and raised her hand. She was holding her phone. 'You remember how the gates work? That I can open them remotely? I'll give you two minutes' start, then you'll find out whether your little friend can stop Vic from tearing you a new one.'

When they reached the road, Winters pulled hard on his bike's brakes, swerving to a halt in a scatter of gravel, looking back at the lane tunnelling through the trees. Nothing moved in the slanting shafts of sunlight; there was no sign that Cleo had let her dog loose. But it wasn't the dog he'd been trying to outrun.

He said to the kid, 'She must have been lying. Do you think she was lying?'

'She wanted to hurt you.'

'Yeah. She's a piece of work, like her husband. And she was scared, too. Wanted to get rid of me. I think she was lying, but I need to make a couple of calls.'

He was carrying his old personal phone, in case Izzy called again. He'd copied some of the contacts from his work phone into it, including the details Detective Sinclair had sent him in what seemed like another era, and wasted five minutes navigating a stubbornly dumb automated gatekeeping system before reaching an agent which politely refused to put him through to DI Sinclair or DI Briggs, said that someone would return his call as soon as possible.

'Tell them it's about my sister,' Winters said, but the agent had already disengaged.

His next call, to the police station in Maldon, connected him to Detective Sergeant Grace Fairbrother in only two steps. After he'd explained why he was calling, she put him on hold, came back on line a long minute later and told him that there was no report of the death of Isabel Winters in the system. Explained with stony patience, after Winters asked her if that was what she'd been told to say, 'I fed your sister's name into LEADS. The national database. If her body had been found and identified it would have been flagged up there.'

'I'm trying to confirm something someone told me.'

'What exactly did they tell you?'

'Just that she was dead.'

'Did they give any details? How it happened, when and where?'

'I think it must have been very recently. No more than two or three days ago,' Winters said, thinking of Izzy's message.

'And who told you?' Grace Fairbrother said.

Winters briefly considered giving up Cleo, but knew that it might rebound on him. Open up the whole sorry business with Rob Copely and the fucked-up attempt to meet the man's deep dreamer contacts.

He said, 'Someone in the drifter community.'

'Do you have a name for this person?'

'Not really. Not their real one.'

'We have a database of street names that drifters go by.'

'I'd rather not.'

'That's up to you, but it means that I can't take this any further.'

'But if anything comes up. Officially, I mean. If anything comes up in the system.'

'You'll be informed, of course.'

'Call me on this number. I'm on leave at the moment.'

'Try not to worry,' Grace Fairbrother said. 'Drifters are not exactly reliable sources of information.'

'Anything?' S said, after Winters had rung off.

'The police say there's no record.'

'That's good. Isn't it?'

'I hope so,' Winters said, and called his uncle, was put through to a human assistant who told him that Mr Seddon was in a meeting, but any message he cared to leave would be passed on as soon as possible.

'Tell him it's urgent family business. He'll understand.'

Daniel Seddon called back an hour later, when Winters and the kid were halfway back to Heybridge. His uncle saying, 'Have you found Isabel?'

'Not exactly,' Winters said, and explained that he'd heard from someone not especially reliable that Izzy was dead. The kid stood nearby, holding the handlebars of their bike and looking out at a vast field of sugar beet that stretched beyond the narrow tarmacadam road. No one else about. Not a bird in the sky.

'Have you told the police?' his uncle said.

'I left a message with the counterterrorism people, they haven't got back to me yet. The local police say there isn't any record, but I don't know whether or not to believe them.'

The moveless air was packed with heat, but Winters felt a tingling chill in his core. He wanted to tell his uncle about the message from Izzy, but couldn't trust him to keep it to himself.

He said, 'I have a feeling, I don't know why, that it could be true.'

'Who was it who told you?'

'I don't think we should discuss it over the phone.'

'Then we should meet as soon as possible,' Daniel said. 'I'm in Manchester at the moment, a work thing, but I'll be back in London the day after tomorrow. Meanwhile, I'll see what I can find out.'

'Okay.'

'One way or another, we'll get to the bottom of this.'

Winters told S that everything was still up in the air and shook the last joint from the supermarket packet and lit it and drew in smoke to the bottom of his lungs and breathed it out. He knew that it was likely that Daniel would pass the news to Talia Armstrong, ask her to put Bailey on the case, but maybe it wouldn't matter, maybe nothing mattered, as long as he found out about Izzy. One way or the other.

'How can I help?' the kid said.

'I was planning to go look for Dash Baker,' Winters said, and realised that he'd forgotten to ask Cleo Copely if she knew where Dash was, if she'd returned to the Forest of Dean. The woman would most likely have refused to tell him, but still, he needed to be sharper than that, now more than ever. 'But my uncle wants to meet me in a couple of days, in London. So I should stick around here for now. Maybe we could find out if there are any rumours about Izzy floating around the drifter community. If anyone knows anything about this Marquis character. The Instauration and all the rest of it.'

'Okay.'

'You don't have to do this.'

'I know. But I want to.'

Winters took another long drag on the joint and studied the kid. Their slight smile and guileless gaze. He breathed out lungfuls of smoke and said, 'How did you calm that dog?'

'It's a drifter thing. We meet a lot of angry dogs.'

'Like a mind thing?'

'There's a tweak that makes skin bacteria produce pheromones that only dogs can smell,' the kid said, wiggling the fingers of one hand. 'Settles them down. Some of them, anyway.'

'I guess I don't know drifters half as well as I should.'

The kid shrugged.

'We can make a start in the green market,' Winters said. 'There are always a few drifters there, selling stuff they've gleaned from hedgerows or poached, trinkets and keepsakes they've tinkered up. We can talk to them, see if they know anything useful.'

The joint had bestowed a pleasant floating calm. A couple of years after Izzy had left home, their mother had found a lump in one of her breasts. She'd told Winters that it wasn't anything, had insisted on attending a day of hospital appointments for tests on her own. Now, he had the same feeling of suspension that had possessed him while he'd been waiting for his mother to come home. Hoping for the best but expecting the worst. Wondering, with more than a touch of self-pity, what the worst could mean, how it could change everything. When Julia had returned at the end of that long, long day, she had told him calmly that it was nothing. The lump was a benign cyst, she would have a little procedure to draw off excess fluid and that would be that. And so it was. The dire future in which Winters made a funereal journey north to tell Izzy that they had been orphaned died unborn. Banal normality resumed, except that Julia set aside the painting she'd been working on (Emotional Weather Report LXXXI) and spent two weeks perfecting a miniature view of the common in spring, cropped grass starred with purple orchids and yellow cowslips, a clump of hawthorns clad in a froth of the blossomest blossom imaginable, a sapphire sky irradiated with benevolent sunlight. A painting she'd never put up for sale or shown to anyone but her son, and then only briefly, shyly. He hadn't seen it again until years later, when he was clearing out the cottage after her death, and although he'd sent the rest of her paintings to her agent he'd kept that one, along with a sheaf of old charcoal sketches. It was still in the self-storage unit in Acton, strange to think, glowing like a gateway into a better world amongst the clothes and household gear and cheap furniture abandoned when he'd escaped to Europe in the aftermath of the siege.

He told himself that it had only been three days since Izzy had sent that video clip, That she was smart, a survivor. That Cleo Copely had most likely been lying. Even so, he desperately wanted confirmation, one way or another, before meeting his uncle. And if Izzy really was dead, he'd find out everything. The when and the where and the how. Take it to his uncle. Take it to Lady Talia Armstrong and Bailey. Take it to the counterterrorism cops. Burn down the deep dreamers and their fucking world. Burn down everything they believed in.

He stubbed out the half-smoked joint, told S they'd make an early start tomorrow. Hit the green market as soon as it was open for business, then move on to drifter camps and anywhere else where they could plug into the rumour network. But the next day, when he and the kid were eating breakfast at one of the tables outside the pub, big plates of beans and fried field mushrooms on toast, he saw the pair of counter-terrorism detectives coming along the quay towards them and he stood up to meet them, possessed by cold crystalline certainty. Knowing what they had come to tell him. Knowing that Cleo Copely had been telling the truth after all.

Isabel Winters had died in a road accident in Northumberland. Appeared to have been killed instantly when the pickup in which she was a passenger veered off a remote country road in a rainstorm, and struck a drystone wall headlong. The driver, gravely injured and trapped in his seat beside her body, died several hours later. They were found the next day by a farmworker. Isabel hadn't been carrying a phone or any ID, but a counterterrorism alert had been triggered when the local police ran her fingerprints and DNA through the national database.

'Which is when we took over,' DI Sinclair told Winters. 'We're sorry for your loss. And apologise for not contacting you sooner. Unfortunately, there were security issues.'

'It wasn't in the system,' Winters said stupidly. Thinking that this was what it felt like when the world switched to a new track, a different history. A numb, floating, out-of-body experience.

He was sitting with the two detectives at the table outside the pub, half-eaten plates of mushrooms on toast congealing between them. S had performed their vanishing trick when the detectives had appeared.

'We've had to suppress the usual reports,' Sinclair said, with the unruffled calm of an undertaker. 'I'm sure you understand why.'

'When did she, when was the accident?'

'Four days ago.'

'And I'm only learning about this now.'

'We needed to get the full picture,' DI Briggs said.

'And what is it? The full picture.'

'I'm afraid we can't share everything with you quite yet,' Sinclair said.

'No. Of course you can't.'

The accident had happened on the day Izzy had sent her video message. Something had spooked her. Winters was certain of it. She'd sent the video, ditched her phone so it couldn't be used to trace her, gone on the run. Hitched a lift, maybe. He briefly wondered how Cleo Copley could have found out about it before he did. Perhaps Hari Pacek had told her – perhaps the deep dreamers had something to do with the accident. There was so much he didn't know.

He said, more or less at random, 'Who was the driver?'

'Gabriel Middlemass,' Sinclair said. 'Did your sister ever mention the name?'

'Not that I know of. Was he a member of the commune?'

'He was a local man. We haven't discovered any connection to the commune so far, but enquiries are ongoing,' Sinclair said.

'You said this was in Northumberland. Was it anywhere near Wakestone?'

'We can go into that in the interview,' Briggs said.

'Why do you want to interview me?'

Winters was wondering if they knew about his kidnapping, and everything else.

'We hope that you might be able to help us fill in some gaps,' Sinclair said. 'And there's going to be a press conference later today. Full brass and braid. The works. You're invited to attend and give a statement.'

'What good would that do?'

'It will give you a chance to speak on behalf of your sister,' Sinclair said.

'And ask people who might have useful information to come forward,' Briggs said. 'You'll have a much bigger audience than a local news site.'

Winters ignored the jibe. He was seeing himself sandwiched by high-ranking police in their immaculate uniforms. The grieving relative, sweating in the spotlight as he read out a prepared plea for information. Facing the pitiless lenses of cameras and a barrage of questions from every species of journalist.

He said, 'What about the deep dreamers? Are you investigating them?'

'We are still looking into the events leading up to the accident,' Sinclair said.

There didn't seem to be any point in keeping Izzy's message secret, now. Winters told the detectives what she'd said, told them that she'd mentioned someone going by the name of the Marquis, who was most likely one of the deep dreamers. 'Have you heard the name? Do you know who they are?'

'That's one of the things we can discuss in a more formal setting,' Sinclair said.

'We'll need to see this message,' Briggs said.

'It seems to have sort of deleted itself.'

'Our technical people may be able to retrieve it. Do you have the phone on your person?'

'It sounds like I need a solicitor.'

'That's your right, of course.'

'Because I have the feeling that you're thinking of charging me with something.'

'Not at present,' Sinclair said.

'We're hoping you'll see the sense of cooperating,' Briggs said.

'My sister claimed that she'd left Wakestone before the raid and the siege. Can you look into that? Because if it's true, she's innocent. Didn't have anything to do with that whole mess.'

'At present we are focusing on the accident and your sister's movements in the days before,' Sinclair said.

'You should be focusing on the deep dreamers. They were chasing Isabel. They're the reason why she went on the run.'

'We can discuss all of that in your interview,' Sinclair said. 'Now is not the time. Given the circumstances. The shock of the news and so on. Meanwhile, we can organise transport if you agree to attend the press conference.'

'And we'll need your phone,' Briggs said. 'The one with the link to your sister's message.'

'Isabel's uncle. Daniel Seddon. Has he been told about this?'

'I believe two of my colleagues are presently with him.'

'And will he invited to attend this press conference?'

'It would be best if both of you were there,' Sinclair said.

'And if you gave the family statement,' Briggs said. 'Being Isabel's closest relative.'

'Because the media are interested in me, not my uncle.'

Neither Briggs nor Sinclair denied this.

'Where is she?' Winters said. 'Her body. Is it still in Northumberland?'

'We took possession of it,' Sinclair said. 'I'm afraid there will have to be an autopsy. Given the circumstances.'

'She left the commune before the siege. She didn't have anything to do with it. She was being hunted by people who meant her harm. Those are your circumstances.'

'I understand your anger,' Sinclair said calmly.

'Do you?'

'But none of us are as yet in full possession of the facts.'

'If I agree to the press conference, I want to see her,' Winters said. 'I want to see Isabel first.'

There was some to and fro. Sinclair excused himself to make a phone call, and Briggs asked Winters about S.

'They're just a friend. Doesn't have anything to do with any of this.'

'Nice trick, ducking out like that.'

'They're a drifter. People like you aren't especially sympathetic to people like them.'

'How did the two of you come to know each other?'

'I rescued them from a mudbank out in the estuary, after they got themselves stranded. It's a long story, doesn't have anything to do with Isabel.'

'Mind telling me their name?'

'I'll have to ask them if they mind first.'

Briggs let that go, but Winters knew it wouldn't be the end of it. Sinclair came back and said that he had arranged transport and a viewing of the body, asked Winters if he had a suit.

'There's one in a self-storage place in Acton. If moths haven't eaten it.'

'Maybe he should stick with the work jacket and shorts,' Briggs said. 'The media might go for the rugged outdoorsman look.'

'We can find you a loaner suit,' Sinclair said. 'Best be ready for an overnight stay.'

Winters packed a day bag, handed over his old phone after extracting a promise that he would be given a copy of anything the police technicians found, and was driven to London by a uniformed police officer in a powerful unmarked cruiser. The world blurring past at shocking speed. Amazing that people had once thought that this was a safe and completely routine way of travelling.

Neither Sinclair nor Briggs had come with him. Apparently they had a few things to clear up locally. The break-in and the cyberattack on the agency's system and so forth. Winters suspected that there was more to it than that, was worried that his uncle might have told the police about Talia Armstrong's involvement, that they were already looking into the kidnapping and his adventures with Bailey.

He pulled out his new phone, the one he'd bought in a supermarket a few days ago, and texted Teddy, asking him to tell S that he had to go up to London, and he'd appreciate it if they could tap into the drifter network as they'd agreed.

Teddy texted back at once, saying that he'd let S know as soon as they came back.

Maybe I'm confused, but weren't they meeting with you this morning?

They were. They did. Could you also tell them that police might come looking for them.

Hope you aren't in trouble.

Winters hesitated. Studying the back of the driver's head. A glimpse of her eyes in the rear-view mirror. What the hell. The kid might have told Teddy what Cleo had told him.

News will be out sooner or later, but this is in confidence. Police confirmed my sister is dead. Traffic accident. Let S know. Tell them I might have to head north, but I'll stay in touch.

A short pause before Teddy replied.

No problem. Very sorry for your loss.

It was what everyone said when they didn't know what to say about a death, but Winters appreciated it even so.

The mortuary was next door to St. Pancras Coroner's Court, across the road from an embankment topped by railway lines and catenaries of overhead power wires. Another blazingly bright day, dry leaves shed by wilting trees scuttling across the hot pavement on a furnace breeze as the police driver walked Winters to the entrance. No sign above the door. Death needed no advertisement. A mortuary assistant led him in silence to the viewing room. A pair of armchairs and a small table between them with a potted orchid and a box of tissues. An animated mural of woodlands wrapping three walls and a large blank window of whitened glass centred on the fourth. The assistant explained that his sister's body would be on view shortly, and withdrew.

Winters stared at the whited-out window, willing it to open, aware of sunlight glimmering through fresh green leaves at the edges of his vision, shifting stars dappling a carpet of bluebells that stretched into green shadows between trees. He told himself that the creepy feeling that there was something watchful lurking in those shadows was nothing more than stress and nerves.

It wasn't like his last visit with his mother, who'd been laid out in a coffin in a room with soft lighting and floral displays, dressed in a skirt and blouse he'd given to the undertakers, looking unnaturally neat and somewhat shrunken. The inevitable end of the long course of her ever-diminishing health. All her wild energies dispersed. He'd felt an aching loss then, sure, but also a measure of relief. This was different. The suddenness of it, after Izzy's message. All his hopes snatched away. The collapse of every possibility but this last. It was like one of those old cartoons where a character ran over the edge of a cliff and hadn't yet looked down, realised that they were in mid-air. Time was stilled and everything else in the world had been flung to the far corners of the universe, leaving only this room, blandly hyperreal as a spaceship cabin, its woodland mural like a reminder of the world long ago left behind in the starry deep, and the institutional blue carpet, the bentwood armchairs upholstered in a deeper shade of blue and the polished wood table and the square box with a tissue protruding like a frozen waft of smoke. The hum of air-conditioning felt as much as heard. Winters in his costume of shorts and green jacket, mouth dry, palms sweating. Trapped in this interstitial moment.

At last the glass blinked and cleared, revealing the assistant in a small room with white-tiled walls, standing at the head of a cantilevered trolley draped in a sheet that covered the contours of a body. Her body. Izzy.

'When you're ready, sir,' the assistant said, his voice coming from a speaker somewhere behind Winters, startling him. Winters said that he was, and with a stage magician's dexterity the assistant folded down one end of the sheet to reveal a face.

It wasn't her. It wasn't but it was. The older version of Isabel he'd seen in that holiday photograph and the brief video message, waxen and pale and severe in the pitiless light. Eyes closed, never to open again. Mouth downcurved, lips faintly blue, slightly parted, as if about to take a breath that would never come. Her hair cut short in a stiff crewcut and dyed black. How many years since it had last been its original foxy auburn? A bloodless gash on her forehead and smaller cuts on her cheeks and chin like chips in marble. Winters wondered how much pancake the morgue had used to make her presentable. Knew she would have hated that – after a very brief teenage flirtation she'd given up on all makeup except lipstick.

It had been eight years since he'd seen her last, coldly furious in the dark of that night at Wakestone Farm, but the sight of her now collapsed all time. She was here and she wasn't. Whatever had animated her body was utterly gone. She had escaped. Nobody could reach or use her. Not the police, not the deep dreamers and the Marquis, not even her brother.

He thanked the assistant and the window blanked and he knew he was not alone in the room. Knew that there was someone behind him and also knew, before he turned to confront it, blazing green out of the green shadows of the wood, who and what it was.

There was a bright light, like the light some claimed to have seen in the moments before they were pulled back from the brink of death, the heavenly glow at the far end of the post-mortal rabbit-hole where beloved ghosts waited to welcome the orphan home, but there was a pinkish cloud floating behind it, a cloud resolving into a face, a woman's face pulling back as the light, it was a small torch, blinked out. Winters was lying on a hospital trolley in a bay bordered by blue curtains. He had been stripped of his jacket and shirt and patches were stuck to his bare chest and his left wrist.

The woman was a young doctor dressed in green scrubs, a pale pretty blonde with the bruised eyes of the perpetually sleep-deprived, briskly telling him that he was in University College Hospital's Accident and Emergency Department, he'd had a serious seizure and had been unconscious for almost two hours. Asking if he remembered what had happened and where he had been and what he had been doing, did he have a history of epilepsy, had he experienced any unusual signs, an aura, a strange odour, a sudden headache?

Winters didn't want to tell her about the Green Man or the dose of shroom extract whose residue had almost certainly conjured him, saying instead that the last thing he remembered was viewing his sister's body in the mortuary, nothing like this had happened to him before. The doctor seemed to accept the lie, asked him to start counting backwards from a hundred by subtracting seven each time, had him grip her hand, follow the movement of her forefinger with his eyes, flex his arms and legs, wriggle his toes. She angled a tablet towards him, pointed to spikey lines travelling left to right and clusters of numbers, told him that his EEG, ECG and blood pressure were all normal and he didn't seem to be suffering from any aftereffects apart from possible transient global amnesia, but he needed to stay in the hospital for rest and recovery and further tests.

'You'll be admitted to a ward as soon as a bed becomes available. And I've booked you in for a scan, to eliminate the small possibility that there's a physical cause. Someone will take a blood sample, and I'll check in with you again in a little while,' she said, and whisked out of the bay.

Winters sat up. He had a slight headache and a taste like burnt iron in his mouth but otherwise felt fine. Had a moment of dizziness when he stood up, but it quickly passed. His clothes and day bag were stuffed between the trolley's frame and mattress. He ripped off the patches stuck to his chest and wrist and dressed, listening to the ordinary bustle beyond the curtains, the blended murmur of several conversations, a phone ringing, the beeping of hospital machinery. He parted the curtains, saw a hospital corridor, Bailey conferring with the doctor and the police driver at the far end, and scurried off in the opposite direction.

No one challenged him or tried to stop him as he followed exit signs to an ambulance bay. He used his phone to beep through the gates of the underground station on Tottenham Court Road and rode two stops to King's Cross, bought a train ticket and a new phone. After his train had drawn out of the station he transferred his contacts and credit from his no-contract phone to the brand new one, which he christened by tendering his resignation via text, and calling his uncle.

'I won't ask you how you are,' Daniel said. 'This is all pretty bloody, isn't it?'

'Did the police invite you to their press conference?'

'I'll be there. Giving you whatever support you need.'

'The thing is, why I'm calling, I have to be somewhere else,' Winters said, and explained that he believed that the press conference would be scripted by the police. That they wanted publicity, to boast that they had caught up with one of England's most wanted, had no interest in explaining that Izzy was being chased by a group of fanatics, or in clearing her name.

'I know now that she left Wakestone before the raid and the siege,' he said. 'Motte had begun to doubt her loyalty, and she walked away from everything he stood for. Was innocent of the charges the police wanted to bring against her. If you're going to take part in that press conference, that's what you need to say.'

'Do you have evidence for this?'

Winters told his uncle about the video message, said that it was a one-time thing that had deleted itself after he'd played it, but the police were trying to retrieve it.

'I doubt if that would count as evidence of her innocence in a court of law,' Daniel said.

'Not on its own. But it confirms what Rob Copley, her common law partner in the commune, told me. Ask Talia Armstrong and Bailey. Both of them were there.'

'Would this Copley fellow be willing to make a full and proper statement?'

'I don't know. He'll be in France by now, but his wife lives here, and I think she knows as much about it as he does. The point is, that press conference could be a way of putting the idea out there. Getting the news people interested. Proving it can come later.'

'I'll need to speak with Talia. And it really would be best for Isabel if you attended the conference. Spoke for her.'

'A few days ago, someone kind of kidnapped me and handed me over to Rob Copely, who was supposed to deliver me to the deep dreamers. And Copely's wife told me that Izzy was dead before the police did, and I think she'd been visited by deep dreamers, or someone close to them. So I reckon that they had something to do with Izzy's death. Directly or indirectly. Either the accident happened when she was running from them, when they were chasing her, or it wasn't an accident.'

'Surely that's something the police should be investigating.'

'I'm still involved in this deep dreamer thing. They seem to think I can be useful to them, and not just because of Izzy. Ask Talia Armstrong and Bailey if you want to know all about that.'

'Actually, I do know a little.'

'Yeah. I'm sure you do. The deep dreamers wanted to get hold of me because they couldn't find Izzy, and thought I was the next best thing,' Winters said. 'And now that she's dead, do you think that they'll leave me alone?'

He wanted to find out what Izzy had been doing, in Northumberland. And the anniversary of the siege was in a couple of weeks, he was wondering who would be drawn to Wakestone, if any of the deep dreamers might pitch up. But he didn't tell his uncle where he was going and what he hoped to discover because Danny might pass it on to Talia Armstrong. Who was definitely still interested in him, given the sighting of Bailey at the hospital. And he didn't tell his uncle about the hallucination which had triggered his blackout, either, because Danny really would think he was crazy. The face that had erupted from the woodland projection in the mortuary had been no more than a shroom flashback brought on by shock and stress, but it had made him realise that he needed to put an end to the deep dreamers' fever dreams. A final confrontation. A cleansing. Some kind of exorcism.

When the train stopped at the next station, he hopped off and dropped the no-contract phone into a recycling bin and hopped back on again. Bailey had taken it from him when she'd rescued him from Copely and he was worried that her technical pal might have infected it with some kind of stalkerware. Something that could be used to track him, monitor his calls and texts. It would explain how she'd found him in the hospital, so swapping phones might buy him a little time, help him to evade her and the police. He was gripped by a fugitive's paranoia, couldn't help wondering which of his fellow passengers might be an undercover officer, and when he got off the train at Berwick-upon-Tweed he half-expected to find Bailey waiting outside the station entrance, or a black cruiser with Sinclair and Briggs leaning against it.

He followed a broad road simmering in late afternoon heat to the town centre, found a shop that sold outdoor gear. A man with a thinning cap of white hair stood behind a counter, studying something on a tablet, taking a few moments before he looked up at Winters and asked if he could be of any assistance.

'I need camping gear.'

'Then you've come to the right place.'

'Also a good pair of walking boots.'

'Are you planning to hike across country, or is this for casual use?'

'For hiking, I guess.'

'What kind of terrain?'

'All kinds.'

'Roads?'

'Yeah. Beginning with the one outside.'

'May I suggest walking shoes rather than boots,' the man said, and guided Winters to a display and took down a kind of slipper, matt black with a studded orange sole. 'This is an excellent all-terrain choice, designed and manufactured by a small Swiss company. Lightweight, waterproof, air cushioning and ergonomic elastomers for support and comfort, conformable outsole lugs. It is somewhat expensive, but I highly recommend it.'

'Can I try it on?'

'Of course. What size do you take?'

Winters bought the walking shoes and two pairs of merino wool hiking socks, a lantern and a heating stone and a solar-powered charging strip, a bivvy bag, a pair of softshell hiking trousers and a rain poncho, an aluminium water bottle, a pair of alloy mess tins and an alloy mug, a small assortment of freeze-dried food, and a sling bag to carry his purchases and the contents of his day bag. He'd left his work knife at Cynsea, along with almost everything else, and added a pocket knife with a drop-point carbon steel blade and a beechwood handle to the bill, asked the man if he sold paper maps.

'We do, as a matter of fact. Some of my customers want a souvenir of their journey, and a few still like to do their own navigating. Will you also be needing a compass?'

'Yeah. Better give me one of those too.'

The man had totted up Winters' purchases and said, 'From your jacket, I assume you work for the Biodiversity Agency.'

'I used to be a ranger.'

'Used to be?'

'I recently quit.'

Even though it had been necessary, the words were bitter in his mouth. And he felt guilty about ignoring his supervisor's calls and texts, knew that he owed her and the agency an explanation, but that would have to come later.

'I can still give you a discount, as long as you have your agency ID,' the man said.

Winters felt a prickle of caution. He couldn't avoid leaving footprints in the panopticon's vast grid of surveillance, but he wanted to tread as softly as possible.

'That's all right. Just tell me what I owe.'

The final tally was astonishingly high. Winters paid it from the account where he'd salted away credit from sales of Julia's paintings, feeling only slightly guilty. Izzy wouldn't need her share now, and he hoped she would have approved of the cause it was funding.

He studied the paper map and turned his back on the sea and set out, crossing the River Tweed on the Old Bridge and following an unfamiliar B road. It would take him further to the south than he wanted, but would be a nicer walk, hopefully without any road trains or much of anything else in the way of traffic. On his way out of town he stopped at a corner shop and bought tea bags and energy bars, cheese and oatcake biscuits and a packet of joints. Found a chippie and bought a parcel of prawns and chips, sat on the bench outside the shop and ate every greasy scrap, the most satisfying meal he'd had in a long time. He smoked one of the joints and left the rest of the packet for someone else to find, he wanted to be sharp and alert in the days ahead, and went on.

He left the town's fringe of houses and bungalows behind, followed the road as it crossed the A1 and ran on past fields and farms, gently rising and falling. It bent to the south after passing through a hamlet, and straightened out before doglegging through a village where he spotted a cluster of caravans parked alongside a stone-walled barn. The caravans housed seasonal workers, most of them drifters, but none of them knew anything about deep dreamers or Wakestone Farm, or if they did they didn't want to discuss it.

'We're here to work, man,' one of them, a burly bare-chested man said. 'Doesn't leave time for your kind of nonsense.'

Winters disengaged as politely as he could and went on, passing through a strip of woods that looked like a good place to make camp, but sunset was a ways off and he decided to keep going. The shopkeeper had been right about the walking shoes. They gripped his feet like well-worn gloves and lent a little bounce to every step and he had the feeling of a wind at his back, urging him on. He'd been caught up in the plans and needs of others ever since the break-in and the news about Izzy had shattered his comfortable routines, the little life he'd made for himself, but he was free of all of that now. Free of every obligation but the task he'd set himself, gaining distance from the muddle and confusion of the past with every step.

When he reached the village of Etal he left the road and in the deepening dusk followed a footpath across a couple of fields to the bank of the River Till and in a stand of pine trees used the heating stone to boil river water and cook freeze-dried butternut squash curry. After he'd eaten he brewed a cup of green tea and slowly sipped it, savouring his solitude. He thought about checking out reports of the press conference but it was late and he was tired, didn't want to puncture his good mood. He finished his tea and shook out his bivvy bag and laid it on a patch of soft duff and snuggled down and quickly fell asleep.

He woke in the night with a freezing start and the sense that something was moving out in the dark. He lay in his bivvy bag, eyes wide, a scatter of stars chilly and remote in the moonless sky beyond the carbon silhouettes of pine trees. The river chattering to itself, a faint creaking of branches, and there, there, a soft distant scurrying. Stopping, starting again, fading away. Only an animal, he told himself. A fox, or maybe a weasel, there were still a few weasels here in the north. Nothing that meant him any harm, but even so it was a little while before he could fall back into sleep.

When he woke again blades of early morning sunlight were slanting between the trees and sunlight was flashing off the river beyond and there were voices nearby, a man and a woman walking their dog, passing without seeing him. He washed his face with water scooped from the river's shallows, brewed a mug of tea and ate an energy bar. Decided he couldn't put it off any longer and steeled himself to check for news of the police conference. There wasn't much. A couple of paragraphs on the BBC's site and in a few of the larger newsfeeds, links to chatter in the undergrowth of social media he didn't want to look at. Nothing about the deep dreamers, but the BBC piece mentioned that the family believed that Isabel Winters had escaped from Wakestone before the siege, so at least Daniel had done his bit.

Feeling somewhat encouraged, Winters switched off his phone and dug a squat hole and covered it over after using it and packed up and went on, following the path across fields as it bent back to the road. The sky clouded over and it began to rain. He pulled on his new poncho and put up its hood, but soon afterwards thunder grumbled overhead and the rain intensified, slashing down, bouncing off the road's tarmacadam and flattening grass and weeds along its edge. He walked on grimly, rain lashing his face and starting to soak through his poncho and hiking trousers. When he saw a disused byre in the corner of a potato field he quickened his pace and ducked through a gap in the hedge and dashed into the byre's open doorway.

It took him a few moments, as his eyes adjusted to the crepuscular shadows inside, to realise that someone else had already taken shelter there. An old man with elf-locked white hair and a patriarch's beard, seated on a rotten straw bale and dressed in an oilcloth coat and corduroy trousers and cobblestone boots. Saying, when Winters apologised for the intrusion, that he didn't own the place.

'Make yourself comfortable in this nook until the rain passes on. Shouldn't be much more than an hour or so.'

'Long enough to brew some tea, if you'd like some,' Winters said.

'That's right kind of you.'

Winters stripped off his poncho and jacket and spread them out to dry on a straw bale, filled a mess tin with water from a leaking downspout outside the byre's door and dropped in the heating stone and a couple of tea bags and sat across from the old man. His name was Cole Mordue. Northumberland born and bred, he said, and presently on the ramble.

'I have a caravan in Bamburgh, but sometimes I get the wandering itch and take to the roads for a while.'

'Going on the drift.'

'As they call it nowadays. But there were always people like us.'

'Like Romany people?'

'Anyone with a restless soul. I was born in Bamburgh and I'll likely die there, but I've been all over. And not just the local countryside. I was in the Navy eighteen years. A full term of service. Saw plenty of the world.'

'Bamburgh is on the coast, isn't it?'

'It is. I'm heading back there now. How about you?'

'The old farm at Wakestone. Do you know it?'

'I've heard of it. Not much there now, I reckon.'

'Do you know the story?'

'If you mean the siege, I'll own to having heard a fair few stories about that sorry affair.'

'My sister was sort of involved. Not the siege, she left before that. But she was at one time a follower of Kasey Motte.'

'I know that name,' Cole Mordue said.

The tea had come to a boil. The old man ferreted a chipped enamel mug from his rucksack and allowed Winters to fill it and reached inside his oilcoat and pulled out a hip flask and unstoppered it and added a measure of amber liquid to his tea and offered the flask to Winters. Shook it like a baby's rattle.

'If you fancy a little something to lace your brew.'

'That's okay.'

'Each to his own,' Cole Mordue said and tucked the flask away and blew on his tea and took a long sip and closed his eyes with a little shudder of appreciation. 'That hits the spot. Mighty kind of you.'

'My sister was Isabel Winters. She died very recently. A road accident somewhere around here.'

'I'm sorry to hear that. So you're on what might be in the nature of a pilgrimage.'

'I suppose I am. A local man, Gabriel Middlemass, was also involved. He was the driver.'

'It was recent, wasn't it, the accident?' the old man said.

'Just a few days ago.'

'Heard talk of it in a local hostelry. I believe the party you mentioned owned a smallholding over West Newton way.'

'Can you show me this smallholding on a map?'

'I can show you West Newton,' Cole Mordue said, and after Winters had unfolded the map and spread it on the straw bale he studied it and smudged a spot on a road that cut along the northern edge of the National Forest, not so very far from Wakestone. 'There it is. West Newton. I passed through it myself hardly a week ago.'

'And that's where the smallholding is?'

'Somewhere around and about. Middlemass, it's a local name. People there would know him.'

'I was told that he and my sister were caught in a rainstorm. The pickup he was driving came off the road and they were both killed.'

'Bad business.'

'It was. Do you know where it happened?'

'That I can't help you with.'

'I'm trying to find out about it. Whether anyone else was involved. Especially people calling themselves deep dreamers.

Are there any of them around here? Maybe they're camping out at Wakestone.'

'I don't know about any deep dreamers, but people come from all over to visit the place. Especially this time of year. The anniversary. None of them much liked by those living around and about.'

'As I've found out.'

'It was about some sort of weirding, wasn't it?'

'They thought they'd changed the world. And wanted to do it again.'

'And your sister was involved.'

'Until she got away. Or thought she had.'

A small silence descended. Threads of water unspooled through gaps in the stone roof tiles of the byre, falling to little streams that meandered across the packed earth floor. Curtains of rain swept across the potato field and the fields beyond and flashes of lightning briefly revealed the outline of the distant hills where Winters' destination lay.

Cole Mordue finished his tea and began to talk about the women in the family his brother had married into. Said that they were part of a long line of midwives and healers, told Winters about a book owned by his brother's wife, a hand-written compendium of recipes and cures more than two hundred years old.

'People say that those old nostrums aren't a patch on modern medicine. And in many ways they're right. But some of those modern drugs come from the same plants used by healers in times past. Not just a couple of centuries past, but many more than that. I'm talking about thousands of years. People in those far-off times didn't have all the advantages we do, but they weren't lacking in sense. If they thought a herb was of use and the knowledge of that was passed down, generation after generation, then there must be something to it.'

The old man said that he had learned something of the use of local plants from that book, and mosses and fungi too. Although it was harder to find many of them now, given how things had changed. How much had been lost.

'We had puffins and seals in abundance on the coast where I grew up. They're entirely gone hereabouts, and those few that're left can only be found in the far north. I remember when there were so many starlings the trees where they roosted would be entirely black with them. When they took flight, you would have thought those trees had exploded. Hardly any of them around, now. It's the same with owls. As for curlews and goshawks, they're gone entirely. Mountain hares, too. People said they weren't to be found here, mountain hares, but they were. It was just that they were scarce and shy because they were culled by the big estates that kept moorland for grouse shooting. That's one thing I don't miss. Those big shooting estates. It wasn't only hares they culled. Every kind of bird of prey, and crows and polecats and foxes too. My father said in the old days the keepers would nail everything they killed to fence posts, like the shrike hangs its prey on thorn bushes. Supposedly to scare away the rest. Hard to believe, but it's true. Well, those estates are gone, and the moors and everything that lives on them are what they call retreating northwards. Like seals and puffins. We have the National Forest instead, and I don't know what to think of it. I turned seventy this year, and I've seen changes I couldn't have imagined when I was growing up. Countless losses. You said that Kasey Motte and his followers claimed they'd changed the world. Did they think they'd changed it for the better?'

'That's what Motte said, yes.'

'All I can say about that, it's hard to believe things could ever have been worse than they are. I've seen something of the world, thanks to my years in the Navy. And lived through the troubles we had here, too. Not just Panic Summer, but the years before. You'll be too young to remember those times, I reckon, but back then I would have disbelieved any who said I'd survive to the age I am now.'

'I was only a kid, but I remember Panic Summer,' Winters said.

'They say things have got better since, but what they mean by that is things haven't got as bad as they once threatened to do. We survived, but we have to live with the consequences of what went before. The losses that are still being tallied.'

'I'm familiar with that idea,' Winters said.

He was thinking of the little ceremony at the end of the rangers' meetings, the loss protocol, but the old man thought that he meant Izzy, and apologised and said that he hoped that Winters would find the answers he was looking for.

'I get to rambling in my mind. As is not uncommon, at my age. When you've seen so much as I have, you can't help but try to make sense of it. To make it all connect.'

'To see the patterns underneath everything.'

'Aye,' Cole Mordue said, with a sharp shrewd look. 'That's why I'm out here, walking about in the world. And also because I like to see what's left of what once was. What's survived of what we did to this world. Which is mostly weeds, and creatures tough enough to withstand us, or canny enough to find a way of adapting to us and our works. I remember, when I was a bairn, seeing my first green parakeets. The first to arrive where I was born and bred. I'm sure you'll be familiar with them.'

'Sure.'

'It was strange and exciting, seeing those flashes of green in flight. Hearing their harsh cries and quarrels. People said they wouldn't survive the winter, but they did. Survived and thrived, in all the years since. Survivors. Yes. That's what we have now. All that's left. Survivors. And we're lucky to have as much as we do, considering all we've done to the world.'

After an hour or so the storm moved off to the south and the rain slackened and the threads of water falling through the broken roof frayed into erratic drips. Winters pulled on his damp jacket and packed up his kit and said goodbye to the old man and by the middle of the afternoon was following a single track road that climbed through the Northumberland National Forest. Seeing a farm he recognised off in the distance, a plantation of young ash trees grown taller since he'd last seen them, and then the familiar line of hills against the skyline.

It was like re-entering a dream. The gate was off its hinges and lying in tall weeds which had sprung up between its bars, and the track between thickets of trees had shrunk to a narrow path trodden through nettles and brambles. Winters ducked under overhanging branches and clambered over a young pine fallen slantwise, and then the trees thinned out and the path turned and there, beyond a security fence topped with coils of razor wire, were the remains of the commune. The vegetable plots which had been scattered amongst stands of trees were mostly overgrown by weeds and volunteer saplings and bramble thickets, but a broad stretch of grass had been cut down and half a dozen tents and a dun-coloured yurt were pitched there. These ruins were inhabited.

Winters ducked through a gash someone had snipped in the fence, and cut around the farmhouse. Its windows were boarded up and the front door hung aslant on a single hinge and most of the slates were gone from one side of the roof, presumably dislodged by the blast at the end of the siege. The cottages and outbuildings on the far side of the farmhouse were roofless burnt-out shells, and beyond them weedy hummocks of overturned dirt ringed the shallow crater where the turf-roofed meeting house and dormitories had once stood.

The crater seemed smaller than it had looked in the clips broadcast the morning after Kasey Motte's self-willed apocalypse, when it had still been on fire in places and half obscured by drifts of smoke. Patches of weeds and rough grass had colonised its slopes. An oval pool of water at the bottom darkly reflected clouds sailing the hot blue sky. Winters could make out a scorched jut of concrete on the far side, but there was no other trace of the buildings. He was surprised that he didn't especially feel anything. Neither sorrow nor anger. Perhaps it would be different if Izzy shared this common grave, but he knew now that she didn't. She had been close to Kasey Motte, had believed in his fantasies, had been involved in almost everything he had done and planned, but she had escaped his final act.

Motte had fostered connections with an assortment of like-minded conspiracy groups and individuals, including a man who worked for a private satellite launch facility to the east of the Northumberland National Forest and had passed on information about the facility's routines and weak spots in its security, and helped to establish a backdoor into its drone and CCTV systems. The facility's slim, single-stage rockets, which boosted microsatellites into orbit, were propelled by sustainably generated solid fuel manufactured in Scotland. Motte had planned to steal part of a fuel shipment and set fire to the rest so that no one would know about the theft, but although his inside man had given him the schedule for the next delivery, he either didn't know or had failed to pass on the news that it had been delayed by a day. When Motte's rag-tag crew broke into the facility, armed with shotguns, printed handguns and tasers, knives and machetes and homemade capsicum spray, several workers and a full complement of security guards were still on-site, transferring cakes of rocket fuel into a bunker. One of the guards was shot in the leg during the brief struggle; another was felled by a blow to the head that left him permanently disabled. Two more guards and one of the fuel handlers were taken prisoner, but the rest took refuge behind locked doors in the facility's administration building. They raised the alarm while Motte's crew were still securing their loot, and Motte's inside man hadn't told him that there were tracking tags embedded in the fuel cakes. The raiders barely made it back to Wakestone ahead of the police.

Motte and his followers hunkered down inside the mushroom farm, the meeting house and the dormitories, which were linked by hand-dug crawlways. Clerestory windows were boarded up and crude traps set at every door, and after two officers were injured while trying to force an entry the police set up a perimeter and negotiations began. Motte released the fuel handler who'd been taken hostage, but refused to surrender, issuing increasingly demented demands and threatening to end the siege with a great and glorious sacrifice.

A few days before the raid, he'd published a rambling manifesto on several sympathetic sites. Appended to a self-serving autobiography and theories about dreamwork and the mutability of history and much else were claims that, with some help from his fellow dreamers, he had reset history and healed much that was wrong with the world, and their last and greatest reset would make the most radical change of all.

The ultimate sacrifice which no one, not even Motte and his crew, would survive. In a shared, precisely orchestrated dream, they would reach back nine hundred thousand years, to a time when glaciation and punishingly long droughts had threatened to wipe out the ancestors of modern humans, and use this hinge-point to create a new timeline, a new history of the world, in which the human species did not survive this bottleneck but died out. The world as it was would become the world as it should have been. A world without global heating and the great thinning of biodiversity. A green world, dreaming its long dream of being.

After a stand-off that lasted for a little over three days, the police collapsed crawlways they'd located with LIDAR, and forced entry to the mushroom farm and one of the dormitories. Two of Motte's crew were killed and the rest, with their leader and his hostages, made their last stand in the meeting house. Motte read out the names of what he called his saviours and before cutting contact told the negotiator that they would celebrate their success and shed their earthly shells in flame, and all the works of man would vanish in the birthing of a new green world. Twenty minutes later he or one of his followers ignited three hundred kilos of stolen solid rocket fuel and an unknown amount of ammonium nitrate fertiliser. The explosion and fire injured more than a dozen police officers and incinerated everyone inside the meeting house.

The only human remains discovered by extensive excavations and forensic analysis of the ashes and shattered foundations of the meeting house and the other buildings were a few handfuls of charred, unidentifiable bone fragments. Meanwhile, the world rolled on as it always had. Badly damaged and impoverished by industrialisation, exploitation, fossil fuel burning and displacement of wild places by cities and agricultural land. The consequences of this despoilation ongoing, the efficacy of international, governmental and communal efforts to slow and eventually halt and reverse it still unclear. Some of Motte's admirers and fellow travellers believed that he had been captured and was imprisoned in a government black site where scientists were making use of his powers, or that he had escaped and was living in hiding, would make good his promise to redeem and renew the world in due time. Others thought that he and his followers were martyrs to the cause. He had become a symbol of resistance. Part Mahatma Gandhi, part Robin Hood, part Jack o' the Green. Murdered by the authorities because they'd been afraid of him.

The crater where he and his followers and hostages had died had become a memorial. A place of pilgrimage for drifters, dreamers and various groups of radical green campaigners who gathered there on the anniversary of the siege. Winters found a run of knee-high wicker fencing with a laminated photograph of the man propped at one end, stapled to a square of plywood and framed by spraypainted wreaths of flowers and leaves. The long blond hair with the centre parting. The smile which didn't reach the blank eyes behind those stupid purple glasses. A few fresh bunches of wildflowers lay beneath the photograph, amongst stubs of candles and spent nightlights set in cracked soot-stained jars and tumblers, and the gaps in the fencing's weave were stuffed with small folds of paper. Most had been ruined by months and years of sun and rain, but some posted more recently were still intact and Winters squatted on his heels and plucked out a few and read what was written on them and put them back.

The Saviours will never be forgotten.

In loving memory of my cousin Janine Ridgley, murdered by the state.

He isn't dead, he's just asleep.

When he rose, he saw that several people had gathered in front of the tents and were watching him. One came forward as he walked towards them, asked if he was the law.

'Not in any way,' Winters said. 'Are you in charge here?'

The man was bare-chested, wearing cycling shorts and shower sandals. His forked beard was dyed bright red and he was studying Winters with a kind of good-natured arrogance.

'No one's in charge. Or you might say we all are. Why I ask, and don't take this personally, the state sends all kinds of people to check up on us.'

Winters put his hand over the logo on the breast pocket of his jacket. 'I used to work for the Biodiversity Agency, but I quit,' he said and introduced himself, explained that he was Isabel Winters' brother. 'She was a follower of Kasey Motte, once upon a time. And died not far from here, just a few days ago. I've come to find out what happened.'

'You mean the road accident.'

'That, and what led up to it.'

The man thought about that and stuck out a hand and said, 'Ty.'

'Good to meet you,' Winters said, and shook his hand.

'I don't know if we can be of any help,' Ty said. 'But you're welcome to break bread with us and tell your story.'

There were a round dozen people in the little encampment. Most were drifters, but there were also a young couple in high-end hiking gear and a tall fellow dressed all in black, come all the way from Denmark to mark the anniversary, as he did every year. The red-bearded man, Ty, explained who Winters was and why he'd come to Wakestone, and they settled on logs and folding stools arranged around a camp fire. Winters refused the offer of a joint that was being passed around but accepted a mug of rosehip tea. His first sip conjured a memory of working side by side with Izzy in the kitchen, washing and halving the hips they'd collected from dog roses that grew on the local common, scooping out the seeds, and he told the woman who'd handed him the mug about his sister's foraging.

'Isabel liked to wait until after the first frost, or the end of November, whichever came first. She said it made them sweeter.'

'That's right enough,' the woman said. 'I made that tea with some I picked and dried last winter.'

'Isabel used them to make rosehip jelly. Always gave a couple of jars to one of our neighbours, because it helped to ease his arthritis.'

'Sounds as if she knew her plant lore,' the woman said. She was about Winters' age, slender and sharp-faced, her frizz of black hair contained by a head scarf.

'She could name every plant, and knew their uses,' Winters said. 'Could collect the makings of a salad on a short walk on the common, or in the woods. She said it wasn't free food but food given freely. I'm still trying to figure out my life, but she was one of those people who know what they want to do from the off. She joined the local Nature First! group when she was twelve years old, was at their stall in the market every Saturday, handing out leaflets, getting people to sign petitions. Could out-talk anyone who criticised the group, what it did and what it stood for. Food given freely, that was one of her talking points. Nature gives to us, she'd say, and we have to learn how to give back to nature.'

'She was right about that, too,' the woman said.

Winters took another sip of the sour-sweet tea, looked at the people sitting around the fire.

'Why my sister came here, joined the commune, the original commune, she wanted to be part of something that showed one way of doing that. Living lightly on the land. Returning more than you took from it. And from what I could tell she and her friends were doing some good work before Kasey Motte took over.'

'Did you ever visit?' someone said.

'Several times.'

'Did you meet Kasey?' someone else said.

'I mostly stopped visiting after he took over.'

'But did you ever meet him?'

'Just the one time,' Winters said, and several people spoke at once.

'What was he like?'

'Did you talk to him?'

'What did he tell you?'

'I can't tell you if he believed what he preached, but he certainly knew how to make other people believe in him. If he had a talent, that was it. But you probably know more about him than I do.'

'I do not think dreams can reset history,' the Danish man said solemnly. 'But he helped us to understand the power of lucid visions. How to visualise the world as you want it to be, and share that with others. When you can see where you want to go, you can draw a line between the world you are presently living in and the world you want to live in. And then you can take the first step towards your goal.'

'Your sister was a believer,' the red-bearded man said. 'But I don't think you are.'

'No, I got away. And Isabel got away too, just before the end. She managed to evade the authorities for eight years, until she was forced to abandon the life she'd made for herself. And was killed in that road accident.'

'You think the state had something to do with it?' Ty said.

'Have you heard of people who call themselves deep dreamers? They're what you would call believers.'

'We know who they are,' the Danish man said. 'But we do not have anything to do with them.'

'They were looking for my sister. Wanted to get hold of her. And wanted to get hold of me too. Still do, for all I know. I want to find out about them. Find out if they had anything to do with the accident.'

'All kinds of people come to celebrate Kasey Motte's life and ideas on the anniversary of his martyrdom,' Ty said. 'But the deep dreamers aren't welcome here.'

'They claim to have discovered secret knowledge in his writings,' the Danish man said. 'But refuse to share any of it. They are proud and selfish, and unlike true followers want only change that will benefit themselves.'

Winters wondered what the relatives of Motte's original crew and the hostages he'd taken would think about these true followers. He doubted that many would be as sympathetic as the cousin of Janine Ridgely. He definitely wasn't, but kept his peace. It wasn't an argument he wanted or needed to have.

He said, 'Is there anyone who might know where I could find them?'

'There are people who sort of keep track of what they are doing,' Ty said. 'One or two of them usually pitch up for the anniversary.'

'I'd like to meet them,' Winters said.

'You may have to wait a while.'

'That's okay.'

'And I can't guarantee that they'll know anything that'll be of use to you,' Ty said. 'But if you've had a run-in with the deep dreamers, they'll most likely want to talk to you.'

After the little crew had shared their supper with him, flatbread baked on hot stones, a stew of lentils and wild greens, Winters wandered off into the patchwork of trees and vegetable plots gone to weeds and called Teddy. He wanted to talk to S, find out if their canvassing of the drifter camps had yielded anything useful, but Teddy told him that the kid was gone.

'Some kind of private investigator called yesterday, wanting to speak with them. Afterwards, S said they had to leave. Thanked me for all my help, as if that amounted to very much, and was gone before I could ask what was up.'

'What was the name of the investigator?' Winters said, although he already knew.

'Bailey. Said she was a friend of yours.'

'More of a business acquaintance than a friend. We shared a common interest until we didn't. Did S tell you what they talked about?'

'They did not. It wasn't a long call, two minutes or so, but it spooked them. That and your warning about the police.'

'And did they say where they were going? Were they planning to meet up with Bailey?'

'All they said was they had to go. Didn't say where or why. Do you think they might be in some kind of pickle?'

'I hope not.'

'So do I,' Teddy said. 'I've developed a fondness for them and their funny little ways. Not to mention their help. But they have the wildness in their blood. As so many drifters do. They remind me of this cat I had, when I was a kid. Well, "had" is the wrong word. He was a feral creature, didn't belong to anyone. An unneutered tom. Raggedy-eared from fights with rivals. I put out food for him when he started to hang around the garden, and we became friendly. But that was as far as it went. He wouldn't set foot in the house, vanished if anyone else came near. And then one day he didn't come by at his usual time, and that was that. Never saw him again.'

'Yeah, I know what you mean. Talking of coming by, have the police paid you a visit?'

'Not yet.'

'Any trouble from them, call me. You have my new number now.'

'What trouble can they cause me? I'm just an old man going about his business. I have a licence for my gleaning, I pay taxes on the weed I sell. But this talk of police, and your recent loss, and now I am hearing you quit your job – I can't help wondering what kind of trouble you're in.'

Winters would miss his work, and the island, but he knew that giving it all up was the right thing to do. He was pretty sure that his disciplinary hearing wouldn't have gone well, he needed more time to find out about Izzy, about her death, and he couldn't go home again. Cynsea was no longer a refuge. The world had found him again. It was time to move on. But he couldn't tell Teddy, the old gossip, any of that.

'I guess I have a lot going on,' he said. 'If S comes back or gets in touch, I'd appreciate it if you'd have them call me.'

'I will,' Teddy said. 'And be sure to call me if S gets in touch with you first. Let me know they're okay.'

Winters was unsettled by the news. He didn't need Bailey back in his life. Didn't want her interfering with his plans, such as they were, and very much didn't like the idea of S being involved with her. He hoped that Teddy was right, hoped that talk of police and Bailey's phone call had spooked the kid and they'd decided to move on before the law found them, but he couldn't shake off his unease. After he bedded down in the woods, spreading his bivvy on a deep litter of dry leaves that had collected behind the trunk of a fallen tree, the possibility that the kid had been suckered into one of Bailey's dangerously crackpot conspiracies was the last thing he thought about before he fell asleep, and the first thing on his mind when he rose early in the next morning.

The skinny Danish fellow was the only one awake in the encampment, patiently feeding the remains of the communal camp fire with scraps of dry wood, nodding to Winters as he went past with his sling bag over one shoulder.

'You look like you are going somewhere.'

'There's something I need to do, but I should be back before dark.'

'If you are missing supper I can save you a plate,' the man said, but Winters was already walking on.

He filled his water bottle at the mossy cistern which had been used by the commune to irrigate their crops, ate an energy bar and consulted his map, taking directions from his new compass, and set out for West Newton and Gabriel Middlemass's smallholding. Crossing the single track road and climbing the swell of rough grassland beyond. It was going to be another hot day. The sun soon burned away the fret which had crept in and blanked the sky overnight, revealing a panoramic mosaic of tracts of forest and patches of moorland. Dry stone walls rambled along contours. A recent burn had scarred a distant hillside. Despite the previous day's rain the grass and weeds were cracklingly dry, browned by drought. Some of the slopes of sheep-cropped turf terminated abruptly in low cliffs footed in aprons of scree. Winters stood at the edge of one such and took in the view, wished that the hot wind could strip away everything that was haunting him, carry it off into the vast space and deep time of this remote country.

The shadows dancing under a cluster of birch trees were cast only by their windblown leaves. A starry glint in a belt of trees far below was the reflection of sunlight off the windscreen of a vehicle travelling along a narrow road. The tiny figures on a distant slope were no more than mundane hikers.

He shrugged off his jacket and folded it lengthwise and draped it over the strap of his sling bag and went on, struck a signposted path that seemed to lead in the right direction, swinging around the brow of a hill and contouring across a slope cut by the deep gashes of washouts that ran down to tangles of broken trees, reminding him of similar wreckage seen while walking in the Black Hills with CeCe. Trees snapped off at the trunk. Trees fallen whole, roots clutching plates of earth.

The path descended through a scant woodland of pines and birches and fern banks, crossed a slope of scrub grass that fell to a blackwater lough ringed on its far side by pine trees that stood above their perfect reflections. He saw a red kite hanging above the crest of the slope, cupping the wind with its wings, suddenly sliding sideways towards the water and trees below. He came across a patch of brambles and picked a handful of berries that had ripened early. Their sharp taste triggered a picture of Izzy wading amongst thorny runners in some other country, a summer long past. Her windbreaker tied around her waist, purple juice staining her smile as she fed her younger brother her best finds.

'Oh Izzy,' he said to the empty sky, the uncaring world.

He drank from his water bottle and went on. Passing clumps of birches standing amongst boulders spattered with lichens, following a footpath that ran down rough pasture to an old tarmacadam road. He checked his map and turned right, following the gentle curves and switchbacks of the road, grassy slopes and scraps of woodland rising on one side, views across fields stretching across the floor of a valley towards low hills on the other. It was as if he'd stumbled into a dreamworld polder, or had been cast back to a time before global heating and the great extinction, the resource wars and everything else. Dry stone walls spattered with grey and orange lichens. Lush grass along the verges. Nettles, patches of fireweed, cow parsley holding up saucers of small white flowers. A short stretch of the road tunnelled in green light between stands of trees and when he emerged from the far end he saw a neat whitewashed cottage with a clutter of small sheds off to one side, the slope behind it, divided into vegetable plots and paddocks bounded by neat wooden fences, rising towards dark green conifer forest. At the beginning of a short gravel drive a sign painted on a stone slab advertised vegetable boxes, honey and hats for sale.

No one came to the door after he knocked, but when he leaned at the gate to one side and called out a woman emerged from one of the sheds. She was in her late thirties, early forties, wearing dungarees and floral-patterned wellington boots and a wide-brimmed straw hat. A dog, a Border Collie, at her heels. Winters started to explain who he was, and she told him that she recognised him from the news.

'You're the brother.'

'Of Isabel Winters, yes. So I guess you know why I'm here.'

She told him that she was Ellie Laidlaw. One of Gabriel Middlemass's nieces, looking after the place until all the legal stuff was sorted out.

'Gabriel didn't leave a will, his wife died nigh on twenty years back and they didn't have any kids. So you can imagine it might take a while.'

'I'm sorry for your loss.'

'I hold no malice towards your sister, you understand. But I can't help thinking that if she hadn't come back here he would still be alive.'

Winters didn't know what to say to that.

'I suppose you have some questions to ask,' Ellie Laidlaw said.

'If you don't mind answering them.'

'I can try my best. I knew about your sister, but I never met her. Do you eat cheese?'

'Sure.'

'Not everyone does these days. Come in then. Don't mind Jess, she won't bite unless I tell her to.'

She led him around the back of the cottage to a small paved terrace. Pink and red geraniums in tubs. An old cast-iron latticework table and matching chairs where Winters sat, watched by the dog, while Ellie Laidlaw spent a few minutes in the kitchen and returned with a tray. Oatmeal biscuits and crumbling white cheese, black grapes, small sweet tomatoes cut in quarters, a jug of ice water. The cheese was sheep's cheese, Ellie said.

'From one of the certified flocks that keep the moors as they should be. The tomatoes and grapes are grown right here.'

'It's very good,' Winters said, around a mouthful of oatmeal and sharp, salty cheese. He was aware that he smelled of sweat and woodsmoke, wondered if Ellie had noticed it.

'Well,' she said. 'Ask on.'

'How much do you know about Wakestone, and what happened there?'

'If you mean the siege, about as much as anyone else, but no more than that. I know your sister was supposed to have died in it.'

'I thought so too,' Winters said, and explained that the police had discovered that Isabel had been living in Scotland under an assumed name, working in a displaced persons camp, until she'd gone on the run a few weeks ago. 'The police suspected that I might be sheltering her, but I didn't even know, until they told me, that she was alive. And I had no idea where she was until a couple of days ago.'

'No more did we. At first, the police told us that she was a hitchhiker Gabriel had picked up. And it seemed likely, because it was the kind of thing he'd do. But then there was that press conference, in London. We were only given a few hours warning beforehand. Told who Uncle Gabriel's hitchhiker really was. You can imagine our surprise.'

'That may be my fault. I don't think that the police were planning to make my sister's identity public quite so soon, but I found out what happened to her.'

'They said, the police, that it was all because of who she was. What she was involved in.'

'I expect they did. You said that you never met her, but you knew about her. I guess your uncle knew her too.'

Ellie Laidlaw plucked a grape from the platter and ate it in two bites. Her fingernails were cut short, no nail varnish. No wedding ring, either. She said, 'It must have been fourteen years ago when they first met. A good few years before that man came along and took charge of her commune. Did you know that they were friends?'

'I had no idea. I visited several times while it was still a commune. And as far as I remember, my sister never mentioned your uncle.'

Winters was wondering if Rob Copely and Dash Baker, Charlie Lowe and the other survivors, had known about Isabel's friendship with this older man. Almost certainly, even though no one had ever said anything about it to him. But why would they? As far as anyone in the commune was concerned, he had always been an outsider. Even to his sister.

He said, 'How did she come to know him?'

'It was because of the bees. The commune over at Wakestone bought package bees from a local breeder, wanted them to live half-wild. Gave them hollow trees and logs instead of hives, let them keep a good portion of their honey for winter instead of feeding them sugar syrup. Two years in a row, they died out. The third year, your sister came to Uncle Gabriel to ask him what she was doing wrong. He had the touch, when it came to bees. Was famous for it. He advised her how and when to supplement her colonies' stocks of honey with sugar cakes and protein patties to give them the best chance of survival over winter, and showed her how to bait and set hornet traps. The big ones that moved up here on account of the changing weather are a plague on local honeybees. They snatch them from the air, raid hives, generally cause havoc. Only way to deal with them is to trap the queens in early winter and spring. Anyhow, that was how your sister and my uncle met. Because of the bees.'

'And they became friends.'

'Gabriel's wife had passed and he was living on his own, which may have had something to do with it. A sweet kind man he was, but not much of a one for company. I don't live but ten kilometres away, have lived there all my life, but I rarely saw him. Mostly at Christmas. We'd have him over, or someone else in the family would. Christmas, and weddings and funerals. He'd turn up for those. Otherwise, not so much. But somehow your sister befriended him. Started visiting on the regular.'

Winters thought of Rob Copely's claim that Izzy and Kasey Motte had been lovers and said, 'Were they close?'

Ellie smiled. 'You mean like boyfriend and girlfriend?'

'I suppose so. Yes.'

'The police asked the same thing. And I'll give you the same answer I gave them – nobody in the family knew what they were to each other. Gabriel told us the story of how they met, but never said much else about her, never brought her to visit with any of us. How old would she have been, back then?'

'In her early twenties.'

'And my uncle would have been in his fifties. A May-December romance, it isn't unknown, is it? But I can't tell you if that's what it was, or if it was just an unlikely friendship.'

There was a short silence as the two of them considered that. The secret lives of other people.

'Anyway, it didn't last,' Ellie said. 'After that man took over the commune, your sister stopped coming by. What Gabriel thought or felt about that I don't know. He never said anything about it to anybody.'

'Kasey Motte liked to keep his followers close,' Winters said. 'I visited just the once after he pitched up. I thought that Isabel had invited me, but it turned out to have been Motte's idea. He believed I might be useful to him, but Isabel helped me to get away. That was the last time I saw her, apart from a message she left a few days ago, just before the accident.'

'What did she say, in this message? If you don't mind me asking.'

'She told me not to think of looking for her, but to find out what I could about deep dreamers. This group of people who were searching for her. Before the police visited me, told me Isabel was still alive, someone associated with deep dreamers broke into my place, trying to find anything that might lead them to her. And left their slogan behind.'

'"The Instauration Is Coming."'

'Yes. How did you know?'

'Someone burgled this place a couple of weeks before the accident. Turned it upside down, painted that selfsame slogan on one of the walls in the living room. Gabriel tried to cover it up with obliterating emulsion, but you can still make it out.'

'That would be about the same time my place was broken into. After Isabel had gone on the run. Was she staying with your uncle then?'

Ellie shook her head. 'She was camping up in the hills. After the accident, police searched the area with dogs and drones and found her tent. Seemed like a lot of fuss at the time, over a hitchhiker, but now we know why. Gabriel was likely taking supplies up to her, or maybe leaving them in a cache some place, where she could pick them up.'

'So he wouldn't lead anyone to where she was staying.'

'He was canny like that. But it's just a guess. And I don't know why he and your sister took off like they did, either. The police wouldn't say. Do you think these deep dreamers might have found them?'

'I think it's possible. Could I ask you about the accident? The circumstances.'

Ellie sat up a little straighter in her chair. 'I knew we'd be getting around to it.'

'I'm sorry, but I need to find out how it happened. According to one of the local newsfeeds, it was on a road called Collingwood Rise, not far from here.'

'That's right. A road Gabriel must have taken a thousand times, in all kinds of weather.'

'There wasn't any mention of it, but I'm wondering if another vehicle might have been involved. Whether someone was chasing them, or maybe forced them off the road.'

'Someone like these deep dreamers, you mean?'

'Yeah.'

'One thing I can tell you straight, there wasn't. The beginning of that road, it takes a sharp turn through a farm, and like all farms around here it has security cameras. One of them caught my uncle's pickup going past, and according to the police there wasn't any sign of anyone chasing it. It could be that a deer or a sheep wandered into the road and Gabriel swerved to avoid it. Or he was going too fast in the rain and skidded, as the police reckon. But the plain fact is, he wasn't being chased. Your sister turned up after all these years and asked him for help. And help her he did, even when they needed to leave in such a hurry, in the middle of the night and the middle of a rainstorm, that it got them both killed. The daft old fool,' Ellie said, with the force of a curse.

The dog, sitting by her chair, pricked up its ears and gave a small startled yelp.

'I'm sorry,' Winters said.

Ellie absent-mindedly rubbed the dog's head. 'You can't ever know what's in people's hearts. And I suppose you can't blame them for acting on it, neither. I'm sorry I can't be of more help, but that's all I know.'

'Thank you for your time. And your honesty.'

'Maybe I could ask you a question.'

'Of course.'

'Your sister,' Ellie said. 'Do you think she was a good person?'

When Winters left the smallholding his sling bag was bulging with cherries and windfall apples, an assortment of vegetables and a jar of honey. He was wearing one of Gabriel Middlemass's hand-woven straw hats, too. Ellie Laidlaw had refused to take his credit for any of it, saying that it would only complicate the business of probate.

So many of his questions were unanswered or unasked, and most of the answers had generated further questions, but at least he had learned that Izzy had found refuge with someone she could trust, in the familiar surroundings of a country where it was easy to hide. He suspected that someone, a deep dreamer or one of their allies, had come there looking for her, which was why she had needed to leave with such reckless urgency, and why she'd asked him to find out what he could about them, in that hasty last message.

He thought about that as he walked towards the farm at the junction with Collingwood Road. And thought about Ellie Laidlaw's last question, too. He'd told her about Izzy's love of nature and all things in it. How much he had learned from her. How that love had turned into grief and anger as Izzy learned more and more about the history and extent of the world's damage, and how that grief and anger had been the foundation for her belief that trying to fix the world and save everything that would otherwise be lost was the best way to spend her life. He'd described her campaigns and actions, explained that when she'd joined the commune at Wakestone she had wanted to set an example by living as humbly and lightly in the world as possible. That before Kasey Motte's arrival the commune had been a pocket utopia where ideas could be trialled and demonstrated. The sacrifices that entailed. The devotion and discipline. The abnegation of self necessary for the creation of a better world.

All of this was, he knew, an idealisation of the life Izzy had chosen. A life he had barely glimpsed in his brief visits. He didn't know half as much as he would have liked, could only speculate about how the communal will towards self-sacrifice and dedication had left Izzy and the others vulnerable to Kasey Motte. How the man had tailored his claims to their desires. Telling them that he knew how to save the world from itself and how they could help him. Using drugs and psychological violence to bind them to his vainglorious narcissism.

Izzy and her comrades had been Motte's victims, but they'd also shared his fantasies. Become willing accomplices. And even though Izzy had been exiled from Wakestone before the siege, she must have known something about his plans. Had probably, given her place in his so-called inner circle, helped to draw them up. Winters hoped that the years she'd spent in Scotland living under an assumed identity had involved some kind of atonement, but knew that it was unlikely that he'd ever find out. All he could tell Ellie Laidlaw was that his sister had tried to be good, but he didn't know how well she had succeeded.

'I understand if you think that isn't enough,' he said.

'I'd like to think Gabriel saw some goodness in her. That she didn't trick him or force him to do what she wanted.'

'I hope so too.'

'And what will you do now?'

'I want to find out if deep dreamers will be amongst the visitors to what's left of my sister's commune.'

'For the anniversary of the siege.'

'Yes. I've already met some people who told me deep dreamers aren't welcome there, but maybe they'll come to pay their respects anyway. Without letting on who they are. And I've been promised an introduction to a couple of people who might know more about them.'

'Does finding them matter now?'

'It matters to me,' Winters said. 'Not only because Isabel asked me to do it, but also because it seems that they think I can help them somehow. The siege should have put an end to Motte's crazy ideas, but it didn't. There are still people who believe that they can make use of his rituals and his drugs. They have to be stopped. Not because they might be able to do what they claim, but because of who they might hurt and who they've already hurt, while trying.'

It wasn't far to the junction with Collingwood Rise, a single-track road that passed a scatter of cottages and an imposing house set in rolling lawns and evergreen topiary before bending sharply between farm buildings. In the cobbled farmyard a young woman elbow-deep in the gears of some kind of portable conveyer belt pointed him towards the office, a converted steel shipping container painted blue with a single window cut into its side. Inside, there was a beat-up sofa at one end and a man, the farm manager, sitting behind an old wooden desk at the other. He listened sympathetically to Winters' explanation for the visit, confirmed that recordings from two of the farm's security cameras had captured Gabriel Middlemass's pickup passing by.

'Our insurance company insisted that we put them up after someone ran into the side of the barn on the corner, and tried to sue for the damage. As if we deliberately put the barn in his way,' the farm manager said. He was a broad-shouldered man in his forties, shirtsleeves rolled up above his elbows, hands clasped before him on the desktop. 'I can show you the footage of Gabriel's pickup, if you like.'

'Thank you. But I'd rather not.'

'Of course. I understand.'

'I was told that it was late at night, and raining,' Winters said.

'Yes it was. Close to midnight, and rain fair stotting down. A right cloudburst. Gabriel had his headlights on full beam and you could see the spray when he hit a sheet of water at the road junction.'

'And there definitely wasn't another vehicle following.'

'The police ran the footage for the next hour as I recall, but didn't see anything they were interested in. We don't get much in the way of traffic.'

'Where the accident happened – how far is it from here?'

'A couple of kilometres up the road. Are you walking?'

'That's how I got here.'

'I'll give you a lift if you like.'

They drove along the narrow road in a small van with the farm's logo on the sides and straw on the floor behind the seats. A pungent smell of sheep. Papers sheaved along the top of the dashboard. The road snaked up between patches of forest, views of hills. Every bend seemed like the ideal site for an accident. They took the righthand road at a junction, rattling over a cattle grid, passing a bothy and sheep pens, unfenced slopes of rough grass where a couple of hundred sheep were grazing. The road grew narrower and began to slant down, open moorland on the left creased by the winding path of a beck, a wall of conifers on the right falling away to fenced pasture as the road climbed in a long curve under the hot, cloudless sky, running on through an open gate and bending right in a sudden descent. Winters' heart quickening as the van slowed and glided to halt in a passing place. A thick growth of rhododendrons and bracken sloping down from the road, a conifer plantation covering the hillside rising beyond.

'See the break in the bushes?' the farm manager said. 'That's where it happened. The police said Gabriel must have been going at a fair old speed.'

The two of them sitting side by side, looking out through the windscreen. A faint wuthering of wind at the open windows. No other sound.

Winters said, 'Where does the road go?'

'Bends around south to College Valley, on to Cuddystone Hall. Not much beyond that. A bunkhouse for hillwalkers and the like at Mount Hooley. Runs out just before the border.'

'The border with Scotland?'

'None other.'

Winters thought about that, then thanked the farm manager for the lift and unclicked his seat belt and cracked open the door.

'I don't mind waiting a short while, if you want a ride back,' the farm manager said.

'That's okay. After this, I'm going to walk cross-country to Wakestone.'

'You know the way?'

'I can find it.'

Winters waited while the van performed a three-point turn and moved off, then crossed the road. Bunches of flowers were laid along the far edge. Roses. Carnations. Lilies. All the messages were for Gabriel Middlemass. From friends and family. No one had known who his passenger was. No one had known Izzy.

He studied the smashed path through the rhododendrons and bracken, the tyre tracks scored deep in the grassy verge. No skidmarks on the road. The pickup had simply shot straight off it. He tried to imagine that night. Darkness all around. The pickup's headlights tunnelling through drenching rain whipped by wind. It could have been a sheep on the road. A deer. An especially hard gust of wind, or simple tiredness. Or there might have been a vehicle which had intercepted the fugitives from the other direction. Some kind of ambush. Impossible to say.

He walked slowly and carefully down the smashed track, between a dense growth of rhododendron bushes and a stand of bracken. It wasn't very long. Five or six metres. Torn leaves, broken branches. The bushes had partly sprung back into shape, but the track through the bracken was smashed flat all the way to the drystone wall. Stones had spilled from a breach in the wall and there were bright scars gouged in stones on either side.

Winters stood in hot sunlight amongst broken bracken fronds, breathing in their faint sharp grassy odour. Set his hand against the warm stone of the scarred wall.

Oh, Izzy.

Izzy and Gabriel Middlemass might have been planning to hole up somewhere out here. In that bunkhouse mentioned by the farm manager perhaps. But Winters thought it more likely that they'd been heading to Scotland. Izzy had been discovered, or feared discovery, and had doubled back towards a place she knew. A place where she might get a more favourable hearing if she was arrested. Most of the roads that crossed over into Scotland were monitored by cameras, there were permanent customs checkpoints and roving patrols, but in wild empty country like this long stretches of the border were unlikely to be watched or even fenced.

Winters wondered if this was the route Izzy and Rob Copely had taken when they'd left the commune, just before the siege. Wondered if she'd learned about it from Gabriel Middlemass. He walked back to the road and sat on the grass by the passing place and drank water from his bottle and listened to the silence of the empty countryside. Picturing once again the pickup careering along the narrow spine of tarmacadam in darkness and slashing rain. Plunging straight into the rhododendron thickets. Vanishing like a conjuring trick. Then he tried to unsee that simple scenario. Run an alternate version. Although nothing had been following the pickup when it passed the farm, it might have been tagged and tracked, heading towards an ambush. A vehicle skewed across the narrow road or parked beside it, switching its headlights on, full beam, as the pickup sped towards it, the glare filling the pickup's windscreen . . .

After a little while he unfolded his map and traced a route that would take him over the hills back to Wakestone. Judging contour lines, looking for footpaths. It was a much longer walk than the walk from Wakestone to the smallholding, but he reckoned that he could get back before nightfall.

He was folding the map when he heard a distant mosquito whine and looked up and saw a van emerging from the shadows cast by the conifers at the top of the road's rise. A newer, larger vehicle than the farm manager's workhorse. White. Boxy. Slowing as it approached. He stood up, ready to run, his hand in the pocket where he'd stowed his new knife, as it rolled to a stop beside him and its side door slid open.

'Hello, Marc,' Bailey said.

★

He was stashed in a small bedroom under the eaves of a cottage. Shackled to the headend of an old brass bed by handcuffs and a chain improvised from zip ties, the arrangement just long enough so that he could reach the covered sanitary bucket or stir aside the net curtains and peer out of the corner of the dormer window. There wasn't much to see, just a narrow stretch of block-paved hardstanding between the cottage and an old stone byre, and a row of raggedy Scots pine trees that rose above the byre's slate-tiled roof and hid any view of whatever lay beyond, but Winters was certain that the cottage was somewhere in or close to the National Forest.

After he'd been bundled into the back of the van the drive had been short and bumpy, no more than twenty minutes on potholed minor roads. He'd been handcuffed to a bench on one side of the rear compartment. A sheet of plywood screened off the driver, and the windows of the back doors and the sliding door were blanked by aluminium foil and duct tape. Bailey and a tall, rangy man in a long-eared animal mask, either a hare or a rabbit, sat across from him, and Bailey had done most of the talking. Telling him that Talia Armstrong had come to believe that the deep dreamers might be of some use, she'd got in contact with them via Rob Copely, and Winters was the price of admission.

'Admission to what?'

'I think you know.'

Winters looked at Bailey's companion. Hard to know, with that goofy mask, buck teeth and stand-up ears and black gauze over the eyeholes, if the man was looking back at him.

He said, 'The thing you want to do, trying to copy Kasey Motte's reset? It won't work. It never did and never will. It was all drugs and mindfucking.'

'I'm not paid to have an opinion,' Bailey said. She was dressed in a tweed suit with a herringbone weave, notched lapels broad enough to land a drone on and leather buttons like the caps of small dark mushrooms.

'I wasn't talking to you,' Winters said. 'I was talking to your sidekick or whatever he is.'

'You'll find out what we can do soon enough,' the man said, lips moving behind the mask's buck teeth.

Winters said to Bailey, 'Is S part of this?'

'I thought they might be with you,' Bailey said.

'So you couldn't persuade them to go along with you.'

'I asked them if they knew where you might be headed, after you absconded from hospital. And warned them that they'd be walking into a world of shit if they tried to help you. They claimed they didn't know where you were, but it wasn't hard to figure out. Given the news about your sister. I had a friend, the one who helped me before, check the cameras at Newcastle and Berwick stations, and there you were.'

'The fucking panopticon.'

'Which helped to save your skin the last time you got into trouble. I could have caught up with you at Wakestone, but there were some skeevy people camping there and I didn't want a scene. I admit you gave me the slip this morning, but I knew where you were going. The one place you had to see.'

'What's it like, working for the deep dreamers?'

'I'm working for Lady A, as always. Someone who's had more than her share of hurt and loss. You should know all about that, seeing as that's what brought you here.'

'You could have refused to have anything to do with them. Walked away. But you didn't, so you're as much a part of this as anyone else.'

'I know you're feeling hard done by. Upset that you've been out-smarted. But look at it this way. You wanted to find the deep dreamers, and now you have.'

At the end of the ride Bailey fitted Winters with a blackout sleeping mask, helped him out of the van and guided him across a brief space of hot, open air, warned him to duck his head as she pushed him through a doorway. There was a stutter of applause, people, deep dreamers, celebrating this success, and Winters was steered up a narrow staircase and chained to a bed before Bailey removed the sleeping mask. She took his shoes and socks, too. In case, he supposed, he somehow figured out how to lock-pick the handcuffs, and made a run for it.

The room's walls were painted in a shade of grey that might have been fashionable decades earlier. The bed took up most of the space. The only other furniture was a ladder-backed chair by the window and a small bookcase, its shelves empty apart from a few old austerity paperbacks in uniform blue, against the opposite wall. An amateur watercolour of sheep grazing on a hillside tacked above it. It felt like the kind of place owned by people who lived somewhere else, visited for a few weeks every year but otherwise neglected.

He could hear voices elsewhere in the cottage. Could make out a few words, but not enough to grasp any sense of the conversation. It reminded him of the times when he'd been a kid up in his bedroom, listening to his mother argue with one of her boyfriends. She hadn't had many, and none of them had lasted long. Her paintings had always been the most important thing in her life, and the arguments were usually about that, usually why the boyfriends left.

For a long time he tried to ignore the bottle of water next to the sanitary bucket, but the room was hot and stuffy and at last he gave in to his thirst, telling himself that if they wanted to drug him they could stab him with a needle, didn't need to spike his water. Hours passed. He was half asleep when footsteps on the stairs roused him, and he sat up as three people crowded into the room, squared his back against the brass rails of the headend.

Two men and a woman shoulder to shoulder in the narrow space at the foot of the bed, animal masks over their faces. A badger and a frog. An owl. The man in the badger mask said, 'Do you know why you are here?'

He was taller than the others, stooping under the low ceiling. Shoulder-length black hair parted in the middle. Hands clasped over his paunch were tattooed with eyes in the style of ancient Egypt. The edge of a bandage under the cuff of his shirt.

'I know who you are, Mr Pacek,' Winters said. 'Looks like Cleo Copely's dog gave you a souvenir when you paid her a visit. It was you who roughed her up, wasn't it? And told her that Isabel was dead. Was it before or after you helped Megan Rix and her boyfriend move out?'

'The woman is of no consequence,' Hari Pacek said. 'And if someone told her about your sister, perhaps it was to warn off her and her tiresome husband. Let them know that all was in hand, and how much trouble they would be in if they tried to interfere again.'

'I thought Rob Copely was one of you. Part of your thing.'

'He claimed that he could deliver you to us,' the woman in the owl mask said. 'But he reneged on our agreement as soon as you fell into his hands. Demanded additional payment, only to lose you almost immediately afterwards.'

Winters looked at her. At her mask, with its cruel beak and inscrutable stare. 'Are you the Marquis?'

'It is a position, not a person,' the woman said. 'One that all three of us presently hold.'

'If you turn me loose before this goes any further,' Winters said, 'I promise not to tell.'

'You'll be free to go after you've done your duty by the Instauration,' Hari Pacek said.

'If that works out, we'll all be dead. That was Motte's plan – complete extinction. The whole point of his Great Green Reset.'

'We are not as extreme as Kasey Motte,' the man in the frog mask said. An old guy with a white crewcut, wearing an asymmetric jacket patched with jagged red and yellow blotches that were slowly crawling over and around each other. 'At the end of our series of resets the world will be a greener, better place. Everything that has been lost restored. No more overpopulation. No exploitation of resources. No global heating. Just select groups of people living in harmony with nature and each other.'

'You're gradualists,' Winters said. 'Do you know how much Kasey Motte hated gradualists?'

The three masks looking at him like a child who'd spoken out of turn.

'He killed their leader,' he said. 'That's how much.'

'You will be the template,' the woman said. 'You are a creation of this world, by dreamers from the world before. As such, you can help us to open the way.'

'Open it in dreams,' Hari Pacek said.

'Do you know how insane that sounds?' Winters said.

'You have already passed the first test,' Hari Pacek said.

'What test?'

'The card.'

'You mean that silly trick with the Tarot?'

'It was no trick. There was no forcing, no sleight of hand. You chose freely. And you chose the card you were always destined to choose, given who you are.'

'Given your place in this world,' Frog Mask said. 'And your absence in the world that was.'

'You bear the imprint of your sister's part in the reset that created this iteration,' the woman in the owl mask said. 'Everything you think you know, the memories of the life you think you have lived, comes from that.'

'And you met with Kasey Motte,' Frog Mask said. 'And were instructed by him.'

'He didn't tell much of anything, apart from boasting about how special he was,' Winters said.

He tried to put a little steel in his voice, an edge of defiance, but the deep dreamers' mad claims, their serene certitude, had triggered his old doubts and fears about what Motte might have done to him after the Green Man had appeared in the woods and he'd passed out.

'There may be others like you, but you're the only one we know of,' Hari Pacek said. 'The only person who was created in the dream which created this world. Who sprang into being in the moment of the old world's dissolution. Someone who can help us to find the right path. The template for our collective dreaming.'

'And afterwards, you will be free to go,' Frog Mask said. 'Free to discover the changes you helped to make.'

'If I'm the template, what was my sister?' Winters said.

'She knew Kasey Motte's secrets,' the woman said. 'It would have saved us much trouble if she had been willing to share them with us.'

'But after I met with you, and you passed the test, we knew that you could help us if she would not,' Hari Pacek said.

'It would have been better if she had come to us. Accepted our invitation,' Frog Mask said. 'But it is what it is.'

'She saw you for what you are, didn't want to have anything to do with you. But you were closing in on her, and she decided to get back to Scotland, thought she'd be safer there. And you tried to stop her, didn't you?' Winters said, anger taking hold of him like the sudden onset of a fever. 'You ambushed her. You caused the crash. And when you realised you'd killed her, you ran away. Left her friend sitting beside her body. Left him to die alongside her.'

'We were close to finding your sister, yes,' Hari Pacek said. 'And it does seem that she tried to escape us. But we were not involved in the accident.'

'That's all it was,' Frog Mask said. 'An accident caused by rain and speed on a dark road.'

'We wish it had been otherwise,' the woman said. 'And we are sorry for your loss. But we must move past that.'

'You killed her,' Winters said. The devastation of seeing the place where Izzy had died was still raw and immediate. He had to make sense of it. Someone had to be accountable. 'All of you. Hounded her to death because of your stupid ideas. You want to build a better world? Founded on what? My sister's death, and the death of the man who was trying to help her? The deaths of Kasey Motte and his followers, his hostages? The billions of people you fantasise about erasing? I don't want anything to do with that. Whatever it is you want me to do, I won't do it.'

Silence. As if he'd shouted into a deep well, and it had swallowed his words whole. Not the faintest echo returning.

The deep dreamers looked at each other, masked faces inscrutable. The frog and the owl turned and left and three more people came in. Rabbit Mask from the van, a burly man masked with the grey muzzle and yellow eyes of a wolf, and a woman in a fish mask, who carried a small tray with a leather strap and a hypodermic syringe on a fold of white cloth.

'You can cooperate,' Hari Pacek told Winters. 'Or we can hold you down.'

Winters tried to fight them, but it did no good. Rabbit and Wolf forced him against the rails of the brass headend and pinned his arms above his head, Hari Pacek grabbed his legs when he tried to kick out, and the woman, ignoring his protests, tightened the strap around his left arm. The syringe's needle pricked the soft hollow inside his elbow, something cold flushed into his veins, and when the woman removed the strap everything in the room shot away, dwindling into universal nothingness.

He was lying on his back in dim light. There was the sound of running water and a small fish was swimming in a bright circle above him. Turning and turning as it chased its tail. A voice telling him to relax and watch the fish. It turned and turned and turned. Silver scales shimmering, tail and fins wimpling like translucent veils. The voice softly telling him that he could relax completely, let his eyes close, let everything fall away, and the fish turning in its bright circle flickered out and after a timeless interval he woke up.

He was still on the bed. Slivers of evening sunlight defined the edges of the blackout blind that blanked the window. Nothing above him but the shadowy slant of the ceiling. He planted an elbow on the mattress and pushed himself up until he was sitting against the rails of the headend. He felt spaced and faintly nauseous. Gripped by a weaker cousin of the existential hangover he'd suffered after sampling Jude Lee's weird and wild drifter weed. He remembered with a growing edge of anxiety the brief fierce struggle and the woman looming over him, the strap and the syringe. He'd been drugged. He'd been drugged and hypnotised, and something had been done to him. To his mind.

When the door cracked open he squinted in the light that fell across him and saw that it was Bailey, carrying a tray in both hands.

'Soup and bread if you want it,' she said.

'What's in the soup?'

'I don't know. Vegetables.'

'Mushrooms?'

'Do I look like the fucking chef?'

'Just give me the bread.'

Bailey perched at the end of the bed, resolute as a carven figurehead, watching as Winters gnawed at the heel of bread and sipped warm brackish water from the bottle.

'How are you feeling?'

'Why would you care?'

'You passed some kind of test. Lady A will be here tomorrow. The rest of the deep dreamers too. Showtime.'

'Whatever they promised your boss, they can't deliver it. They're stringing her along, playing on her hope that her son is still alive. I understand that hope because I lost my sister, twice over. So I know what the loss of someone you love does to a person, especially when there's no body, no hard evidence of death. The blind hope that there's a chance, however small, that they're still alive. The bargains you try to make with the world, to reverse time, fix the mistake . . . I know what it can drive you to, against all reason. I mean, here I am. But this won't bring her son back. And I think you know that. So before she gets too far down this road, we can put an end to it. All you have to do is give me a way of getting free. A key for the handcuffs. That knife you took from me. I'll do the rest.'

'I would have thought you'd be eager to find out,' Bailey said.

'Find out what? If this thing of theirs is real? Even if it worked – and I don't believe it, not for second – but if it did, they want a world with fewer people in it. Like billions of people fewer. Motte wanted to erase everyone. Including himself and his followers. Or at least he said he did. These people aren't as ambitious, or quite as crazy, but still. If you piled up all the crimes in human history, it wouldn't come close to matching the pure evil of what they want to do. But we can stop it. A key or a blade. That's all I need.'

'Isn't going to happen,' Bailey said. 'For one thing, your current state, you look like you couldn't work your way out of a paper bag. And even if I wanted to help you, which I don't, there'll be someone sitting outside your door all night, and that window is screwed down.'

'So give me a screwdriver.'

'All this while, you've been stumbling around like a blindfolded man in a room full of rakes. And look where it got you. But I have to admire your determination, wrongheaded though it is.'

'When they realise that this thing of theirs hasn't worked, do you think they'll let me walk?'

'Then you better do your best to make sure it does,' Bailey said. 'Now, how about trying this soup? It's your big day tomorrow. The first of what I understand will be a fair number of sessions. You need to be match fit.'

After Bailey had taken away the untouched bowl of soup, Hari Pacek and the woman in the fish mask returned, accompanied by the two thugs, Rabbit and Wolf. The woman was carrying a tablet with a flesh-coloured cap cabled to it, told Winters that she was going to obtain a baseline for his slow sleep waves and a read of his REM activity, said that they would be networked to his co-dreamers to induce the necessary synchrony. Rabbit and Wolf braced him as she scrubbed his hair with dry shampoo and set the cap on his head. It tightened and adjusted itself with a peculiarly horrible vigour, and when the woman flicked her fingers across the tablet he felt as if a prickling swarm of ants had invaded his scalp. A wave of tiny stabbing shocks, and another, and another. Rabbit and Wolf tightening their grip on his arms so he couldn't try to tear off the cap.

After a short while the woman said that she had good readings across the board and Hari Pacek's stupid badger mask, lit from below by the tablet's flicker, floated towards Winters in the gloom.

'A little something to help you sleep,' he said, and flourished a hypodermic syringe.

When Winters woke again the cap was gone and he was on his back with his arms stretched out. His wrists were fastened to the rails of the bed's headend by zip ties and broad nylon straps were stretched tightly across his chest and his thighs. The thug in the rabbit mask brought in a breakfast tray, paying no attention to Winter's questions as he undid his straps and freed one of his hands, and raised the blackout blind to let morning light flood the room.

After Winters ate half of a dry croissant and drank most of a paper cup of milky tea, Rabbit Mask zip-tied his free hand and Hari Pacek and the woman in the fish mask came in and there was the business with the strap and the needle, the fish chasing its tail in a bright circle and the sound of water running somewhere unseen. When Winters came to he was alone again. Bonelessly drowsy, sort of scattered, he lay staring up at the ceiling, wondering what had been done to him. People were clattering about elsewhere in the cottage, and there was a faint odour of smoke, as if someone had lit a wood stove. At last, Hari Pacek returned, still wearing his badger mask and dressed now in a raw linen shirt and matching drawstring trousers. He dropped a neatly folded bundle of clothing on the bed and told Winters that it was time for him to shine.

'Just a small test today. Proof of concept. A more ambitious session tomorrow. Will you dress yourself, or will we have to do it for you?'

It was as if Winters was being prepared for a meditation class, or some gentle form of martial exercise. The same kind of shirt and trousers as Hari Pacek. White slippers. After he dressed he was led downstairs, through a living room cluttered with shabby, mismatched furniture, out into the hot afternoon. The van which had delivered him and several bubblecars and a battered 'streamline' microbus were parked nose to tail on the hardstanding. He could see now that moorland slanted away beyond the cottage. Reefs of smoke were drifting out from the ridgeline and there was a strong smell of burning and a faint flutter of ash flakes.

'Don't worry,' Hari Pacek said. 'It's only a small fire, and the wind is blowing it away from us. And soon it won't matter.'

He gripped one of Winters' arms and Rabbit Mask gripped the other and they marched him past the vehicles to the byre. It was dim inside, the air cooler. Whitewashed stone walls, two rows of hospital beds. Infusion stands hung with pouches of clear liquid. Caps and cables, neatly coiled like sleeping snakes, lying on pillows.

There was a tightness in Winters' chest, an airy hum in his head. A sudden spurt of dread and anticipation. It was happening. It was really happening.

The woman in the fish mask, dressed in linen shirt and trousers, was waiting for him at the end of one of the rows of beds. After he'd been strapped to the bed, she fitted the cap over his head. As before, it squeezed and stung his scalp, and after studying her tablet the woman pushed up the left sleeve of his shirt and swabbed the crook of his elbow and inserted the needle of a cannula into one of the fat blue veins, taped it down and attached it to the line from the pouch hanging overhead.

Winters wanted to know what was being fed into his arm and the woman told him briskly that it was IV fluid to prevent dehydration and maintain electrolyte balance during the dreaming, and set a kidney-shaped steel tray on his chest. Picked up a hypodermic syringe filled with pale yellow fluid and said that this was the shroom extract and injected him without fuss or ceremony, a long cool push of poison flowing into his bloodstream.

For a little while there was no effect. Winters lay with his head turned, watching as the woman ministered to Hari Pacek on the bed next to his. One by one, the other celebrants filed through the door. All of them dressed in linen shirts and trousers, all of them masked. Either to hide their identities from each other, or because it was part of this comically sinister ritual. Shuffling in their slippers, climbing onto the hospital beds, awaiting their turn.

There seemed to be other people crouching in the shadows under the beds, and there was a fluttering at the edges of Winters' sight, as if leaves were lifting and falling on a wind he couldn't feel. He wasn't alarmed. Was floating inside a humming calm. A bubble of white noise. He wondered if this was how Izzy had prepared for the first reset. Maybe she'd been excited. Expectant. Resolute in her belief that she was about to dream a better world into being. And when she woke, Kasey Motte had somehow convinced her and the rest of his followers that they'd woken into a world they'd remade. Or maybe they'd shared some kind of psychotic delusion, a refusal to believe that their beliefs were worthless. Izzy had made a bad mistake when she'd fallen for Motte's bullshit, no question about it. But when everything had blown up at the end, she'd finally seen through his mindfuckery. Had taken back control of her life. And perhaps, in the years afterwards, before the deep dreamers came looking for her and everything fell apart, she'd found some kind of peace. Drowsily adrift on the wash of shroom extract, comfortably numb, Winters wanted to think so. It was something to cling to in the wreckage of this whole sorry mess.

More than half of the beds around him were occupied. And now Talia Armstrong wheeled in, her skeletal chair purring towards him, Bailey pacing behind it like a pall bearer armoured in tweed.

Talia Armstrong's hand moved on the tablet strapped to the wheelchair's arm, conjuring her synthetic voice. 'No doubt you think I'm mad.'

'These people, the people you think might help you, are responsible for Izzy's death,' Winters said.

It took some effort to get that out in one piece. He was having trouble speaking. Sorting out the right words.

Talia Armstrong reached out, lightly patted his shoulder. It was like being brushed with a bundle of twigs. Her face was framed by the jostling flutter which had invaded his sight, like a lone pale star seen through a telescope. Her synthetic voice said, 'She may be with us when we wake.'

'It's nice. Nice to think so.'

'And William, of course. I gave them everything they needed. And they should have passed it on to you.'

'I don't remember anything they told me, when I was under the fish.'

'The fish?'

'The thing they did. Hypnosis or whatever. Point is, it doesn't matter. Because it won't work.'

Talia Armstrong tapped once on the tablet. A preprepared soundbite. Behind her, Bailey was giving Winters her best dead-eyed look.

'I tried everything. Bailey's investigations. Spiritualists. Someone who claimed they could telephone the dead. Someone who claimed to see messages in the static of old televisions. The kind with vacuum tubes. And now this. But I am very hopeful that it will at last give me what I've been searching for. And you are the key. Everything necessary for its success is buried inside you at a level deeper than thought. Waiting to be released, in dreams. And you will be rewarded in the next world.'

Winters knew that he couldn't reach her. She was lost inside her grief.

'This thing,' he said, looking straight at Bailey. 'You can stop it.'

'Dream well,' Talia Armstrong's synthetic voice said, and her wheelchair spun around and Bailey followed her to her assigned bed.

The woman in the fish mask returned. She was wearing a cap now. Its cable hung over her shoulder as she checked his drip, told him that he was linked to everyone else in the byre.

'You are the channel for our shared dream. The lightning conductor.'

Winters tried to summon some kind of smart remark but came up empty. Everything was bleeding into a dusky shimmer and he seemed to be slowly sinking through the hospital bed into a void as deep and dark as a grave. The last thing he saw was the woman clambering on to the neighbouring bed and jabbing a cannula into her arm, and then he passed out of the world.

And woke with a start from a dream that was fading as he tried to grasp it, something about flying over water, but if there was anything more to it than that it was already gone, leaving only an unfocused feeling of loss. His heart was pounding and the air stank of bonfires. Smoke wraiths were chasing each other through oaken joists and struts above him and all around there was a panicky commotion as ghosts heaved up from deathly sleep and quit their slabs and jostled towards a shaft of inflamed sunlight that fell through the door like pilgrim souls at the threshold of heaven or hell.

He tried to sit up, struggling against his restraints. There was a sharp tug in his elbow, something tearing loose, and a ghost with the toothy face of a rabbit materialised and the restraints fell away and he was dragged off the bed, hauled stumbling towards the furnace light. Shouts and screams, ghosts frozen or flinching away as a carpet unrolled across their feet, fraying and breaking apart into hundreds of tiny creatures that were devoured by the shadows under the slabs, and then he was outside, in an acrid smog lit by erratic pulses of blue light and coronas of flame cradled in the tops of trees.

'Stay calm,' the rabbit ghost said, but Winters hardly heard it.

Ghosts with the faces of animals and birds and fish were shuffling past shells of huge dead animals that squatted in front of a white sepulchre, past brutes in yellow helmets and bulky armour trimmed with yellow bands that left trails of light in the smoky air. He saw a ghost with an owl's face ranting at one of the brutes, saw an ogre dressed in a kind of suit woven from hair and dead grass walk past at a deliberate pace, a frail body limp in their arms, and then the ghosts fluttering around him shouted and ducked as a wave of birds swooped low. Ravens and crows and starlings passing in a beating of wings and rustle of feathers. A snake-necked heron, legs trailing. A pair of red kites on wings wide as outstretched arms. Dozens of smaller birds, bobbing and weaving through the smog. The rabbit ghost had ducked like the rest, and Winters stood alone, amazed and laughing, and a small slender shadow in the shape of a person oozed or materialised from the shadows under the largest shell.

'Come with me,' S said, and took hold of his hand. 'Hurry.'

Worms of flame sidewindered down the moorland slope, leaving stretches of smoking char and little islands of fire behind them. There were things in the flames that Winters didn't like to look at, and as he and S neared the crest of the slope something passed through him in a mad rush. A horde of phantoms bursting out of his chest and gaining form and solidity as they galloped away up the slope, mounted on small sturdy horses and elks with ragged palmate antlers, clad in leather and patchwork armour and helmets worked from wood and bone. This motley horde raising spears trailing pennants black as night as they urged on their mounts, some blowing horns and the rest calling out to him, and he pulled away from S's frail grasp and chased after them.

S followed him for the rest of the long summer day. Slept when he slept and rose when he rose the next morning and went on. Followed him south and west through woods and moorland. His pale linen shirt and trousers were streaked with ash and dirt and the left arm of his shirt was bloodstained at the elbow, where a cannula had been pulled out. He lost his slippers early in the afternoon of the second day, but although his feet were bruised and scraped and cut by stones he went on at a steady pace. Sometimes stopping and looking about with childlike wonder. Laughing at or calling out to things S couldn't see. Crouching by a stream and holding a brief whispered conversation with the swift clear water before lowering his face to it and drinking as an animal drinks. Trying to wrap his arms around the swollen mossy trunk of a grandfather oak, tears cleaving clean wet tracks down his smoke-stained face.

It was all very interesting.

He gave no sign that he was aware of his companion, but slowed and stopped whenever he spotted hikers and climbers or farm workers, no matter how distant, and watched them as warily as any wild animal until they had passed from sight. That night he slept on a patch of dry moss in the lee of a fallen tree trunk, and was possessed by dreams. Shivering and thrashing. Speaking in tongues.

S sat nearby, watching. Wondering what he might be dreaming inside the dream that possessed him.

When Winters stirred the next morning, he seemed to be truly awake. Wincing as he sat up, tenderly touching the cut and bruised soles of his feet and looking around with a haunted expression, relaxing a little when he saw S sitting cross-legged on the ground a couple of metres away. Pristine morning light dropped between the slender young trees around them, gilding patches of bare ground, patches of grass and dog's mercury. Maps of leaves floated above, incandescently green against a cloudless blue sky.

'Where are we?' Winters said.

'The forest.'

'The National Forest?'

'You walked a long way.'

'How long has it been?'

'Two days and two nights. More or less.'

'I thought it was longer. They really jacked me up, didn't they?'

'I guess.'

'Is that my sling bag?'

'I found it in the cottage while you were dreaming with the deep dreamers.'

'Was that before or after you started the wildfire? That was you, wasn't it?'

'The wind blew it in the wrong direction at first, but then the wind changed.'

'And you snuck in while everybody was panicking, and found me. Toss that bag over here. There's something I need to check.'

S watched as Winters rummaged in the sling bag, pulling out a phone, asking it to tell him about Isabel Winters. Holding it close to his ear as he listened to the small, precise voice of the phone's agent. His eyes closed, his mouth clamped in a thin line.

Asking the agent if it was certain, asking if there was a clip, then asking the agent to play it, S watching him as he watched it.

'That's enough,' Winters said after a couple of minutes. He switched off the phone and looked at S. 'Well, she's still dead.'

'Your sister.'

'Yeah. I never believed the deep dreamers' bullshit. Not for a single second. Not even when they drugged me, put me at the centre of their stupid little ritual. But I had to be sure.'

'You thought you might have brought her back.'

'I wanted to believe and at the same time I didn't.'

'Because of the dream. The dream you were walking through.'

'It seemed so fucking real. Another world. A green world, like the world Kasey Motte talked about . . .'

Winters was looking off through the trees. Searching for something that wasn't there.

'You haven't eaten for a while,' S said. 'Why don't I fix some breakfast?'

While the kid collected dead branches and broke them up and built and lit a small fire, Winters ate an apple and a handful of cherries from the stash Elli Laidlaw had given him, scooped honey from its jar with two fingers. S boiled water in a mess tin and added a packet of freeze-dried red lentil soup and Winters ate the soup slowly and with great relish. Afterwards, S boiled more water and steeped two tea bags in it. They poured half the brew into Winters' alloy mug and he took it and sipped absent-mindedly.

At last, he said, 'How did you get here? How did you find the deep dreamers?'

'You told Teddy you might have to head north. Then Bailey called me, seemed to think you had gone to Wakestone.

Asked what I knew about that. She was going to look for you there, and I thought I better go too.'

'But not with Bailey.'

'No. It was something I wanted to do. I had some cash money, but I didn't really need it. I walked. Hitched rides. There are always kind people. I got lucky with a road train that took me more than half the way, reached Wakestone the day after you'd left it. Two of the people there told me about the deep dreamers. They'd been studying them for a long time, as if they were the worst kind of enemy.'

'I think I know the people you mean. I was supposed to meet them.'

'They knew what the deep dreamers were planning to do, where they were. You'd left Wakestone and hadn't come back, so I thought I might find you there.'

'And you did.'

'Bailey was there too. I saw her carrying the woman from the airfield.'

'I think I saw that. Bailey and Talia Armstrong. Who changed her mind about the deep dreamers. Came to believe that they could bring her son back. He died in the Wakestone siege, and the deep dreamers promised to change things so he didn't. So she set Bailey on me, and here we are.'

'Yes. Here we are.'

'You knew I was dreaming. Sleepwalking. But you didn't try to wake me.'

'Thought it best if you woke when you wanted to. You seemed to be searching for something.'

'You were following me, and I was following the Wild Hunt. You know what that is?'

S shook their head.

'Something from old stories. Myths. Ghostly hunters led by one of the old gods, or someone from history or legend. They passed through me or came out of me after you helped me to get away from the deep dreamers. I remember some of that. There were firefighters, and I thought they were ogres or devils. And the deep dreamers, fleeing the scene in their silly costumes and masks. I remember trees on fire, and a swarm of what I think were mice, and the birds. A mob of birds, different kinds, flying low and adding to the deep dreamers' panic. Did that really happen, or was it part of my dream?'

'It was real.'

'All of it?'

'All of it.'

Winters remembered gulls lifting from the mudbank where S had been stranded. If they ever had been stranded. And that crow flying off when he'd seen them waiting for him outside the pub, the day before he'd heard about Izzy's death. Her true death.

He said, 'Did you have something to do with those birds, and all the rest?'

S shrugged, the way they did. A twitch of a shoulder. 'Animals flee from wildfires. Birds too.'

'I guess I was out of my head on the deep dreamers' drugs, but still sort of awake. The Wild Hunt passed through me, and I followed them into another world. It's already fading, but there are some things I think I will always remember.'

'What was it like?'

'A forest, older and bigger than this one. Parts of it seemed to come from the deep past, and there were also things I saw, or thought I saw, after Kasey Motte slipped me a dose of his special shrooms. Like the Green Man and the Wild Hunt.'

'You were following the Wild Hunt. Where did it take you?'

'Its riders were always ahead of me, but even when I couldn't see them I knew where they were. I could hear their horns. Their shouts. Their songs. I thought that they were leading me towards Isabel. My sister.'

'Did you find her?'

'If I did, I don't remember it. I do remember seeing some other people, though. Men and women and children, walking in a line through the trees. They were small, and pretty much naked. Long hair with shells and nuts and dry flowers woven into it. Strings tied around their waists. Blue tattoos all over their bodies. Patterns of lines and dots. Spirals and little circles. Tattoos that seemed to be moving, slowly changing shape. Changing from one pattern into another. I saw them but they didn't seem to see me. Except one, an old woman at the end of the line. She turned and stared at me and began to chant. Words that stung me like stones or bees. Drove me away. I don't know if they were our ancestors, or the chosen people of the green world of the deep dreamers' Instauration. But whatever they were, I must have seemed like some kind of ghost to them. To that old woman. An unwelcome spirit creature.

'That was the thing about the forest. It was haunted. Everything in it, the huge old trees with moss dripping from their branches, bushes and ferns and flowers in the understorey, everything seemed to have a little flame of consciousness burning inside it. And everything was connected to everything else. A vast organism, big as the world, got up from millions of separate lives. I came to the edge of a cliff and there was a blanket of treetops below me, stretching away to the horizon. No sign of civilisation. No buildings. No roads. Just trees and thin scarves of mist. And a flock of birds, thousands of them in a great cloud, circling a tree bigger and taller than all the rest. A murmuration, like in the old days, blowing this way and that before settling into the giant tree's branches.'

Winters paused, seeing that vast unpeopled forest in his mind's eye, coming back to the world when S refilled his mug with the rest of the tea.

'Don't you want any of this?'

'It's fine. You were telling me about the forest being haunted.'

'I drank from a stream that dropped in little waterfalls to a pool where something I couldn't see was singing in no language I knew. There was an albino deer, a stag, standing in a clearing. Lit by a shaft of sunlight. Its rack of antlers like polished ivory. Its eyes like two black flames. It looked at me and I couldn't bear its gaze and sort of sidled into the trees and went on.'

'You were still following the Wild Hunt.'

'As best I could, until it grew too dark. I slept on a bare hillside under a sky full of stars. More stars than I'd ever seen. A vastness of stars.'

'Did you dream, in the dream?'

'Not then. Or if I did I don't remember. When I woke it was still night and the stars were swirling like flecks of foam caught in a strong current and I watched as they poured away somewhere beyond the horizon, until only the moon was left. It must have risen while I was asleep, and it was the colour of old bone. A piece of old bone jammed in the empty black sky. And I heard the horns and cries of the Wild Hunt and got up and went on through the forest. Kind of feeling my way in that bone-coloured light until at last the sun rose and I caught a glimpse of the hunt and followed it somehow, or thought I did, through the endless trees. Along the way I came across more animals. Shaggy elephants no bigger than sheep, grazing on fallen apples. Hippos splashing about in a pool. Crests of coarse black hair along their backs. What I think were aurochs, in a glade around a big fallen tree. Big beasts with shaggy coats. Horns pointing forward. There were plans to bring aurochs back, once upon a time. Or at least, breed animals that looked like aurochs from crosses with different kinds of cattle. But the ones I saw seemed to be the real thing. Part of the ancient megafauna which had survived in that forest, that green world, because they hadn't been hunted to extinction. I circled around them and went on until it grew dark again, and I slept again. At least I think I did. And in that second sleep I fell into a dream.'

'A dream within the dream.'

'Yeah. Was the first closer to reality, because it contained the second? I can't tell you. Anyway, in the dream inside the dream it was morning, much like it is now, and I found the Wild Hunt. Found where it was waiting for me. Men and women in leather and armour, on horses and Irish elks. Another long-ago extinct species, those elks. All of them bulls, with enormous antlers, like carvings of giants' hands. This was in a grassy clearing. A big meadow, really, with a huge tree in the centre of it. I don't know if it was the tree I'd seen before, the one circled by that murmuration of birds, but it was bigger than any tree has a right to be. The riders seated on their elks and horses were ranged in a line in the tall grass, looking towards me as I stepped out of the shadows under the trees into the sunlit meadow. One of them was taller than the rest, wearing a suit of armour. Steel polished mirror bright. A circlet of gold crowning his helmet.'

'Do you know who he was?'

'Some old-time king I guess. His face was hidden behind the grill of his visor, but I knew that he was watching me.

Knew that he knew who I was. And another rider raised a horn to his lips and blew a long blast and they wheeled away one after the other and rode off into the trees and left me standing there.'

'Was that the end of it?'

'You mean the dream inside the dream? No, not quite. I saw steps cut into the trunk of the huge tree, a broad stair spiralling up its trunk, rising between branches wide as streets, and I began climbing it. Sunlight in my face on one side of its turns, cool shadow on the other. I don't know how long I climbed, but quite soon the forest was far below me, and part of it was hidden by clouds.

'I suppose I was still hoping to find Isabel. And when I climbed around what seemed like the hundredth turn of the stair, I saw something moving in the sunlit sea of leaves beyond the stair. A face patched from golden light and green leaves. Large eyes so black they seemed to be all pupil, fixed on me. A gaze that seemed to know everything about me.

'I'd seen him before. The Green Man. And there he was, in this other place. In the dream inside the dream. The first time, he was triggered by Kasey Motte's shrooms. An archetype out of folk history or folk memory, like the Wild Hunt. I hadn't seen him for a while, but after Rob Copely dosed me I started catching glimpses of him, and at last he appeared again, manifesting out of a video display. And this time, in that dream inside a dream, he spoke to me.'

'What did he say?'

'Do you know how it is, in dreams? Ordinary dreams, I mean. Where you have to be somewhere for some reason. To find someone or do something, but you lose your way, and everything's urgent and unclear. This was something like that. The Green Man spoke to me, and I think he had something to say about the forest I'd found myself in. Some kind of revelation. And then I woke up, from the dream inside the dream and the original dream. Woke and found myself here, with you. And what he'd told me slipped away. I've been trying to remember. But it's gone.'

'Perhaps it wasn't anything.'

'Yeah. Perhaps. Things that seem meaningful in dreams often aren't, after you wake up. But I'm awake now, and I still think that what the Green Man told me was important. The true nature of that dream forest, the significance of my journey through it. The deep dreamers claimed that they were going to change the world. Finish what Kasey Motte had begun. I was supposed to be some sort of catalyst. The dreamer whose dream would be shared and amplified by other dreamers. I didn't believe any of it. Not when Motte told me about it, way back when. Not when the deep dreamers kidnapped me for their weird ceremony. Maybe it's because I'm still high on the shroom juice they stuck in my veins, or maybe it's something that was planted in my mind when they put me in a trance, but I can't help wondering if my dream changed things. If this is the world as it always was and always will be, or if it's become something else. Something I walked into while I was dreaming.'

'I'm still here,' S said.

'I have this sort of vague feeling that the Green Man might have told me something about you, too. Why I found you stranded on the mudbank. Why you followed me here.'

'I only wanted to help.'

'I'm wondering if you didn't try to wake me because you think that Kasey Motte's resets were real. That they really changed the world. And you wanted to see if my dream would change things too.'

'Do you think that it did?'

'I know that it didn't undo what happened to Izzy. Even though it's the one thing I'd change, if I could. I sort of went crazy when I learned that she hadn't died in the siege. I was mad angry at her, but I also wanted to help her. Wanted to see her again. Wanted to fix what had broken between us . . .'

Winters knuckled his eyes and took a deep breath and blew it out.

'And now she really is dead and I don't know how I'm going to deal with that. But I'm also relieved, if you want to know the truth. Relieved that all the things I remember, even the crash in which she died, they haven't changed. Because if we can change the world by some kind of magical dreaming, it might not be in the way we expect, and we'd have to live with the consequences. If I'd dreamed Izzy back into life, maybe Kasey Motte would still be alive, too. Or maybe the deep dreamers would be able to get what they wanted, erase billions of people and become the rulers of an unspoiled world.'

'You think that nothing has changed,' S said. 'That everything that happened has still happened.'

'Are you disappointed?'

'It is what it is.'

'I hope so. But I can't help wondering about something Rob Copely told me. According to him, when the commune's shared dream reset the world's history, each dreamer added something distinctive. A unique little change. Like flourishes in a signature, or the faces stonemasons give gargoyles during the construction of a cathedral. He claimed that he'd brought back tigers. I thought at the time that it was a silly story, something to make him seem more important than he was. But what if my dream wasn't powerful enough to change the world's history, but might have added some small flourish instead?'

'Like those aurochs.'

'Yeah. Or dwarf elephants. But it could just as easily be something inconspicuous, like this moth that recently was declared extinct. The Lesser Lichen Case-bearer. A tiny creature hardly anyone knows or cares about. If my dreaming changed anything, I'd like it to be something like that.'

'If that's so, it would be hard to find.'

'Yeah, that's kind of my point.'

'But it might be something more than that. Aurochs and elephants and who knows what.'

'Or it might be nothing at all. Do you know how to get to Wakestone from here?'

S thought for a moment, then swivelled and pointed to the shadows beyond a cluster of birch trees. 'Reckon it's that way. More or less.'

'Only one way to find out,' Winters said, and followed them back into the world.

Author's Note

Cynsea Island displaces an existing island, but the salt marshes and most of the other places in the Blackwater Estuary mentioned in this novel can be found by anyone who cares to visit. Many of the locations in London and Northumberland are likewise grounded in reality: you can track down the location of Hari Pacek's flat easily enough (but I don't recommend calling on him), or follow most of Marc Winters' walk from Berwick-upon-Tweed to Wakestone Farm, although at some point you'll find yourself on another path.

I'd like to thank my agents Oliver Cheetham and Simon Kavanagh for taking care of business. Also Marcus Gipps, Zakirah Alam and Grace Barber for editing, Colin Murray for copy-editing and Saxon Bullock for proofreading, Nick Shah, Ola Galewicz, Deborah Francois and Helen Ewing for cover and design, Paul Hussey and Katie Horrocks for production, and everyone else at Orion for their help in bodying this dream into reality.